CW01018723

THE CHOSEN

D. B. SCOTT

THE CHOSEN

AUSTIN & MACAULEY

A CIP catalogue record for this title is
available from the British Library.

ISBN 978 1 905609 444

www.austinmacauley.com

First Published (2009)
Austin & Macauley Publishers Ltd.
25 Canada Square
Canary Wharf
London
E14 5LB

Printed & Bound in Great Britain

DEDICATION

To Pam, for the black dog days.

It is a raw night, not the kind of night to be outside. The old man, sitting in his favourite armchair, leans over and puts another log on the fire. He can hear the wind outside, howling through the fir trees and bare silver birches, whipping down the Perthshire glen, from across an angry North Sea. Rain turning to sleet patters off the window panes. His housekeeper has left early, snow is forecast. She's left his dinner in the oven, but it is still there because of the phone call. He looks at his watch again. Where is he, dammit? He must have phoned at least two hours ago.

Just then, he can hear the sound of a car, above the noise of the wind, coming up the drive, the headlights flashing across the wall in front of him. He gets up slowly and crosses the lounge to the hall to meet his visitor. He opens the sturdy, timber door and is buffeted by the wind. Before him he sees a young man, wearing a dark overcoat, his hair already slicked by the sleet.

'You're Bradbury?' he enquires.

'Yes, sir,' the young man replies nodding, beginning to shiver in the cold.

'Well, you'd better come in.' The old man steps aside, letting the younger man gratefully enter the hallway.

'Is it always like this, you know, the weather?' Bradbury grins, smoothing his hair down.

'It was your choice to come here,' the old man replies, his flinty grey eyes expressionless. 'You can hang your coat up there,' pointing to a row of coat hooks, as he pushes the door shut. Bradbury does as he's told and then follows the old man into the lounge. He's glad of the warmth of the room, rubbing his cold hands together.

'You can have one, if you want' the old man says, sitting down and pointing to the whisky bottle beside him.

'No thank you, sir, I have to drive straight back.' Bradbury does not want to be here any longer than he has to; he could be marooned here at this rate.

The old man nods slowly, takes a sip of his whisky and looks at the young man. 'So, you have a message for me. Very urgent you said.'

'Yes, sir.'

'Well? I haven't got all bloody night!' The old man picks up the bottle and pours another generous measure into his glass.

'We've had a message from Master, sir.' Bradbury stands there, expectantly.

'Jesus Christ!' says the old man, slowly puts down the bottle and buries his head in both hands.

PART ONE

Events, dear boy, events
Harold MacMillan

CHAPTER ONE

'This is your bloody fault!' Forsyth glares at me across his vast desk. His office is also vast, which I suppose reflects his position as head of MI6. As usual, Forsyth is immaculately groomed, dark suit, faint pinstripe. We are the same age, but he looks younger than me. Still tanned from his vacation in the Bahamas, silver grey hair recently trimmed. His pale blue eyes stare at me through gold-rimmed spectacles. A well-manicured hand throws a newspaper towards me. It's a copy of the Sun, which surprises me. Didn't think red tops sullied Forsyth's fingers. 'Britain Defenceless!' the headline screams at me.

'Could be a straight quote from your bloody memo!' Forsyth snaps. I know when Forsyth is angry, his Scottish burr overtakes his otherwise clipped, Cambridge accent.

I don't bother to pick up the paper, Forsyth is probably right. It's Monday morning and I'm still suffering from Saturday night. On Saturday, I am officially divorced. A pub crawl follows with a few of my remaining friends. Since Angela and I have split up, I've offloaded a lot of our friends. They were mostly hers anyway, took her side of the argument.

And so, I arrive at my last watering hole, The Star in Holborn. Bill, Sandy and Ted have dropped off, one by one. They have wives to go home to, I have an empty flat. The Star is an old-fashioned pub, hard to find these days. It's busy during the week, filled with city types in pinstripe suits. But at the weekend it's quiet, the regulars knowing that they won't be disturbed. A refuge from whatever they're hiding from or trying to forget about. Maybe that's why I've ended up here. The interior hasn't changed for decades, red flecked wallpaper competing with dark oak panelling. The lighting is subdued, almost gloomy, easy to hide away in a corner, forget about your troubles. I stand at the horseshoe bar and order a whisky from a pretty barmaid, who is too young for me or maybe more accurately, I am too old for her. She sounds Australian, her accent of sunshine and youth. My mood is therefore dark when Ben Saunders walks in. Saunders is a reporter for The Sun, I remember him from his coverage of the Iraq War. He also knows Angela, from her PR company, been to our parties when I've been in town. I haven't seen him for months. He gives me a nod and settles down on a bar stool beside me.

'Sorry about Angela,' he says simply, lights a cigarette. The smoke drifts up to the blue haze which has settled over the bar. Saunders is quite tall, a squarish face, tanned skin, pale blue eyes matching his denim outfit.

'Didn't know this was one of your haunts.' I sit down beside him, ignoring his comment about my ex-wife, and order a couple of whiskys.

'Not always one for the bright lights,' he gives me a wry smile.

We trade whiskys, small talk. My pretty barmaid is now being chatted up by a guy half my age, she laughs, flicks her hair. God, I feel old. Saunders is talking to me, something about Iraq. Ah, Iraq, the tipping point of my life. The reason for my predicament, including my divorce. As my sphere of operations is Europe, I shouldn't have been involved in the Middle East. But all section heads had been asked to review the current intelligence on WMD in Iraq. I'd laughed out loud when I read the report. My laugh was heard in the corridors of power, my political masters were not amused. Told to stick to Europe and so I did. Hence my famous memo, written with tongue-in-cheek. Due to the overstretch of the British armed forces, Britain was defenceless, ripe for invasion. Maybe by the French. It was meant as a joke, but Forsyth had latched on to it. Another question mark against me.

'So, how's Mr Forsyth?' Saunders tries to catch the eye of the barmaid who's now exchanging phone numbers with her new friend. My mood is now black.

'Arrogant Scottish prick!' I stare into my empty glass.

'Yeah,' Saunders nods in agreement, 'you know that I met him in Baghdad? Must have been about six months ago.' He rubs the stubble on his chin.

'Looking for his precious WMD, was he?' I laugh at the thought.

'Something like that,' Saunders pushes another whisky towards me. 'Heard that you were a dissenting voice regarding the dodgy dossier.' Saunders stubs out his cigarette and looks at me.

'Rumours, Saunders, rumours. And you know that I couldn't possibly comment.' I finish the whisky in one gulp.

But now looking at the newspaper, I obviously had and more, during the rest of the evening, which I must admit is still a bit of a blur. I quickly scan what Saunders has written, sketchy not detailed. Not enough for Forsyth to pin it on me, yet. And Saunders won't give up his source. No, I'm safe for now. Why did I do it? The alcohol? My divorce? Forsyth's promotion? Maybe that young guy in the bar, brushing past me, the smug look of conquest on his face, the barmaid, her pink tongue licking her red, solvent lips. I don't know and maybe I don't care.

My continued silence propels Forsyth from his black leather and chrome chair. He stalks across the deep pile carpet and stands in front of the large picture window, surveying the Thames, master of all in front of him, the king of the castle.

'You're sailing close to the wind, Richard. I can't have that, I run a tight ship.' Forsyth turns to face me, adjusts a jacket sleeve, a gold cufflink catches the morning sun. 'Your floor is due to be renovated next week, more offices. The government is giving us more staff, as we've requested.' A faint smile crosses his face, his empire has just got bigger. 'Maybe you should move out to Newton House, less incovenience and all that, eh?' The smile remains fixed.

Forsyth couldn't care less about my convenience. I know when I'm being edged sideways. I wonder if he got his suntan from the desert?

'Project Phoenix must be about finished now?' Forsyth resumes his position behind his desk, toys idly with a silver letter opener, not looking at me, waiting.

'Almost,' I reply, breaking my silence.

'Good,' Forsyth carefully lays the opener on the desk and pushes an unmarked file towards me, 'something else for you to look into.'

I pick up the grey manila file and open it. Inside is a single piece of paper, there is a type written message:

'Master is back in the game. Is Mother still playing? If so, contact me through The Times Personal Column.'

'Looks like your old friend Baxter's ghost is still alive.' Forsyth's smile is now more of a smirk.

'Where did this come from?' I decide not to rise to the bait, not give Forsyth the edge.

'Ah, I seem to have got your attention, at last,' Forsyth settles back in his chair, adjusts his waistcoat. 'Last Friday it was delivered to our ambassador in Paris. It didn't mean anything to him, of course, so he passed it onto the Foreign Office and they passed it on to us. And I'm passing it onto you.' Forsyth folds his arms in front of him, indicating that this piece of paper is now my responsibility.

'To do what?' I reply innocently.

Forsyth frowns, elbows rest on the desk, chin sits on clenched fists.

'Well, contact Baxter, if he's still alive. Is he?' He asks through gritted teeth.

'I haven't heard from him for years.'

'Christmas cards stopped, did they?'

'Something like that.' I fold my arms, touché.

'Well, whatever.' Forsyth decides to stop the verbal sparring. 'Speak to Personnel, they'll have his address or his death certificate.' The smirk reappears.

'And?'

'Whether Baxter's alive or dead, contact this Master, whoever the hell he or she is and find out what he or she wants. Christ, Richard! This is 1960's stuff, the Cold War, the Iron Curtain, it's all so passé. Who the hell cares now, eh? Maybe this Master wants to make a deathbed confession or sell his story to the newspapers, The Sun, for instance?' Forsyth smiles to himself.

God, how I dislike this man!

'Anyway, this file has been open for over thirty years. Just close it, tie it up in a nice piece of ribbon and hand it over to Records.' Forsyth looks down at his desk and opens another file, I am dismissed.

I get up slowly, leaving the copy of the Sun on his desk; maybe Forsyth can do the crossword. As I close the door behind me, I can hear Forsyth's voice.

'And don't fuck it up, Stevens.'

Bastard!

Friday morning, the door to Newton House, off Devonshire Square, has been recently painted. Blue, royal blue. A brass plaque to the right identifies the occupants as The Department of Trade and Industry – Statistics Department. There is a keypad below, I punch in six numbers, the door opens with a soft click. The smell of fresh paint greets me in the hallway; it used to be of cigarette smoke. The ground floor always seemed to be a hive of activity then. People, phones, laughter, shouting. Now there's almost silence. Just the hum of computers. People, half my age, sitting in rows staring intently at their screens, not a word passing between compressed lips. The lighting is harsh, fluorescent. Not like before. Everyone then seemed to have a black anglepoise, casting small pools of light on cluttered desks. Everyone's face in shadow, just like the world they lived in.

I stand there for a few moments, watching the 21st century at work. Maybe it is time to get out, take my pension and run. There is no receptionist and so I ascend the grey-carpeted stairs to the next floor. This used to be a self-contained flat, living and dining room, two bedrooms, bathroom and kitchenette. A safe house, used by our friends who came across the Iron Curtain seeking freedom and democracy. They got it at a cost, information, some of it priceless. And then they went to America; they always wanted to go to America. This door has not been repainted and is locked. I wonder if I can find a key. I turn towards the stairs to the top floor. The stairs are uncarpeted, just stained timber treads, long scuffed by leather soles. My footsteps echo down the stairwell, timber creeks under my weight. There are two offices on this level, the larger to the left. This will be my office; it also used to be Baxter's. The door to the smaller office is open. A woman sits at one of two desks, typing. She is Gladys Jones from Vauxhall Cross, a plain-looking woman, grey hair tied in a tight bun, wearing a shapeless dress with a floral pattern that vaguely reminds me of my mother's lounge curtains. A spinster if I remember correctly, not really surprising with that sour, turned-down mouth. She's never liked me, the feeling's mutual. She will have been Forsyth's choice, just to keep an eye on me. She gives me a curt nod of acknowledgement; I do not reciprocate. As I enter my new office, nothing seems to have changed in thirty years except for a new desk and carpet. Someone obviously likes royal blue. The walls are still the same battleship grey, the filing cabinet from the last war, battered and scarred. I open the top drawer, somebody has delivered my Project Phoenix files. The other two drawers are empty, a bit like my life at the moment. I sit behind the desk; tropical fish drift across my computer screen. Two files rest on walnut veneer in front of me. One contains the latest update from Toulouse, the other is stamped TOP SECRET – MASTER AND MOTHER. I turn over the dog-eared cover. I should know the file by heart, Baxter gave it to me verbatim. Late nights in this room, Baxter with his feet on the table, a half bottle of whisky sitting on the desk between us. Baxter gazing at the ceiling, puffing on an endless supply of cigarettes. The file was officially closed in 1968. I can see that there were periodic reviews in the following years – 'No Further Action' stamped in red across blank pages with unintelligible signatures, persons unknown. Even these had stopped in the mid 80's. And then the letter from the British Embassy in Paris, dated two weeks ago.

I hear Bradbury before I see him. Bounding up the stairs, whistling something tunelessly. He stands in the doorway, flushed, unplugging something from his ear.

'Sorry, sir. I-pod,' he grins sheepishly, taking a metal object the size of a cigarette packet from his pocket.

'You're late,' I tap my watch.

'Well, the tube broke down and…'

'Next door and bring me a coffee.' I nod to my left. I return my attention to the file. I can hear muttered good mornings and the whine of the Welsh valleys, another reason I don't like Gladys Jones. Bradbury reappears.

'Coffee, sir?'

'Across the landing, that's where it used to be anyway.'

'Ah, yes,' Bradbury turns to retrace his steps. The tuneless whistle recommences; this could get quite tiresome. At least he hasn't got that thing sticking in his ear. I close the Master and Mother file and glance at the latest messages from Toulouse. Looks like the Americans are going home with their tails between their legs again. Sometimes they can be real amateurs. I shake my head.

'Fraid the china is not the best, sir,' Bradbury puts a white chipped mug in front of me. 'We are, however, self-sufficient in tea and coffee with milk and orange juice in the fridge.' Bradbury looks pleased with himself, eases into the chair in front of me.

'Probably supplied by her next door.' I nod to my left.

'Bit of a dragon, sir?' Bradbury whispers as he leans forward.

19

'A Welsh one as well,' I reply in a loud voice. 'Now, to business. Have you read the file?'

'Well, not all, sir,' Bradbury puts down his own mug. 'I've made some notes though.' He pulls a black notebook from his jacket pocket.

'Humour me,' I lean back in my chair, close my eyes and wait for him to begin.

CHAPTER TWO

The Star, Saturday night. I am standing at the bar, nursing a large whisky with a splash of water. I look around me, nod to a few of the regulars who acknowledge me and then return to their papers or private thoughts. My pretty barmaid is not here tonight. Instead there is a tall, gangly youth behind the bar with various metal studs attached to his anatomy. He says that he is a student, from Warsaw. He says he's working here to improve his English. I wish him luck. He looks at me, shrugs and starts polishing some glasses, deciding that this will be more productive.

I'm not sure why I'm here. I've sent Bradbury off to Scotland. Baxter has retired to Glen Clova in Perthshire. Took three days for him to agree to see anyone. Hasn't changed, obviously. Well, it will be good experience for Bradbury. Maybe I'm hoping that Saunders will walk through the door and I can ask him what the hell he was playing at. I've made no contact with Saunders since last Saturday; don't want Forsyth to have an inkling that we had met. There is an old man sitting beside me, emanating a slight odour that I can't quite place but it's definitely not aftershave. He's staring at a half-full glass in front of him which he suddenly finishes in a swift gulp. He wipes his mouth with a calloused, leathery hand and with a cough, a wheeze and a gruff 'G'night,' slides of his barstool and disappears behind me. The faint odour persists. I think that I will leave too when I catch sight of a woman, sitting in a far corner. Women in the Star are not a rare occurrence but women sitting on their own – well that is unusual. But there is something about her; I think I know her. It's not easy through the blue haze and dim lighting, her head down, but... I pick up my glass and wander across. As I approach, she looks up.

'It's Richard, isn't it?' A slight smile crosses her face.

'Yes, long time. Do you mind if I sit down?' I stand in front of Helen, just as pretty as I remembered her.

'Please.' She moves across the banquette, moving her tall glass to one side.

'Sorry, I'm not intruding, am I?' I sit down on the faded red leather, place my whisky on the small round table between us.

'No, no, please. It's just that I don't meet many people here whom I know.' She gives another nervous smile, takes a sip from her glass.

Her blond hair is cut shorter than I remember but her face is the same, pale complexion, pert little nose, and sensuous mouth. But it's her eyes that I remember the most, pale green, feline. She's wearing a well-cut black trouser suit, black patent shoes sit firmly on the wooden floor. At her side is a red handbag, which she opens, and takes out a packet of cigarette and a gold lighter.

'You don't mind, do you?' She takes out a cigarette.

'No, please, carry on.'

'I stopped smoking after I was married,' she lights the cigarette, ' but after John died…'

'I am so sorry that I couldn't come to the funeral, but I was abroad at the time…'

'I know, but thank you for the card,' she takes another sip, this one longer than the first.

'I meant to call you, but I…' I shrug my shoulders.

'It doesn't matter, I know you and John were friends. Anyway, I probably wouldn't have had a chance to talk to you at the funeral, there were so many people there, his regiment, the top brass, even the Minister of Defence turned up. Mind you, the television cameras were there,' she shakes her head, draws deeply on her cigarette.

'How have you been coping, it must be a year now?' I break the silence between us.

'Oh, the first few months I was numb. Both families were very supportive, but the worst part was when I was alone, especially at night.' She leans forward, takes another sip from her glass.

'And the newspaper?' I remembered that Helen had worked for The Times.

'I had compassionate leave and when I went back everyone was very nice but then they all forget; they've got their own problems. And then one of the editors wanted to do John's story, you know, from the widow's perspective. So I quit. Bloody ghouls! Even in death, they want your pound of flesh,' she stubs out her cigarette in the plastic ashtray, clasps her hands together. She gives a slight shake of her hair, as though collecting her thoughts. 'I've gone back to teaching English, at a local comprehensive. Very dull.' She turns to me with a slight smile, 'Enough about me, what have you been doing, Richard?'

'Oh, the usual, plodding away with the Foreign Office. Also very dull.' I give a slight smile, studying the glass in front of me.

'John said that you were a spook.' The voice is soft, green eyes transfix me.

'Ah, John was always very perceptive, a good imagination,' I give a short laugh but it sounds hollow.

'And Angela?' Helen changes tack, lights another cigarette, blows the smoke away from me.

I remembered now that Helen had known Angela before I'd met her husband. Helen had written an article about Angela, high-flying PR consultant, blue chip clients, that sort of thing.

'Angela and I are now divorced,' I say simply.

'Oh, I see.' Helen taps some ash into the ashtray.

'You don't sound surprised.' I watch her closely, it's the way she said it, as a matter of fact.

'When was the last time we all met?' She turns towards me, her eyebrows slightly arched.

'Er, about eighteen months ago. We had a summer party in our house in Surrey.' I remember that afternoon, beautiful and hot, but ghastly people. I'd flown in the night before from Toulouse, just wanting a quiet weekend, but Angela had arranged it otherwise. By lunch time, the smart set had invaded, with fake laughter and jollity pervading the house and grounds. At least Helen and John were there to provide some sanity. I seem to remember that John and I spent most of the afternoon sitting under an umbrella at the far end of the pool deck. As I was the host, the waiters at least kept up a steady supply of champagne. The more we drank, the more I realised how troubled John was about the events in Iraq. I was aware of Helen in the distance. She was quite beautiful that day, working the crowd, as they say. Every so often, she would turn with a smile, and wave to John. I envied John that day. Looking at her through champagne-filled eyes, did I have carnal thoughts? Maybe.

'It was Simon Jones, wasn't it?' Helen brings me out of my reverie with a jolt.

'Yes, how did you know?' An image of Simon Jones floats in front of me, tall, handsome, hale and hearty, the kind of man who walks into a room and is noticed, takes command. Everything that I didn't do, according to my wife. Maybe it was the life that I led, in the shadows, never in the spotlight.

'Woman's intuition,' Helen continues.

'Meaning?'

'A woman knows when another woman is having an affair. It was obvious that afternoon,' Helen stubs out her cigarette.

'Mm, it was evidently obvious to everyone except me,' I say bitterly.

'That's often the case, Richard,' her voice is gentle, her hand rests briefly on my knee, it feels like an electric shock.

'It's strange how we have lost both our partners,' I try to recover my composure. 'Mine through carelessness.'

'I lost John through carelessness as well,' Helen stares at me, her voice hard, bitter.

24

'What do you mean?'

'God, is that the time?' Helen looks at her watch, 'I must be going. I'm having dinner with an old school friend. That's what I'm reduced to, phoning up old school girls for dinner dates.' Helen smiles but it is a sad smile. She eases out between the table, straightening her jacket then leaning over to pick up her handbag and cigarettes. 'Well, it's been nice meeting you again…'

'Listen, maybe we could have dinner sometime?' I start to get up. She just looks at me, slipping her cigarettes and lighter into her bag. God, what a fool I am! Why on earth would she want to have dinner with me?

'Why not,' she says eventually with a smile. 'It's ages since I've had dinner with a man, make a change from discussing other peoples' children and the state of education. Yes, I'd like that,' she leans forward and gives me a peck on the cheek. I smell perfume for the first time in a long time.

'Great, maybe next week?'

'Call me. You've got John's old number? Sorry, must dash.' She gives me that little wave, just like she used to give John.

I sit down as she walks through the bar, heads turn as she passes, she has that effect on people, and then she's gone. I pick up my glass and… what do I feel? Not sure. Helen is the first woman that I've had a conversation with for a long time. And a beautiful woman at that. And that whiff of perfume, oh dear. Have I carnal thoughts? Yes. For that I feel guilty, knowing John as I did. But now he is dead. Anyway, I'm being stupid. I must be twenty years older than Helen. She couldn't possibly be interested in me, could she? I look at my glass, finish it in one. I wonder how Bradbury is getting on?

CHAPTER THREE

'Jesus Christ, is that all he said?' I look at Bradbury, across my empty desk. 'Didn't you give him the whole message?' Monday morning's good humour has vanished, thoughts of Helen are quickly banished from my mind.

'Of course, sir. Told him – Master is back in the game, needs to talk to Mother. He just looked a bit stunned by what I had said. Mind you, the whisky bottle was already half-empty, so maybe…?' Bradbury tails off into silence, letting the inference hang in the air between us.

I look at my young assistant, so new to the game, cocksure, doesn't know the history. Maybe just as well. 'So, he says Jesus Christ and then?'

'Well, after I gave him the message, he just sat there for a few minutes, sipping his whisky. And then he said that he would have to think about it. I told him that the message came via you. I gave him your card. He just said – 'tell him I'll phone.' And that was it, so I left, mission accomplished, so to speak. By the time I got back to Glasgow, I just managed to get the last flight to London. The weather was bloody awful.'

I sit there for a few minutes, my gold Parker pen tapping the desk, thinking about Sir James Baxter's reaction. To be expected? Probably, after all this time. I'd hoped that Baxter would remember me, even after all these years, as someone that Baxter would trust. Maybe not, these scars ran deep.

'What's his house like?'

'Well, it was pitch dark, difficult to tell. Not very big, grey stonework, remote as hell.'

'That sounds like Baxter, never one for ostentation,' I remember with a wry smile. 'And Baxter himself?'

'Old, coughed a lot, drank even more.'

'Baxter could always hold his drink, had a head like granite.'

'You obviously knew him, sir?'

'Oh, yes. When I first joined Intelligence in the early seventies I was made his assistant. He worked in this very same office. I was next door with a guy called Digsby, I think. I didn't realise until later that Baxter had been put out to graze here.'

'Why here?'

'Newton House, then, was full of some interesting characters, square pegs in round holes, so to speak. Thinking the unthinkable. The ground floor was known as the Brain's Trust. They came up with some weird and totally unworkable schemes, ha! We fronted fictitious companies, selling arms to people that the government wanted to help but politically couldn't. Arming and financing opposition groups, especially in Africa. We provided public deniability. These were wild times! And Baxter was nominally in charge, but he sat up here for most of the day. Reading transcripts, intercepts, still looking for Master.'

'You said that he was sent out to graze, why was that?'

'You've read the file?'

'Yes, but quite a bit seems to be missing.'

'Ah, you've noticed, very good, Bradbury.' I notice Bradbury's usual pallid skin turns pink. 'Yes, somebody has been busy with the black felt marker. Anyway, I'll be brief. In 1968, Master, our prime source across the Iron Curtain suddenly dried up. You'll remember that Master would only deal with Baxter, alias Mother. Some of the information we got was priceless, like gold dust. It stopped the Cold War becoming the Nuclear War. At one time, the Americans thought Baxter was god. But Baxter didn't like sharing with the Americans, blamed them for what happened in '68.'

'What did happen?'

'As I said, the information stopped, nothing, silence. The betting here was that he or she had been found out and had probably been killed. Baxter blamed the Americans. It was the time of the Czech crisis, remember Dubcek? Baxter claimed there had been a leak in Washington. But who knows? Maybe we're now going to find out.'

'And Baxter?'

'With Master gone, Baxter's claim to fame had also disappeared. The knives were out. Baxter had made a lot of enemies in his time. He didn't suffer fools gladly. Revenge for those on high was sweet. And so he ended up here. Ha, feels like history is repeating itself.'

'Sorry, sir?'

'Nothing, Bradbury, just a private joke.'

'And Newton House?'

'Became too small. Everybody was moved out to offices in Kings Road. Remember Sandline International? Well, MI6 was involved.'

'Really? There was all that fuss about Sierra Leone, wasn't there?'

'Oh, yes, Bradbury, there's a lot of worms in cans around here.'

'So, what do we do now?'

'I'm not waiting, put a reply in The Times, tell Master that Mother will meet him.'

I look again at my young assistant, sitting there with an inquisitive look. Eager, just like I was, many years ago. I lay my pen on the table and pick up the white, chipped mug, warming my hands in the process. This morning my office is cold. I've discovered that the heating is either on or off, there is no happy medium. I take a sip of coffee, which is rapidly cooling, and gaze at the ceiling. I see a damp patch above me, which I haven't noticed before. I stare at the ceiling again, make a mental note to get that damp patch fixed.

I think back again to these late nights in Baxter's office, this office, making serious inroads into a bottle of malt whisky. Baxter chain-smoking Senior Service cigarettes, his feet resting on his desk as he leaned back in his chair, telling me about another of his exploits. Everything seemed so simple then, you knew who the enemy was, the lines were drawn. Now it's all Sigint, signals intelligence, all very sophisticated. Humint, human intelligence, bodies on the ground, is a dying breed. Look at Bradbury, he's the future. God help us.

Sir James Baxter sits in his favourite chair, pours himself some more whisky. He leans back, studies the card left by the young man. So, Richard Stevens still works for 6, does he? Thought he would have been long gone by now. Bit of a rebel, just like me, I suppose. A faint smile crosses his lips. I've said I'd phone, maybe tomorrow. Not sure why I haven't called him already. Bit of a shock that message, a ghost from the past. Maybe I don't want to confront it. He looks at his glass, empty again. Another refill? No, better eat, otherwise I won't remember if today is this week or last week.

Suddenly the door bell rings. Baxter puts down his glass, looks at his watch, eight o' clock. Who the hell can that be? Margaret, his housekeeper? But she has her own key. Mind you, she's always losing it, probably forgotten her knitting again. Baxter stands up, staggers slightly across the lounge. One dram too many, he thinks to himself, no doubt will get a row from Margaret. He switches on the hall light, the doorbell rings again.

'I'm coming, I've only got one pair of legs, you know.' Baxter mutters to himself. He unlocks the front door, the wind blows it open, it's started raining again.

'Forgotten your key again, eh?' Baxter peers into the darkness, his befuddled mind sees the figure in black, standing to one side. 'You're not Margaret, who the hell are you…?' Sees the gun, dark metallic, glinting in the pale moonlight. A flash of bright orange, then nothing.

The figure in black steps forward, looks at Baxter lying in the hallway, a neat hole between his wide vacant eyes, blood pooling on the beige carpet. He listens for any other sound but knows that the house is empty. He's been watching Baxter's house for two days now, knows when the old woman leaves, knows Baxter doesn't have any visitors. Who'd come to this godforsaken place, anyway? The man shivers slightly, Christ it's cold! He steps forward, leans down beside Baxter, eases the wallet out of his back pocket, takes out several twenty pound notes, drops the wallet on the carpet. He stands up, takes one last look at Baxter, closes the door behind him, looks at his watch. Now for London.

I look through the Personal Column of The Times, no reply. I put down the paper, the desk phone rings.

'Stevens.'

'Is that Mr Richard Stevens?' An accented voice enquires, definitely north of the border.

'Er, yes, who is this?' I take a sip of cold coffee.

'Detective Sergeant MacKay, Perthshire police.'

'Perthshire police?' I sit back in my chair, mystified.

'Did you know Sir James Baxter, Mr Stevens?'

'Yes, I used to work with him…'

'Well, I regret to inform you that he was found dead this morning,' MacKay pauses, 'We believe that he was murdered.'

'Bloody hell!' I look towards the ceiling then close my eyes.

'Quite,' MacKay continues. 'We were aware of who Sir Baxter was, so my Superintendant phoned the Home Office first thing. They gave us your name. Mind you, we found your card in the house. Have you seen him recently?'

'No, my assistant visited him last week.'

'Care to tell me the reason for the visit?'

'Not over the phone. I'll get the next flight up to Edinburgh.'

'You'd better. Phone me back the details, we'll have a car waiting for you.' MacKay breaks the connection.

I stare at the now silent phone. Baxter dead? Oh my God!

'Coffee, sir?' Bradbury breezes into my room, late again.

'Get me on the first flight to Edinburgh.' I slam the phone down.

'Edinburgh, sir?' Bradbury retreats towards the door.

'Yes, Edinburgh, all hell is about to break loose!'

My visit to Scotland lasts the whole day. A police Range Rover picks me up from Edinburgh airport and whisks me off to Glen Clova. We pass, at high speed, through bleak-looking countryside; it starts to rain. By the time we reach Perth, it has turned to sleet. It's snowing in Glen Clova. We climb a rutted dirt track, I now understand the reason for the Range Rover. I meet MacKay, a dour humourless Scot who briefs me on the facts, which are few. The housekeeper discovered the body yesterday morning at around eight o'clock. She's being treated for shock in Perth infirmary. Baxter was killed by a single gunshot, almost between the eyes. One hundred pounds was withdrawn by the housekeeper the day before for Baxter and is now missing. Could be a random break-in gone wrong, says MacKay. There have been several burglaries in the area, addicts feeding their habit but no violence, certainly not murder. This worries MacKay, it also worries me. He quizzes me about Bradbury's visit and so I tell him it was about some previous case that needs to be cleared up. Could there be a connection with Baxter's murder? I reply no, but MacKay doesn't look convinced, and maybe neither am I, but I don't admit it. Did Baxter have any enemies? Yes, plenty, but no one that I can actually think of who would kill him, not now anyway. In the end I feel a bit sorry for MacKay. The snow has covered any tyre tracks or footprints, the nearest neighbour lives five miles away, witnesses are going to be hard to come by. At least with the bullet, they will be able to identify the gun.

Bradbury's description of the house is apt. Even in daylight, it looks grey, not particularly welcoming. Probably why Baxter chose it. I take a look inside, see the dark stain on the hall carpet, Baxter now lying in the Perth mortuary. The interior of the house is basic but comfortable; Baxter was never one for extravagance. I ask MacKay to send all Baxter's papers down to London, Official Secret's act and all that. MacKay barely nods. I look outside; the snow is falling heavily now. MacKay suggests maybe I'd better get back to Edinburgh. I gratefully accept the offer, don't want to be here any longer than I have to. MacKay sees me to the door, tells me that he'll probably have some more questions once he's finished with the house. I reply that will not be a problem. A brief handshake and I leave.

Thursday morning and the bad weather seems to have followed me down from Scotland. By the time I'd reached Edinburgh last evening, my flight was delayed due the snow. I didn't get back to the flat until midnight; haven't slept well either, thinking about Baxter. I look out of my office window, watch the rain drift across the street, thinking about yesterday's visit. Still can't believe that Baxter is dead. All these memories, so why no sorrow? I know MacKay doesn't think it was a simple break-in; heard him mutter under his breath, more like a professional hit. And if he's right, who killed Baxter and why? My eyes come back to The Times in front of me, and read Master's message again. He arrives tomorrow on the first Eurostar from Paris. Bloody great! What do I do now?

CHAPTER FOUR

I've sent Bradbury to Waterloo, to meet the first Eurostar train of the morning from Paris. Bradbury is looking for an elderly man, black woollen coat, black homburg, red scarf. Should be easy, even for Bradbury. The phone on my desk rings.

'Yes?'

'I've met him, sir. We're in a taxi, on our way to Claridges.' Bradbury sounds breathless.

'Well, don't lose him then. I'll be there in half an hour.' I replace the receiver. I look at the ceiling, the damp patch is getting bigger.

Now comes the tricky part. How will Master react when he is told that Baxter is dead. I've decided not to tell him the manner of Baxter's death; I'll see how things go first. I get up and put on my coat.

'I'll be at Claridges, if anyone wants me.' I look at Gladys, sitting at her computer, typing away.

'Some people have all the luck.' She says in that whiney Welsh voice, her face unsmiling.

I give her an icy stare, and make for the stairwell.

Forty-five minutes later, I'm sitting in a comfortable armchair in the suite reserved for a 'Mr Smith.' I've chosen Claridges as Forsyth is picking up the bill. Forsyth never attends these preliminary meetings, only at the end when he can pick up the credit and plaudits.

'He's in the bathroom,' Bradbury whispers.

'Has he said anything?' I look around the tastefully furnished room.

'Only that he's looking forward to meeting Baxter, sir.'

'Shit!'

The bedroom door opens. An elderly man appears, wearing a dark suit, white shirt, grey tie, black shoes. He stands there, very upright, a military bearing.

'Ah, Mr er...?' I stand up and cross the room to meet him.

'Smith will do in the meantime. And you are?' His English is good, a slight guttural accent. Definitely German.

'Richard Stevens and you've already met my assistant, Mr Bradbury...'

'Where is Baxter?' Mr Smith's question cuts across me like a knife.

'Ah, well, I regret to inform you that Sir James Baxter has recently died. We were going to...'

'Inform me?' The old man stares at me, his face expressionless.

'I, we, thought that this meeting should still go ahead. Sir James would have wanted it that way.'

'Really?' The old man crosses the room slowly and sits down in one of the armchairs. 'I read The Times every day and not just the Personal Column. Everything, including the Obituaries. I've not seen any mention of Baxter.'

'We've withheld his obituary until after this meeting.' I stand there for a few moments. This is not a good start. Herr Smith appears to be a tough old bird. 'I apologise that you weren't forewarned. I realise that this may have come as a shock to you.' I sit down opposite him.

'Not really,' the old man pauses, ' Sir James was about my age. I was just hoping that he was still alive. So, he never got to meet me after all.' Mr Smith slowly shakes his head, 'Pity.'

'Yes.' Silence ensues.

'I assume, Mr Stevens, that you are therefore with the Intelligence Services?'

I am suddenly aware of the old man's penetrating pale blue eyes, the lined face, the close cropped hair.

'Yes, I'm with MI6, to be precise.'

'I see.' The old man nods his head. Another silence. 'So why have British Intelligence sent you to meet me? And not Mr Forsyth?' The pale blue eyes stare me, the question hangs in the air.

I sip coffee from a porcelain cup. For hotel coffee, it's not bad. The arrival of room service has eased the tension in the room. Mr Smith is drinking tea, milk no sugar. Bradbury has found another chair in the bedroom and is now sitting behind me.

'You will understand,' I carefully put my cup and saucer back onto the table, 'that your message caused quite a stir when we received it. I mean, it's almost forty years since you were heard from.'

'I know that, but you still haven't answered my original question.' The old man pours himself more tea from a silver teapot.

'I am one of the few left that remembers Baxter. You see, when I first joined the Service, I was an assistant to him, when he returned to London from Berlin.' I sit back my armchair. 'It was thought, therefore, that I was most suited to meet you.' And basically, because no one else was bloody interested, but I bite my tongue.

'I see,' the old man mulls over what I have just said. 'And so, when do I meet Mr Forsyth?'

'After this initial meeting, I will report back to him and…'

'And if I have something sufficiently interesting to say then he may condescend to meet me, yes?'

'I wouldn't quite put it like that…'

'Never mind! Enough of this minuet, this dancing round the edges! Once you've heard what I have to say, I'm sure Mr Forsyth will make time to see me. So, how do you want to start, Mr Stevens?'

'A name would help.'

'Ah, of course! I keep forgetting that you never knew who I was,' the old man smiles for the first time. 'I am Ernst Kruger, formerly a senior officer with the East

German Intelligence Service, known more commonly as the Stasi. You don't look surprised, Mr Stevens.'

'It was assumed that you were either German or Russian, so, no, I'm not surprised.'

Bradbury has resumed his seat and takes out a Sony tape recorder, presses record.

'Your young friend can check your archives, you'll find my name there. But I should start at the beginning. I was a captain with the RSHA, German Intelligence, in April 1945. I was at the Eastern Front, when the Russians attacked through the Seelow Heights, I was captured and imprisoned. I was then moved to a prisoner of war camp near Leipzig. I would be working there as a translator; the Russians were desperate for German speakers. They had thousands, hundreds of thousands of German prisoners. They weren't bothered by the other ranks, they were only interested in the officers, particularly SS officers. When I arrived in Leipzig, I was put to work immediately. It was easy to spot the SS men, it was the tattoo on their arm that gave them away. I thought that there was a certain irony in that, both Jews and Germans dying because of a tattoo.' Kruger pauses to take a sip of tea. 'It's important that you understand the background. May I proceed?' Kruger looks across at me.

'Please do.' I settle back in my chair.

'The interrogations went on for months, into years. Then a MVD officer visited me in 1948, at the time of Berlin Airlift. Tension was high. The officer was a Major Kutzsenov. He told me that the authorities were impressed by my work. That I was to be sent to Berlin, to be part of the new security apparatus. I was overjoyed as I'd only recently been told that my wife and son had survived the war and were still in Berlin.' Kruger leans forward and pours himself more tea.

'I joined the Ministry for State Security and was made captain just as I had been in '45. Kutzsenov became my mentor. He was a very good teacher. In

1949, the German Democratic Republic was formed; the enemy was in the West. It would be in the early 50's that Baxter came to my attention. Kutzsenov used to ridicule the Western intelligence agencies. Amateurs, he used to call them. He boasted then that the KGB had highly placed informants in MI5 and MI6. I heard later about the defection of Burgess and Maclean. Philby, however, was a closely kept secret. I watched Baxter from afar, he was hitting his head against a brick wall. His agents were picked up immediately as they crossed the borders; a lot of young lives were lost. But he kept trying; I began to admire his doggedness, he never gave up. So, I decided to help him.'

'But why?' I ask the question that has puzzled many before.

'Ah, why? I suppose it's quite simple, really. You see, I'd fought for a fascist state and was now employed by a communist state. The ideologies may have been different, but the aim was the same – control of the people. The Stasi were no better than the Gestapo, maybe worse. East Germany was a Russian armed camp, Moscow ruled. I could see in West Germany the rebuilding, the freedom. That's what I wanted, one Germany. To get that, the Russians had to leave. I was prepared to do anything to achieve that.'

'And so, you contacted London'

'Yes, through my son. He was young, very brave. When he'd finished his degree, he joined the Stasi. I thought that it was better for him to be in the organisation than out of it. In hindsight, I was wrong.'

'And so, you started passing information over to Baxter. How did you get it?'

'By now, I was a colonel, respected and trusted by the Russians. Kutzsenov had started drinking by then; he was careless with his talk when he was drunk I also knew people in the East German armed forces, disillusioned like me. But I had to be very careful, one false move and I was dead. I slowly built up a network of sympathisers.

They never knew each other. They'd pass on pieces of information; I'd give what was relevant to Baxter.'

'But you never took any money. Why?'

'Why? Money was never the object, Mr Stevens. A united Germany was the object!'

'Of course. And then 1968, you vanished. What happened?' I lean forward in my chair. I will be the first person to actually hear what happened to Master.

'Ha, I'm not sure really. By 1968, Kutzsenov was now a general. He was also drinking heavily. He had developed a penchant for little girls, provided by the Stasi, of course. At the beginning of July, he was suddenly recalled to Moscow. I never saw him again. I was arrested two days later. I was taken to Hohenschonhausen, the Stasi jail in Berlin and charged with crimes against the State. They said that I was a spy, aiding and abetting the Western Powers. I still don't know how they found out, maybe a colleague at work, one of my sympathisers, Kutzsenov? Maybe. I was beaten and tortured, but I never confessed. Never gave them Baxter's name or my associates. I was tried in secret, sentenced to life imprisonment. I thought I was lucky, if I'd been sent to Lubyanka, I'd have been shot. But they did something worse.' Kruger goes quiet, takes out his handkerchief and wipes the tears from his eyes. 'They shot my wife and son.'

'My God,' I sit there stunned.

Kruger has excused himself to go to the bathroom. I stand up and wander over to the window. I look down on the traffic jam below, the busy pavements, ordinary people going about their ordinary lives.

'Do you believe all that stuff, sir.' Bradbury is still sitting, putting another cassette into the recorder.

'Why not? I don't think Herr Kruger has come all this way to tell us lies. Anyway, we can check out a lot of what he has said. I want you to got to Archives, look up what we've got on Ernst Kruger. Also check out the Stasi files, a lot of information was released by the German government in the early 90's.' I turn and look at Bradbury. 'He certainly wasn't faking the part about his wife and son. Just remember, Bradbury, in these situations you have to be patient. Kruger is telling us his story, at his pace. We've reached the middle of his story, it's the ending which going to be the really interesting part.'

Kruger reappears, he suddenly looks his age, the previous erect figure now stooped. He makes his way slowly across the room and sits down.

'I realise that this is not easy for you, Herr Kruger. Maybe you would like a break?' I sit down opposite him.

'No, no, I'm fine now. Some of these memories are still very painful.'

'Of course, I understand. Would you like something to eat?' I glance at my watch.

'Yes, that would be good. Just a sandwich will do, I don't have much appetite these days.'

'Something to drink?'

'A glass of white wine, if I may. Dry.'

'Order a platter of sandwiches, Bradbury, and see if they've got a bottle of Chablis.'

The sandwiches arrive, the wine is poured. Kruger asks about Baxter, what happened to him when he returned to London. I give him the sanitised version, don't mention that Baxter was eventually kicked out. Tell him about Baxter's house in the Scottish glens, don't mention the dark stain on the hall carpet. Kruger sits there, taking an occasional sip of wine, maybe visualising Baxter in retirement. I finish the last sandwich; I've barely touched my wine, must keep a clear head.

'Maybe, we could continue, Herr Kruger?'

'Yes, of course.' The old man pours himself some more wine, then settles back in his chair. He's quiet for a few moments, recollecting his thoughts.

'I was in that stinking prison for over twenty years. There were times when I'd thought I would never survive,' Kruger shakes his head. 'But then I would remember, these people, these animals, who laughed at me, who told me that my wife and son had been shot. Then I got down on my knees and prayed, yes prayed, that I would survive and one day tell the world what these bastards had done!' Kruger stares at his glass, then takes another sip.

'And I did survive. One day in the middle of December,1989, my cell door was flung open. A stranger stood in front of me. He told me that I was free. Free! Can you imagine?'

'And you walked out free?'

'They took me to hospital in an ambulance. I was there for two weeks. When I was fit enough, I had a visit from two Germans. I knew they were from Intelligence, the BND. Even after 22 years I could spot them from a mile off,' Kruger gives a short laugh. 'They were polite, though, gently probing. But they really weren't very interested in me. I'd been out of circulation for too long. Spy games of the 50's and 60's were in the distant past. No, they wanted the names of the Stasi executioners, the torturers. I told them who had arrested me, told them that I didn't know who had executed my wife and son. They said that they would look into it. I never saw them again. The day that I was passed fit to leave the hospital, a young lady visited me. She was from some government agency or other. Told me that I was entitled to a State pension and that I could return to my old flat. She was very kind, they were all very kind. It was very difficult to get used to that after all these years.'

'And so, you stayed in Berlin?'

'Yes, of course, it was my home. The Wall had come down. We were free! I was both happy and sad. Sad about my family but happy that Germany was finally going to be united.' Kruger smiles and nods to himself and refills his glass. 'It took me a year to regain my health. The next few years are not important,' he gives a dismissive wave.

'I was always a keen bridge player. There was a bridge club near my flat. I went there three or four times a week, sometimes just for the company. It must have been 1995 that I bumped into Klaus Pieck. He was ex Stasi, we'd met briefly in the sixties, now also retired. We had a drink together, talked about old times. We never discussed my imprisonment, strange, when I come to think of it. I think he'd told me at one stage that his wife was dead and his son was in the Army. The following year, Pieck became ill and died shortly afterwards. I went to his funeral. There weren't many people in the church but I met his son, Otto, he would have been in his late forties, tall and thin. I assumed that I would never meet him again, but I was wrong.' Kruger puts down his empty glass, declines a refill from Bradbury.

'We now move to May 1998. I left the club one night, and outside Otto Pieck was waiting for me. I must admit, I was quite surprised. We talked about this and that and then he asked if he could walk me home. I said of course, I was delighted with any company. As we walked, I could tell that there was something troubling Pieck. When we reached my block of apartments, I was about to bid him good night when he grasped my arm and said could we discuss something professional, in private. He looked around him as if he was being watched. I was intrigued, my old intelligence antennae were alerted. I took him up to my flat, made coffee, we had a schnapps. My flat is quite small but it's comfortable enough. Pieck sat on the small settee, I sat opposite. He was obviously nervous, said how much he had appreciated me coming to his father's funeral. He said that his father had told him about me, about my imprisonment, that I had never given up any names and thus saved quite a few lives. Most important was that I could be trusted. I thanked him for his kind words. I poured out another schnapps. Otto Pieck said he had been an officer in the East German army. His father had persuaded him to join the Stasi, which he had done reluctantly. He eventually specialised in Middle East affairs. And then the Wall came down and Germany was re-unified. He assumed that he was out of a job, but the BND recruited him, his experience and contacts would be useful to them. So, life was good again or so he thought. He then told me that, at the beginning of '98, an enquiry from Mossad had crossed his desk. The Israelis had information that an unknown Arab terrorist group were in the market for a nuclear device.'

'I remember that, it was in February,' I interrupt him. 'We, the French and the Americans, all received a similar enquiry. The Israelis were always paranoid about some dissident group getting their hands on a nuclear weapon.'

'Maybe they have a right to,' Kruger pauses. 'Anyway, Pieck told me that he had just returned from Rome. A holiday, mixed with some business. He'd contacted one of his old sources, an Arab, Mohammed Habtoor. The meeting took place outside the Vatican, always very crowded; a good place to meet. Habtoor was a wheeler-dealer, mostly second-hand arms. He'd supplied the guerillas in Afghanistan and others, made a fortune, but now he's semi-retired. So, Pieck then cut his holiday short, for he now had a name.' Kruger stops and stares at me.

'Who?'

'Osama Bin Laden'

There is total silence in the room.

'Good God!' I eventually say.

'God may not help us, Mr Stevens. You see, much has happened since. Otto Pieck died one month ago. I think he was murdered.'

CHAPTER FIVE

I'm sitting alone at my desk. I've had to make my own coffee this morning. The Welsh dragon doesn't work on Saturdays, thank God. In fact, there doesn't seem to be anyone else in the building. It's very quiet, the only noise comes from the outside, the occasional peel of laughter from a passerby below. A good time to think, and I have much to think about.

I am thinking about what Kruger has told me so far. So why is he here? There was a eight-year gap between the first mention of Bin Laden and now, so what had happened in between? I've sent Bradbury to Archives this morning, to find out about Ernst Kruger. Bradbury is not best-pleased; he was supposed to be spending the weekend with Mummy and Daddy, in Surrey. Well, tough.

Well, I'd better get going. I check the radiator, still cold. Glad I'm leaving. I slip on my coat, thinking, I wonder what Kruger is going to say? A nuclear bomb hidden in Berlin? Maybe Bin Laden is alive and well in Bavaria. I chuckle to myself at the thought. Just as well Forsyth isn't around, he'd tell me I'm wasting my time. I haven't told Kruger that Forsyth isn't here. For Forsyth is on one of his favourite jaunts, to Washington. Forsyth loves Washington, loves Langley. Sitting at the same table with the real power brokers of the world. Forsyth thinks he's a big fish over there. I liken him more to a minnow, swimming in shark-infested waters. A quick glance at my watch, time to go.

I sit in the same armchair as yesterday. There is a breakfast tray in front of Kruger, he finishes the last piece of toast. He has offered me coffee, but I've declined. The first coffee of the day already sits uneasily in my stomach.

'I hope I'm not spoiling your weekend, Mr Stevens?' Kruger leans back in his chair, wiping some crumbs and butter from his mouth with a white linen napkin.

'No, not at all.'

'Mrs Stevens…?'

'Divorced.'

'Ah, yes. That often happens in our line of work.' Kruger nods his head slowly. 'And Mr Bradbury?'

'Will be joining us later.' I look at his watch, he's late. 'But maybe we should get started.'

'Of course. Where did I finish?' Kruger leans forward and places his now neatly folded napkin on the tray.

'Otto Pieck.'

'Ah, yes, poor Otto.' Kruger pauses for a moment. 'You will have realised that more than ten years have passed since I first met him.'

'Yes.'

'When Pieck passed on the name of Bin Laden to his superiors, nothing happened. Now, I'm sure that you are well aware, Bin Laden's name was already known to the West, even then. His threats to America and Israel were in the public domain. So, Pieck was worried and upset.'

'Why upset?'

'He felt like an ousider. You must remember that he was from East Germany and an ex Stasi employee. He felt that he'd been employed as a token, you know, the good West Germans helping out their poor cousins from the East. And he was still a communist, poor fool. He thought then that some of his colleagues were fascists. He'd come to me because he didn't have anyone else to talk to, now that his father had gone. Maybe he was looking for another father figure. I may have become that over the years that followed. Anway, I told him not to be disheartened, to keep working, keep his head down, that sort of thing. I told him that he could come and see me whenever he wanted to. As it happened, he was a keen bridge player, like his father, and so he used to come along to my club. Afterwards, we would go back to my flat and chat. It became something of a ritual.'

There is a knock at the door. Bradbury enters. Good mornings are exchanged. Bradbury takes off his coat, sits down beside me. I give him a glare. He quickly takes out his cassette recorder.

'Please continue,' I nod to Kruger.

'We now come to the beginning of June 2001. He came to the club one night; he was late. I could see that he was agitated, he played terribly. Back at my flat, he told me that something big was going to happen, that Bin Laden was involved.'

'Where was he getting his information?' I lean forward, I think I can guess what the something big is.

'Pieck, remember, specialised in the Middle East. The Stasi had a lot of dealings with Syria, Iran, Iraq and Libya. He'd kept up his old contacts when he joined the BND. He said that, lately, he'd been picking up a lot of traffic, chatter on the airwaves. He'd made enquiries but his contacts, even Habtoor, were suddenly unavailable. The BND also knew there was something going on, so did the French. And yet, the Americans did nothing. I've always found that very strange.'

I almost add that the British did nothing as well, but decide to keep quiet.

'Then, I saw Pieck shortly after 9/11. He was quite shaken, well, weren't we all. He felt that certain people in the BND had known more than they were letting on.'

'What did he mean?'

'You remember, later, that two of the hijackers had been in Hamburg?'

'Yes.'

'The BND hailed this discovery as a great intelligence coup. The Americans gave them a big pat on the back. Pieck thought it was a joke. He told me that the BND had a file on those two six months before. They did nothing.'

'Who knows about all this?'

45

'Myself and Pieck. And you know what happened to Pieck, Mr Stevens.'

Deja vu, I'm thinking. Just like yesterday. Kruger drops these little bombshells every so often. Maybe he's just making sure that I'm paying attention.

'After this, Pieck was moved sideways, so to speak. He was assigned to an anti-drug smuggling section. The BND were trying to infiltrate some of the Eastern European drug gangs, particularly the Albanians.'

'Why did Pieck think he was being moved sideways?'

'It was obvious. He was asking too many awkward questions about 9/11. He was certain that there was a pro-Arab clique in the BND. There was a cover-up going on. Someone, maybe high up, wanted him out of the loop.'

'So, what happened next?'

'This is where we start treading in deep waters, Mr Stevens. I don't need to tell you that the drugs business is a multibillion dollar industry. It involves the Mafia and other international criminal gangs. It has also attracted terrorist groups. The BND and the German police were paricularly interested in the criminal gangs operating abroad. Pieck, therefore, had dealings with the Russian intelligence service, the FSB. And whoever thought that they had put Pieck out to pasture were wrong. He was very active over the next few years, put quite a few smugglers behind bars. In 2006, there had been an increase of drug trafficking in Munich. It was thought that an Albanian group was involved. The FSB suspected that there was a connection between Odessa and Tirana, that the Russian Mafia were involved. It would be about December that a report landed on Pieck's desk. There was to be a sting operation, involving a certain Mohammed Habtoor.'

'I thought he was the arms dealer?'

'Very good, Mr Stevens, you are paying attention.' Kruger gives a thin smile. 'Now, Pieck had known

Habtoor for many years and, as far as he knew, he'd never dealt in drugs. Something was amiss. So, he met with Habtoor in Vienna, that would be the end of December.'

'And what happened?' I glance at my watch

'Patience, Mr Stevens, patience. I think Pieck was going to warn off Habtoor. I suppose a sort of friendship had developed over the years between them. You have to remember that the Stasi had used Habtoor to supply various dissident factions in the Middle East, just to keep the pot boiling, so to speak. So, Pieck never told me what he said, only that Habtoor was very grateful. But, Pieck did receive something in return. Habtoor described it as a quid pro quo, something that he had never told anybody. He told Pieck that he'd been approached by a German for the supply of a nuclear device in 2001. Should Habtoor have a client who was interested, the device would be provided, free of charge.'

'Bloody hell!' I sit there in disbelief.

Kruger ignores this outburst and continues, 'Habtoor told him that the man he met called himself Herr Schmidt. Habtoor had made enquiries and found out that this was a false name, not surprising, really. The meetings were always in the Hotel Kaiserhof, in Vienna, and that on the last two or three occasions, Schmidt appeared to have stayed overnight. Habtoor gave Pieck the dates of these meetings, but said contact had been broken after 9/11. At this point they parted company, Habtoor promising to keep in touch with Pieck, should he hear again from this Herr Schmidt. So, Pieck goes to the Kaiserhof, shows his credentials to the manager, tells him he's investigating a drug smuggling gang. Now, five years have passed since Schmidt's last visit. Finding out about him will not be easy. But Pieck is lucky because all guests who stay in the Emperor suite receive Christmas cards every year and there is Schmidt's name. And the address is the Berlin office of KK Industries.'

'KK Industries?' I must look mystified.

'Come, come, Mr Stevens, you must have heard of Kurt Kohler?'

I turn to Bradbury, scribbling away in his notebook. Bradbury stops and looks up. He put a hand in his jacket pocket and takes out his mobile.

'KK phone, as good as Nokia but cheaper.' Bradbury smiles as he puts his phone back

'Ah, yes, of course, KK hotels,' I suddenly remember.

'Kohler is, what you English would say, a magnate.' Kruger continues, 'very wealthy, very powerful. Not just in Germany but also in Europe. He also has political ambitions.'

'So, Pieck thought it was Kohler who met Habtoor?'

'Oh, no. If it was Kohler, he wouldn't be involved personally. No, he would use an intermediary.'

'Who, then?'

'When Pieck returned from Vienna, he started investigating KK Industries. Not easy, as Kohler is a very private person. Although recently, he's had a much more public profile. And in public, he's always accompanied by a certain Herr Haller.'

'Haller?'

'Yes, Franz Haller. He's Kohler's private secretary, at least that's what he's officially called. But Haller has a police record, admittedly in his youth, for smuggling and violent assault.

'So, Pieck suspected that Haller was the intermediary.'

'Yes. So he sent a recent photograph of Haller, at some charity ball, to the manager at the Kaiserhof. The manager confirmed that, according to his assistant manager, who had been the receptionist at the time, the photograph resembled Herr Schmidt.'

'And, I assume, that if it was indeed Haller, he was there at the behest of Kohler?'

'Correct.'

'I see,' I say slowly, 'but actually, I don't see. What on earth is Kohler doing by being involved with the purchase of a nuclear bomb?'

'The same question that confronted Pieck. And sometimes, you have to look back at history to get the answer, Mr Stevens.'

'Meaning?'

'Kohler's father was General Heinrich Kohler of the Wehrmacht. He was also a Nazi, through and through.'

'Like father, like son, then?'

'I haven't finished yet, Stevens. In 1945, he surrendered to the Americans. Some thought this was out of character with him, considering his war record and how highly he was thought of by Hitler. After the war, he set up a construction company, the rest they say, is history. But there was always a mystery of where he got the money to set up the company in the first place.'

'So, you think this Kurt Kohler is a closet Nazi?'

'When I returned to West Berlin,' Kruger ignores the question, 'I was shocked to see the swastika daubed on walls. You see, in East Germany, all vestiges of Nazism had been eradicated. But it had reappeared in West Gemany. I never thought that I would see again 'Juden Raus' sprayed on a wall, quite shocking.' Kruger shakes his head. 'And then these skinheads parading through the streets, arms outstretched, frightening.'

'But you don't take these people seriously, do you?'

'People didn't take them seriously in the the 30's, and look what happened, Mr Stevens.'

' Quite, but Kohler doesn't parade about as a Nazi, does he?'

'Oh no, he's too clever for that. He's far more dangerous, powerful and wealthy and undercover.'

'Undercover?'

'There are various neo-Nazi associations in Germany today, Mr Stevens, you'd be surprised. These people still worship Adolf Hitler and are proud, if that's the right word, to show it. But there are others who shun the spotlight, they're the ones to be worried about.'

'And you think Kohler fits the latter category?'

'Pieck thought so and he convinced me. You see, after the war, there were all these rumours about Odessa and such like. There was also a rumour that Hitler had chosen certain individuals, in the army and business, to escape to the West, before the war ended. They were to be the nucleus to fulfill Hitler's wishes. There was never any proof, of course, nothing was ever written down.'

'And you think Kohler's father was one of them?'

'Yes, I have come to that conclusion. It would explain why he surrendered. I think that he was told to.'

'Er, Herr Kruger, this is an extraordinary story,' I finally say.

'It's not a work of fiction, Mr Stevens, believe me. You see, Habtoor called Pieck again. He told Pieck that Schmidt had been in contact, the deal was back on the table.'

'What? A nuclear bomb?'

'Yes, and because of it, Pieck died.'

'And how did he die?'

'Two weeks after he told me about Kohler's connection and Habtoor's call, he fell under a train at the Banhoffstrasse. The newspapers reported it as suicide, his office said that he'd been depressed at the time. I knew this was rubbish. The last time I'd seen Pieck he was very excited, had something to go on, expose even.'

'So, you think he was pushed and if so, by whom?'

'I'm sure that he was pushed. Maybe by someone in the BND or by Haller, he's certainly capable of it.'

'But why didn't you go to the police?'

'What with? I'd no evidence and I didn't want to end up like Pieck.'

'So, you contacted us.'

'Yes. I didn't know if Baxter would still be alive but I thought that my message would at least make people curious and it did. So, when do I meet Forsyth?'

'He arrives back tomorrow night, I'll arrange a meeting on Monday morning. Would you like some lunch or…?'

'No, thank you. I've said enough, I will tell the rest of what I know to Mr Forsyth. I need some fresh air, I think I'll take a walk, take in some of the sights, you see I've never been to London before.' Kruger stands up, indicating that the meeting is over.

'One more thing, why Paris?'

'What do you mean?'

'Your message came through the British Embassy in Paris.'

'Ah yes,' Kruger pauses, 'you see after Pieck was murdered I went on the run, so to speak. I was being followed, don't know who by. So I went to Paris, needed to get out of Germany, stayed in a little nondescript hotel on the Left Bank, waited for your reply.'

'Are you still being followed?' Maybe I should tell him the truth about Baxter.

'I don't think so, not in Paris anyway,' Kruger smiles briefly.

'Well, we'll keep an eye out for you, Herr Kruger. I'll come by tomorrow morning,' I stand up, Bradbury follows suit.

'Goodbye for now, Mr Stevens, thank you for being so patient. Please inform Mr Forsyth of the importance of our next meeting.' Kruger gives a slight bow.

Bradbury and I walk down the hotel corridor in silence. As we approach the lift lobby, Bradbury says, 'Do you think all this is true, sir?'

'If it is, Bradbury, then we could all be in deep shit!' I press the lift button, 'and I shall have great pleasure in landing this right in Forsyth's lap.'

The main lobby is busy with guests arriving, guests leaving, people waiting, people heading for the restaurants. Bradbury looks at his watch.

'If I hurry, I could catch the three o' clock train.'

'You're not catching any train, Bradbury. You will wait here and follow Herr Kruger on his sightseeing trip.' I ignore the look of disappointment on Bradbury's face. 'Look out for anyone tailing him. They did teach you how to follow someone, I hope?'

'Of course, sir.'

'Well, don't bloody lose him! When he gets back here, you can wait in the lounge until he goes to bed. I'll have someone cover for you during the night. I want you back here at 9:00 am tomorrow.'

'But sir...' Bradbury starts to protest.

'And speak to the manager. I want all phone calls from Kruger's room monitored.' I turn to leave. 'By the way, give me your recorder. I will also be working, Bradbury. I'm going back to the office to type up my report. Phone me there if anything happens.'

I look at the computer screen, the final paragraph of my report is finished. I lean back in my chair and yawn, it's been a long day. I wonder how Bradbury is doing, hoping that he hasn't managed to lose Kruger. This lack of manpower is all Forsyth's fault. All this surveillance of suspected terrorists, a waste of time. Should just lock the bastards up. I eventually stand up and stretch myself. Right, time for home, just print out my report, send it across to Forsyth's assistant, Henshaw. Let him be the bearer of bad news, I smile to myself.

Ernst Kruger hurries along the crowded pavement. He hadn't realised that London would be so busy, is looking forward to the tranquility of his hotel room. As he's jostled and bumped, Kruger thinks about his meeting this morning and the day before. He's satisfied, so far, just given enough information to Stevens, his debriefer, to keep him interested until his boss Forsyth appears. Kruger prides himself on being able to assess people within minutes of meeting them, a skill which was a necessity in the past. But he's having trouble with Stevens, can't quite work him out, and that's annoying him. And what about Forsyth, the head of MI6? Read a bit about him, seems young for the job. Hope he can handle what I'm about to tell him. He'd better, otherwise an awful lot of people are about to die.

Kruger quickly enters the hotel, glances back, sees Bradbury loitering outside a shop window. Kruger shakes his head, he sticks out like a sore thumb. From a crowded pavement, Kruger is confronted by a crowded lobby. A bus load of Americans has just arrived; raucous voices reverberate around the reception area. Kruger navigates himself around the many suitcases strewn over the floor, a young bellboy is manfully loading up a trolley. Kruger extricates his room key from a harrassed-looking receptionist. The equilibrium of Claridges appears to have been upset. Kruger heads for the lifts, one arrives almost immediately and thankfully empty. He gets out on the fourth floor, walks along the corridor, inserts his room key, opens the door. The room is in darkness, the outside light fading fast. He finds the light switch by feel, presses it, nothing happens. Strange, I'm sure the lights were working before I left. Makes his way slowly across the thickly-carpeted floor, opens the bathroom door, finds the light switch. White, bright light cascades down from silver recessed downlighters. That's better, he thinks to himself. He stands in the doorway, looking at his reflection in the mirror in front of him. Doesn't see the figure in black emerge from the gloom behind, only sees the glint of the piano wire as it is looped over his head. He does feel the wire slicing into his throat, feels the knee in the small of his back, his upper body being pulled backwards. His hands try desperately to pull at the wire, but his assailant is too strong. The oxygen supply is now cut off from his brain, consciousness slips away, bladder and bowels empty simultaneously. Kruger's last living thought, through the blinding pain, is seeing the face of his murderer, smiling. I know that man!

The man in black feels Kruger go limp, pulls the wire ever more tightly, through skin then thorax. Blood sprays out against the mirror; Kruger's once white shirt turns violent red. The man lets go of one of the wooden handles of the piano wire, Kruger's body slowly slides to the floor. Blood quickly pools on the white marble floor. He steps over the body, stands in front of the wash basin, rinses the piano wire clean, puts it in his jacket pocket. He examines his black leather gloves, rubs away some specks of blood. Checks his jacket and trousers, both clean, good. Peers at the mirror, smooths his hair back. Takes one last look at Kruger, his nose twitches at the smell emanating from the almost decapitated body. Looks back at the mirror, smiles again.

'Better phone Berlin then,' he says to himself.

'Mr Stevens!'

I look across the busy hotel lobby, watch my young assistant running towards me. I glance at my watch, it's just after nine o' clock, Sunday morning, my day of rest, fat chance! 'Where's Kruger?'

'Well, I was waiting for you, sir, I…'

'Come on, Bradbury, we haven't got all bloody day!' I head for the reception desk, Bradbury in my wake. The receptionist rings Mr Smith, room 404, no reply. I stand there for a few moments, maybe Kruger has gone for a morning constitutional or maybe he's having breakfast. A quick look around the restaurant confirms that Kruger isn't having his morning cornflakes. But a group of Americans appear to be demolishing the buffet table. I suddenly regret just having a cup of coffee before I left.

'Let's try his room.' I survey the mayhem as Bradbury glances around then picks up two croissants from the large wicker bread basket. He offers me one, but I decline.

The hotel corridor is empty, the only sound from a muffled television somewhere. Bradbury has finished his breakfast, buttered flakes stick to his tie.

'Mr Kruger?' I knock on the door of room 404. Silence. I knock again. Nothing. I try the door handle, locked.

'Where can he be, sir?'

'If I knew that, I wouldn't be bloody standing here, would I?' I pace around the corridor. 'Go and get the manager, and bring a key!' I wave Bradbury off. Where the hell is Kruger? Forsyth will now be back later today. His officious little assistant, Henshaw, had phoned me earlier, saying that he was coming back on an earlier flight. Would have to go to the office first though, to change. Ah yes, change into his interrogation suit, the dark grey pinstipe, crisp white shirt, some club tie or other, black patent shoes. His action man look, huh! I see Bradbury hurry back down the corridor, a young officious looking man in tow.

'This is highly irregular, you know. Our hotel guests' privacy is…'

'Look Mr…eh,' I glance at the badge on the manager's jacket, 'Mr Reynolds, Mr Smith is a guest of Her Majesty's government and I need to find him, now!' I flash my identity card in front of him.

'Well, it's still…' Reynolds straigthens his jacket.

'Just open the bloody door, Reynolds!'

The young man steps back, mouthing words which don't come out. He looks at me, then Bradbury, decides maybe it would be better just to unlock the door. To maintain some vestige of dignity, he makes a great show of choosing the correct key.

'Thank you, Mr Reynolds, wasn't so painful, was it?' I brush pass him into an empty bedroom. The bed hasn't been slept in, curtains are drawn, pale morning sunlight filters into the room. But it's the smell that I notice first, the smell of death. Very unpleasant, never forgotten. I walk towards the bathroom, the door is open, the light is on. I see the blood first, a deep red swathe across the white floor. I push the door open, see the shoes then the trousers. Kruger's head is at a very strange angle, it's then that I notice that it is barely attached to his torso. Bradbury is behind me, his recently consumed breakfast is quickly deposited on the bedroom carpet.

'Jesus Christ!' I can hear the hotel manager shout.

'Call the police, Reynolds,' I say simply and step back from the door. Reynolds, ashen-faced, just nods, turns and runs out of the bedroom. I walk slowly across to the bed and sit on the edge. Bradbury stands there looking distinctly unwell, dabs his mouth with a handkerchief, starts shivering.

I've seen death before, once in Cairo and once in Buenos Aires, theirs not ours. Both clean head shots, not like the abattoir in there. I try to collect my thoughts. Was it just yesterday that I was sitting in this same hotel room? Kruger recounting his extraordinary story, a story that was to be finished today and now never will be. How has it come to this? I shake my head. Forsyth will go ballistic and it will all be my fault, again. I need some help.

'Bishop here.' The voice is strong, commanding.

'Sir Edward, it's Richard Stevens here.'

'Stevens? God, are you still around? What the bloody hell do you want? It's Sunday afternoon, you know.'

'Yes, sir. I apologise for calling you, but something has cropped up…'

'You people always call at the most inconvenient time. I've got a table at the Ivy tonight, taken me bloody weeks to get it…'

'I am sorry, sir, I wouldn't have phoned you unless it was urgent.'

'Oh, it's always urgent with you people, go on then.' Bishop gives an audible sigh.

'We were debriefing a German. He went for a walk and wound up dead.'

'And?'

'He was murdered, rather brutally. I'd like you to do the autopsy.'

'I see. Well, you're doing your best to spoil my weekend. She is young and very pretty, you know.'

'I apologise again, sir. The man is called Kruger, the body is at Guy's.'

'I assume you'll do all the necessary paperwork, don't want to be accused of body snatching.' Bishop gives a faint laugh.

'I'll arrange everything, sir.'

'Good. Where will you be?'

'In the office, I'll give you my number.'

'Is Forsyth involved?'

'He will be.'

'God help you, then.' Bishop hangs up.

I stare at the silent receiver and then slowly put it down. Damn! Why me? I think to myself. It started with a simple message, now there are two dead bodies. And if what Kruger said was true, then there could be a lot of dead bodies before this is finished.

CHAPTER SIX

'So, what's this all about, Richard?' Forsyth's fingers thrum on the desk top, a sign of his impatience. Forsyth's eyes are red, he stifles a yawn, he's just flown in from Washington. I'm sitting in front of him. Henshaw, his assistant is to his right, standing, a smirk on his face.

'You've read my report? I enquire politely.

'Haven't had time, but Henshaw has briefed me,' the thrumming continues. 'I'm away for less than a week and now we have two murders on our hands, huh!' Forsyth turns to Henshaw, shakes his head. 'And some cock and bull story about a closet Nazi wanting to give al-Qaeda a nuclear bomb, really!' Forsyth rolls his eyes to the ceiling.

'Well, because of this cock and bull story, Baxter and Kruger are now dead.' I'd like to wipe that smirk off Henshaw's face.

'Meaning?' Forsyth looks at me as if I'm some kind of simpleton.

'Someone knew Kruger was coming to London, knew what he was going to tell. This someone didn't want Kruger and Baxter to meet.' I'm trying hard to keep my cool.

'But Kruger met you.' The thrumming stops.

'Yes, and that obviously wasn't meant to happen. Whoever it is maybe made their first mistake.'

'Maybe,' Forsyth nods slowly, purses his lips. 'And you say that the debriefing wasn't complete?' Forsyth raises an eyebrow.

'No, whatever else he had to say, he wanted you to be present.'

'So, we have one of the wealthiest men in Germany, who out of the kindness of his heart, wants to donate a nuclear device to al-Qaeda. Why?'

'Maybe that's what Kruger was going to tell you.'

'Any ideas?'

'None at the moment. Still can't get my head around why Kohler would be involved with such a thing.'

'Quite and that's the problem. We only have Kruger's word about all this, there's no proof.'

'Except that we have two murders…'

'Granted, but I need proof about Kohler. You'd better get started, Richard. Contact our embassy in Bonn, see what you can find out. Low key, remember, this could be a political hot potato.' Forsyth leans forward, opens one of the several files in front of him.

'And the Americans?' I ask, but I know the answer.

'Leave them to me,' Forsyth looks up at me, ' and I also don't want Mossad tramping all over London.'

'Doesn't leave me much to go on, does it?'

'Well, we'll see just how good you are, won't we.' The bastard's hanging me out to dry! A casual wave of the hand, I am dismissed. I stand up, make for the door.

'One last thing, if al-Qaeda get this nuclear device, where's it headed for?' I turn and look at Forsyth.

'That does not bear thinking about, Richard.' Forsyth's face is for once a mask.

I'm back at Newton House, drinking coffee, trying to keep warm. The bloody heating is off again. I sit at my desk, thinking about my meeting with Forsyth. Strange, no histrionics, no recriminations. Forsyth was quite calm about the whole thing. He's up to something, but what? My thoughts are interrupted by the phone ringing,

'Stevens.'

'Richard, I was given this number by Vauxhall Cross, something about Newton House.'

'Henri, good to hear from you.' Henri Lefevre, my opposite number in French counter intelligence. 'It must be important if you're phoning on a Sunday.'

'Yes, my wife is not happy, we're supposed to be going to her parents for dinner. But something has cropped up.'

Project Phoenix. A year ago, Airbus had approached the French government expressing concerns about industrial espionage. Somebody was trying to buy information about the new jumbo Airbus, probably the Americans. It wasn't the first time our friends across the water had dabbled in a bit of spying on their European friends. They'd done it in the 90's, also in France, caused quite a political stink. It would appear that they were at it again. I'd become involved to protect British interests, British Aerospace were making the wings and Rolls Royce the engines. I'd known Henri for about a year now, had become good friends. He's sharp as a pin and his English is better than my French.

'I'm listening, Henri,' I shiver slightly, it's bloody cold in the office.

'You remember the French and the Italian engineers that we picked up?' Thanks to Henri's doggedness and surveillance, we'd caught two engineers red-handed in separate bars in Toulouse. Money was being exchanged, Americans had left in a hurry.

'Yes and both are going to jail.' I switch on my computer, open my Phoenix file.

'Well, the Italian has been talking some more,' Henri pauses.

'And?' I scroll my screen, looking for names.

'He claims there's a third on the American payroll,' another pause, 'and that he's a Brit.'

'Oh shit!' I can feel a headache coming on.

'I thought that would be your reaction.'

I can hear a chuckle from Henri down the line. Damn! I thought we'd wound up Phoenix. I'll have to go through all the Brits working in Toulouse again. 'He wouldn't have a name, would he?' I say in more desperation than hope.

'Ah, if only things were that simple, Richard. No, evidently his American handler let it slip at one of their meetings, but no names mentioned. And, by the way, O'Reilly has been seen in Toulouse again.'

'O'Reilly! What's that Irish bastard doing down there again? Thought our old friend Kelly had pulled him out of there.' O'Reilly works out of the American embassy in Paris, something to do with promoting American trade. Kelly pulls his strings from Langley. Henri is sure that O'Reilly was at the meetings, just before the two engineers were caught. And we know he's really with the CIA.

'Precisely. They must be still running somebody. But whom?'

Bloody Americans! I've got enough on my plate now with this Kruger business. I click on my suspects file, scroll down the names, 'Bear with me, Henri, I'm looking now. Let's see, we know from our information that it wasn't the wing design.'

'Yes, and the Frenchman and the Italian were working on the navigational systems.'

'So, it must be the engines. I'm looking at the Rolls Royce personnel. Now, there were four that were senior enough but three of them left three months ago. We're left with Andrew Johnston. He also worked on the new Eurofighter engine, Pratt and Whitney would certainly be interested in him.'

'But, you checked him out, didn't you?'

'Of course! Nothing untoward, no bulging bank accounts, no flashy cars. Married, two children, lives in Manchester.'

'Maybe he's just very careful, Richard?'

'Maybe,' I quickly scan through the life of Andrew Johnston - Grammar school education, degree in engineering, worked for Rolls Royce for twenty years, now senior design engineer. Yes, Pratt and Whitney would like to get inside his head.

'You think it's him?'

'Could be, didn't you tail him for a couple of week last summer?'

'Yes, but nothing untoward. Spent most of his time in the office, even Saturdays except when he went down to the coast. Played golf on Sundays.'

'Did you say golf, Henri?' For some reason, my interest is piqued.

'Yes, Richard, we do have golf courses in France, you know.'

'I know, I know, what did your people do when he was playing golf?'

'Sat in the bar, maybe had a couple of beers. When he'd finished, they followed him home.'

'But, who was he playing with, Henri?'

'Listen, Richard, I'm not a, what do you say, golfer. Who would he be playing with?'

'You usually play with other people, Henri, golf clubs don't like you playing on your own, especially when it's busy. And I'd like to know who his golf partners were.'

'Meaning?'

'Our friend O'Reilly plays golf.'

'Ah, now I think I can see light at the end of the tunnel.'

'Precisely. It takes about four hours to play a round of golf, plenty of time to discuss things of a mutual interest. I wonder.'

'So, what do we do?'

'We need surveillance, 24 hours.'

'I don't have the men now, Richard. My superiors think Phoenix is completed...'

'I'll send Mitchell down from Paris to help.'

'Okay, okay, I'll see what I can do. Maybe I can use Yvette.'

'Who's Yvette?'

'She's one of our more athletic officers. Maybe she'd like to take up golf. She's also very pretty, has a most persuasive mouth.'

'Henri, Johnston is happily married.'

'You haven't seen Yvette's mouth. Maybe I'll introduce you when you're next in Paris.'

'Henri, sometimes you have a one-track mind.'

'But, Richard, I am French. Anyway, what is this Newton House that you're working in? Have you been a bad boy again?'

'Yeah, something like that.'

'Richard, you must stop standing on Monsieur Forsyth's toes.'

'I can't help it.'

'You sound… distracted, Richard.'

'I've got two murders on my hands, Henri.'

'Murders? You're now a policeman also?'

'Is that gallic humour, Henri?'

'Sorry, Richard, anything I can do to help?'

'Maybe, not now, I've to check out a few thing first.'

'Whenever. I must go, my wife is waving her handbag at me. Tell me when Mitchell is arriving. I'll start the surveillance tomorrow. Au revoir.'

I replace the silent receiver, deep in thought. First Baxter, then Kruger and now I've got Phoenix rising from the ashes. I realise I'm now bloody cold, time to go home.

'Stevens! I've been trying you for ages!'

'Sorry, Sir Edward, I was…' It's Monday morning, I could hear the phone ringing coming up the office stairs.

'Some of us have been working through the night, you know and I had to cancel my dinner date.

'Sorry, I…'

'Never mind, I've got some preliminary findings for you.' Sir Edward pauses, clears his throat, 'Your German was in a bit of a mess, wasn't he?'

'Yes, you could say that,' I ease into my chair.

'Well, he was garrotted with piano wire, something like a cheese cutter but stronger. I can tell you that he was dead before the almost decapitation took place.'

'Why would that be?'

'Did this German have information for you?'

'Yes.'

'Important?'

'Could be.'

'Mmm, I think the post death violence was a warning.'

'What do you mean?'

'If anyone else talks, they'll end up like Kruger and, excuse the vernacular, a message to you, don't fuck with us!'

'Charming.'

'I don't think you're dealing with very charming people, Stevens, I'd be very careful.'

'Well, thank you, Sir Edward, for the warning and being so prompt.'

'Not at all, does Forsyth know?'

'About Kruger? Yes, but it's my show now'

'Glad I'm not in your shoes then.'

'Thank you…' but he's already hung up. I sit back in my chair, stare at my empty desk. Well, that's a great start to the week.

'So, this Kruger fellow was murdered, was he?' The tall figure in a dark pinstripe suit, shock of white hair, stares out of his office window at Whitehall below him.

'Yes, sir,' Forsyth sits uncomfortably in his chair. This is not going to be an easy meeting.

'Baxter and Kruger die within days of each other. Coincidence?' The tall figure turns towards Forsyth.

'Baxter was shot, Kruger was garrotted. We assume the deaths are connected. Someone didn't want them to meet.'

'Mm, but who?' The mandarin sits down at his desk, gives Forsyth an icy stare.

'They knew Kruger was coming to meet Baxter. Could be someone in the BND, maybe someone from this neo-fascist group.' Forsyth shrugs his shoulders.

'As I understand it, Kruger comes to us because he doesn't trust his own intelligence service. Correct?'

'Yes, sir.' Forsyth shifts again in his seat.

'And yet Kruger is in the country for less than two days and winds up being killed. Bit careless, what?' The icy stare is now almost glacial.

'Well, we didn't know why he was coming here…'

'Who was in charge of the debriefing?'

'Stevens, sir.'

'Stevens! That renegade! I thought he was counting sheep in the Falklands.'

'We're a bit short-staffed at the moment, sir, and Stevens had worked with Baxter.'

'Not a wise choice, Forsyth. The debriefing should have been carried out by yourself or your deputy.'

'But, I had to go to Washington and…'

'I've noticed that you are spending a lot of time there. Be careful of your friends across the pond.'

Forsyth just nods, taking his knuckle rap in silence.

'Who's dealing with it from the Met?'

'Superintendant Kennedy. He's being difficult about the murder investigation.'

'I'll speak to him. Remind him that the New Year's honours list is due. That tends to focus people's minds.' The mandarin gives the faintest of smiles. 'So, where do we go from here?'

'Not easy, we've not got much. Bin Laden is in the market for a nuclear device. There is some connection with a neo-fascist group in Germany. We do have two names, Kurt Kohler and Mohammed Habtoor.'

'That's Kohler of KK Industries, isn't it?'

'Yes, sir.'

'Be careful there, Forsyth. Kohler is a good friend of the German Chancellor, he's also met the PM.'

'Well, we don't know if he's actually involved but…'

'And Mohammed Habtoor?'

'A Saudi by birth. Arms dealer, bit of a slippery customer. We don't have a current photograph of him. Nobody seems to know where he is. Last time I heard, it was either Yemen or Egypt.'

'Well, I suggest you'd better find him. Try our Israeli friends.'

'They could be difficult.' Forsyth doesn't want Mossad on his patch, they're always bloody difficult and so secretive.

'Well, it's your call....'

'What about our American friends?'

'I think we should leave them out of this for the moment.'

Forsyth sits back, he is silently pleased. He'd a rough ride from the Americans about this Toulouse business. Maybe time to remind them that MI6 are still in business. 'What happens if the device is meant for America?'

'Then you'd better bloody well find it!' the mandarin slams his fist on the desk.

'And the Germans?' Forsyth shifts again in his chair.

'Too risky. Let's see how far Stevens gets.'

' I thought you said...'

'If things go pear-shaped, Forsyth, you'll need a scapegoat, won't you?'

'Quite, sir'

'I thought so too. Now, I have a dinner engagement. Anything happens, you're to contact me immediately.' The mandarin watches Forsyth leave the room. How I dislike that man. Another bloody Scotsman thinking he's running the country, ha! Forsyth was never my choice, would have preferred Digsby, safe pair of hands, does what he's told. Not like Forsyth and his predecessor, think they know better than Whitehall, the nerve! That dodgy dossier, what a cock-up. The number of favours I had to call in to bury that nonsense. No, Forsyth will need to be kept on a short leash.

Now, what to do about this Kruger business? Could be a lot of bloody nonsense, of course. But, I have to be careful here, if there is any truth in it, things could get very messy. The problem is Kohler. The prime minister stayed at his castle outside Munich during his last visit to

Germany. If the press get a whiff of anything, they'll have a field day. There's also a political agenda here; Kohler could one day be chancellor of Germany. I need to talk to my friend, but I'll keep Kohler out of it. I'll give him the Arab, that should keep him busy. The mandarin nods to himself, satisfied with his thought process and reaches for the phone.

CHAPTER SEVEN

Dick Kelly sits at his desk, leafing through the pile of papers in front of him. It's the same every morning, reading the overnight reports which have come into Langley. He sighs as he finishes and puts the reports in his out tray. Nothing seems untoward with the world this morning, as long as you exclude the Middle East and the elusive Numero Uno. Yep, things are quiet, maybe too quiet. He flicks on his computer, the screen comes alive. He clicks on his mail, 32 messages this morning, about average for a weekday. Messages from all around the world, Paris, Madrid, Rome, the list goes on. All the messages had been encrypted, but by the time they reach his screen, they have been decoded. Kelly is part of a 24/7 business. So, as he scans these messages, he thinks Europe is pretty quiet too. But that is about to change.

There is a buzz from his direct line. Only a select few have this number, and that doesn't include his wife. He leans forward and picks up the receiver.

'Richard?' A voice enquires.

'Sir Clive! And how are you today?' Kelly immediately recognises the clipped English accent.

'Fair to middling, and you?'

'Not bad,' there's a pause, 'I assume you're not calling to tell me that Forsyth is back on terra firma.'

'No, no.' Sir Clive lets out a faint chuckle.

'Listen, if Forsyth spends any more time over here, I'll think he's after my job.'

'Maybe I could arrange an export licence.' Another faint chuckle.

'Very droll, Sir Clive.' Kelly has a faint smile on his face. 'So what gives?'

'Ah, yes. I've just had a meeting with Forsyth, something has cropped up.'

'Go on.' Kelly reaches for his pack of Marlboro and lights his first cigarette of the day.

'We have been debriefing a German, a Herr Kruger, an ex Stasi officer. After the initial debriefing, he appears to have been murdered, in Claridges.'

'Well, if you're going to go, I suppose Claridges isn't a bad place.'

'Richard, please be serious'

'Yeah, okay. So how was he murdered?' Kelly takes a deep drag of his cigarette.

'Garrotted, almost decapitated, I believe'

'Ouch, nasty,' Kelly taps some ash into the desk ashtray.

'Quite.'

'So, why was he murdered?'

'Ah, now we come to the nub of the matter. This Kruger claimed that a friend, a BND officer, had been murdered. This BND officer had uncovered a plot to give, not sell mind you, a nuclear device to an Arab terrorist organisation. He was going to tell us more until his untimely demise.'

'You're kidding me?' Kelly stubs out his cigarette.

'I'm afraid not. It would appear that Forsyth and his people are taking this seriously.'

'So, who's giving this weapon?'

'That Forsyth wouldn't divulge. He's playing this one close to his chest.'

'Meaning?'

'You're out of the loop, Richard, on this one. For the moment at least.'

'I see.' Kelly grips the phone tightly. That little prick Forsyth!

'He did let slip one name, though. A certain Mohammed Habtoor, mean anything to you?'

'Maybe, I'll have to check.' Alarm bells start ringing in Kelly's head.

'I think he's an arms dealer.' There is a certain distaste in the voice from London.

'Yes, but we thought he was out of the game. Maybe not. What about the Israelis?' Kelly lights another cigarette, his hope of one pack a day going up in smoke.

'Forsyth doesn't much like our friends in Mossad, so I'm not sure. One other thing, Kruger said that he thought that certain elements in the BND couldn't be trusted.'

'Mmm. Is Forsyth handling this himself?'

'Oh no, Richard. This could be too hot to handle, he'll keep this at arm's length. Stevens is in charge.'

'Stevens! Isn't he the one that skewed us on the Airbus thing?'

'Richard, I did forewarn you not to meddle in France's backyard, that they'd play hardball.'

'Yeah, I know. But I had Boeing up my ass, we had to do something.' This episode still rankled with Kelly. His people had virtually been kicked out of Toulouse for industrial espionage. And Stevens had helped the French.

'Okay, Sir Clive, leave this with me. We'll stay in touch.'

'Please do.' There is a soft click, the connection is broken.

Kelly replaces the receiver and sits there fuming, that bastard Forsyth! Playing this close to his chest, huh! He wants the glory for this one, another coup for MI6! We'll see. Kelly picks up the phone again and presses three numbers.

'Connors, get in here! And bring what we have on Mohammed Habtoor.'

Five minutes later, Connors enters Kelly's office. He's holding a slim file.

'Not much, sir.' He looks pointedly at Kelly's cigarette. 'I thought the building was all non-smoking, sir.'

'You got a problem, Connors? Would you prefer the meeting in your office?

'No, sir, I just…'

'Sit down! What have you got?' Kelly blows some smoke across his desk, another little prick!

'Eh, Mohammed Habtoor, sir. Born Riyadh in 1950, son of a wealthy Saudi businessman. Went to Cambridge, England, in 1970, received a degree in Law, 1st class honours. Set up a law practice in Riyadh in 1976. Went AWOL in 1980. Rumoured to have been seen in East Germany, probable contacts with the Stasi. Resurfaced in Lebanon in the mid 80's. Thought to be supplying arms to Hezbollah, the start of his other career, so to speak. Then seen in Pakistan, the CIA knew he was supplying arms to the Mujahideen. They used him to supply Stingers. He vanished for a while, the KGB were looking for him. In the 90's, thought to be supplying the PLO and Hamas. Then nothing.'

'What? He just vanished?' Kelly stubs out his cigarette.

'Yes, after 1998, nothing. The only photograph of him that we have is ten-years old.' Connors hands over a passport-sized photo to Kelly.

'Well, I wouldn't pick him out in the streets of Riyadh.' Kelly examines the grainy image of an Arab-looking man. 'So, why does a rich young Saudi give up a lucrative law practice and vanish, eh?' Kelly looks across at Connors.

'Maybe he got involved with the fundamentalists.' Connors shrugs his shoulders.

'This Habtoor sounds like a forerunner of Bin Laden. I wonder if the two were in England at the same time? Check out the dates.'

Connors takes out a notepad and starts writing.

'You're new here, Connors. I like to think out loud. So, write down names and dates and then we'll see what we've got. Now in 1980, Habtoor goes missing, maybe in East Germany. Maybe for training, maybe for financing, but he's probably pretty wealthy in the first place. I think for a time he was a Stasi operative, helping them stir things up in the Middle East. But Habtoor has his own agenda and so when the Russians invade Afghanistan, he helps his Arab brothers. Habtoor is an intellectual, though, doesn't get involved in the fighting, just supplies the weapons.

'Bin Laden was in Afghanistan at that time.' Connors stops writing and looks up.

'Very good, Connors. Maybe they met. Anyway, Habtoor supplies Stinger missiles, courtesy of us, and Russian helicopters start falling out of the sky. I'm not surprised the KGB were pissed off. And so he goes into hiding, maybe his Stasi minders tipped him off. A year or two later, he's selling arms to Hamas and Hezbollah, again. This involves the Syrians and the Iranians. This Habtoor has pretty heavy friends.' Kelly lights another cigarette, ignoring Connors' frown. 'And then in 1998, he vanishes again.'

'Yes, sir. There's an addendum in the file dated July 1998, from Mossad. That was the time they were on alert about a possible purchase of a nuclear device by some radical Arab group.'

'Now I remember. Habtoor's name cropped up then, the rumour was he was fronting for Bin Laden. Maybe after '98, he was handling only one client, I wonder?' Kelly sits there for a few moments.

'Apparently, the Israelis wanted him for the supply of Semtex for the suicide bombers in Israel.' Connors reads a note in the file.

'Yes, he's been a busy boy, our Mr Habtoor. But where is he now?' Kelly picks up a pen from his desk and twirls it between his fingers. 'Let's see what you've written down, Connors.'

Connors stands up and hands over his notebook. Kelly looks through Connors's scribbles, makes an occassional note with his pen.

'A couple of things strike me, Connors. One is the CIA's dealings with Habtoor, and Bin Laden's name keeps cropping up. Time for some airbrushing, Connors.'

'Airbrushing, sir?' Connors looks mystified.

'Time to lose the CIA's connection with Habtoor. Your immediate task is to go through the past classified files on Afghanistan. Find all references to Habtoor and have them deleted.'

'But isn't that illegal, sir?'

'Of course not, Connors. We live in a democracy, we're free to do anything!'

'Can I ask what this is all about, sir?' Connors doesn't look convinced.

'For the moment, that's on a need to know basis.' Kelly taps his nose. 'Now, get out of here. You've got a lot of reading to do. Oh, and your notebook stays with me.' Kelly dismisses him with a wave. Kelly sits there thinking, watching Connors close the door behind him. Kelly stubs out another cigarette and picks up the phone.

'Get me Harding, Angie.'

'Yes, sir.'

Moments later, his phone rings, he picks it up.

'Harding?'

'Is that you, Kelly?'

'Yes, I heard you were back in town.'

'You heard right.'

'We need to talk about Afghan 1.'

'Long time ago, Kelly.'

'Maybe, but a name has cropped up. Let's say Tysons Corner, usual place about six?'

'You paying?'

'Of course.'

'I'll be there.' Harding hangs up.

A man of few words, Harding, thinks Kelly, I hope he has more to say when we meet.

At five minutes past six, Kelly walks into Joe's Bar. From the outside, it's just as nondescript as the rest of Tysons Corner mall. Inside, it is dark and gloomy; it's meant to be. There is no music, no slot machines. A small muted television is showing a football match. This is a man's bar, where he can forget work, wife, mistress or all three. Or where you have meetings that you don't want other people to know about. The long bar faces the entrance, James the barman is behind, polishing glasses. Kelly nods to a couple of regulars sitting at the bar, nursing beers.

'What will it be, Mr Kelly?' James drops his cloth on the bar top. James knows all his regulars by name.

'Eh, bourbon and a beer, thanks.' Through the gloom, Kelly can see Harding sitting in a booth at the back, near the fire exit. Kelly smiles to himself, Harding always covers his ass. As he approaches, Harding looks up and folds his Post, takes a sip of the beer in front of him.

'So, how's Baghdad at this time of year?' Kelly says, as he slides along the bench seat opposite Harding.

'Hot,' replies Harding, picking up his paper and putting it in his jacket pocket.

James appears and puts a glass of bourbon and a Coors beer in front of Kelly.

'You want another?' Kelly points to Harding.

'No, I'm fine, for now.'

'Put it on my tab, James.' Kelly gives him a nod. He looks across at Harding, still much the same as the last time he saw him. Broad shouldered, tanned, cropped fair hair, ice blue eyes.

'I hear you made Assistant Director. Still patrolling Europe for us?' These blue eyes fix Kelly with a stare.

'Something like that.' Kelly downs the bourbon in one. 'And you?'

'Here and there.' Harding takes out a packet of cigarettes and lights one, blows smoke towards the ceiling. 'So, who's piqued your interest?'

'Mohammed Habtoor.' Kelly takes a sip of beer, looks at Harding.

'He's a bit out of your territory, isn't he?'

'That's why I'm talking to you.'

Harding just nods, takes another drag on his cigarette.

74

'We provided him with Stingers in Afghan 1, correct?'

'Correct.'

'Did you meet him?'

'Several times.'

'And?'

'Typical-looking Arab, if there is such a thing. Average height, sallow coloured skin, black hair, trimmed beard, moustache and dark brown eyes. The usual.'

'How did you meet him?' Kelly takes out his second packet of Marlboro for the day and lights up.

'In Quetta, Pakistan. We had a supply depot there, not too far from the border. We were always looking for people to run the weapons across the border. He came highly recommended.'

'Did you know that he'd worked for Hezbollah?'

'Christ, Kelly, we didn't ask for work references! We were desperate for anybody. Habtoor proved to be reliable. What we gave him was delivered into Afghanistan, not like some of the others we used, half the stuff used to go missing.'

'So that's why you gave him the Stingers?'

'Yes, we trusted him.'

'Did you ever meet Bin Laden?'

'No, but I heard about him.'

'Would Habtoor have met Bin Laden?'

'Maybe. Bin Laden received some of the missiles, so yes, probably.' Harding finishes off his beer. 'Where is this leading to, Kelly?'

Kelly pauses, stubs out his cigarette, wondering how much to divulge.

'Habtoor may be involved in a current operation,' Kelly finally admits. 'I'm just trying to get a handle on the guy.'

'You mean you can't find him.' Harding smiles across the table.

'How do you know?'

'Oh, a lot of people have been looking for Habtoor, but they've never found him. He was very smart, you know. Not like some of the arms dealers I've dealt with. No smart suits, no flash cars. You'd bump into him in the street and he'd be dressed as a beggar. He stayed in no star hotels, fleapits, always moving. When the Soviets pulled out finally from Afghanistan, we heard the KGB were after Habtoor, they'd discovered his connection with the Stingers. That would be the end of '89. I never saw him again.' Harding signals for another two beers.

'Did he ever mention being in East Germany?'

'Nope. He did speak perfect English, though, some French. Ha, there was this French guy in Quetta, trying to sell Mirage jet fighters to the Mujahideen. We dealt with some crazy fuckers.' Harding laughs, his eyes looking into the distance.

James puts another two bottles of Coors on the table; they're ice cold to the touch.

'Tell you one thing, after Habtoor disappeared, there were rumours that he'd been tipped off. We had kept tabs on him and he was last seen in Karachi, near the East German embassy in the company of a European. Then he vanished. And from Karachi you can fly almost anywhere.' Harding takes a sip from his fresh beer.

'And then the Berlin Wall came down,' Kelly says thoughtfully.

'So, you think Habtoor had a Stasi connection?'

'Well, in 1980, I don't think he went there for a holiday.'

'But the Stasi are now defunct.'

'Yes, but what happened to them all? Become train drivers, postal workers? No, the BND hired most of them.'

'So you think Habtoor's minders are still around?'

'Maybe that's why no one can find him.' Kelly lights another cigarette, looks at the now half-empty packet. 'And all I've got is a ten-year-old photograph, huh!'

'You can bet he's changed, Kelly. He's a rich man, false passports, plastic surgery. Ha, look at Michael Jackson for Christ's sake!'

'I know, I know. Look, you know the region better than most. I'd really appreciate if you hear anything…'

'Sure, Kelly, sure.' Harding finishes off his beer. 'I must be going.'

'One more thing,' Kelly watches Harding as he picks up his cigarettes and lighter, 'if you were in the market for a nuclear weapon, who'd you go to?'

'You kidding me?'

'Just hypothetical, you know,' Kelly tries to laugh.

'Does this involve Habtoor?' Harding lights another cigarette, places the pack and lighter back on the table.

'Maybe, look, as I said, this is hypothetical…' Kelly takes another swig of beer, already regretting his question.

Harding says nothing for a few moments, studies his empty Coors bottle, then looks across at Kelly, takes a deep drag of his cigarette. 'Anybody else know about this… hypothetical situation?'

'Me and now you.' Kelly meets Harding's stare. Silence ensues. 'You haven't answered my question,' Kelly takes another swig of beer.

Harding looks at his half-finished cigarette, drops it into his Coors bottle, it fizzes for a few seconds. 'Well,' he sighs, 'the North Koreans, for one, they're crazy fuckers, do anything for hard currency. But difficult to deal with. We're also keeping a pretty close eye on them. India or Pakistan? Maybe, but they've cleaned up their act since the Iraq war. Not the Chinese, they'll sell the technology, but not their precious weapons. No, my best guess would be the Russians.'

'What, with Putin in charge?' Kelly shakes his head.

'No, Kelly, it's about what happened before Putin, the Yeltsin years. You and I know, Russia was a fucking mess then. He was drunk half the time, sold off the State companies, including the oil and gas fields, to his friends.

There were, are, a lot of rich oligarchs around. The Red army, meanwhile, was broke, soldiers weren't paid for months. You could buy anything, uniforms, T 52 tanks, Hind helicopter gunships. Ha, talk about Ali Baba and the forty thieves. Christ! This was the ultimate arms bazaar.'

'But, nuclear weapons?' Kelly finishes his beer, the gassy liquid sitting uneasily in his stomach. 'I know there were rumours…'

'Look, the reasons that America and Russia signed the Nuclear Disarmament Treaty were to stop the arms race and also destroy nuclear weapons to a mutually agreed level. Now, in America, we can account for every screw, nut and both in our weapons systems. But in Russia, huh, our people found inventories missing, officials didn't know where stockpiles were, a fucking mess! You ever been to Siberia, Kelly?' Harding lights another cigarette.

'No, I haven't…'

'Well, I wouldn't recommend it for a holiday. The staple diet of the Red Army there was vodka. These guys couldn't even count the number of fingers on one hand, they were so pissed. So what if a missile went missing, who knew, who cared?'

'You think that could have happened?'

'My nuclear nightmare, Kelly. That some crazy son of a bitch actually got hold of one, doesn't bear thinking about.'

'But, if someone did, why haven't they sold it?'

'It's a seller's market and the number of buyers has just got bigger. Someone could make big bucks. In the arms business, it's all about timing. Anyway, as you said, it was all rumours, nothing ever proved. Now,' Harding glances at his watch, 'I really must be going.'

'What happened to you after '89, anyway?' Kelly watches Harding ease his lanky frame out between the table and the banquette.

'Kuwait '91, went back for Afghan 2, then Iraq.'

'And where to now?'

Harding stands beside Kelly and bends down, whispers in his ear, 'I hear Damascus is an interesting place to visit at this time of year. Oh, and by the way, if Habtoor is involved in any of this, you'd better find him quick. That motherfucker will sell anything, and I mean anything, to anybody.' And then he's gone.

Kelly sits there for a few moments, sees Harding's paper lying on the seat, knowing that he won't come back for it. He suddenly feels cold; he looks across at James. 'Bourbon, make it a double.'

I fucking need it.

CHAPTER EIGHT

La Taverna, Saturday night, the following week. I've decided that I need a break. What better than to meet up with Helen? We've met for a quick drink in the Star and then a ten minute stroll to a little Italian restaurant at the end of Old Bishop's Lane. I say hello to Gino, the owner, who shows us to a table in the corner. The restaurant is only about a third full, mostly couples like ourselves. Gino has ensured that all the tables are set apart, difficult to overhear other conversations. For La Taverna is a favourite rendezvous for private assignations.

'It's not very busy,' Helen leans over and whispers.

'No, you're right. You see, this is a city restaurant and it's packed during the week, lunch and evenings. But the city closes down over the weekend, so there's not many people around and it's a bit out of the way for tourists.'

'So why's it open?' Helen looks around her.

'Well, Gino's mother runs the kitchen and she believes in only one day of rest in the week and of course, that's Sunday. So poor Gino has to work on Saturdays.'

'He doesn't look very happy,' Helen watches him as he serves the table nearest us.

'I think he'd prefer to be at home watching the football. I think this year he's supporting Chelsea, last year it was Arsenal,' I shrug my shoulders. 'But his real passion is cars and last year Mama allowed him to buy a Ferrari. On Sundays, he spends all day driving around the M25. I've never understood Italians.'

'So, Signor Stevens and how are you tonight?' Gino appears at our table.

'Fine, and you?'

'Not so bad,' Gino shrugs his shoulders as if he's carrying the weight of the world on them.

'I'd like you to meet my friend, Helen Thompson,' I say, pointing across the table.

'Ah, bellissima!' Gino leans forward, smiles and kisses Helen's proffered hand. I do believe she blushes. For several moments, Gino gives Helen his rapt attention.

'Er, Gino…?' I lean forward trying to catch his eye.

'Ah, scuse. Yes, tonight, the antipasto is very good and we have the best baby clams, so I suggest the spaghetti alle vongole.'

I look at Helen who smiles in agreement.

'Excellent and the wine?' Gino finally takes his eyes off Helen and turns reluctantly to me.

'A Barolo, I think, Gino,' knowing that this is his favourite.

'Another excellent choice, I have a '93, perfetto.' He turns to leave and gives me a smile and a wink. Gino loves beautiful cars and beautiful women, and looking across at Helen, I can understand the smile and the wink. She's slipped off a short, black leather jacket, revealing a bright red dress, cut to the knee, showing off her long, slim legs. A V-neck gives a hint of cleavage. A pale green eyeshadow further highlights her eyes, red lipstick matches her dress. She's the most beautiful woman here and she's with me. My thoughts are interrupted by a Barolo, poured by Gino. He doesn't ask me to taste it, he knows it's good. Helen and I toast each other with the deep and fragrant wine.

'So, you and John frequented The Star,' I break the silence between us.

'Yes, sometimes when he came back from one of his tours, we'd meet in town. He liked that pub, the peace and quiet, just him and me, talking. He took some time to accept normality after what he'd been through,' she looks past me, remembering. 'He said that you'd introduced him to The Star, after one of your meetings. Quite a coincidence that you and I should end up seeing each other there.'

'Or fate?' I say quietly.

She nods slowly, not saying anything, takes another sip of wine.

Gino appears bearing a large platter full of cold meats, stuffed peppers and olives. 'Enjoy,' he says, as he lays it down between us.

I let Helen serve herself and then I choose some slices of salami, parma ham and some black and green olives. We eat for a few minutes in silence, each with our own thoughts. After the first glass of wine, Helen relaxes. She talks about her school, her pupils. Her father has now retired and she goes to Bath to visit her parents when she can. Gino clears away the first course, more smiles to Helen.

'At least you've made him happy tonight.' I refill Helen's glass, she blushes slightly again.

Gino reappears with two steaming bowls which he presents with a flourish; now he's showing off. The pasta is cooked to perfection as are the clams. One bottle of Barolo becomes two.

'That was very good,' Helen finally says, wiping her mouth carefully with her napkin.

'Glad you liked it. If you ignore the decor, can't think when this place was last painted, it's worth it for the food.' I top up our glasses again. We decline dessert and Gino produces two black coffees. Helen settles back in her chair.

'Do you think I could have a cigarette?' Helen puts her black bag on the table.

I look around me, there's only one other couple left on the far side of the room.

'Why not?' I shrug my shoulders.

Helen takes out a cigarette, lights it, blows smoke towards the ceiling. I notice the man across the room, fumbling with his jacket pocket and then producing a packet of cigarettes. He smiles, waves the packet at me and offers a cigarette to his lady companion.

'Maybe you'll start a new fashion, smoking in restaurants,' I smile at Helen. 'Just be careful the thought police don't come in.' I give her a wag with my forefinger. Helen laughs for the first time since I've met her.

Now for the difficult bit.

'When I said that I'd been careless about Angela, you said something similar about John.' I pick up a little packet of sugar and carefully empy it into my coffee cup. Helen leans forward, drinks some more wine, but says nothing.

'I'm sorry, I shouldn't have asked…' I stop stirring my coffee.

'No, it's alright. It's just that I've never talked about it with anyone,' she pauses looking at me, making a decision, ' but I think I trust you, John did.' She takes another sip of wine. 'You see after the funeral, I met one of John's friends, Mike Scott. He was with John when he died. He swore me to secrecy about what happened. They were on a joint mission with the American Special Forces just south of the Syrian border, trying to stop insurgents crossing into Iraq. It was at night. Mike said the weather was bad, messed-up the radios, so there was a foul-up with the coordinates for an ambush. John ended up in the wrong place at the wrong time, he was the one who was ambushed. By the Americans. They killed him. It's called blue on blue, I think.' Helen fumbles around in her bag, takes out a handkerchief, dabs the tears welling in her eyes.

'My God, that's terrible.' I sit there nonplussed. 'Didn't you speak to anybody?'

Helen dries her eyes, sits looking at her handkerchief, clenched in a fist. 'I was on pills for a few days, wasn't thinking straight. And then I plucked up the courage to phone John's commander. He was kind and sympathetic to begin with but when I raised the subject of John's death, he became distant, abrupt. 'Couldn't possibly comment' and 'suffice to say that John died for Queen and country.' He cut the phone call short. I should have known that the SAS wouldn't reveal any details. I tried my local MP, but he was useless. I couldn't tell the parents, it was an upsetting time for everybody. I think it would have killed John's father if he'd learnt the truth. And so I didn't tell anybody. I'm sure my editor thought there was a story somewhere, maybe he had a tip-off. The Americans killing a British officer would have been front page news. But I didn't want any stories, I just wanted John remembered as he was.' Helen has forgotten about her cigarette, it's almost down to the tip, a line of ash has dropped onto the tablecloth. She quickly stubs it out into her saucer. 'Sorry, there doesn't seem to be an ashtray...'

'Never mind about that, god, what you've been through.' I lean across and take her hand in mine, giving it a gentle squeeze.

'Thank you, Richard, I feel a bit better now,' Helen gives me a wan smile, slowly releases her hand from mine, finishes her wine. 'Anyway, enough about me, what about you?' She sits up in her chair, looking somehow refreshed, as if some weight has been lifted from her shoulders.

'Oh, this and that, dreadfully boring...' I try to be offhanded.

'Richard, John told me that you worked for Intelligence, so?'

'Ah, I see, well he shouldn't have...'

'Oh, come on, Richard, I was his wife after all. He told me about his work, well, the palatable bits, not the nasty stuff.'

'Yes, well...'

'How did you meet him?' Helen fishes for another cigarette.

'John? Oh, that must have been, when? December 2002. He gave us a briefing on Special Forces in Iraq.'

'I thought John said that you specialised in Europe?' Helen lights her cigarette.

I look at her, she actually seems interested. I suddenly realise that I would never have told Angela any of this, she was never interested in what I did. I suppose that I could have been a carpet salesman, for all she cared. 'Yes, he was right, but in this case I was brought in to think outside the box.'

'Meaning?' She looks intently at me.

'Well, Iraq was naturally handled by our Middle East section. But their eyes were becoming filled with sand and camels, so, I was brought in to provide fresh eyes and ears, lateral thinking, outside the box, so to speak.'

'I see. And?' she says slowly.

'John was there with several of his colleagues. When it came to his turn, he told us that he had just returned from Iraq. The British and the Americans, at that time, were denying that we were running covert operation in Iraq. But, we knew otherwise. John's sortie had been to a factory about 40 miles west of Baghdad. This factory was supposed to be producing anthrax. It was at night of course, in and out by helicopter. I was surprised how easy it was for us to get in and out of the country. It was then that I wondered how much command and control the Iraqis really had. Anyway, he'd taken some Iraqi scientists out into the desert and interrogated them, but they denied all knowledge of any biological production. The Americans had gone through the factory and found nothing. John confirmed that this had been his third covert operation and they had found no evidence of biological warfare production.' I finish off my coffee.

'I didn't know exactly what John was doing but I knew it had to do something with Iraq. I had many sleepless nights,' Helen shakes her head.

'Just remember, John was a very brave man,' I remind her.

'I know, I know. It was just such a waste.' She draws heavily on her cigarette. 'So, why did we go to war?'

'I thought at the time that it was quite bizarre. We had the United Nations searching by day and we were searching by night and yet we all found nothing.'

'John said that you got into trouble over the so called dodgy dossier.'

'Yes, got my knuckles rapped. I read the draft report; it just didn't stack up. I knew John didn't think there were any weapons of mass destruction, could see it in his eyes, hear it in his voice. We talked about it one night in the Star, maybe after one drink too many.'

'You knew that John was still operating in Iraq after the war was supposed to be over?'

'Yes, he told me. In fact the last time I saw him, at that party in the summer, he was quite depressed about the security situation. About the incursions from Syria and Iran, said the whole thing was a bloody mess.'

'That's the final irony about the whole thing,' Helen toys with her handbag. 'He was very unhappy about what he was doing. Said he would do one more operation and then he was out of the army. He'd been offered a good job in a security firm run by a friend of his, in London. It would have been perfect for us. Maybe I would have stopped work, we were talking about starting a family. Just one more operation, he said. And the rest, as they say, is history.' She stubs out her cigarette, grinding it into the saucer.

We sit there saying nothing, Helen uses her hands to smooth down imaginary creases in the tablecloth. I suddenly notice that we are alone in the restaurant, only Gino hovering in the background, surreptitiously looking at his watch. I signal to him for the bill. Once I've paid, we both stand up slightly awkwardly, I help her on with her jacket. She turns around, looks up at me, her green eyes melt into mine. She grips my arm, pulls me forward and whispers,

'Maybe we could have a nightcap somewhere?'

CHAPTER NINE

I can hear a shower running in the distance. I open one eye and then the other. Have you ever had that panic attack in the morning after the night before? Not knowing where you are. As I come to, I'm relieved to see that I'm in my own bed. I'm alone but someone is in my shower. It must be morning, light filters through the window blinds that never quite shut properly. I look to my left, see my trousers, my shirt and then the red dress. My God, Helen! I sit up, rub my face, there's a dull throb in my temple. Images of last night flash through my befuddled brain. Leaving the restaurant, in a taxi, entering my flat, coffee and brandy, more brandy, sitting on the sofa. Helen leans across me, I kiss the back of her neck, she turns and kisses me on the mouth. Tie being undone, fumbling with shirt buttons, unzipping the back of her dress, the two of us stumbling through to the bedroom.

The shower stops, silence, then I hear Helen humming to herself. The bathroom door suddenly opens, she appears through billowing steam. She's wearing a towel wrapped around her body, dries her hair with another. Not many woman are beautiful when they come out of the shower, Helen is the exception. She sees that I'm awake and smiles across the room.

'Thought I'd make some coffee,' she points towards the open bedroom door.

'Great, that would be great,' For some reason, I pull the bed sheet over my chest, which seems strange after the intimacy of last night. I watch her as she leaves the bedroom, notice her little wet footprints on the parquet floor. I get out of bed, discover that I'm naked. I'm never naked in bed. I have a quick shower and shave. I slip on clean underwear, a pair of khaki slacks and a grey sweatshirt. I gather up my clothes from the bedroom floor and put them on a chair. I look at the red dress and put it on the bed. I leave her white, satin underwear. I don't know why. I enter the kitchen. Helen is sitting at the breakfast bar, legs crossed, her towel riding precariously high. I divert my gaze. She has a mug of coffee, and is smoking a cigarette.

'Caffeine and nicotine, the way to start your day,' she smiles at me.

'I think I'll just have the caffeine,' I return her smile and make for the percolator. I'm not sure what to do or say, this is a completely new experience for me. This beautiful woman, half naked, sitting in my kitchen on a Sunday morning, well any morning to be exact. I take a quick gulp of coffee, wait for the caffeine to kick in. 'I'm not sure…' I turn to face her.

'Thank you for last night, Richard,' she puts out her cigarette in an old green onyx ashtray that I found last night. I think it was a wedding present.

'Oh, I'm not very…' I start to say.

'Richard, you were just fine. Kind and gentle, just what I needed.' She slides off the stool and stands in front of me, adjusts her towel. I find it hard to avert my eyes from the swell of her breasts.

'But, I must be going,' she presses against my body and kisses me on the lips.

'Can't you stay?' I look at the kitchen clock. Christ! It's eleven o' clock. Anna, my daughter, will be here in an hour.

'I'd love to, but I've got school work to prepare for tomorrow, sorry.' She slides away from me and disappears towards the bedroom. I want to follow her, but hold myself back. Maybe last night was just about two lonely people needing each other. Helen reappears at the kitchen door, slips on her jacket, looks at her watch.

'God, I'll be late for George,' she fumbles inside her bag. 'Where are my keys?'

'George?' My heart sinks, who the hell is George?

'George, my cat. I've never been out all night before, he'll be starving,' she looks at my expression and starts to laugh. 'You didn't think…?'

'No, no. Just didn't know that you had a cat… named George,' I start to laugh too.

'Well, must be going,' she walks towards me, arms go around my neck, we kiss.

I taste her lipstick, smell that perfume. She stands back, 'Don't worry, I'll see myself out.'

'I'll phone you.'

'Please. Next weekend, I'm not doing anything,' she smiles, as though reading my thoughts. That little wave and she's gone.

I stand there for a few moments, the flat seems empty already, just her lingering scent remains. I wander through to the bedroom and lie down on the bed. I roll over to where she had lain, smell the perfume on the pillow. I lie on my back and stare at the white ceiling, thinking about her. Her small, firm breasts, urgent hands and mouth, that golden triangle between her legs…

The harsh ring of the entry phone brings me back to reality. I slowly make my way to the hallway.

'Hello?' Maybe it's Helen.

'Dad, it's me! Hurry up, I'm freezing!' No, it's my daughter.

'Okay, okay.' I press the entry buzzer, she'll be here in a couple of minutes. I have a quick look around the flat, in case Helen has left anything, find the ashtray in the kitchen, empty it into the bin.

'Hi, Dad,' I hear Anna before I see her, ' brought your Sunday reading.' She comes into the kitchen carrying a mound of newspapers. 'God, they're heavy,' she dumps them on the breakfast bar. I look at my daughter, she's wearing a black bomber jacket, faded jeans cut low, exposing her midriff. Not surprised she's cold. She's pretty, like her mother, but has black hair from me, although now I'm more grey than black.

'Well, this makes a change,' she says as she takes off bright red gloves.

'What do you mean?' I eye the headlines of the Sunday Times, nothing about Baxter or Kruger.

'Well, usually when I come around on Sunday, you're still in your dressing gown. Look at you, dressed. God, you've even shaved this morning.' She smiles as she slips off her jacket then leans over and gives me a kiss on both cheeks.

'Well, I…'

'And, I smell perfume,' she stands back, gives me a quizzical look.

'Perfume?' I reply with all the innocence that I can muster.

'Well, Dad, unless Opium have started making aftershave…?' She hangs her jacket on the breakfast stool.

'Opium?' So that's the distinctive scent. I must remember that.

'Yes, Opium. You never were very good at perfumes, Dad, were you?' She's now teasing me. 'And a hint of cigarettes.' Her eyes look around the kitchen, looking for other signs. 'Speaking of which, where's the ashtray?' She takes a packet of cigarettes from her jacket.

'Eh, on the worktop.'

'Usually, it's in the drawer,' she lights her cigarette and slides onto the stool, 'So, who is she then?' Waiting expectantly.

'What do you mean?' I try to busy myself by sifting through the papers.

'Oh, come on, Dad. I think we have established that a woman has been here, come on.' Anna leans forward on the edge of her stool.

'She's a friend.' I decide to be frank, persistancy is one of the traits Anna has inherited from her mother; this could go on all day.

'Which friend?'

'You probably won't know, Helen Thompson.'

90

'Helen Thompson? Now why does that ring bells?' Anna puffs on her cigarette, thinking. 'I know! She's the one who interviewed mum, she works for The Times.'

'Used to,' I correct her.

'But she's young, well younger. How old is she?'

'Oh, about 35.'

'God, young enough to be your daughter or old enough to be my sister. And she stayed the night?'

'Er, yes.'

'Dad, you are the quiet one,' Anna slides off her chair and gives me a hug. 'I think it's great. About time you came back to the living. Since you and Mum split up, you've been like a hermit, all work and no play.' She stands back, looks at me. 'Well, that takes care of this afternoon.'

'Meaning?'

'Shopping, Dad,' She folds her arms and nods.

'Shopping, but it's Sunday.'

'See what I mean. When was the last time that you were out on a Sunday?'

'Well…'

'Months, I bet. You just sit inside, wallowing through the papers or files from the office. There is life out there, you know. Well, this afternoon, you and I are going shopping.'

'What for?'

'Dad, look at you! These slacks must be at least ten years old and that sweatshirt.'

'Well, they're comfortable…'

'And ancient. No, you need a new wardrobe.' Anna says it with an air of finality. I know when I'm beaten. 'We'll have lunch first, I hear the George and Dragon has reopened at the end of Narrow Street, supposed to be really trendy. Then we'll go to Canary Wharf.' She starts to put her jacket on.

'Couldn't we do this next week?' I look across at my pile of unread newspapers.

'Dad, you can read them when you get back. Come on!'

Ten minutes later, we're strolling along Thames Walk. The sun is shining, but a brisk wind whips up the river. Anna holds onto my arm, her only concession to the cold is one of my scarves wrapped round her neck, although I think it would be more appropriate around her waist.

'Thought you would be seeing Christopher today.' I zip my old anorak up to the neck.

'He's history, Dad,' Anna's voice is muffled in my scarf.

'Oh?' I can never keep track of Anna'a boyfriends. 'Thought he was nice, had plenty of money.'

'Oh, yes, but his first love was his Porsche, the second was his rugby and I came third.'

'Ah, I see,' I dig my hands deeper into my pockets. The sun disappears behind thickening clouds; I'll be glad to be inside. We cut over near the Four Seasons Hotel. At least here, we're sheltered from the wind. The George and Dragon looks the same on the outside but inside it's completely changed. Polished wooden floors, chrome tables and chairs, zinc-topped bar. I prefer The Star. Anna finds us a table, I discover that the chairs are as uncomfortable as they look. She surveys the blackboard menu.

'Mmm, let's have the lobster tails, my father is making me feel decadent,' she licks her lips and then smiles at me.

'Well, that's a first,' I return her smile, slip off my anorak.

'That has to go,' Anna points at the anorak.

'Whatever you say, my dear,' I raise my hands in mock surrender. I order the lobster tails for two and a bottle of Sancerre. We talk about this and that as we eat. Anna and I have always had an easy relationship, despite my difficulties with her mother. I feel better after my first glass of wine, my head cleared from last night.

'Wasn't Helen married?' Anna leans back as the waiter clears our plate.

'Yes, her husband was a soldier. He was killed in Iraq, last year.'

'Oh, how sad,' she pauses. 'Did you know that I've met Helen?'

'Really? When?' I top up her glass, then mine.

'She asked mum to meet her in town, you know before the article in the papers. Mum wanted me there for moral support. She's quite a stunner, Helen Thompson, you know.'

'Yes, Anna, I had noticed.' I hide my pleasure behind my glass. A comfortable silence falls between us.

'We'd better be going,' Anna looks at her watch. 'Are you paying?' she slips on her jacket.

'What are fathers for?' I reach for my wallet.

'Thanks, Dad. I'll meet you outside. You can't smoke in these places now and I'm dying for a cigarette.'

We enter Canary Wharf shopping mall from the south side, on the lower level.

'Where did all these people come from?' I'm surprised how busy it is.

'How often do you come here, dad?'

'Not often, there didn't seem to be many shops last time.'

'That must have been ages ago You can do all your shopping here now. Now, where are we? I think it's the next level. We'll start at Thomas Pink.' She pulls me towards the escalator.

'But that's expensive, isn't it?'

'You know I love spending other people's money,' she gives me a wink.

'Remind me,' I reply, resigned to my fate.

Two hours later, I sip a coffee, looking out over my balcony. I love this view of Limehouse Harbour. In the summer, I sit outside, watching the boats coming in and out through the lock. The harbour master is busy, adjusting the water levels between the harbour and the Thames. I've never been interested in sailing, but I like watching other people. This evening, however, everything is quiet. In the distance, through the gloom, I can see a blue and red train of the DLR, the interior lights shining brightly, carriages empty. Unlike tomorrow morning; carriages full of workers, like bees coming to the hive, Canary Wharf.

The light is fading fast, low grey clouds scudding in from the west. I turn around surveying several shopping bags on the coffee table, my afternoon purchases. A couple of shirts, a pair of slacks, a jacket and two pairs of shoes. I think that I got off lightly. Anna has gone back to her place, happily clutching a new skirt that she wangled out of me. I sit down on the sofa and look around me. Maybe this flat could do with a new look, too. Angela and I had bought the flat as an investment and also as a place to sleep over if we were late in town. I had used it often. Angela had found somewhere else to bed down, but I wouldn't discover that until later. The divorce settlement gave Angela the house in Surrey, I kept the flat. Anna describes the interior as Swedish minimalist. Yes, it does look a bit bare, maybe some paintings would help to brighten it up.

It's now dark outside. I get up and switch on the lights. I'm not very hungry. I think I'll have a pizza somewhere, maybe later. I wonder if I should call Helen, again maybe later. My thoughts turn to last night. Why did she choose me? She admitted that this was the first time that she had been with a man since John's death. Why me? I'm not exactly that good looking and what about the age difference? But, I'm not complaining. I look again at my purchases; my daughter was right. A new woman in my life, a new beginning.

But first, I have work to do. I've quickly scanned the newspapers. Some bright spark in the Observer has made a connection between the deaths of Baxter and Kruger. Where do they get their information from? And then I remember about Saunders, enough said. The past week has been like being back at school, catching up on my twentieth century history reading. Not much else to do, really. The police investigations into the murders don't seem to be going anywhere; the perpetrator hasn't left a single clue. Except for the bullet that killed Baxter, from a Walther PKK. The German connection is too obvious, even for McKay. The police may have many unanswered questions, I have only one. What was Kruger going to tell Forsyth?

Did Kruger know where this nuclear bomb was going to be used? If so, and it's in the hands of al-Qaeda, the obvious choice is America. Bin Laden would have no hesitation in exploding such a device in New York or Washington. But why would Kohler want that? Could it be that America would retreat into isolationism, as it has done before, after such a devastating attack? The American people are already tired of foreign adventures after Afghanistan and Iraq. With the Democrats in government, they may decide to pull up the drawbridge. That would leave a power vacuum, who better to fill it than a resurgent Germany, led of course by Herr Kohler? It sounds mad, but I don't think I'm dealing with clinically sane people.

I'm not sure how many times that I've listened to the tapes of Kruger's debriefing, but there's one phrase that keeps coming to mind – 'You have to look back into history, Mr Stevens.' So, what does history have to do with Kurt Kohler and Osama Bin Laden? I'm missing something here, what the hell is it?

PART TWO

The best laid plans o' mice and men
Robert Burns

CHAPTER TEN

14th April, 1945, Berlin.

General Heinrich Kohler hears the sound of distant gunfire to the east as he hurries down the concrete steps to the Führer bunker. At the entrance, an SS officer stops him, demanding his papers. The officer is unsmiling as he studies Kohler's orders. An SS sergeant takes his briefcase and looks inside, then empties the contents onto a wooden table. Kohler stands there, his impatience mounting. This is the second time he's been stopped, searched. The first time they didn't even allow Haller in. Don't they know I'm a loyal party member? Do they think I'm a threat or something? Look at these two, must be half my age, just young pups! The young officer hands back Kohler's orders. He barks a command to the sergeant who picks up the papers scattered on the table and hands them over to Kohler. He looks through his situation reports, quickly putting them into order, and then back into his briefcase.

'Pistol,' demands the officer, pointing to Kohler's holster.

'Anything else?' Kohler enquires with as much civility as he can muster, as he hands his Luger to the sergeant.

'You're late,' the SS officer stands, legs astride, an ebony swagger stick slapping his thigh.

'Late! You're bloody lucky that I made it. I've been shot off the road twice getting here!' Kohler angrily shuts his briefcase. 'And you are?' Kohler studies the arrogant young face in front of him.

'SS Gruppenfuhrer Muller, Herr General, at your service,' he replies giving a mock bow.

Kohler can hear the sergeant sniggering behind him. The impudence of these people! A couple of days at the front would sort them out!

'Now, we've wasted enough time. Follow me...
please.' Muller turns, without waiting for Kohler to reply
and descends the next set of stairs.

Kohler fumes to himself as he follows Muller. His
eyes adjust to the gloom, how he hates this place! This is
his third visit, each time to give the situation report on
the Western Front. Each time as depressing as before. To
suffer the rants of his Fuhrer. What am I supposed to do
anyway? he thinks bitterly. For a fleeting moment he
remembers the summer of 1940, as they rolled through
France; then we were invincible! Now he has a ragtag
army, not enough men or equipment. He starts down
the corridor, the atmosphere is damp and fetid.

'This way please, General,' Muller says looking to his
left.

'But the Situation Room is down there,' Kohler
points straight ahead.

'Please.' Muller turns and beckons Kohler to follow.

They walk down another dimly lit corridor, the bare
concrete walls damp with condensation. The officer stops
in front of a grey, painted steel door, already beginning
to corrode, and knocks once with a black gloved hand.

'Enter.' Kohler hears a guttural command from
within. Muller swings the door open. Kohler enters a
bare room, except for a table and two chairs. A single
light bulb hangs from the ceiling, light flickers
intermittently. Behind the desk sits Martin Bormann.

'Herr Reichsleiter, I...!' Kohler was not expecting
this.

'Heil Hitler! Please, General, sit down.' Bormann
points to the chair in front of the table. Kohler sits down,
confused, his briefcase resting on his knees.

Bormann glances up at Muller, 'Thank you, Gerd,
you can wait outside.'

Muller closes the door behind him, looks at his
watch. The briefing usually takes about fifteen minutes
and then I'm out of here, thank god. Just like the rats,
down the corridor, deserting this fast sinking ship.

Muller paces in front of the door, the sound of his black boots echoing off the concrete floor and walls. He puts a hand inside his trouser pocket, takes out a gold cigarette case, lights a cigarette with a matching gold lighter. He can hear raised voices from inside the room. Maybe Kohler is not going to be so easy after all. Kohler is the last one, eleven others have gone before him. At least Kohler is an army man, Muller thinks to himself, not like those others, lily-livered bankers and accountants. Muller draws heavily on his cigarette, smiles, the raised voices are quiet, Bormann always gets his way. Kohler is younger than Muller expected, mind you there are not many generals left. Maybe he's been picked because of his youth, not like these old buffoons in the Situation Room, moving around fictitious armies, defending positions already lost. Ach! Muller drops his cigarette on the floor, grinds it out with his left boot. He looks at his watch again, seventeen minutes have passed. Just then the door opens, Kohler steps out into the corridor. He looks shaken, as they all do, slightly disorientated. Muller steps forward to close the door, sees Bormann give him a nod.

'This way, Herr General,' Muller retraces his steps down the corridor. Kohler says nothing, head stooped, absorbing what Bormann has just told him. They ascend the stairs; the sergeant is waiting for them, he hands over Kohler's pistol.

'You understand what you have to do, General Kohler?' Muller eyes up Kohler looking for any signs of doubt, any indication that he might baulk at the last moment. For if there are, Kohler will not leave here alive.

'Yes, I understand completely,' Kohler meets Muller's gaze.

'Well, you'd better get moving then. Here is your Fuhrer pass, you'll need it to get out of Berlin,' Muller points upwards to outside.

Kohler gives him a curt nod and starts up the stairs. Muller watches the receding figure. Well, my good

101

general, although you don't know it, we are destined to meet again. My work here is now complete. I have to hurry, Switzerland beckons; a new life is about to begin.

Kohler slowly ascends, his head still spinning from Bormann's instructions. Haller, his adjutant, is waiting for him above ground. Several SS soldiers stand around, machine guns at the ready. An officer steps forward.

'Papers?' he demands, a hand outstretched.

Kohler hands over his pass, the officer studies it.

'One of the lucky ones, Herr General,' he smiles briefly, glancing over his shoulder. Kohler follows his gaze, sees a figure in uniform, across the rubble, hanging from a lamp post.

'That's what we do to deserters now!' The officer smiles again, hands the paper back to Kohler. He stands aside to let Kohler pass. Kohler motions Haller to follow him.

'Well?' Haller hisses as they walk to the staff car.

'Wait until we're in the car. You don't want to end up hanging from a lamp post, do you?' Kohler says quietly.

They step over bits of masonry, the odd piece of metal, hear the sound of more heavy gunfire from the east. The air is acrid with smoke, from burning buildings, burning flesh. Kohler's nose twitches with distaste. Haller gets in the driver's side, Kohler walks around the front and eases himself into the front passenger seat.

'Well? What happened in there? You look, well... different,' Haller says, as he starts the engine.

'Everything is now different, Haller, the ground rules have just changed. But first, we have to get back to Magdeburg,' Kohler stares in front of him.

'You've got orders to attack?' Some of the old excitement returns to Haller's eyes.

'No, come on, let's get out of bloody place! Let's find us some Americans. I've been ordered to surrender!'

CHAPTER ELEVEN

'…and, of course, all your father's shares pass to you.' Otto Schmidt, the Kohler family solicitor, pauses as he reads the last will and testament of Heinrich Kohler and looks across his desk at the only heir to the family fortune, the son, Kurt Kohler.

Kohler says nothing, just nods his head for Schmidt to continue. A week has passed since his father died. And I wasn't even there, he thinks bitterly. Opening another KK hotel, this time in Rome. The frantic phone calls, but even his private jet couldn't get him back to Berlin in time. Sitting at his father's hospital bedside, seeing the once robust figure, shrunken in death. He'd wept unashamedly. I never even had the chance to say goodbye. A stroke, the doctor had said, he wouldn't have suffered, he'd never regained consciousness.

'Your mother will continue to live in Schloss Kohler, outside Munich, as long as she wishes. It will eventually, of course, revert to you. Your father has left an annual sum of…'

'No matter, my father will have made sure that my mother will live in considerable comfort,' Kohler interrupts, thinking about his mother. They'd met at the funeral, two days ago. It was the first time he'd seen her in a year, she'd aged considerably. He'd never been close to her, found her to be a distant figure in his life. His father had dominated him, made him the man that he now was. Kohler nods again, indicating Schmidt to continue.

'With regard to the other properties, the villa on Lake Wannesse, Lake Geneva and the apartment in London are yours, including the contents. I have a large inventory of paintings and other art works. It will take some time to assess their value. I should warn you that the duties on your father's estate could be considerable.'

'We'll see. Keep in touch with my company accountant, you have his number?'

'Yes, of course. I…'

'Look, Herr Schmidt, the only reason that you're acting as the family lawyer is because of the friendship between my father and your father. Since your father's death, it was convenient using your firm. My own personal affairs are, however, handled by my company lawyers and accountants. They're young and sharp, that's why I pay them so much. They will be looking over your shoulder, so I do not expect to pay one more mark than I have to. Do I make myself clear?'

'Of course, Herr Kohler, of course,' Schmidt looks flustered, takes out a handkerchief and dabs the sweat forming on his brow.

'Good, I want your interim report in my office by Monday.' Let this little bastard sweat over the weekend, Kohler smiles to himself. 'Now, is there anything else?' Kohler stands up, straightens the cuffs of his jacket, ready to leave.

'Yes, sorry, there is this…' Schmidt stands up, scrabbles around an overflowing desk of papers and file. 'Ah yes, here it is.' Schmidt produces a plain white envelope, 'It's addressed to you.'

Kohler takes the envelope, sees his name written on the front in his father's handwriting. He quickly tears it open; inside there is a white slip of paper. He stares at the two lines, again written by his father,

Wannesse

60 30 19

'What is this?' Kohler looks at Schmidt.

'I don't know. I've not found any reference to these numbers so far in your father's papers. I thought that you might know.' Schmidt shrugs his shoulders.

'Doesn't mean anything to me, how strange,' Kohler shakes his head, puzzled but intrigued. 'Well, keep looking, call me if you find anything.'

One hour later, Kohler sits at his desk, looking out over the skyline of Berlin. His office building, KK Towers, is now the tallest in the city. His office, private meeting room and reception area take up the whole top floor. There are, however, two floors above this; his penthouse. But Kohler is not thinking about any of this; his mind is preoccupied by the piece of white paper in front of him. What do these numbers mean? Too short for a phone number. Maybe a safe combination, but Father never mentioned about having a safe at home. Kohler's thoughts are interrupted by his desk phone ringing.

'Magda, I told you that I wasn't to be disturbed!'

'I'm sorry, sir, but there's a Herr Schreiber calling…'

'Schreiber? Do I know him?'

'He's not on your list, sir, but…'

'So?'

'He says it's about your father and that it's urgent.'

'Oh, very well, put him through… Kohler speaking.'

'Ah, Herr Kohler, I must apologise for disturbing you. I know that you are a busy man.'

'Yes, yes, you said it was to do with my father,' Kohler certainly doesn't recognise the voice.

'I just wished to express my deepest condolences.'

'Well, that's kind of you. Were you at the funeral? I thought that I'd met everybody.'

'I was, but I watched from afar. It was very moving, he was a great man.'

'Quite. Did you know my father?'

'Oh yes, I knew him.'

'Strange, I don't remember father ever mentioning your name.'

'He wouldn't have.'

'I see, well, thank you for your call…'

'Herr Kohler, I believe you are now in possession of six numbers.'

'How do you know anything about that?' Kohler sits back in his seat, stunned.

105

'Ah, I know a lot about the Kohler family,' there is a faint chuckle at the end of the line.

'Who are you, anyway?' Kohler grips the phone tightly. He's used to being in command of the situation, but this is getting out of his control. 'How do I know you're not some phoney, trying to get some money from our family bereavement?'

There's silence for a few moments, Kohler smiles to himself, maybe I was right.

'The numbers are 60 30 19,' Schreiber says softly.

Kohler leans forward, closes his eyes. 'How do you know these numbers?'

'I gave them to your father,' the soft voice replies.

'Look...Herr Schreiber, I...'

'I think that we should meet, Herr Kohler, sooner than later,' the soft voice now has a hard edge to it. 'Let's say six tonight, at the Wannesse house, that would seem appropriate.'

'But, I have a dinner engagement this evening...' Kohler starts to protest.

'I know, but I won't take up much of your time. This is more of an introductory meeting, shall we say. Till six, then.' Schreiber hangs up.

Kohler stares at the silent receiver, slowly puts it down. What the hell is going on? Who the hell is Schreiber? He says he gave these numbers to my father, but why? For what? He buzzes his intercom.

'Yes, sir?'

'Magda, can you trace that call?' Kohler feels a cold sweat on his forehead.

'One moment, sir... yes, a public phone box in the Potsdammerplatz.'

Of course! He wouldn't use a phone that I could trace, he's obviously not that stupid. What else did he say about tonight? He knew that I had a dinner engagement tonight. How the hell did he know that! 'Magda?'

'I'm still here, sir.'

'Where's Haller?'

'He's on his way back from Munich. Should arrive early evening.'

'Tell him to phone me, immediately he gets back.'

'Yes, sir.'

'Have my car ready at 5.30. Tell the staff at Wannesse, that I'll be there around six.'

'Your dinner is at eight, sir…'

'I know, dammit! I'll be back in time!' Kohler breaks the connection. He sits there for a few moments trying to collect his thoughts. Well, Father, what have you been up to? And why didn't you tell me about Herr Schreiber, who seems to know so much about us? Kohler picks up the piece of paper on his desk, folds it carefully and puts it inside his jacket pocket. And what's so important about these bloody numbers?

The black Mercedes drives past the open ornate iron gates. Kohler can see the large villa ahead, in front of the winding driveway. The villa on the shores of the lake had been one of his father's first purchases. As the car comes to a smooth stop under the covered portico, Alfred, his father's old steward, steps forward and opens the car door.

'Good evening, sir,' Alfred gives a slight bow as Kohler sweeps past him.

'Put these files on my desk in the study and tell Thomas to be ready with the car in an hour or so. And make sure it's been cleaned.'

Kohler doesn't wait for Alfred's reply as he enters the house through the double panelled doors. He stands for a moment, surveying the grand entrance hall. This space always gives him pleasure, the black and white chequered marble floor, the sweeping white Italian marble staircase, the double storey space crowned by a glass dome. The centrepiece of the hall is a Louis XIV ormolu round table on which rests a large, black lacquered vase containing freshly cut orchids, their scent already pervading the house. Satisfied, he looks to his left and sees one of the maids giving the lounge a final clean. To his right, the dining room, the table still set for six. I wonder who my father had invited. Alfred bustles past him, the files under one arm, his footsteps echoing off the floor. Kohler follows him towards the door under the staircase. Alfred opens the door to the study and waits for Kohler to enter. Kohler walks to the large desk in the middle of the room and surveys the maple panelled walls, the fitted bookcases. He looks out of the large picture window, the tall fir trees casting long shadows from the setting sun, across the well manicured lawn. Alfred places the files on the desk and stands to attention.

'Will there be anything else, sir?'

'Yes, I'm expecting a Herr Schreiber at six. Please show him in here when he arrives. Oh, and Alfred, if he arrives by car, take a note of the registration number. And, I'll have a whisky and soda, not too much soda.'

'Of course, sir.'

Kohler hears the study door close softly and sits down at his father's old desk. How many times did I sit here, opposite my father, discussing the future? He runs his hands over the smooth, polished mahogany top, feeling the occasional indentation, maybe from his father's pen. His father, up to the day he retired, wrote everything in long hand, often at this desk, late into the night. Kohler can remember the nights here, when he was young and couldn't sleep, creeping down the stairs to go to the kitchen for a glass of milk and maybe a biscuit, passing the study door. Seeing the light underneath it, knowing that his father was at work, knowing there would be hell to pay if he was disturbed. So, what was he doing so late at night, what was he thinking?

There is a soft knock at the door, Alfred enters carrying a tray. He approaches Kohler and carefully lays the tray on the desk. A white gloved hand places a silver coaster, with the family crest, in front of Kohler. A crystal glass, three quarters full of whisky and soda is placed on top of it. Alfred lifts up the tray and stands back, again his heels click to attention. He raises his right hand to his face and coughs discreetly.

'Yes, Alfred?' Kohler leans forward and tastes the whisky. Perfect, just like the way his father drank it.

'You mentioned that a Herr Schreiber was expected, sir.'

'Yes, Alfred. Do you mean he's been here before?' Kohler's pulse quickens.

'Oh yes, sir, on many an occasion. That is, after your father had bought this house and it had been renovated, sir.'

'So, who is this Schreiber, did my father tell you?'

'No, sir. He'd just say that Herr Schreiber was coming and to let him in. They always met here, in this study.'

'And Schreiber, what's he like?' Kohler takes another quick sip of whisky.

'Undistinguished, I'd say, nondescript would be a good word. He was younger than your father, though. He wasn't the kind of person that your father usually associated with,' Alfred pauses, 'and if I may say, sir, your father was often in a bad temper after Schreiber's visits, used to shout at the staff, most unlike him. Fortunately, Schreiber has not visited here for some time.'

'Did you ever overhear what they talked about?'

'Oh no, sir. Whatever they talked about was only within these four walls. I used to show Herr Schreiber out, when they were finished. Your father never came to the front door with him. It was obvious that they were not friends. I assumed it was all to do with business.'

'I see,' Kohler ponders on what Alfred has just revealed. 'Did my father ever mention some numbers to you?'

'Numbers, sir?'

'You know, maybe for a safe combination.'

'Eh, no sir. I wasn't aware that your father had a safe in the house.'

'No, nor did I. As far as I'm aware, he kept all his personal papers in the office,' Kohler toys with the crystal glass in front of him. 'So, 60 30 19 means nothing to you?'

'I'm afraid not, sir.' Just then, there's the soft buzz of the front door bell. 'That could be Herr Schreiber, sir,'

'Yes, Alfred, if it is, bring him in here,' Kohler settles back in his chair, takes another sip from his glass. He hears muffled voices from the entrance hall and then a knock at the study door.

'Enter,' Kohler carefully places his glass on the coaster.

'Herr Schreiber, sir.' Alfred appears, followed by a man of average height, stocky build, wearing a brown hat, brown gloves and beige raincoat. From below the raincoat, Kohler notices dark blue trousers and brown brogues. Not exactly a fashion icon then, Kohler stifles a smile. Kohler indicates the chair opposite him. Schreiber sits down rather heavily, takes off his hat and looks around for some place to put it. Alfred quickly steps forward and takes the offending article. Alfred stands to one side, hat in one hand, tray in the other, looks expectantly at Kohler.

'That will be all, Alfred,' Kohler waves him away. He studies the man sitting in front of him. Alfred was right, what on earth was my father doing with someone like this? Schreiber pulls out a rather dirty looking handkerchief from somewhere, wipes his face, then blows his nose, noisily. His breathing sounds asthmatic, maybe he's just out of breath. His face is plumpish but his eyes have a cunning, furtive look to them. Schreiber leans to one side, looking for a pocket for his handkerchief. Kohler notices the faintly frayed collar, tie slightly askew. He's also still wearing his gloves. No, not one of my father's typical guests.

'So, Herr Schreiber, I understand from Alfred, that you have been here before,' Kohler breaks the silence between them.

'Ah yes, Alfred, very observant but also discreet,' Schreiber nods to himself.

His voice is quite soft, just as it was on the phone. Kohler can't quite place the accent, maybe southern Germany. Schreiber's eyes focus on Kohler's now almost-empty glass.

'At least your father had the courtesy to offer me a drink.'

'I am not my father, Schreiber, and I don't consider this a social call. I have several questions for you, and once answered satisfactorily, you can leave.'

'Ha, that sounds more like your father! Impetuous, arrogant,' Schreiber smiles, then laughs but it's more like a bark.

'Don't you dare talk about my late father like that!' Kohler rises from his chair.

'Calm down, calm down, Kohler, we've only just met,' the smile turns to a smirk.

Kohler sits down again, glances at Schreiber. Mmm, maybe I have to reassess the situation. I have to remember that my father dealt with this man for many years. I have to find out why. He slips a hand inside his jacket, takes out the piece of paper, opens it and lays it on the desk.

'You said that you gave these numbers to my father. I simply want to know why and what they are for.'

'That's better, Herr Kohler, but I really would like one of those,' Schreiber replies, pointing to Kohler's glass.

'I wouldn't mind a refill myself,' Kohler smiles faintly, presses a button on the old, black bakelite intercom, 'Alfred, two whisky and sodas.'

'I thought that you would be interested to know who I am, first of all.'

'The floor is yours, Herr Schreiber,' Kohler leans back in his chair, waiting.

'I first met your father in Berlin, April 1945, just three weeks before the war ended.' Schreiber unfastens

111

his raincoat, settles himself, 'I was an officer in the SS. The night after I met your father, I was sent to Switzerland, in civilian clothes, of course. The next day, your father surrendered to the Americans.'

'Yes, he told me but never said why.'

'No, he wouldn't have, because he was sworn to secrecy. That's why you never knew about me, until now.'

There's a knock at the door, Alfred enters carrying his tray, this time with two glasses. He places one glass in front of Kohler, removing the now empty one. Another silver coaster is placed in front of Schreiber, followed by the other glass.

'That will be all, Alfred.'

'Prost,' Schreiber raises his glass after Alfred has left the room.

'So, why did you and my father meet?'

'I was there to ensure that your father knew what he had to do.'

'Meaning?' Kohler picks up his glass.

'Your father was to be one of der Auserwahlte.'

'The what?'

'One of the Chosen, Herr Kohler.'

'I don't understand…'

'Your father was one of twelve men, chosen to carry out Adolf Hitler's final order!'

'Which was?'

'The Final Solution, of course! The extermination of the Jews!' Schreiber barks out a laugh.

'My father agreed to this?' Kohler sits there, disbelieving what he has just heard.

'Of course, your father was a Nazi, through and through! He'd sworn an oath of loyalty to the Fuhrer, he had no choice.' Schreiber sits there with a smug look on his face. Kohler stares in front of him, picks up his glass, swallows half the whisky, notices his hand is trembling as he puts the glass back on the desk. My father, my god! Several thoughts cross his mind at once. This would explain his strict upbringing at private schools, the tutors extolling the virtues of national socialism. His father's refusal to employ Jews or any other race for that matter. Like pieces of a jigsaw, completing the final picture

'Are you shocked, Herr Kohler?'

'I am, but maybe not surprised. Certain things about my father now make sense. But why didn't he tell me anything?'

'He couldn't, he'd been sworn to secrecy, they all were. Until it was necessary, like now.' Schreiber picks up his glass, finishes the whisky in one, wipes his mouth with the back of his hand. 'Your father was the best though, the rest, pah! He was the driving force, the one with the ideas. He tried his best.' Schreiber nods thoughtfully.

'And your role in all this?'

'Thought you'd never ask, Herr Kohler. I was one of the Knight Protectors of the Chosen. There were six of us, you'd probably call us minders, today. Just to keep the minds of the Chosen on their task. I was also the banker, hence my reason for going to Basle. Your father was released by the Americans soon after the war and he returned to Munich. I met him there at the end of 1946. I gave him a suitcase full of American dollars. My other colleagues were doing the same across Germany, to the rest of the Chosen. It was a risky business, but we did it. I made several trips to your father, always with the same suitcase.'

'So Kohler Construction was…'

'…financed by the Nazis! Very good, Herr Kohler. Where do you think all this came from?' Schreiber looks around the study. 'Your father had never been a wealthy man, he needed a helping hand to get started, all the Chosen did. That was the idea. The Chosen were to set up companies, be successful, become rich. Then implement the plan.'

'But they obviously never did implement the plan, did they?'

'Mmm, before we talk about that, maybe I should explain about the numbers.' With that, Schreiber gets out of his chair and walks behind Kohler. He stands in front of the panelled wall, takes down an old photograph of the house. Kohler sees, for the first time, a keypad recessed into the panelling, he gets up slowly.

'60 30 19.' Schreiber says, as he punches the numbers into the key pad.

The panelling moves slightly and then a door opens silently. Kohler walks forward, peers into the darkness. He hears Schreiber behind him.

'The original house had been built in the 19th century, for a Count von Flossenberg. This had been the chapel. When your father bought the building, it had been damaged during the last war and been neglected by the then current owners. Your father took pride in restoring the house to its former glory, but the chapel was his real joy. Please, enter.'

Kohler tentatively steps forward, Schreiber follows. The door slides shut, silently, behind them. Subtle uplighting switches on automatically, highlighting the semicircular floor plan, the walls are deep red.

'He used separate contractors, for the walls, the floor, the lighting. No one saw the finished article except for him, me and now you.' Schreiber stands to one side, watching Kohler, open-mouthed, trying to absorb what he was seeing for the first time. 'All the artwork and memorabilia were chosen by your father. I purchased them from all over Germany.'

Kohler stands there for a few moments, notices in the middle of the room a simple chair in front of a simple table. In front of the table is a large portrait, which dominates the room. He slowly moves towards the table, sits down on the chair, looks up at the figure in front of him. 'It's very good,' Kohler speaks for the first time, 'almost lifelike, so three dimensional.'

'Yes, probably the best portrait of Hitler ever done.'

'Who was the artist? Such confident brush strokes,'

114

'Young fellow called Leeb, he was discovered by Goebbels. The painting was finished after only four sittings, amazing really. If you walk around the room, the eyes seem to follow you everywhere.'

'Leeb? I'm not familiar with his other works.'

'You wouldn't be. You see, they discovered later that his grandmother was Jewish. He ended up in Auschwitz, even the painting couldn't save him. Shame really.'

Kohler suddenly feels cold, reminded why he's here. He stands up slowly, walks towards the flag to the left of the painting.

'Your father's regimental colours, now that was difficult to get hold of.'

'And the painting?' Kohler looks at Schreiber.

'Ah, trade secret,' Schreiber smiles, a gloved hand taps his nose.

Kohler just nods, walks around the curved wall, which is decorated with framed photographs. All black and white, all including his father.

'You can follow your father's war, looking at these photographs. The last one on the left was his favourite, though.'

Kohler sees his father, stern-faced, receiving his Iron Cross from a smiling Hitler. Kohler turns away, sits down on the chair again, 'But why did my father do all this?' His arm sweeps around the room.

'To remind himself of what he had to do. This was his sanctuary, where he did his thinking, formed his plans.' Schreiber wanders over, leans on the desk beside Kohler.

'But he and the rest of them did nothing.' Kohler looks up at Schreiber.

'Not quite true. You see, the idea of the Chosen was flawed from the beginning. No one had foreseen what would happen to Germany after the war, being split in two, east and west. For the first ten years after the war, it was all about rebuilding, democracy. The German people were in denial about the Nazis. I told your father that he was on a mission impossible, but he was stubborn. By the sixties, his company was one of the biggest contractors in West Germany; he was already very wealthy, as were the rest of the Chosen. He decided that the time was right to attack the State of Israel. He bribed several Egyptian generals, the Six Day War resulted, but that was a fiasco. In 1973, he tried again, this time with the Syrians, another fiasco. He'd spent a lot of money, he needed to build up the war chest again. And so, in the 80's he thought of a different approach. He would use the various Arab terrorist groups to bleed Israel dry. A war of attrition, he called it. Ha, if Yasser Arafat knew where some of his money came from! That war continues to this day, but he never managed to deliver the knockout punch. Your father was the last of the Chosen, he outlived them all, and now he is dead.'

'What happened to the rest of them?'

'As I said, the original idea was flawed. Most of the Chosen were not up to it. They became... dispensable, shall we say.' Schreiber smiles faintly.

'Meaning?'

'I don't think we have to go into details, suffice to say that they are no longer with us. And so, to the present. You, Herr Kohler, are the only living heir of the Chosen. And we expect you to deliver the knockout punch!'

'Me! Are you being serious?' Kohler leans back in his chair and is about to laugh.

'I would never joke about such matters, Herr Kohler.' The look on Schreiber's face, however, stills any laughter.

'But where would I start?'

'There's a drawer in the desk, look inside, please.' Schreiber slides off the desk, stands in front of Kohler.

Kohler looks down, sees a simple brass handle below the desk top. He pulls the drawer open, inside is a manila folder. He lifts it out, the folder is thick and quite heavy. He lays it on the desk and opens it. On the first page, he immediately recognises his father's writing, it's dated the 15th October 1965.

'It took your father twenty years to write down his first thoughts. The rest of the file contains his plan of action. Ever the soldier, it's like a military campaign. The file also contains all that he did, where and why it failed. All the payments are noted; you'll be surprised at some of the names. You can read the whole file later, just look at the last page.'

Kohler flips the file over, takes out a crisp sheet of paper.

'It's last month's statement from the International Bank of The Cayman Islands. Look at the bottom line.'

'There's over fifty million dollars in this account!' The figures dance in front of Kohler's eyes.

'I told you that the Chosen had made a lot of money. That account is now yours. That is now your war chest!' Schreiber stands there, smiling at Kohler.

'You're pretty confident that I'm going to do this, aren't you?'

'I don't think that you have a choice, Herr Kohler. You have to finish what your father started. It's now a question of family honour, isn't it?' Schreiber looks down at Kohler's face, sees the uncertainty. Now to play the ace.

'Ever been interested in politics, Herr Kohler?'

'What? Politics? No, never had the time. Politicians are either stupid or corrupt, or both.'

'Yes, quite. Your father thought of entering politics in the seventies, it's in the file somewhere. But, he decided that he carried too much baggage, ex Nazi general and all that. You, however, would be perfect. Tall, handsome, debonair and very wealthy.' Schreiber nods to himself.

'And?'

'I and my colleagues think that the next century will see the birth of a new Germany. They say that history eventually repeats itself. Look at Germany today, it reminds me of the '20's. On the surface all is well, there is prosperity, but it's skin deep. There is a lot of resentment underneath. The Wall coming down was a godsend to us. The former East Germans think they are the underclass. Unemployment is more than twice that of the West. It has become a fertile recruiting ground for our people, especially the young. Instead of the Jews, they'll vent their anger on the immigrants, especially the Turks, they'll be a nice soft target. You don't have to build autobahns this time, but you can build new factories, give them full employment. You'll be a hero. Just think, Chancellor Kohler has a certain ring to it, doesn't it?' Schreiber looks at Kohler, now staring at the portrait in front of him. I may not have your fine clothes or the right accent, but I'm sharp, maybe sharper than you. I've had to be, to survive this long. Mmm, you've had the carrot, now for the stick. 'Unfortunately, some of my colleagues don't think you're suitable, unproven.'

'What! I'm running one of the biggest companies in Germany...'

'I know, I know, and very successfully too. But have you got what it takes to make a new Germany? But, a significant strike against Israel would convince them.'

'You think so?'

'I know so. Look, we have the people, the organisation, we could form a new party tomorrow. We'd clean up in the cities in the old East, we'd just need a couple in the west, say Munich and Hamburg. We'd win by a landslide. We just need the right leader to follow.'

Kohler just sits there for a few moments, 'I'll think about it, Herr Schreiber. I'd like to read my father's file first.'

'Of course, no rush, no rush. Look at the time, I must be going.' Schreiber starts to button up his coat.

Kohler stands up, glances at his watch, it's eight thirty. Shit, the dinner party, Helga will be screaming. Kohler follows Schreiber out of the old chapel, the panel slides shut behind them. Schreiber crosses the study towards the door.

'What was the significance of the numbers anyway?'

118

'Ah yes,' Schreiber stops and turns, 'they were the numbers of the Chosen's account in Basle, the Banque Suisse Agricole. That account is long closed and Credit Suisse took over that bank in 1983. Don't worry, the original money is untraceable,' Schreiber pauses, tightens his belt. 'By the way, don't send that bloodhound of yours, Haller, after me, he'll never find me. Your father tried to and he failed. I shall be in touch. Good night. I'll see myself out, I always do.' With that, he's gone.

CHAPTER TWELVE

'How much have you had?' Haller points to the half-empty whisky bottle sitting on the desk beside Kohler.

'Enough.' Kohler rubs his eyes, he feels tired, but it's not from the alcohol. An hour has passed since Schreiber left, Haller has been here for half of that time. Kohler has told him what he needs to know, well most of it.

'Thought you had a dinner party tonight?' Haller cradles a whisky glass in his hands.

'Yes, I cancelled it. After all the guests had arrived. Had Helga screaming down the phone at me.'

'Trouble on the home front?'

'Oh yes. Helga may have a great body, but she's thick as red cabbage.'

Haller laughs, 'Time for a change?'

'Definitely, see that's she's out by tomorrow night, Franz.' Kohler looks at his empty glass, then at the bottle, but decides against a refill.

Haller just nods, he knows what to do. Since Kohler's two acrimonious divorces, he's had a succession of girlfriends. They usually last six months, Helga will only last three. Kohler had decided that it was cheaper having girlfriends than paying off ex wives. Haller was the bearer of the bad news, but a parting gift of a diamond necklace tended to soften the blow. 'Any preferences, this time?' Haller asks the question, but knows the answer.

'Blonde, six foot tall and knows how to fuck!' Both Kohler and Haller laugh.

'So, now we've got the important business out of the way, what about Herr Schreiber?' Haller looks across at Kohler, sees the laughter fade from his face.

Kohler says nothing for a few moments, just sits there. Finally, he stands up and wanders over to the large window, looks out over the floodlit garden. 'I've just turned 50, Franz. What other challenges have I got in life, eh? I own one of the biggest construction companies in Europe, I've just opened the 30th KK hotel, in Rome, the sales of KK phones should overtake Nokia within the next three to five years. I've so much money, I don't know what to do with it!'

'You've always found some new challenge before.' Haller finishes his whisky, puts his glass on the desk.

'What? Attend some charity ball? Open another new wing of some library? Have my photograph taken with some dumb politician or even dumber film star? I can't have children, my first wife proved that. So, the Kohler line stops with me. It's my duty to finish what my father started.' Kohler turns around, faces Haller across the room.

'I never knew that you felt so strongly about the Jews.'

'I do, it was drummed into me when I first understood the spoken word. You know what my 13th birthday present from my father was? No? A copy of Mein Kampf! Aged 13!' Kohler paces in front of the window. 'Some of what Schreiber said to me makes sense now. I live in a bubble, Franz, not in the real world. I read papers, but don't see the words. I watch television, but don't hear it. I have a penthouse with the best views of Berlin, a chef, a valet, housemaids. I fuck women other men can only dream about. I'm chauffeured from one meeting to the next in a bulletproof, bomb proof car, with my own bodyguard. I travel abroad in my own private jet, stay in the best hotel suites. When was the last time I was in a shop, Franz?'

'I don't remember, I…'

'I don't remember, either. Who bought the birthday, Christmas presents for my father, the flowers for my mother, the baubles for the girlfriends, mmm?'

'Well, I did…'

'Precisely! I can't even remember when I walked a hundred metres along a pavement. You know, I don't think I've even been on a bus or a train, and I've just turned 50 years of age.' Kohler slumps down in his chair.

Haller looks at his boss, has seen that look on his face before, that deep, hidden anger. Kohler's public persona is that of a suave, debonair, gentleman. But Haller has seen the other side, the dark side. Seen grown men, on building sites, reduced to tears just because a door or a window has been put in the wrong place. Watched as Kohler threw an interior designer down a stairwell, just because a carpet had been laid the wrong way. The designer survived, but will walk with a stick for the rest of his life. No, best to let Kohler get it out of his system, he'll come down to earth eventually.

'Germany is sleepwalking to disaster, Franz, and do you know why? Uncontrolled immigration, our borders are like a sieve. Turks, Arabs, any fucking raghead are welcomed with open arms, given jobs, housing. Whilst good Germans stand idle, some even homeless. All under the benign eyes of spineless, liberal politicians. It has to stop!' Kohler bangs a fist on the desk He reaches across the desk, grabs the bottle.

'Maybe, you've had enough, Kurt,' Haller says softly, watches the fire slowly die in Kohler's eyes.

'Yes, you're right, maybe I've had enough for tonight.' He slowly puts down the bottle, shakes his head, rubs his face with his hands.

'I understand what you're saying, Kurt, I understand, believe me. It's just this bit about Israel. This is dangerous, Kurt, very dangerous.'

'It didn't seem to worry my father.'

'Maybe he was just lucky. If the Israelis find out about any of this, they'll come after you. They'll kill you.'

'Then, they'd better not find out, had they?'

'Just think about it, Kurt, please.'

'Don't worry, Franz, I won't do anything rash. I told Schreiber that I would read this first,' Kohler taps the file on the desk, 'before I decide anything.'

'So, what do we do now?'

'Phone Magda, first thing. Tell her that I'll be working at home tomorrow. Cancel all my appointments. I don't want to be disturbed.'

'And me?'

'Get rid of Helga, then find Schreiber.'

'Thought Schreiber said that he couldn't be found?'

'Franz, a man of your undoubted talents, that should be easy. But, you may have to use Deep Throat.'

Haller smiles, Deep Throat, an old friend of his who now works for German Intelligence. He's provided useful information in the past. It was he who found the Italian politician who obtained, for a fee, the planning permission for the Rome hotel.

'Ok, I'll call him tomorrow.' Haller gets up to leave.

'You can stay in the guest room tonight, Franz, I'll want to talk to you tomorrow morning. But in the meantime, I have some bedtime reading.'

Next morning. Kohler finishes his first coffee of the day. The dining room has been prepared for breakfast. Alfred has been up since six. A place has been set opposite Kohler for Haller. Alfred appears, silently, and places a china pot of tea on the table. Haller never drinks coffee.

'Herr Haller will be down shortly, sir.'

'Thank you, Alfred. By the way, I know that you're due to retire, but I may be spending more time here than I thought. I'd like you to stay on.'

'I would be honoured, sir. I know no other life, I wouldn't know what to do with myself if I retired.' Alfred looks relieved.

'And the rest of the staff?'

'They'll be no problem, sir.'

'Good, that's settled then. You can go now.' Kohler watches Alfred leave the dining room, maybe with a slight jaunt to his step. Looks like I've at least made someone happy this morning, Kohler sighs, pours himself more coffee.

'Just got hold of Magda,' Haller breezes in, 'all appointments cancelled for the day. Nothing too important, except for De Vries, he'll be pissed off.' Haller sits down opposite Kohler, pours himself some tea, adds a little milk, but no sugar.

'Well, he'll just have to wait,' Kohler thinks briefly about the little Dutchman. He wants a KK hotel in Rotterdam. Kohler already has one hotel in Amsterdam and thinks, for the moment, that one is enough in Holland. 'You can have something cooked, if you wish, Franz?'

'No, toast is fine, thanks.' Haller carefully chooses a slice from the silver toast rack, butters it, then adds a thick layer of plum jam.

'How did you sleep?'

'Like a baby. I'd like to buy that bed off you.' Haller manages to say, between mouthfuls of toast.

Kohler smiles and looks at Haller, as he chooses another piece of toast. Although Haller is an employee of KK Industries, he's also Kohler's friend and confidant.

'And how do you feel this morning, Kurt?' Haller reaches across for the butter.

'Felt better, I must admit, don't think a half bottle of whisky was a very good idea.' Kohler sips some more coffee.

'No, not like you.'

'Well, yesterday was rather exceptional, don't you think?'

'A slight understatement, Kurt.' Haller finishes the last piece of toast, wipes some butter from his fingers with a crisp, white linen napkin. 'How did the bedtime reading go?'

'I'm about halfway through, I'll finish the rest today. There's a lot of detail, my father was quite meticulous. Some interesting names have cropped up already. There's a couple in the Bundestag who got their hands dirty. I've filed them away for future reference. They might come in handy one day.'

'I did some thinking last night, before I fell asleep.' Haller neatly folds his napkin, places it beside his plate.

'And?'

'If you do go through with this, you're going to need some help.'

'Apart from you, you mean?'

'Yes,' Haller pauses, looks across at Kohler, 'what about your French friend?'

'Who, Dubois?' Kohler looks surprised, sits back in his chair.

'Why not?'

'But, you don't like him, you've never liked him.'

'I know! I think he's a crook. I know he's a crook. I've warned you before about dealing with him.'

'Look, Dubois Construction and Kohler Construction have done several big projects together now. He's never been a problem, anyway he makes me laugh. If that's what you think, why even mention his name?'

'Being a crook, he knows some very dubious people. Ha! You think that I know some shady characters, I'm an amateur compared to him.'

'If, and I emphasise if, I proceed with this,' Kohler taps the manila file, sitting on the table to his left, 'what about your friends?'

'For what you're talking about? No, out of their league.'

'Anyway, my father didn't need any help, why should I?'

'He had the Chosen.'

'Granted, but at least they were all Germans.'

'That's another reason I don't like Dubois, he's French.'

'Ok, Franz, you have made your point, now can we....'

'Just one last thing, Kurt, please. I hear that Dubois may have got himself mixed up with the Russian Mafia.'

'How? That's news to me.' Kohler leans forward.

'The Russians have been moving into the French Riviera, you know, buying up hotels and apartment blocks, paid in cash. Everyone down there knows it's the Mafia. My sources tell me that Dubois has just won contracts for two large villas, near St Tropez, the owners are from Moscow. I also hear that the Russians won't stop in France, they're already eyeing up Spain and Portugal.'

'This is all very interesting, Franz, but really of no concern to me. What Dubois does...'

'It's just that if he is dealing with the Mafia, I hope your friend doesn't get his fingers burnt or worse.'

'Thank you, Franz, your concerns are duly noted. May we proceed with more pressing matters?' There's now an edge to Kohler's voice.

'Of course, I'm sorry, Kurt,' Haller knows when to shut up.

'Good. Now, Herr Schreiber?'

'Deep Throat is not answering.'

'Well, keep trying. This morning, I want you to go down to the offices of our family lawyer, you know that halfwit Schmidt? Well, he may not be the family lawyer for much longer. In any event, go through my father's papers, see if there is any reference to Schreiber, I'll phone ahead, tell Schmidt to expect you. I'll be here all day, going through the file. Come back here by six, we can review what we've found out. I'll tell Alfred to have dinner ready by eight. Oh, and don't forget about Helga, Franz, will you?'

'You're difficult to get hold of today.' Haller lights a cigarette.

'I'm busy.'

'Still got time for lunch, though?'

'How did you guess?'

'You know that I only phone you at home or lunchtime. In the park are we?'

'Yes, I'm feeding the pigeons. What do you want?'

'Information about a name.'

'Ha! You always want information about a name.'

'This one goes back a while, April 1945, Berlin. An SS officer by the name of Gerd Muller, now calls himself Schreiber.'

'One of your more unusual enquiries,' there's a pause. 'Do you have a first name?'

'No'

'A photograph?'

'Not yet.'

'What about fingerprints?'

'He always wears gloves.'

'Ah, a careful man, this Herr Schreiber.'

'Yes, that's why I'm phoning you.'

'Naturally. This may take a few days.'

'Where were you this morning, anyway?'

'In the office.'

'Rather early for you?'

'There's a bit of a flap on, trouble brewing in the Middle East, again.'

'Really? Anything thing to concern my boss?'

'Not unless he intends to build a hotel there. By the way, have you sent me my last package, for Rome?'

'You'll receive it tomorrow. Your mother's still at the same address?'

'Yes. I must go, I'll be in touch.'

Haller sits at Schmidt's desk, puts away his now silent phone. He looks in front of him, papers are strewn everywhere, and I'm only halfway through. He looks at his watch. Christ, it's already after midday. I wonder if Schmidt does lunch?

Kohler closes his father's file, leans back in his chair, stretches his arms and yawns. Christ, I'm tired. He rubs his eyes, maybe I need glasses. No, contact lenses would be better. It's already dark outside, the only light in the study comes from a desk reading lamp. Haller has just arrived, sits opposite Kohler. He also looks tired, yesterday's suit now crumpled, he's taken off his tie.

'So, nothing in my father's papers about Schreiber?'

'No,' Haller stifles a yawn. 'But you're right, though, Schmidt is a nitwit.'

'Well, he has until Monday, then I'll decide what to do about him. And Helga?'

'Packing as we speak. I've just come from the penthouse, I was late because of that idiot Schmidt. There were the usual hysterics, throwing stuff around, but the Tiffany box did the trick.'

'It always does.'

'Yes, well, your valet is keeping an eye on her, she'll be out by tonight.'

'Good, one less problem to think about.'

'Speaking of which?' Haller points to the file in front of Kohler.

'Ah yes,' Kohler picks up several pages of notes that he's made during the day, 'quite fascinating.'

'You're going to go ahead with this, aren't you?' Haller shifts uneasily in his chair.

'Yes, I am.' Kohler pauses for a moment. 'You see, Franz, I've decided that the prize is greater than the risk.'

'Meaning?'

'Why, it's obvious! To become the leader of a new Germany!' Kohler smiles at Haller.

'Schreiber is using the oldest trick in the book, you know, the carrot and the stick.'

'I realise that, but in this case, the carrot is much bigger than the stick. You don't look happy, Franz.'

'I will go along with whatever you decide' Haller shrugs his shoulders. 'You gave me my life back, it is also yours to take.'

'Don't get melodramatic on me, not now.'

'No, I'm fine, it's just the risks involved...'

'The risks will be great, I know that, but think of the prize!'

Silence ensues between the two men, both deep in thought.

'So, what are you going to do?' Haller finally says.

'I don't know yet,' Kohler sighs. 'Schreiber said something to me, what was it? Ah, yes. My father had told him that the key to the solution was in this file, but that he couldn't find it.' Kohler scans the notes that he has made. 'There are names here which don't mean anything to me, they could be Egyptian or Syrian, they're probably all dead now. Bank transfers, company names, some phone numbers crossed out. There was one thing, where is it? Yes, I made a note of it on the last page.' Kohler quickly sorts out his papers. 'My father made some large money transfers to the Argus Trading company, there's a Credit Suisse account number in Geneva. Each time after Argus, father has written a name, M. Habtoor, and underlined it. Mean anything to you?'

'Never heard of the Argus Trading company and certainly never heard someone called Habtoor.'

'No, I wonder if he's still alive? And why did my father underline his name?'

'Well, think about it, Kurt. What was the money being used for?'

'To finance various terrorist groups, you know, Hamas, Hezbollah…'

'Maybe Habtoor was the go-between?'

'Mmm, maybe. Some of the money must have been used to buy weapons and explosives.'

'So, maybe our friend Habtoor is an arms dealer.'

'Yes, could be,' Kohler sits there, thinking. 'Schreiber thought my father's plan to use these terrorist groups against Israel was brilliant. But that it was a war of attrition, not the knockout blow that he was looking for.'

'You should just nuke them!' Haller laughs.

Kohler stops reading his notes in mid sentence, looks up slowly at Haller.

'What did you say, Franz?'

'I said just nuke them! I was only kidding, Kurt, I mean...'

Kohler places his notes carefully on the desk. 'You know, Franz, sometimes you can be quite brilliant! My father had the key all the time. It wasn't the use of terrorist groups, it was how to use them, how to arm them. Just think, giving a nuclear bomb to one of these groups, destination Tel Aviv! It would bring Israel to its knees! Franz you're a genius!' Kohler gets up from his chair, paces around the room.

'There is just one problem, Kurt.'

'Yes, what?' Kohler stops, faces Haller.

'Where do you get a nuclear bomb?'

Alfred has been and gone. Last night's bottle sits on the desk, Kohler and Haller sip their whiskys.

'Ever the pragmatist, Franz.'

'Well, you can't go down the local supermarket and buy one off the shelf.'

'No, quite,' Kohler studies the light, reflecting off the cut crystal from the glass in his hand. 'So, we're agreed on the plan. It's the method of implementing it and where to get the material.'

'What about Schreiber?' Haller tops up his glass.

'I don't want to say anything to him, yet, not some half-baked scheme anyway. I'll wait until everything is ready. It'll be a nice surprise, don't you think?'

'What about my earlier suggestion, Dubois?'

'Why?'

'Well, if he is involved with the Russians? What do they say about the Mafia, they'll sell you anything, including their mother, or is it their grandmother?'

'Involving Dubois could be risky, he might not keep his mouth shut.'

'He will if you pay him enough.'

'That's true, I'll think about it. Now let's eat. I'm starving.' Kohler finishes his whisky in one swift gulp.

'If you don't mind, Kurt, I've got another engagement tonight.' Haller smiles as he stands up.

'Who is she?'

'A new barmaid, in my local stubbe. She's got big breasts!'

'Now why does that not surprise me.' Kohler laughs, then thinks about sex. He feels quite aroused after all this talk. No Helga tonight, what about a bit of my favourite speciality? No, not in Berlin, too risky. His erotic thoughts are interrupted by Haller.

'By the way, our friend is looking into Schreiber, says it will take a few days. He's busy, something about trouble brewing in the Middle East.'

'Ha, I'll give them a brew that they'll choke on!'

CHAPTER THIRTEEN

'Monsieur Kohler, this way please,' Jacques, the maitre d', leads him through the busy restaurant. Jacques knows his important guests by sight, knows their food preferences and which wine to serve. Kohler is definitely 'A' list. Although barely 9 o' clock in the evening, the restaurant is already full. Several couples sit at the zinc-topped bar, sipping cocktails, waiting for a free table; they may have a long wait.

Le Canard Blanc is Kohler's favourite restaurant in Paris. On the Left Bank, it's situated in a little alley off St Germain. The clientele is mostly local, affluent Parisians. Very few, if any, tourists know about it. If by chance they did find it, they would be told, regrettably, that the restaurant was fully booked, a Gallic shrug of the shoulders. As Kohler strides between the tables, several people look up at the tall figure, dressed impeccably in a charcoal, pinstripe suit. Few however will recognise him. Jacques pulls open the red velvet curtain at the far end of the dining area, allowing Kohler to pass. He opens the door in front of him and enters a small private dining room, the table set for two.

His fellow diner is Marcel Dubois who is standing beside the fireplace, sipping champagne from a crystal flute. He smiles broadly as Kohler enters.

'KK, mon ami!' Dubois is one of the very few people allowed to refer to Kohler as KK.

'Marcel, always good to see you!' Kohler grasps Dubois's outstretched hand, they embrace in the middle of the room. Kohler steps back and looks at his friend. 'Marcel, you've put on more weight since we last met!' admonishing him with a forefinger.

'I know, I know,' Marcel rolls his eyes to the ceiling, 'Louise is always complaining. But I'm a Frenchman, for

Christ's sake! You know, food, then sex, then we worry about our health!'

'You'll never change,' Kohler laughs, shaking his head. He picks up the bottle from the ice cooler, sitting on a small table beside Marcel and pours himself some champagne.

'So, shall we?' Dubois points to the table. Kohler nods and they sit down opposite each other.

'When was the last time we met, KK, it must be months?' Dubois arranges his crisp white linen napkin.

'My father's funeral.'

'Of course! I'm sorry, how could I forget. Such a sad occasion. But he had lived to a ripe old age.' Dubois picks out a piece of bread from the silver basket on the table. He breaks off some and chews it carefully. 'Good, fresh from the oven.'

A side door opens. A white jacketed waiter enters, carrying three plates. He lays one each in front of Kohler and Dubois, the third, slices of crisp toast, is placed in the middle of the table.

'Foie gras, KK, the best in France. Comes from a little farm near Sarlat.'

Another waiter appears, carrying a bottle of Monbazillac and pours two glasses of the amber liquid.

'Sante.' Koller and Dubois toast each other.

The meal progresses. The foie gras is followed by magret de canard with roasted potatoes in duck fat. A St Emilion from Dubois's vineyard is served to accompany the duck. The conversation revolves around personal matters, as the wine flows. The meal finishes with dessert, the chef's own Armagnac ice cream topped with crushed walnuts. Dubois belches softly and wipes his mouth with his napkin. As the plates are cleared, he orders coffee and two cognacs.

'So, KK, is this business or social?' Dubois lights up a cigar.

Kohler looks across at Dubois and toys with his balloon brandy glass.

'Business, Marcel. I was hoping that I'd met you sooner than this. But I had to go to America, we're looking at possible sites for new hotels. Then it was the Far East; Tokyo and Beijing are possibilities.'

'Ha, KK! You're always flying somewhere.' Dubois shakes his head and chuckles to himself.

'And then, when I got back, you were away in Portugal. You seem to be spending a lot of time down there, now.'

'Your bloodhound keeping track of me, is he?'

'Let's just say that Haller likes to keep apace with events. So, what are you doing down there?'

'Oh, this and that,' Dubois gives a dismissive wave of his cigar.

'Come on Marcel, I hear that you're involved with some Russians.'

'Mmm, so?' Dubois studies the end of his cigar.

'Marcel, this is like drawing teeth!'

'Alright, alright! I'm doing work for some Russians, so what? Listen, KK, you should come down with me next time. The money! No expense spared, marble bathrooms, gold fittings,' Dubois smiles and rubs his thumb and forefinger together.

'Where does the money come from?'

'That I don't ask and don't care. Look, they don't quibble and they pay their bills on time, what else could a contractor ask for?' Dubois chortles into his glass. 'If you do come down, I'll show you the latest villa that we're building, in the Algarve. It's huge, like something out of the Arabian Nights. And it's for a general.' Dubois gives Kohler a wink

'Really?' Although he appears disinterested, Kohler is beginning to think that Dubois might be useful after all.

'Yes, a Red Army general, a guy called Novchenko.'

'So, how does a Red Army general afford a large villa in the Algarve?'

'Ah, well, he might be in the army, but he also owns a haulage company. And business must be good with the amount of money that he's spending.'

'I see, sounds an interesting character. Maybe I'd like to meet him.'

'Of course, of course! He often comes through Paris on his way to the Algarve. I'll arrange it next time.'

'Marcel, I'd appreciate it sooner than later.' Kohler finishes his cognac.

'Of course, KK, anything you say.' Dubois does likewise. He then looks at his watch, 'The car is waiting for you.'

'Everything is arranged, as usual?' Kohler rises from the table.

'The location is different, but the driver knows where to go.' Dubois and Kohler shake hands across the table.

'I'll contact you when I get back to Berlin.' Kohler gives Dubois a smile as he leaves the room.

The driver stops outside a dark timber door. Kohler gets out into an unlit alley, somewhere still on the Left Bank. The car drives off, he is alone. He sees the speaker phone to the left of the door. He presses the button and says 'Romulus', his password for the night.

There is a soft click as the door opens. Kohler looks around him, the alley is still empty. He enters and hurries up the dimly lit stairs. He comes to the landing, he sees Stephan standing in front of him. But the Albanian can't see Kohler, for Stephan is blind, never knows who the clients are. All arranged by a third party.

'Romulus, you are late.' Stephan's hand is outstretched.

Kohler puts the envelope, containing the money, into Stephan's palm. Stephan rolls the envelope around between his fingers counting the money by feel. He is satisfied.

'Room three. Svetlana, she's fresh this week, from Kosovo.' Stephan stands aside, letting Kohler mount the next set of stairs.

Kohler enters room three. The room is empty except for a large bed in the middle. Standing beside the bed is a young girl, her face heavy with make-up. She's wearing a short white cotton nightdress. Kohler approaches her, taking off his jacket, slipping off his tie. She slowly pulls the nightdress over her head, she is naked underneath. Kohler is quickly aroused by her nakedness, he pinches her rouged cheek, she tries to smile at him. He roughly throws her down on the bed. He undoes his black leather belt, gripping the buckle in one hand, I'm going to enjoy this, oh yes!

One hour later, Kohler stands outside, straightening his tie. The car pulls up and he gets into the back. As the car drives away, Kohler is preoccupied, still excited, thinking of what he has just done with Svetlana, and so he doesn't notice. But Haller would have noticed, seen the red glow of a cigarette in the doorway opposite, someone watching.

The car disappears from view. The watcher drops the cigarette on the ground, crushing it with his heel. He steps out from the shadows into the moonlight and looks at his watch – 2:17 am. He writes the time down in his notebook. He's already noted the car registration number. He slips the notebook into his overcoat pocket and pulls up his collar. That's it for the night then, I think, as he walks down the alley, his footsteps echoing off the cobblestones, and whistling softly to himself.

CHAPTER FOURTEEN

The bath is hot, but not too hot. Kohler lies back, luxuriating in its warmth. The bathroom is just off his bedroom, through a dressing area. Kohler always stays at the George Cinq when he's in Paris, always the same suite. He slowly washes his arms then upper body. He's been thinking about the girl, now his thoughts turn to his meeting with Dubois. Can I trust Marcel? I have in the past, he muses, had to. The deals, the joint ventures. But that was business, this is different. This could be mass murder.

Kurt's finishing year was spent in Geneva. His 21st birthday party was a glittering occasion in Berlin. That's when Kurt first met Marcel Dubois.

Heinrich Kohler and Henri Dubois, Marcel's father, had met in 1943, in South West France. Kohler's division had been sent there to recoup after a hard winter in Russia. Dubois had been a successful builder before the war, in Bordeaux. During the war, times were hard for Dubois, so he ventured into other areas to make money. He'd quickly discovered that the German High Command had an insatiable appetite for fine wines. And Dubois had a nose for good wine and soon the finest Pomerols and Margaux were finding their way to German tables and Kohler became one of his best clients.

Marcel had said, during one drunken evening with Kurt, that after the war, several Frenchman thought his father had been a traitor, but Henri Dubois had been clever, he'd played both sides. He'd helped downed British pilots escape back to Britain by fishing boats from Biarritz. He was a hero in some eyes. He'd restarted his business and had flourished, expanding into other areas of France. He'd also bought a vineyard near St Emilion, bargains were easy to find after the war. Heinrich and

Dubois had met again at a trade fair in Paris. Over the years, they had become friends and business associates.

Kohler smiles as he remembers the holidays he and Marcel shared together. Kurt loved the west coast of France, particularly around Arcachon in July. Plenty of pretty girls from Paris to share. It was during these times, late at night after too much wine, they dreamed of the future.

Kohler opens his eyes, feels the bath water cooling. He glances at the gold Rolex on a table beside the bath. Time for breakfast. He eases himself out of the bath and dries himself with a large white bath towel. He slips on the monogrammed bath robe and walks through to the lounge. A breakfast tray is already waiting for him, orange juice, coffee and croissants. He finishes the orange juice and looks outside at the morning sunshine. Kohler pours some coffee, time to wake up Haller.

'You were late last night.' Haller sits on the sofa, watching Kohler finish his breakfast.

'You know Marcel, we ended up in some nightclub.'

Haller says nothing. This has happened before in Madrid, Rome and now Paris. Kohler goes missing for a few hours, always late at night. Kohler is not a nightclub person, so what does he get up to? And Haller is worried, he doesn't like not knowing where his boss is.

'You were right about Dubois, up to his eyeballs in Russians.' Kohler gets up, crosses the room to the dressing area. He slips off his bathrobe.

It's then that Haller notices the faint scratch marks down Kohler's back. How did he get them, I wonder?

Kohler dresses quickly, comes back into the room, sits opposite Haller.

'Anyway, I've got a name out of Marcel, a Russian general called Novchenko. Could be interesting.'

'Why?'

'Why? What's wrong with you this morning, Franz? You seem... distracted.' Kohler gives him a quizzical look.

'Sorry, I...' Haller is still thinking about the scratch marks.

'Never mind. Anyway, this Novchenko is having a large villa built. Marcel claims that this general owns some haulage company or other, that's where the money comes from.' Kohler leans forward, ties his shoelaces. 'Remember last year, when I went to Moscow?'

'Yes, you hated it.'

'Right, and do you know why? The corruption! Everyone was on the take, the whole place was a fucking shambles. That hotel site in Red Square was a fiction, for which some government flunkey wanted to relieve me of one million dollars, ha! I said then that I'd never work in that godforsaken country. But, I remember then that there were rumours that the army wasn't being paid, there was even talk of revolt. Maybe our Russian general would like to earn some more money?'

'How?'

'My, we are slow today,' Kohler shakes his head. 'The Red army means weapons... nuclear weapons, dear Franz.'

'You think...?'

'I don't know. Anyway, I've asked Marcel to set up a meeting, no harm in that. We have to explore every avenue.' Kohler stands up, walks across to the window. 'We have to speed things up, Franz. I know, I know it's partly my fault, I've been so busy with other things.' Kohler turns around, pauses. 'Anything further about Schreiber?'

'No,' Haller shakes his head. 'My source says that this Muller died in April 1945 and he has nothing on anyone called Schreiber. He said he'd call me if anything else cropped up, but, so far, silence.'

'Mmm, I've been thinking about this Habtoor. If he's alive, I think we should contact him.'

'How?'

'If he's an arms dealer, maybe Deep Throat knows about him.'

'I'll call him.'

'Good, now, I have to go to the Louvre. I hear they've found an unknown Renoir and it could be for sale.'

'Haller, if it's about Muller…'

'No, another name.'

'Go on.'

'M. Habtoor.'

Silence

'Are you there?'

'Yes, why are you asking about him?'

'I just want to know who he is.'

'Haller, what are you involved in? First you ask me about some SS officer and now it's about a Saudi arms dealer.'

'So, he is an arms dealer.'

'You didn't know?'

'I guessed so.'

Silence

'I may want to contact him, can you help?'

'Haller, a word of advice. Mohammed Habtoor is a dangerous man, his friends and associates are even more dangerous.'

'That's a risk I'll have to take. So, how do I contact him?'

'You don't contact people like him, they usually contact you.'

'But, how can he contact me, if he doesn't know about me?'

'Wait one moment.'

Silence

'My fee is double for this information.'

'Agreed.'

'Do you have a pen?'

'Yes.'

'Write down this phone number. Got it?'

'Yes.'

'That's all I can give you. Don't call me again about this man, I'll hang up. One more thing. If you do have dealings with Habtoor, do not cross him. You won't live to tell the tale.'

Kohler paces around the hotel room, Novchenko is late. He glances at his watch again, 'He was supposed to be here at one, now it's one-thirty. I do not like people who are not punctual.' He looks across at Haller, who just shrugs his shoulders. Just then, there's a knock at the door, Marcel sweeps into the room, followed by two men.

'Apologies, KK, Paris traffic, impossible sometimes! Now, may I present General Andrei Novchenko and his associate Feodor. And Andrei, this is Kurt Kohler and his associate Franz Haller.' Marcel smiles at the four men.

Kohler studies Novchenko as he approaches. About the same height as Kohler, but broader, thickset. His head a square block, with close-cropped silver hair, eyes flinty grey. He's dressed in a charcoal grey suit, open-necked white shirt. His associate, Feodor, is dressed similarly, they could be brothers. Kohler takes Novchenko's outstretched hand, hard, calloused, a vice-like grip. After the introductions, they all sit down except for Dubois, who's looking for somewhere to sit.

'Thank you, Marcel. Maybe you could wait downstairs in the bar,' Kohler settles back on the sofa, Haller sits to his left.

'But I…' Marcel looks flustered.

'Thank you, Marcel.' Kohler glares at him.

'Right, well, gentlemen, I shall see you later.' Marcel leaves the room with as much dignity that he can muster.

'Forgive me, General, I would prefer this to be a private discussion.'

'As you wish.' Novchenko replies in clipped German.

'Would you like some light refreshment, tea, coffee?'

'No, thank you. May we proceed, I have a plane to catch to Faro this afternoon.' Novchenko looks at his watch.

'Of course. You know who I am?'

'Certainly. I do not agree to such meetings unless I know who I am meeting.' Novchenko gives a faint smile. 'As you are aware, Marcel is building a villa for me. I am not intending building another one, if that's what you were thinking.'

'No, not quite.'

'Didn't think so. And if it's not to do with the trucking business, I'm not sure what business interests we would share.'

'No, nothing to do with trucking, I'm more interested in your present line of work.'

'What, being a general?'

'To be precise, the Red Army.'

'The Red Army, ha! What possible interest could you have in the Red Army, Herr Kohler?' Novchenko laughs.

'The purchase of weapons.' Kohler stares across the room at Novchenko, notices the smile quickly fading from his face.

'You want to buy weapons? What? Tanks, guns, helicopters? Well, you've come to the wrong person, I'm afraid. Come Feodor, I think we've wasted enough time.' Novchenko rises from his chair.

'A nuclear weapon,' Kohler continues. He watches Novchenko slowly sink back into his chair. If he is surprised by what Kohler has just said, then he doesn't show it.

'If I heard you correctly, you want to buy a nuclear weapon,' Novchenko leans forward, his voice barely audible. Kohler just nods.

'And why would a man like you, Herr Kohler, want to buy such a thing?'

'That is my business.'

'You know, the thought of a German with a nuclear weapon would scare a lot Russians.'

'I can assure you that it is not for use against Russia or, in fact Western Europe.'

'I would hope not,' Novchenko pauses. 'America?'

'No.' Kohler shakes his head.

'There are not many areas of the world left, then, are there?' Novchenko enquires softly.

'No, apparently not,' Kohler sits there saying nothing for a few moments. 'I am prepared to pay twenty million dollars, depending on the weapon's capability, of course'

'A considerable sum.'

'Indeed, but I realise the risks for the supplier.'

'Quite. But I fear that you may be too late.'

'Meaning?'

'To purchase something like that may have been possible in the early 90's. The Yeltsin years were not Russia's finest, chaos reigned. Now, with Putin, things are more difficult.'

'But, not impossible?'

'No, not impossible.' Novchenko says slowly. 'I shall have to think about your request, however, I am not promising anything, you understand?'

'Of course.'

'Good,' Novchenko stands up, Feodor follows suit, 'I suggest that Feodor stays in contact with Herr Haller. If there are developments to our mutual benefit, we can meet again. Now, I must catch my plane.'

Kohler watches Haller usher Novchenko and his associate out of the room. Haller walks back, sits down opposite Kohler.

'So?'

'When I mentioned the money, I could see the dollar signs in his eyes.' Kohler smiles.

'You think he can deliver?'

'Where there's a will, Franz, there's always a way.' Kohler smiles to himself. 'Now, what about our friend Habtoor?'

'I'm meeting him next Friday, in Vienna.'

'Excellent, excellent. I told you, just put down the bait, like a piece of cheese, the mouse will always come around for a sniff.'

'But, he may not bite.'

'Oh, I think so, Franz, especially when you tell him what I have in mind. At last things are moving forward. I may have to contact Schreiber sooner than I thought.' Kohler stands up and walks across to the window. 'What else could you ask for Franz? Paris, a beautiful summer's day, it's good to be alive, don't you think?' Kohler turns around, 'You know Franz, I think that I'll phone up the Louvre. They're asking too much for that painting, But I'll still buy it, why the hell not?'

CHAPTER FIFTEEN

The black Mercedes saloon drops Haller at the entrance to the Hotel Kaiserhof. Haller quickly mounts the red-carpeted steps, the grey liveried doorman doffs his cap as he enters. The hotel foyer is a rather grand affair, the hotel itself dates back to the Hapsburg empire. Haller approaches the pale, pink marble reception desk and checks in.

'Have you any luggage, Herr Schmidt?' The pretty, blonde receptionist looks up at Haller.

'No, as you know, the only reason I'm staying overnight is because there's a problem with the company jet.' Haller looks the blonde up and down. Who said Vienna was boring?

'Yes, your office phoned ahead, you're booked into the Emperor suite.'

'Thank you,' Haller signs the registration card with a flourish, takes in the blonde's smile.

'And, the Middle Eastern gentleman is waiting for you in the Smoking Lounge, it's the second door on the left, beyond the main stairs.' Haller sees the hint of cleavage as the blonde leans forward, pointing to her left. 'I hope you have a nice stay with us, Herr Haller.'

'So do I,' Haller smiles, swings the hotel key around his forefinger. He turns and walks towards the main stairs, then sees the sign for the Smoking Lounge. He enters through double doors; the room is empty except for a man sitting in the middle, amongst various chairs and table. Faded elegance, Haller thinks as he approaches Habtoor. Christ, the amount they charge for the suite, you would think that they could paint the fucking place!

'Herr Schmidt, I assume?' A slim man of average height rises to meet Haller.

'Mohammed Habtoor, I assume.'

'Correct, please, sit.' Habtoor points to a leather chair opposite him.

Haller sits down, studies the man in front of him. A sallow complexion, faint goatee beard, short black hair, dark brown eyes. He's wearing a well cut, dark blue suit, pale blue shirt, lightly patterned blue tie. On the table between them sits a silver coffee service. Habtoor picks up a spoon and slowly stirs a cup of coffee.

'Would you like some coffee, Herr Schmidt?' he enquires politely.

'No, thank you, I only drink tea.'

'Well, I can order some if you wish.'

'No, I'm fine, thank you.' Haller listens to Habtoor, maybe a slight American accent to his English.

'I hope you do not mind conducting this meeting in English, my German is very limited,' Habtoor gives a slight shrug of the shoulders.

'Actually, I'm Swiss, 'Haller replies

'Ah yes, of course,' Habtoor nods, as though filing away this nugget of information.

'Are you staying here, Mr Habtoor?'

'Oh no, a bit too, what shall I say, ostentatious for my taste.' Habtoor gives a brief smile.

But I bet you could afford to, Haller thinks, as he takes in the cut of the suit, the gold cufflinks, expensive aftershave.

'So, we meet at last,' Habtoor takes another sip of coffee.

'You are not an easy man to get hold of.'

'Sometimes a prerequisite, in my line of work.' Again that faint smile.

'Whoever answers your phone is very protective.'

'He is paid well, Herr Schmidt,' Habtoor replies, carefully placing the cup back on the saucer. 'And how did you get my phone number in the first place?'

'He's also paid well, Mr Habtoor.'

146

'Ha, ha! Well said! I like a man with a sense of humour.' Habtoor smiles. Haller notices perfect white teeth. Habtoor pours more coffee. 'Now to business.'

'As you wish.'

'You will understand that the only reason that I am here is that you mentioned the Argus Trading Company to my colleague.'

'As your colleague was being rather vague about your whereabouts or even if you existed, I thought the mention of Argus might do the trick.'

'Well, you were right and here I am.' Habtoor settles back in the brown leather armchair. 'The Argus Trading Company has received considerable payment in the past, for which the Palestinian people are eternally grateful. Regrettably, there have been no payments into that account for several years.'

'That, maybe, is about to change.'

'You, therefore, have my undivided attention, Herr Schmidt.'

Haller looks around the empty room.

'Do not worry, I've arranged it so that we will not be disturbed here. Please, continue.'

'First of all, who was your contact regarding payments?'

'You don't know?' Habtoor looks surprised.

'One of the reasons that I am here is to advise you that your previous benefactor passed away. I am here, therefore, to re-establish contact with your new benefactor.'

'Ah, I see,' Habtoor nods thoughtfully. 'Well, with regard to your question, let's see. It must be over 25 years ago that I was put in touch with a German, living in Cairo. He'd escaped from Germany after 1945. Quite a few such Germans ended up in Egypt after that war, hiding from their past. Anyway, he had a proposition. He had a client who was willing to give money to Palestinian organisations to carry on the fight against Israel. He came up with the name Argus, the account was

147

set up in Geneva, money was paid in. Whenever I needed more money, I just asked him for it. It was quite simple really.'

'And what happened to this German?'

'He died ten years ago, that's also when the payments stopped.'

'I see,' Haller says slowly. This German was probably in the Wehrmacht, Kohler's father must have known him, I wonder who he was?

'Do I take it that the payments are going to resume?'

'Not exactly. You see my client, your benefactor, would like, first of all, to give a gift to the Palestinian people.'

'A gift, is this some kind of joke? What kind of gift? New housing, new schools…?'

'A nuclear bomb.' Haller watches Habtoor for a reaction. There's nothing, except, maybe a slight narrowing of his eyes. Habtoor straightens himself, takes a gold cigarette case from his left pocket, lays it on the table, opens it. From his other pocket he produces an ivory cigarette holder and gold lighter. He takes a cigarette from the case, inserts it into the holder, puts it to his mouth then lights it. He inhales deeply, then blows a perfect smoke ring towards the ceiling.

'You know, Herr Schmidt, I've been in the arms business for over thirty years and I've never received such an offer as you are proposing.'

'There's a first time for everything, Mr Habtoor.'

'Indeed, indeed,' Habtoor slowly draws on his cigarette.

'As I have said, this is a gift, a gift worth twenty million dollars. Your fee to find the right recipient for this gift will be ten per cent.'

'What do you mean by the right recipient?

'There is a condition attached,' Haller pauses, 'The bomb must be detonated in Israel, preferably Tel Aviv.' This time he does get a reaction from Habtoor, whose jaw drops, eyes widen.

'Are you mad?' he finally splutters, stubbing out his cigarette.

'Why should I be mad? Isn't the aim of your people to strike a mortal blow against Israel?'

'Yes, yes, of course! I just wasn't expecting this.' Habtoor takes out another cigarette, dispenses with the holder, lights it immediately.

'Maybe I've come to the wrong person?'

'No, no!' Habtoor puffs on his cigarette, flicks ash into the ashtray. 'I am the right person, I can deal with this.'

'You will realise my client's concern, therefore, that his gift is delivered to the right people, not as they would say in England, to any Tom, Dick or Harry.'

'I understand his concerns,' Habtoor nods briefly.

'Good. Now, we assume that the monies from Argus were used for various Palestinian and Arab factions.'

'Correct.'

'So, who in your opinion would be suitable?'

'You can rest assured that I wouldn't deal with some young Palestinian hot heads. No, for what you are wanting, we need experienced people.'

'Do you have someone in mind?'

'Yes,' Habtoor pauses, stubs out another cigarette, 'I may have one group who could and would carry out such an act.'

'Care to tell me?'

'Not at the moment, I shall have to discuss it with them. The ramifications of this act would be enormous.'

'Well, I know the Israelis will be seriously pissed off!' Haller laughs.

'It is not a joking matter, Herr Schmidt,' Habtoor glares at Haller. 'They'll lash out at anybody, many Arab people could die.'

'That is not my problem, Mr Habtoor. If you want to strike such a blow at Israel, then many people are going to die.'

'Yes, that is true. It will be the will of Allah.'

'So,' Haller stands up, 'I don't think we have anything else to discuss, the ball is in your court, so to speak. When will I expect to hear from you?'

'I have to meet with these people, there is much to discuss and think about, it will take several weeks.' Habtoor shrugs.

'It goes without saying, that we expect you to be very careful who you talk to about this. If any of this information should fall into the wrong hands, the Israelis for instance, it will be very dangerous for us all.'

'Herr Schmidt, the Israelis have been after me for years, I've managed to elude them so far.'

'Well, I wouldn't want your luck to change. Anyway, I'd like your response, the sooner the better, Mr Habtoor. My client is an impatient man.' With that, Haller turns on his heel and makes for the door. Once outside, he pauses. Well, next stage accomplished. Now we have to hope that Novchenko can deliver and we're in business. He wanders past the reception desk, the pretty blonde smiles at him. Mmm, what was her name again? Well, hopefully that takes care of tonight. I wonder how big the bed is in the Emperor suite?

CHAPTER SIXTEEN

The Red Army Colonel stops the Vaz 469 soft top jeep, switches off the engine and gets out. He stretches himself, then lights a cigarette. He looks to the west, watches the sun beginning to set, feels a slight chill in the air. He then looks behind him, along the dusty, dirt track. Where is he?

The Colonel is Andrei Novchenko. He's waiting for his sergeant, Feodor, following behind in a Praga army truck. Novchenko's division, the elite 51st Artillery, had detrained in Odessa that afternoon and were now heading north to their new camp. But Novchenko is heading west, for he has other business to attend to. Novchenko's division have just pulled out of Afghanistan. Moscow has hailed it as a victory, but Novchenko knows otherwise. He'd been awarded a hero's medal for the Afghan campaign; he'd thrown it in the dustbin. Too many of his good men lost in that dirty, senseless war. The Red Army had controlled the cities and the skies, but the Mujahideen were in charge of the hills and mountains. It had been a war of hit and run, sabotage and ambush. And the Mujahideen had been better at it. Novchenko had watched in frustration, as his artillery and Russian tanks proved inaffective in such a war. The border with Pakistan was like a sieve, the Mujahideen received a steady stream of weapons, particularly American Stinger missiles. When the Hind helicopter gunships started to be shot out of the sky, Novchenko knew the game was up. It wasn't a question of if the Red Army would leave, but when. Novchenko had decided that if the Red Army couldn't beat this rabble, it was time to look to his future outside the army. One thing Novchenko did learn in that godforsaken country was about opium. Saw how the sale of drugs had financed the war for the other side. Maybe, he'd thought, this was how he could finance his future. In December 1988, he'd discovered, through an informer, a warehouse near Kandahar, supposedly an opium collection centre for the area. A dawn raid had surprised the Mujahideen guards; in the firefight all had been killed. And Novchenko liberated four thousand kilos of raw opium. As his artillery division rolled out of the foothills of Afghanistan, Novchenko thought that maybe this war had been worth it after all.

Novchenko suddenly sees a cloud of dust in the east, a lorry slowly approaches. 'About fucking time,' Novchenko says out loud. The rather battered-looking truck rolls to a stop behind the jeep.

'Where the hell have you been?' Novchenko shouts, as Feodor jumps down from the cabin.

'I'm sorry, Colonel. The clutch keeps slipping in this clapped-out piece of shit.' Feodor comes to attention and salutes Novchenko.

'Well, never mind, it's got you this far, let's hope it makes it the rest of the way.' Novchenko drops his cigarette, uses his dust- covered boot to grind it into the reddish clay. 'Now, we keep heading west. Just ahead is the Strelsa industrial estate, we're looking for warehouse number eight. You follow me. If you have any problems, flash your lights. I assume they're bloody working?'

'Yes, sir.'

'Who's in the truck with you?'

'Three conscripts, Mongols, thick as shit. I think it was the first time they've even been on a train, ha!'

'You're still sure that you trust who we're meeting?'

'My father did.'

'Your father is dead.'

'Natural causes.'

'That's what you say. Anyway, come on, we're late already.'

The two vehicles continue their way west; dusk is falling. They enter the industrial estate, Novchenko looks to his left, then right, sees warehouse number eight ahead. Novchenko stops outside a dilapidated building, rusty corrugated sheets flap in the light wind. The two large wooden doors, hanging off their hinges, stand open. Novchenko peers inside, sees four men standing beside a black Zil limousine. Feodor's lorry comes to a stop behind him. Feodor cuts the engine and jumps down from the cabin.

'Is that him?' Novchenko lights a cigarette.

'Yes, the one on the left.'

'Let's go then.' Novchenko, with Feodor at his side, enters the gloomy interior. It's almost dark outside, what light is left comes through gaps in the metal siding.

'You're Krasny?' Novchenko stops, addresses the man on the left. He's the tallest of the four, dressed in a grey suit that fits him, unlike the other three.

'You Novchenko?' The tall man answers, flicking away his half finished cigarette. Novchenko just nods, notices Krasny smiling faintly at Feodor. 'You're late.'

'We had a problem with the truck…'

'The stuff in there? Well, bring it in, I haven't got all night.'

'You've got the money?'

'Gregor?' Krasny speaks to the man on his left, who shrugs his shoulders then walks across to the black limousine. He opens the boot and pulls out two suitcases, walks towards Novchenko and drops them at his feet. Novchenko bends down and opens the first suitcase; it's full of used dollar bills.

'Feodor, tell the boys to bring in the bags.'

'Gregor, switch on the headlights, I can't see a fucking thing.'

Feodor reappears with each young private carrying two army canvas bags. Novchenko opens the second suitcase, the contents are the same.

'It's all there,' Krasny says, lighting another cigarette, watching the canvas bags pile up in front of him.

'You want to have a look?' Novchenko stands up and points to the bags.

'But of course... Gregor?' Gregor bends down, unzips the nearest bag, pulls out a slab of raw opium, rubs his fingers in the brown sticky mixture, then sniffs it.

'It's good,' Gregor opens another bag, does the same, this time just nods.

'Well, our business is complete then.' Novchenko turns to Feodor, 'tell them.'

'You three,' Feodor looks at the young privates, 'will wait here for ten minutes, then follow us with the truck, understood?'

'Yes, sir.' They look at each other not quite understanding what is going on.

'Come, Feodor.' Novchenko looks at Krasny, gives him an imperceptible nod. Feodor lifts up the two suitcases and follows Novchenko to the entrance. Just as they step outside, three shots ring out. Feodor puts the suitcases into the rear of the jeep, then jumps into the driving seat alongside Novchenko.

'I suppose that was necessary?' Feodor says as he starts the engine.

'Casualties of war, Feodor, casualties of war. Come on, let's get out of here.' The jeep headlights pick out the dirt road; at the next junction, Feodor turns north.

'So, stage one completed,' Novchenko looks back at the two suitcases. 'One million fucking dollars, Feodor!' Novchenko laughs and slaps his thigh. 'Now for stage two. I'll sign your honourable discharge papers next week. The office is ready and so is the warehouse. This time next week, you'll be the managing director of the newly formed Red Star Haulage Company!'

The two men look at each other and burst out laughing.

The Mafia leader, Viktor Krasny, watches as the jeep disappears into the darkness. He'd thought about a doublecross but had decided against it. Business is good, he doesn't need the Red Army on his back. He's also heard that this Novchenko is a right hard bastard. And if Novchenko could provide this amount of opium, what else could he provide in the future? No, this could be a good investment. He's paid a good price but this amount of opium will give him about four hundred kilos of morphine base, a very nice profit. He looks at his three colleagues and then at the three prone bodies, blood pooling on the earthen floor. He lights a cigarette and says, 'Start digging.'

CHAPTER SEVENTEEN

Andrei Novchenko sits in the living room of his Moscow dacha, sipping black tea from a white porcelain cup. This is one of the old dachas, timber framed, timber sidings, shingle roof. It creaks in the wind. Not like the new dachas which have sprouted up around here. Statements of power and wealth for the nouveau riche. An eclectic range of architectural styles for all moods and pockets. Brazen images, seen clearly from the winding road through the estate, protected by high walls and gates. Guarded by shaven-headed men in dark suits and sunglasses, rain or shine. Bulges in jackets not necessarily from muscles. No, this is one of the old dachas, not seen from the road, hidden by dense conifers, the smell of pine penetrating the interior. No satellite dishes, no radio antennae; just a simple red brick chimney for winter fires penetrates the roof line.

Novchenko sighs as he puts his cup on the saucer, sitting on a rough pine table, made by his grandfather, as was most of the furniture in the dacha. Simple furniture, not necessarily comfortable. Peasant furniture. He looks around him, the interior is quite dark. Timber panelled walls match the rough, hewn timber floor. Two simple windows let in morning, then afternoon light. The walls are unadorned except for photographs of his grandfather and grandmother alongside his mother and father, smiling, in happier times. The dacha had belonged to his grandfather, given to him for services rendered to the Mother Country during the last war. He had been a commissar assigned to Kruschev at Stalingrad. Novchenko's father had also been at Stalingrad, part of the pincer movement that had encircled the German 6th Army. He'd fought his way to Berlin, where he died in April 1945. Novchenko's mother had died a year earlier in childbirth. And so he had been brought up by his grandparents, in this house, gone to a nearby school and at eighteen had joined the army. He was always going to be a soldier – to avenge his father.

Novchenko looks at his watch, Feodor is late. He stands up, hand slipping into his jacket pocket, finding cigarettes and lighter. Behind him is a small alcove, an eating area, a simple table with six chairs. Between the alcove and the kitchen are stairs to above, three bedrooms and a bathroom. Plumbing had been a fairly recent innovation. From the kitchen, you can see an area cleared of trees for the vegetable patch, potatoes, cabbages, tomatoes. Simple vegetables for simple peasant fare of soups and stews. As Novchenko lights his cigarette, he can hear the car arriving, tyres crunching on gravel, motor revving on the incline, then silence. A door slams, a discreet knock on the wooden entrance door.

'Come,'

Feodor pushes the door open and stands there

'Sorry, Andrei, I was held up…'

'No matter, come on in,' Novchenko smiles at his faithful servant.

'You have a new sentry…' Feodor takes off his black hat and places it on the dresser, beside the samovar.

'Yes, Malenkov's mother is sick. I sent him back to Moscow.'

'Always thinking about your men, Andrei.' Feodor smiles.

'They're loyal, aren't they?'

Feodor just nods and holds up his briefcase, 'Last month's figures…'

'Later, let's sit,' Novchenko points to the alcove. On the table, a bottle of vodka and two glasses are waiting. Novchenko and Feodor sit opposite each other, the bottle and two glasses between them. Novchenko stubs out his cigarette on a small silver ashtray, picks up the chilled bottle and pours out two measures of pure clear liquid.

'To Mother Russia,' Feodor clinks glasses.

'Or what's left of it,' Novchenko gulps the fiery liquid in one, feeling it burn his throat.

'Quite,' Feodor averts his eyes from Novchenko's gaze, 'As I said, I have the figures…' Feodor lifts his briefcase onto the table.

'Later, I said,' Novchenko digs deep into his jacket pocket and pulls out his cigarette packet and lighter. He places them on the table, gently tapping the lighter on the gold packet.

'I take it that you have made up your mind then?' Feodor refills their glasses.

'Yes, Feodor, now is the time to quit. We are at the dawn of a new millenium, time for a new life, no?'

'But, you can have anything you want, you…'

'What? In the army? Look at me, I'm still a General. By now I should be a Marshall. But no and do you know why? Ha, every time that bastard Putin sees me, I remind him of the past,' Novchenko snorts as he gulps down the glass of vodka. He bangs the empty glass on the pine top. 'You knew my grandfather?'

'Yes, I had that honour, Andrei.'

'Yes, honour, that's a good word,' Novchenko nods thoughtfully. 'Alexei Novchenko was a peasant, but clever and brutal. He survived Stalin. To survive Stalin, you certainly had to be clever and brutal. And then Kruschev came to power. Alexei was never in the Politburo. He was Kruschev's man behind the scenes, his eyes and ears, sometimes fixer, sometimes power broker. Never in the limelight, always in the shadows. Then they kicked out Kruschev. Alexei followed soon after. He ended up here, looking after a vegetable patch. I think that's what killed him in the end, that fucking vegetable patch.' Novchenko takes out a cigarette and lights it. 'Well, Feodor, I'm not going quietly and growing fucking potatoes! But I want to secure my pension, so to speak.'

'You've been thinking about that German, haven't you?'

'Of course I've been thinking about that fucking German!'

'But you don't even like Germans.'

'Of course I don't! I hate the motherfuckers! They killed my father!' Novchenko downs his vodka and pours another. 'But this Kohler has given me an idea. What do you need to have power, Feodor?'

'Money?' Feodor looks confused.

'Of course money! But I've got plenty of that!' Novchenko inhales deeply on his cigarette, waiting.

'I don't really know, Andrei…'

'Feodor, my dear friend, that's why you never became an officer. You have to be able to see the bigger picture.' Novchenko smiles across the table.

'And the bigger picture is?'

'To have power in this world, Feodor, you need clout. And to have clout, you need weapons.' Novchenko smiles again.

'But we can get guns anywhere…'

'Not guns, Feodor, not like these hoodlums who now run Russia, these apes in black suits.'

Feodor sits for several moments saying nothing. Eventually he reaches across for the bottle and refills his glass.

'What are all these tinpot countries after, Feodor? North Korea? That fucking idiot in Iraq? The mullahs in Iran? They all want nuclear weapons! Why? To have real power, to sit at the top table!' Novchenko finishes another shot of vodka.

'And do you want to sit at this top table?'

'No, no, no! But if I can get hold of a nuclear weapon, I can it sell to the highest bidder, even if it's the German. Play one off against the other. That is real power. And just think, Feodor, we're talking about serious money now. Kohler said twenty million dollars. Alexei would be proud of his grandson!' Novchenko laughs.

'But how…?'

'Where's the list for my farewell party?' Novchenko snaps his fingers.

'Here,' Feodor delves into the open briefcase and brings out two typed pages. Novchenko quickly scans the list of names, 'Mmm, there's somebody missing.'

'Who?'

'Yeremenko.'

'Yeremenko! But he's a…'

'Yes, a little shit with a big prick! But he's also stationed at Krivoi Rog. And he happens to be guarding a mobile SS-24 missile unit.'

'But why should he…?'

'Because our little friend has expensive tastes. A luxury flat in Moscow and a mistress. I also hear that he has a large unpaid gambling debt. But, how does he afford all this? Well, this little shit has been selling off army equipment, on the black market. Yes, I think our friend Yeremenko is ripe for the picking. Add him to the list.'

The Hotel Metropol in Moscow still has some faded glory. It has not been renovated like some of the others, has not succumbed to overpaid interior designers from New York or London. A worn carpet here and there, a light bulb or two missing from the ornate chandeliers. But Novchenko likes it, reminds him of times past. The staff are ancient and still respect the power of men in uniform. Novchenko crosses the marble floor foyer and nods to several comrades, awaiting his arrival. The hotel manager sidles into view.

'The Stalingrad Room is ready, sir, just as you ordered.' The manager clicks his heels and gives a slight bow.

'I wouldn't expect anything else, Oleg,' Novchenko replies, smiling, shaking the outstretched hand and palming several hundred rouble notes which are discreetly despatched into Oleg's jacket pocket.

'You are too kind, sir. Please follow me.' Oleg advances towards the grand staircase; Novchenko follows, several steps behind. Oleg is a good party member, knows when to keep his mouth shut. Always provides a bedroom should Novchenko have a young lady in tow. Never a bill and never a word to the outside world. People like Oleg still respect the army, the army is authority. Not like these hoodlums sprawled in the bar at the Hilton, feet on coffee tables, flicking cigar ash on the carpet. Novchenko clenches his fists at the thought.

On the first floor landing, Oleg approaches the double height doors to the Stalingrad Room and swings them open. Novchenko enters, the room is almost full. Full of his friends, comrade in arms. Men only tonight, but the girls will arrive later. Someone starts clapping and as he walks down the middle of the room, he can hear them chanting his name. He raises his arms, like a prize boxer, acknowledging the applause, nodding to faces on the right and to the left. Faces from Afghanistan and Chechnya, places he'd rather forget. He approaches the top table, his divisional officers are waiting and of course, Feodor. Novchenko raises his hands once more.

'Please, gentlemen, let the proceedings begin!' Novchenko beams.

'Hooorrah!' is the reply.

Oleg claps his hands and the waiters appear.

Caviar and blinis, poached sturgeon and potatoes, roast suckling pig, red cabbage and roast potatoes, delicate pastries with fresh fruit. The best Georgian red and white wines, French cognac with the coffee. Toasts, singing, laughter, jokes. A small Ukranian band tries to compete with the noise. Occasionaly, Novchenko will hear a melody that reminds him of his grandfather's voice. He's chosen the Stalingrad Room in deference to his father and grandfather. A closure of his old life, a beginning of his new life.

Two hundred men are in the room tonight, most are friends, not just acquaintances. Novchenko glances at his watch, just after midnight. Time to say farewell, remind some of favours in the past and maybe favours to be returned in the future. Feodor leans across.

'Yeremenko is at the third table on the left,' he whispers.

'I know, I've been watching him. I think he's drunk already. Tell Oleg to let the girls in. By the way, who's the empty chair at table twelve?'

'That would be Voronov, Dmitri's old commanding officer. He's never forgiven him for leaving Spesnatz. Voronov is also pissed off with you for taking the pick of his other boys.'

'Ach, Voronov is Putin's man, I don't know why I invited him. Anyway, on to more important matters.'

Novchenko passes from table to table, clasping outstretched hands, saying goodbye, seeing grown men with tears in their eyes. Another roar is heard as the doors open, the girls have arrived. Lights are dimmed, carpets rolled up to reveal the dance floor. Now the fun is really about to start. Novchenko approaches Yeremenko's table. He is alone, a glass of vodka in one hand, a cigar in the other. He is surveying the girls, no doubt wondering which is his for the night.

'So Boris, how are things?' Novchenko sits down, pours some vodka into their glasses.

'Ah, Andrei, don't ask me.' Yeremenko's voice is slurred, Novchenko wonders just how much he has been drinking. 'Fucking Siberia!' Yeremenko bangs his now empty glass on the table.

'I heard that you had been reassigned there.' Novchenko refills Yeremenko's glass.

'Reassigned! More like fucking punishment! For Grozny!'

'Yes, Grozny, most unfortunate.' Novchenko nods slowly, sips his vodka.

'It wasn't my fault, Andrei! They gave me the wrong coordinates!' Yeremenko downs another vodka.

'But a hundred of our men died, Boris.' Novchenko says quietly.

'It was the wrong fucking coordinates!' Yeremenko thumps the table with his fist, men at the adjoining table look over. 'Sorry, Andrei, it's just so unfair, those bastards in the Kremlin!'

'And Siberia?'

'Fucking boring! You know last winter it was minus 40 degrees, minus fucking 40 degrees!' Yeremenko sloshes some more vodka into his glass.

'So, how do you keep warm?'

'Ha! She's big and fat!' Yeremenko laughs at the thought, 'Speaking of which, who's the blonde over there?' Yeremenko waves an arm vaguely across the room.

'Ah, that's Tanya, pretty isn't she? Used to be a gymnast, has some interesting positions, I hear.'

'You'll have to introduce me, Andrei,' Yeremenko leans over and gives Novchenko a wink.

'Later, Boris, later.' Novchenko leans back, lights a cigarette. 'So, you're now guarding part of our nuclear deterrent?'

'Yes, guarding. They don't trust me with the firing buttons, not now, ha! Anyway, I'm fucked, Andrei, this unit is to be disbanded. This fucking treaty with the Americans. Nuclear disarmament, huh, under the eyes of American CIA spies!'

'What will happen to the missiles, Boris?'

'Pah! Cut up into little pieces, maybe they make cars out of them!' Yeremenoko is now getting drunk.

'And the warheads?'

'Sent away, made safe. Don't know where, don't fucking care!'

'How many missiles in your unit?'

'Twenty four.'

'What happens if there were only 23 warheads?'

'What are you talking about?' Yeremenko puts down his glass of vodka.

'Maybe liberating one warhead for Mother Russia, eh?' Novchenko smiles across the table.

'Are you crazy?' Yeremenko hisses as he leans across the table, looking around in case someone else is listening. He needn't have worried, since the girls had appeared his fellow officers' minds are elsewhere.

'Crazy enough to pay fifty thousand dollars.'

'What did you say?'

'Here, look.' Novchenko pulls an envelope from his tunic pocket and pushes it across the table.

'How much?' Yeremenko glances inside the envelope.

'Five thousand, balance paid on receipt of the warhead.' Novchenko stubs out his cigarette. He looks around, several of his comrades have already disappeared, taking girls with them.

'This won't be easy you know.' Yeremenko's eyes dart between Novchenko and the envelope lying on the table between them.

'You've got dummy warheads for test firing, yes?'

'About a dozen.' Yeremenko fingers the envelope again.

'Well, it's simple. You substitute one of the dummy warheads for a real one. When you're ready, contact Feodor, he'll arrange to pick it up. What about security?'

'Security, what security? The stockpile isn't even fenced off and the guards are drunk most of the time. Do you know how fucking boring it is out there?'

'Yes, you've told me already. So, we have a deal?'

'Yes.' Yeremenko quickly pockets the envelope.

'Good. As I said, contact Feodor when you're ready.'

'Give me about ten days, okay?'

'Yes, that's fine.' Novchenko looks at his watch. 'Now, I must be going. But you, Boris, enjoy yourself.' With that, he snaps his fingers at the pretty blonde girl, sitting alone at a table. 'This is Tanya, Boris, a little present from me.'

Yeremenko is so engrossed with Tanya's breasts, spilling out of her tight blouse, that he fails to see the look that passes between Novchenko and Tanya.

Fourteen days later, Feodor and Yeremenko are sitting in a backstreet bar in Kiev. Yeremenko is counting the contents of a briefcase.

'Don't worry, Boris, Andrei is a man of his word.'

'Yes, yes, I'm sure.' Yeremenko has one last glance inside the briefcase, then snaps it shut. Yeremenko is sweating, he's never seen so much money in his life. Maybe now he can get rid of that stupid bitch of a wife. And it had been so easy! Feodor had turned up at the appointed time, after midnight, when most of the guards were in a drunken stupor. Yeremenko had forged instructions from Moscow for the switch of warheads for a test firing, for the visit of a fictitious general. The dummy warheads were outside, lying in their cradles on pallets. The real warhead had been marked with a simple cross in white chalk. Feodor's lorry had a crane fitted; it had only taken ten minutes to load the warhead. Feodor's visit to the camp had lasted just thirty minutes.

'I have to go.' Yeremenko gulps down his vodka shot. It's his fourth, Feodor had been late. He nods to Feodor and stands up, gripping the briefcase to his chest. Feodor watches him leave the dimly lit bar through the blue haze of cheap cigarettes. Feodor gets up as the waiter approaches, pays him for the drinks, a tip not too small, not too big. He doesn't want to be remembered.

Yeremenko grips the steering wheel of his Lada saloon as he weaves his way through the deserted night streets of Kiev. Maybe I can get rid of this rust bucket and get one of these new BMWs, he giggles to himself. Instead of going home, he's decided to celebrate his windfall in the arms of his luscious Tanya. He can't face going home to his fat wife, Ludmilla, and a tiny flat that smelled permanently of boiled cabbage. With his vodka befuddled brain and thoughts of what he is going to do to Tanya, he fails to notice the black Zil car following his erratic progress. Tanya lives off Barraky Street in a block of flats. Yeremenko stops the car outside the entrance. He switches off the engine and gets out, taking the briefcase with him. As he turns towards the pavement, he then notices another car parked further down from him. The street is deserted except for a figure in black, hurrying towards him. He seems familiar, his outstretched hand has something in it.

'What are you doing here?' He sees the bright flash, is aware of a thump to his chest, then extreme pain. As he topples backwards, he thinks he sees Tanya in the doorway. He is dead by the time his body hits the pavement. The figure in black stands over the prostrate body and picks up the briefcase. He looks inside to make sure it was all there, just in case the fool had stashed some in the car. He glances at the doorway, Tanya has gone. She'll phone the police in fifteen minutes or so, an anonymous tip off. Plenty of time for him to get away. As he drives off, Feodor smiles to himself and says,

'Someone must really do something about the crime wave around here.'

The Red Star Detective Agency isn't really a detective agency. It specialises more in blackmail and extortion. Crime had flourished under Yeltsin; Novchenko would often give a silent toast to that drunken baffoon. The employees of his detective agency were ex Spesnatz, Russia's elite special forces. One of the first had been Feodor's son, Dimitri. It is he who is responsible for security of the warehouse in which the nuclear warhead now sits, under a large dirty tarpaulin cover. The warehouse is situated on the outskirts of the city of Odessa. It is one of many warehouse now dotted around the various republics and of course, Russia itself. Novchenko's empire has expanded, his red lorries are now to be seen in Western Europe. They carry everything, fruit, vegetables, white goods, and people, if the price is right. Some, not many, carry concealed drug shipments. For Novchenko has renewed his acquaintance with Viktor Krasny, now the Mafia leader in Odessa. It has been a very profitable reacquaintance. Drugs are big money. Red Star Lines is a container company operating out of Odessa. So easy to ship out to Istanbul. Mules, the drug runners, do the rest.

Life is good for Novchenko, but he has one big problem. What to do with the nuclear warhead? He knew it would be easy to steal one, as it had been. Yeremenko had been a fool, but the world was full of fools. Novchenko has been careful in his choice of warhead for, although the SS-24 had one warhead, this variant actually contained five warheads, each 550 kilotons. So, he could have five nuclear devices, but how to assemble them?

In the good times, when the Red Army was at its peak, Novchenko went to Moscow every six months. Russian boffins always had ways of inventing newer shells, more powerful than the last. Nuclear artillery shells were part of the Army's arsenal. Novchenko remembered a young nuclear scientist who had attended these meetings. What was his name? The Red Star Detective Agency for once did its job. Vlad Borisov was now a science teacher in Kiev.

Novchenko finds him in a one-bedroom flat, ironically, not far from where Tanya used to live. Borisov is now a bitter man. He's been sacked from the Nuclear Institute, not enough money in their budget. Reduced to teaching elementary physics to kids who aren't interested

'A long time, Vlad.' Novchenko says taking in his surroundings. Dirty clothes lying on a heap on the floor, a kitchen sink overflowing with more dirty pots and dishes, several empty vodka bottles lie under the only table. Novchenko wrinkles his nose, there's a strange smell in the flat and it isn't just from boiled cabbage.

'You were the last person I expected, General.' Borisov points to one of two chairs for Novchenko to sit on.

Novchenko notices the stained teeth, just like the open-necked shirt, the frayed trousers, the one shoe without a shoelace. Borisov's skin is pale, face unshaven, once wavy hair now matted.

'So, you don't have many visitors then?' Novchenko takes out his cigarettes, offers one to Borisov, who declines.

'Are you kidding, General? Do you think I want my friends to see me like this?' Borisov laughs, but it's more like a cackle.

'Quite, changed days since we last met.' Novchenko lights his cigarette, hoping the tobacco will nullify the smell.

'Ha, yes! My nice Moscow apartment, the monthly pay cheque, everything was fine until the funding stopped. What money was left was shared out amongst the old guard, to protect their lifestyles, their pensions. Young people like me were jettisoned, put onto the scrap heap. Who wants a nuclear scientist these days?' Borisov says bitterly.

'Maybe I do,' Novchenko says quietly.

'I don't have much of a sense of humour these days, General, so please don't joke with me.'

'I'm not joking, Vlad,' Novchenko looks around the squalid room, stands up and walks towards the only window. The sun is shining outside, although one wouldn't know inside this dreary room. Novchenko uses a forefinger to scrape some of the dirt and grime from the window pane. He can see vaguely across the street, another dilapidated apartment block comes into view, not an inspiring outlook. 'And what do you do now, Vlad?' Novchenko turns and looks at the figure hunched over the table.

'I teach at the State school in central Kiev,' comes the muffled reply. 'Teach, ha!' The bitter voice returns.

'Who wants to learn about physics these days, eh? The girls listen to western music all day, the boys, instead of doing their homework at night, download pornography from the internet. That is the future, Andrei.'

'Yes, there is a lot wrong with Mother Russia today, but, I've come to help you, Vlad Borisov.'

'Meaning?' Borisov looks up, stares at Novchenko.

'I'm offering you employment, to come and work for me.' Novchenko smiles for the first time, enjoying the puzzled look on Borisov's face.

'To do what?'

'You'll remember when you worked for the State, there were a lot of secrets in that head of yours, which you could never divulge.'

'Of course, I would have been shot!'

'Quite, so I'm going to tell you another little secret, just between you and me, and these four walls, understood?'

'Understood.'

'Good,' Novchenko walks over to Borisov and sits down opposite him.

'I have acquired a warhead from a SS-24 missile.'

'What! How?'

'Shh, keep your voice down,' Novchenko takes out another cigarette and lights it. 'The how doesn't matter, it's what I want to do with it that matters.'

'And what do you want to do with it?'

'The warhead of a SS-24 missile contains five warheads, each 550 kilotons.'

'I know that.'

'Of course you do, Vlad. So, with five warheads I want five bombs and I want you to make them!' Novchenko sits back in his seat, puffs on his cigarette.

'Me? Mother of God!' Borisov sits there open mouthed. 'Why me?' He manages to say eventually.

'Because I remember you as a very bright young man, full of ideas, innovation. You can do what I'm asking, can't you?'

'Of course! It would just take some time, that's all. I think I'll have that cigarette after all.'

'What would you need?' Novchenko hands Borisov a cigarette, lights it for him, notices that his hand is trembling.

'Where's the warhead now?' Borisov coughs as he inhales.

'Somewhere safe.'

'Good. I'd need a warehouse with a workshop, cutting and welding equipment, lifting gear...'

'Fine, fine. We don't need to go into details for the moment, you can make a list of what you require later.'

'Is the warhead stable?'

'What do you mean?'

'Any radiation leaks?'

'I don't think so, we check it every so often with a Geiger counter.'

'Well, you have to be careful, these fucking things are prone to leak.'

'I see,' Novchenko makes a mental note for Sergei to check every day from now on. 'Any thoughts about the bomb itself?'

'No, not yet. Extracting the five warheads shouldn't be a problem, I just need the right equipment. I'll also have to think how to detonate the bomb.'

'Meaning?'

'Well, I don't suppose that you want to be near this thing when it goes off?'

'No, I take your point.'

'So, it could be a timing device or a radio controlled explosion. I've heard actually that you can now set off a bomb with a mobile phone.'

'Really?'

'Oh, yes, you just dial the right number and bang!'

'Ha! I knew I'd come to the right man!' Novchenko rubs his hands. 'Now, how do we transport this bomb?'

'Well, it's not going to be that small, not like a suitcase,' Borisov pauses.'We'll need some kind of container.'

'A container, eh?' Novchenko starts to smile, 'What about a 40-foot container?'

'A bit big, but yes.'

'Brilliant! My trucking company has hundreds of containers, worldwide there must be tens of thousands of containers. So easy to transport anywhere we want, so blindingly obvious but so well hidden, I like it.'

'We'd have to have a lead shield, don't want it glowing in the dark!'

'Yes, Vlad, whatever you say.' Novchenko sees Borisov smile for the first time since he's entered the room, sees a bit of fire in these previously dull eyes. 'When can you start?'

'Well, now.'

'Easy, Vlad, easy, I have to arrange things first of all. Now, I'll pay you $5000 a month; you can move into a flat I have in Barraky street, ok?'

'What can I say, Andrei?'

'Ah, it's nothing really. Feodor, remember him? Good, he will come around tomorrow with some new clothes and to pick up anything,' Novchenko looks around the room again, 'you might want.'

'He can burn down the whole fucking lot!'

'Yes, good idea. When's the last time that you had a bath?'

'I don't remember.'

'Yes, well, that's the first thing and then a visit to the hairdresser,' Novchenko gets up, gives Borisov a slap on the back, 'and with a new set of clothes, you'll be a physicist again!'

'Andrei, how can I thank you?' Borisov grabs Novchenko's hand, buries it in his face.

Novechenko can feel the wetness of tears, thinks of patting Borisov on the head, then seeing the greasy matted hair, decides against it. Instead, he lifts up

Borisov's head and stares into his watery eyes and says, 'Don't thank me, Vlad, just build me my fucking bombs!'

'How's your father?' Novchenko sits down at the table, opposite Dmitri.

'Better, thank you, Uncle. They say it was just a heart murmur, nothing serious.'

'Your father works too hard, you know that?'

'He's always been like that, Uncle.'

'Yes, yes. He was the same in the army, but he was the best sergeant I ever had.' Novchenko smiles at the memories.

'And he said that you were the best commanding officer that he ever had.'

'Well, that may be. I treated him then as I treat him now, just like brother. And just as I treat you like my son.'

'You've always been very kind to me, Uncle,' Dmitri pauses, 'Can I ask you a question?'

'Of course, my boy.' Novchenko smiles across the table.

'Why did you never marry?'

'Ha! Not for want of your father trying! Ah, we had some wild times when we were younger and then Feodor met Katriana, your mother. I was on my own so to speak, but the army was my life, by then, my lover. Your mother died about the time we set up the haulage company. Just as well, it stopped your father doing something stupid. Anyway, enough of this sentimental claptrap, I've asked you to the dacha for an update on Borisov.'

'He's another hard worker.'

'One of the reasons that I chose him. Go on.'

'Well, one third of the Odessa warehouse has been partitioned off. That's now his workshop. All the equipment has been installed for cutting and welding......'

'Yes, yes, but how is he progressing?'

'Well, the five containers are in place. He's just finishing the lead lining of the interiors, that's taken longer than he expected. The warheads are ready to be taken out, he's going to install a cradle for each one in each container. He's working on the detonator, wants to know whether it's to be set off by a timer or remote control.'

'Tell him to work on a remote control, in the meantime.'

'Ok.'

'But when will they be ready?'

'He says that he'll finish all five by June.'

'Excellent! Who's helping him?'

'I've assigned two of my men, but Borisov does most of the work himself, he's quite meticulous.'

'He's being paid to be meticulous, Dmitri. But I'm pleased, things are progressing more quickly than I expected. You've done well, my boy. Now you'd better go and visit your father.'

'Yes, Uncle. There is one other thing.'

'Yes?'

'Krasny.'

'What about him?'

'He wants to do two shipments a week.'

'What do you think?'

'We've had no problems with the one weekly shipment. I don't know how much Krasny is paying the Turkish customs officers, but it's obviously enough. The shipment is concealed amongst a cement cargo.'

'Won't they get suspicious of all this cement coming from Odessa?'

'I don't think so. The cement is forwarded to Israel, they're evidently building a lot of new settlements.'

'Yes, I heard, probably for all the Jews we're kicking out of Mother Russia, ha!'

'So, what do we do?'

173

'I leave that to you, Dmitri, it's time that you took more responsibility. You know more about this business than I do. I also want to be kept at arm's length from Krasny, you understand? Good, now just don't take any of that white fucking stuff!'

'Never, Uncle, that's for idiots.'

'Quite, now when you see your father give him my best, tell him I'll visit him tomorrow. I need him fit and well for what is about to happen.'

CHAPTER EIGHTEEN

'Franz?'

'Yes.'

'It's Feodor.'

'Ah, I've been wondering when you would call, my client is getting anxious.'

'The product is almost ready.'

'Excellent news!'

'The product will be of the 550k type.'

'Even better!'

'We require the down payment, two million dollars. I'll send you the bank details. Upon receipt, we can discuss the date, probably June, and place of delivery.'

'Very good, payment will not be problem, just send me the details. The product is bigger than we thought.'

'The bigger the better, no?'

'So, June, eh?' Kohler looks across at Haller

'That's what he said.' Haller studies his mobile.

'And the payment?'

'Sent, it's an account with the Royal Bank of the Bahamas.'

'So, the only loose end is Habtoor, what's he saying?'

'He's still suggesting this group called al-Qaeda, says they're the only ones he can trust.' Haller shrugs his shoulders.

'Trust! It's me that will have to trust them! This gift of mine is now so fucking big, it will take out Tel Aviv! I'm not entrusting it to some bunch of ragheads that I've never heard of!'

'Well, they're not unknown, Kurt, I…'

'I know, I know, I've heard what they're supposed to have done.' Kohler gets up from his desk and paces around. 'Call your contact.'

'He wasn't very happy about Habtoor, I don't know what he'll think about this al-Qaeda.'

'I don't fucking care, Franz, this is too important. Just call him!'

Haller sits on the park bench. In front of him, he watches some children feeding bread to the ducks. His contact sits beside him. He is Helmut Schroener, an intelligence officer with the BND. Haller turns his attention to Schroener, sees a neat little man, neat haircut, neat suit, neat briefcase. From the briefcase, Schroener produces a plastic lunch box, which he opens.

'Ah, Mother has given me tuna today, would you like one, Franz?'

'No, thanks.' Haller shakes his head, instead lights a cigarette.

'They're bad for your health, you know,' Schroener points a sandwich at Haller's cigarette.

'Don't tell me.' Haller flicks some ash onto the ground.

Schroener says nothing, chews on his sandwich for a few moments. 'The reason that I've asked for this meeting, face to face so to speak, is because of your recent enquiry. The group that you're asking about, well, let's say that it's better that they are not discussed over the phone.'

'Why.'

'How long have we known each other, Franz?' Schroener takes another bite of tuna.

'About twenty years?'

'Twenty-two, to be exact. And in that time, I've given you much valuable information.'

'For which you been paid well, my friend.'

'Oh yes, I'm not complaining, don't get me wrong,' Schroener pops the last piece of sandwich into his mouth, chews for a few moments. 'I mean, I don't mind getting the dirt on politicians like that Italian. I don't even mind looking up old records for dead Nazis, you're

176

the one that is paying. But then you asked about Mohammed Habtoor and now al-Qaeda.'

'So?'

'If you're asking about al-Qaeda, then I suppose that you have been in contact with Habtoor.'

'Yes, I got their name from him.'

'Franz, you're stepping into very dangerous territory here.'

'So you told me last time.'

'How much do you know about al-Qaeda?'

'What I've read in the papers. That's why I'm asking you, is all that stuff true?'

'Let's see, where do I begin?' Schroener carefully closes his lunch box and puts it in his briefcase. 'They were first heard of in '93, suspected of being involved in that bomb in the World Trade Centre. Then in '98, the Nairobi embassy bombing and, most recently, the attack on the USS Cole in Yemen.'

'And al-Qaeda was involved in all these attacks?'

'It is the intelligence's opinion that they were.'

'So, they're very organised…'

'And very dangerous, Franz,' Schroener flicks some bread crumbs from his trousers. 'They now operate out of Afghanistan, the Taliban government protect them, so to speak. Osama Bin Laden is also there.'

'I've read about him.'

'Well, he hates the West, particularly America. He'd like to destroy Israel and also take out the Saudi royal family. Bin Laden has a busy agenda in front of him.'

'So, you think they're capable of anything?'

'Oh yes, and more. There's another reason that I wanted to meet you. We think al-Qaeda are plotting something, something big.'

'Where?' Haller suddenly feels cold. Schroener can't know about Kohler, can he?

'Somewhere in Europe, maybe America. There's a lot of chatter on the airwaves, several intelligence agencies are getting very nervous.' Schroener looks at his watch,

'Well, I must get back to the office.' Schroener stands up, straightens his jacket. 'You realise, Franz, that if something bad should happen, further to our discussion, we can never meet again.'

Haller just nods, watches the receding figure of Schroener. He looks around him, the children have gone, he is alone, he feels cold, despite the sunshine. Well, my old friend, I'm sorry, but something bad is going to happen, something very bad.

'Mr Habtoor, I've been trying to contact you for a month.'

'I am sorry, things have been difficult at this end. I've had to move around a lot. You said it was urgent.'

'Yes, the gift is ready.'

'Ah, very good, when can I expect delivery?'

'Well, there's a slight problem.'

'Meaning?'

'My client is still not sure of the recipient.'

'Why not, haven't I given you enough proof?'

'He's still not convinced, I'm sorry.'

'I see, then maybe we do have a problem.'

'Yes.'

'I will have to talk to certain people, you understand?'

'Yes, alright.'

'Good, I will call you back in one hour.'

Haller stands up, walks around Kohler's office. Kohler is in the meeting room with De Vries, who is still trying to peddle his Rotterdam hotel. Haller knows that he's wasting his time, Kohler is in a foul mood these days, won't agree to anything. All because of this fucking bomb! The Russians are ready to deliver and still Kohler dithers over this al-Qaeda group. What more bloody proof does he want? I told him what Schroener had said and still….. I remember the look on Schroener's face, he was scared. And Schroener is a cold fish, always has been;

it would take a lot to scare him. Haller's phone rings again.

'Yes?'

'Listen carefully. You will receive a package on the ninth of September. Have your passport and an overnight bag ready. The package will contain instructions which you are to follow explicitly, do you understand?'

'Yes, but…'

'No questions, please. We will talk upon your return. I think your client will be convinced.'

11th September 2001. New York. Franz Haller is standing, as instructed, at the street corner, waiting.

He had flown in yesterday, on the Lufthansa flight from Berlin. He was staying at the Hilton, downtown and was scheduled to leave the following day. A flying visit, he said to himself. I hate flying visits. But his instructions had been very specific – date, time and location. The message had been very simple, yet puzzling – 'The Towers of Babel will come down.' He looks at his Tag Heuer watch again – 8 :44 am. So? He glances along the busy sidewalk, there's a television crew filming some New York firemen. He takes out a cigarette. Just as he lights it, he hears the sound. The high pitch whine of aircraft engines. He instinctively looks up and sees the twin engine jet.

'Christ, he's low. Too low!' he says out loud.

Other people around him have stopped and are also looking up. He watches in disbelief, as the plane etches its way across the brilliant blue sky and then crashes into one of the towers of the World Trade Center. There is a sudden ball of fire, followed by black smoke. The sound of the explosion reaches him seconds later.

'Good God!' is all Haller can manage to say. The cigarette burns his fingers, it slips and falls unnoticed to the sidewalk. People start screaming, shouting,

'Jesus Christ, did you see that?'

'Hey man, what the fuck was that?'

'Are they filming a disaster movie or somethin'?'

Then people start running, anywhere, everywhere. Haller stands motionless, transfixed amongst the bedlam. The top part of the tower is now on fire. Then he catches a glimpse of a another aircraft, coming in from the south side. It disappears from view but by the sound of the second explosion, he knows it's hit the other tower. More screaming, more panic. The firemen have long gone. Haller instinctively looks at his watch. Twenty minutes have passed, it feels like twenty seconds.

'The Towers of Babel will come down.' He pulls out another cigarette, notices that his hand is shaking. 'Who the hell have we got ourselves involved with?'

Haller sits in a chrome and black leather chair, looking out across the uninterrupted view of Berlin. Seven days have passed since what is now known as 9/11. It had taken him four days to get out of New York. All the flights had been cancelled for three days, nothing was flying above America. He'd been lucky and managed to get the first Lufthansa flight out of JFK.

Haller looks around the office that he knows so well. The decor is minimalist, white walls, double-glazed full height windows, dark grey carpet, off-white ceiling, recessed downlighters. The only colour comes from a large abstract painting of vivid reds, hanging above the desk opposite him. He looks at the desk, its black marble top freshly polished, heavy chrome legs indenting the pile carpet. The desk is empty as usual, except for a black I-Mac computer, the screen angled away from him. The only other object on the pristine top is a black telephone console, an orange light blinking on and off.

Haller looks at his watch. He's late, unusual in itself. Just then, the black mahogany door to his left is thrown open, Kohler enters. He is dressed as usual, crisp white shirt, silver cuff links, grey tie, dark grey linen trousers, black leather loafers. He sits down heavily on the high-backed leather chair behind the desk. He presses a button on the console.

'No calls, Magda' The orange light stops blinking, he looks across at Haller. 'So, it was them?'

'Oh yes, no doubt,' Haller replies, wishing he could have a cigarette. 'I still don't understand why I had to be there, could have watched it on CNN.'

'Hmm, they wanted you there as a witness.'

'A witness?'

'Yes, to witness how clever they are, how inventive, how organised.'

'Well, you must admit it was pretty impressive…'

' And also very stupid!' Kohler interrupts sharply.

'Stupid?' Haller knows from experience not to argue.

'Yes. Look at the reaction of the Americans. You don't hit them in their own backyard. There's Bush, strutting around like some Wild West sheriff. Once a cowboy, always a cowboy! The British, the French, even our own Oskar Fischer, falling over themselves to support the Americans. Stupid, fucking stupid!' Kohler gets up angrily from his chair. Stands against the window, saying nothing, fuming.

Haller knows to keep quiet until his boss calms down. He looks across at Kohler, seeing his well-muscled body, silhouetted against the pale blue autumn afternoon sky. Kohler suddenly spins around and says. 'When's your next meeting?'

'The 18th, Vienna, as usual,' Haller shrugs his shoulders.

'Cancel it'

'But it's all set up…'

'I said cancel it!' The look on Kohler's face brooks no argument from Haller. Kohler slowly walks back to his desk. He puts a hand on the top of his chair, gently swaying it from side to side, thinking. He stares at the abstract painting and says quietly,

'You will cancel the meeting. You will tell him that there will be no further contact between us until further notice. Make it very clear – Don't call us, we'll call you. Also contact the Russians, the deal's off. Understood?'

'They're going to be seriously pissed off.'

'I don't care, just do it!'

'Ok, ok.' Haller slowly nods his head.

'Good, now your laptop?' Kohler sits down.

'Laptop? In my office.'

'Download everything and make a hard copy. Send the hard copy to Schreiberg in Hamburg, he'll be told what to do with it. Then delete everything. Same with your mobile. After you're finished, hand them both to Magda. She'll dispose of them and give you new ones. There must be no connection between you, Vienna and the Russians. Understood?'

Haller again slowly nods his head, 'But why...?'

'Why? Look, the Americans are going to push every button, call in every favour. The CIA will lean heavily on the British MI6, the French DGSE and German BND, even Mossad,' Kohler spits the word Mossad out. 'Your friend in the BND will have to keep his head down. We'll have no protection for a while. We have to be squeaky clean.'

'And the project?'

'Put on ice for a while, until, as they say, things cool down,' Kohler stares across at Haller. 'I'll have to speak to Schreiber. He's not going to be happy. But, I don't want a bunch of fucking Arabs screwing this up!' Kohler looks at his watch, 'I must be going, anything else?'

'You have the Brandts and the Steins for dinner at eight. The menu is...'

'To hell with the menu!' Kohler stands up and starts to leave. As he opens the door, he turns, 'By the way, set up a meeting with Marcel next week, we'll need to talk. You'll be coming too.' With that he's gone.

Haller reaches for the phone, 'He's leaving early, have the car ready. And Magda, get me a new lap top and mobile. No, don't ask why, just bloody do it!'

CHAPTER NINETEEN

'Herr Schreiber, sir.' Alfred stands there, the study door half-open.

Fuck! What does he want? Kohler silently fumes at the desk in his study.

'Show him in, then,' Kohler replies brusquely.

Schreiber enters, dressed as he always is. Doesn't this man have a wardrobe or something? Kohler thinks to himself, as Schreiber sits down in front of him.

'You haven't been answering my calls, Herr Kohler.'

'I have been rather busy.' Kohler points to his desk, strewn with papers.

'Ah yes, the busy businessman.' Schreiber says, the hint of sarcasm is not lost on Kohler.

'Meaning?'

'I've seen your balance sheet, KK industries goes from strength to strength. It's almost a money-making machine.'

'I thought that was the aim, to make money, Herr Schreiber.'

'Indeed, indeed. It's our other aim that concerns us.'

'Look, Schreiber, we've been through this many times. Since 9/11, the game has changed.'

'The game may have changed, but the objective is the same, yes?'

'Of course! But you must understand the difficulties that I have faced.'

'Not the same excuses, please.' Schreiber snorts.

'They're not fucking excuses, Schreiber, these are practical difficulties. After the Americans invaded Afghanistan, al-Qaeda were severely compromised. Since then, it has been difficult to keep in touch. No one appears to know where Bin Laden is, even Habtoor. And now Habtoor has gone missing, Haller thinks he's on the run.'

'Kohler, this was your idea, your grand plan. There will always be difficulties, it's your job to overcome then. You mention al-Qaeda, they have not been inactive, look at Madrid and London.'

'What about the Lebanon?' Kohler angrily replies.

'Ha, a few hundred dead, a pinprick to Israel.'

'It should have been thousands! I paid the Iranians for long range missiles they didn't deliver!' Kohler still fumes over the double dealing by Tehran.

'That is your problem, Kohler. Anyway, time is running out.'

'What do you mean?'

'It is almost seven years to the day since we first met. We were very impressed with you, to begin with, such enthusiasm and dynamism. But since 9/11, nothing.'

'I've told you…'

'No more excuses, Kohler, I'm here to give you an ultimatum.'

'An ultimatum? You, give me an ultimatum, ha!'

'Do not laugh, Kohler, I am deadly serious. I am an old man, the last surviving Knight Protector. Young people now run the organisation, they are not prepared to wait like we did, they want action. You have six months.'

'Six months!'

'Or alternative action will be taken.'

'What alternative action?'

'You can say goodbye to your political aspirations.'

'How can you say that? You may have noticed that I have a rather high profile these days, my new public relations company sees to that. I've been doing my own thinking, maybe I'll just form a new political party of my own. I am wondering whether I need you people after all.'

'And what about your father's unfinished business?'

'My father did not succeed and maybe I shall not succeed. So be it, I see no disgrace in that. The world has moved on since we first met, Schreiber, I think we should move on too, yes? Now, if you have nothing more to say…'

'Oh, I haven't finished yet, Kohler. I was just hoping that it wouldn't come to this.'

'What?'

'It would be most unfortunate if your nocturnal peccadillos were made public.'

'What are you talking about?' Kohler suddenly feels fear for the first time in his life.

'Let's see, Paris, Rome and Madrid. I have the dates here. How old are these girls, eleven or twelve? A serious offence in all these countries.'

'You've had me followed.'

'Naturally, we were originally protecting our investment, so to speak. These nightly excursions without Haller made us curious. You shouldn't have been so careless, Kohler.'

'You wouldn't use this information, it would destroy everything that you want to achieve.'

'What do they say, Kohler? The team is more important than the player. The same applies to you. Now, I have finished,' Schreiber stands up. 'You have six months. Don't worry, I'll see myself out as usual.'

'You look like you've seen a ghost, Kurt.'

'I've had a visit from Schreiber.'

'Oh him, I'd almost forgotten about him.'

'Well, he hasn't forgotten about me!'

'So?'

'He's reminded me of unfinished business.'

'What? Israel?'

'Yes.'

'Oh come on, Kurt! Look, we did our best, so the Arabs fucked up, that wasn't our fault. I thought you'd forgotten about all this shit.'

'He's reminded me of my obligation to my father.'

'Ha! Easy for him to say.' Haller pauses, 'Have you seen the recent opinion polls? You're the most popular man in Germany. Big business is behind you, even the trade unions support you. You can become chancellor without Schreiber, you know that.'

'Maybe I have no choice.'

'Meaning?'

'Never mind. Schreiber has given me six months.'

'Six months? Jesus Christ!' Haller looks at Kohler. What the fuck is going on? Look at him, something has happened but what? He's worried, I can see it in his face. There's another agenda somewhere and I don't know what it is.

'Kurt, I don't need to remind you that you've already taken risks recently. Pieck? Baxter? Kruger?'

'They had to be taken care of, Franz. You knew from Deep Throat that Pieck was getting too close, had confided in Kruger.'

'Pieck was easy, a crowded platform, no one saw me. But Kruger and Baxter, that was more difficult. Maybe I was seen?'

'Franz, that's over a month ago. Magda has checked the English papers, still unsolved murders. We haven't had the police calling, have we?'

'Alright, maybe I was lucky but it was very risky, Kurt.'

'It was a risk worth taking.' Kohler's abruptness brooks no further argument from Haller. 'Look, Franz, everything was in place before, we just have to reactivate it. It will be carried out by others, nothing can implicate me. Once it's done, then I can get Schreiber off my back.' Kohler tries to smile but fails.

'Oh Kurt, the prize is almost within your grasp, you don't need…'

'I have decided!' Kohler slams a fist on the desk-top.

'Ok, ok,' Haller raises his hands in surrender. 'So, where do we start?'

'You'll have to contact Novchenko, then Habtoor.'

'It's five years since I've talked to these people. Easier said than done, Kurt. I've no idea where Novchenko is and Habtoor, well…'

'Well, you'd better get on the phone then, hadn't you?' Kohler glares at Haller.

'Alright, Kurt, anything you say.'

Kohler and Haller have arrived by private jet at Faro airport. Kohler's Gulfstream slowly taxis to a halt. Marcel greets them on the tarmac. He's arrived by a scheduled Iberian flight via Madrid. Even for May, it's already very hot. The Portugese immigration officer gives a cursory glance at the passports of Kohler and Haller, nods to Marcel and hurries back to his air-conditioned office. Marcel leads them to the waiting car, a black Mercedes 500SL. Their driver, lounging against the front door, flicks away his cigarette and gets in. Kohler and Dubois sit in the back, Haller sits beside the driver. Very little is said as they leave the airport; in fact little is said during the journey. Kohler and Dubois assume the car is bugged. They head west, along the N123, catching glimpses of the sea to their left. They pass Quinta de Lago, Kohler can see people playing golf. He's never been one for outdoor sports, prefers the gym for his exercise. They exit the N123 and join the N145, passing through the village of Quita. The road narrows beyond the village, they drive through a plantation of cork trees. Suddenly the driver turns into a narrow track, unmarked. More cork trees, some of the bark already stripped. Ahead, Kohler can see large metal gates, on either side is a high block wall, topped with razor wire. A tall man appears from under the shade of a tree; he's muscular, blonde cropped hair. He's wearing a white T-shirt and faded jeans. Kohler can see the damp patches of sweat on the front of the man's T-shirt; he also cannot fail to notice the AK47 slung from his shoulder. The car rolls to a stop, the driver's window opens with the touch of a button. The tall man, expressionless, peers into the car's interior, surveying the occupants. Some words in Russian pass between the man and the driver. The man stands back and shouts something again in Russian, the gates are opened. The car moves slowly forward. They enter a green oasis, in stark contrast to the cork trees and burnt reddish earth which accompanied their journey. Lush green grass, purple bougainvillea, tall handsome palm trees. Several sprinklers are in operation, sending sprays of water into the air, glistening in the sun like little rainbows. The driveway curves around to the left and Kohler sees the villa for the first time. It's difficult to determine how big the villa is, there seems so many parts to it. There are many changes in roof levels and several towers, like minarets. The exterior has been painted in a strange pink colour, door and windows highlighted by brilliant, white surrounds. Marcel, who built the house, had described the design as eclectic.

The car stops outside the entrance, the doors already open. They step out into the harsh sunlight; Kohler feels the heat rising from the stone-flagged forecourt. In front of him, there is a Porsche and a Ferrari. Another tall, blonde man lounges on the side of the Porsche. He is also cradling an AK47, which he uses to point for them to enter. The three men are wearing business suits; Kohler can already feel the sweat running down his back. They are grateful to enter the cool interior of the house. Kohler finds himself standing in the middle of a huge lounge. The room has been divided into several sitting areas with large leather settees and armchairs, marble-topped coffee tables sit in front of the settees. The room is deserted, except for a stunning young girl sitting at a solitary table for two. On the table is a chess set; she appears to be studying her next move. She looks up and sees Kohler. She takes out a cigarette from the packet in her hand and lights it from a gold cigarette lighter on the table. She stands up languidly, stretching slightly. She is naked, except for a white thong and a pink towel wrapped round her head like a turban. Maybe she's just had a shower. Her body is beautifully tanned, her firm breasts barely move as she drifts past Kohler, ignoring him, a trail of blue smoke in her wake. Kohler can hear Marcel mutter some expletive behind him. Just then a man appears. He's tall, muscular, he's also wearing a white T-shirt and jeans

'I am Dmitri,' He stands there legs apart, doesn't offer a handshake. 'Monseuir Dubois, please wait here. Olga will bring you some refreshments.'

Kohler and Dubois exchange glances. Dubois shrugs his shoulders, sits down in the nearest armchair.

'You two, follow me.'

They step through a large archway, in the centre of the lounge, onto a pool deck. In front of Kohler is a large swimming pool, a dazzling blue. To the right are several Roman steps into the pool. About half a dozen sunbeds have been placed near the edge. Another stunning blonde girl lies on one of them. She's wearing two strips of white material, which barely constitute a bikini. She isn't aware of their presence, she's concentrating on the Sun God. At the far end of the pool, there are three white canvas umbrellas, one large and two smaller. Novchenko is sitting under the large one. Dmitri leads them across the salmon-coloured stone deck. Kohler notices there's another man sitting under the umbrella to Novchenko's left. He also cradles an AK47 on his lap. Novchenko looks up from the papers he's been studying as they approach. He motions Kohler and Haller to sit down. Haller sits down beside the other man, just to even things up. Dmitri gives a slight bow and leaves

'He's Feodor's son,' Novchenko says by way of explanation, laying his papers on the table.

Kohler looks across at Novchenko. He's put on weight since last time but has more of a sun tan. He's wearing a white linen shirt and dark blue bermuda shorts. Kohler is glad of the shade and the cool breeze coming in from the sea.

'The only reason that I've agreed to this meeting is because of Dubois, understand. I'm also very busy,' Novchenko emphasises this, by pointing to the papers in front of him.

Kohler is inwardly seething, having to deal again with Novchenko. Just look at him, the way he speaks and acts, this ghastly house, these men everywhere carrying guns. Just no breeding, no culture. But Kohler knows how to keep his cool.

'Well, Andrei, we had a deal over six years ago which, regrettably, fell through and I…'

'That was your fault! I'd arranged everything and then you say no! After 9/11, you said that things were too hot. So, the deal was off!' Novchenko folds his arms over his broad chest.

'I paid two million dollars as a deposit which, I may say was not…'

'Returned? I told you, the deposit was non-refundable! I had to pay many people. Do you know how much? Huh! What you wanted was very expensive.' Novchenko leans forward and takes a cigarette from the packet lying on the table. The man beside Haller gets up, crosses to the big Russian and lights the cigarette. Kohler notices that he keeps hold of the machine gun, never lets it go. Novchenko puffs on the cigarette, the smell is acrid, maybe Turkish or Russian.

'Well, Andrei, that was in the past. Let's talk about now.' Kohler shrugs his shoulders, tries to smile

'OK,' Novchenko's grey eyes stare at Kohler.

'I am back in the market for a device, similar to what we were discussing before. Can you still supply it?' Kohler leans back in his seat, feeling the cold sweat on his back.

'Ha, Kohler, you are a very funny man! Last time you said things were too hot, the deal's off. Well, Kohler, things are still fucking hot. These terrorists, these motherfuckers, are bad for business! Russia now has the FSB, used to be the KGB, but worse. This Putin is a hard-assed bastard.' Novchenko spits on the ground. 'It's now not easy to get what you want.' Novchenko drops his cigarette and grinds it out with his barefoot.

Kohler sits there, silent. This is not what he had expected to hear. He'd assumed that Novchenko would still be able to supply as before. If Novchenko couldn't do it, he was in real trouble.

'But there again, maybe,' Novchenko taps his fingers on the table and then eases his big frame out of his seat. 'I have to make a phone call,' Novchenko wanders over to the edge of the pool, pulls a mobile out of his pocket, taps in some numbers and listens. Kohler can hear rapid fire Russian, the conversation appears to be one way. Kohler looks at Haller for support, but Franz is staring at the blonde across the pool who has just sat up. She undoes her bikini top, her breasts are firm and round, just like the other girl, they could be sisters. Dmitri appears, carrying a silver tray on which is balanced an ice bucket and glasses. He sets down the tray and pours champagne into three crystal glasses. Kohler glances at his watch, a bit early, but what the hell, it's a '64 Krug. Novchenko turns around and waves Dmitri away. He finally finishes his call, seemingly satisfied. He comes back to the table and sits down heavily. A large hand grasps the glass in front of him, he takes a long gulp.

'So yes, it may be possible.' He finishes his glass in another gulp and refills his glass.

'Excellent. I knew I'd come to…'

'The price is thirty million dollars!'

Kohler is stopped in mid sentence, 'What! But that's ten million dollars more than the price last time.' Kohler for once is stunned.

'Take it or leave it. That is my price.' Novchenko picks up another cigarette, this time he lights it himself. 'Maybe you can find another supplier, good luck. Now, as I say, I'm very busy.' With that he picks up the papers in front of him.

Kohler is thinking furiously. It's not the amount of money, that's nothing to him. It's paying it over to that arrogant bastard in front of him. He looks at Haller who just shrugs his shoulders. It's alright for him, it's not his money.

'So, what do I get for my money.' Kohler eventually asks.

'You're a lucky man, Kohler.' Novchenko puts down his papers again. 'After all this time, I still have one man. He is very good. The deal is the same, 550k and comes in a container. It will still make a very big bang!' Novchenko smiles, but it's not a pleasant smile. 'I'm not a scientist, but if you're interested, I'll send you the specification.'

'And the price?'

'Non-negotiable.'

Kohler sits there thinking, I need more time.

'Ok, send my associate, Herr Haller, the specifications. If they are acceptable, then we may have a deal.' Might as well let the bastard sweat for a bit. Kohler stands up, followed by Haller. Nobody shakes hands. Dmitri reappears and leads the visitors away.

Novchenko watches them disappear into the house. The young man at the table gets up and wanders over to him.

'Tell Dmitri I want to speak to him.'

'Of course, sir.'

'Do you think they'll bite, uncle?' Dmitri returns and sits down beside Novchenko.

'Of course, they have no other choice.' Novchenko answers in Russian. 'These Germans are fucking stupid! We beat them in the last war and now we beat them in business. They treat me like a gangster. Ha, I'll show them who's a fucking gangster!'

'And if they buy it?'

'Go and speak to your father, he'll contact Borisov, he's been told what to do. Now!' Novchenko thinks of having another cigarette but changes his mind. Instead, he stands up and snaps his fingers at the girl on the sunbed. She gets up and saunters over to him. I wonder if she's as good as her sister? He nods to her and then to the nearby sunbed. He glances at his gold Rolex, 'Yes, enough time before lunch.'

Thirty-five thousand feet over Spain. The blonde stewardess pours champagne for Kohler then Dubois. Haller is sitting up front, talking to someone on his mobile.

'Thanks for the lift to Paris, KK.' Dubois inspects the bubbles in his glass.

'My pleasure, Marcel. A little thank you for arranging our meeting.'

'Speaking of which, would you mind telling me what the hell is going on?'

Kohler settles back in the black leather armchair, sips some more champagne. The interior of the Gulfstream seats six, with a work area in front of the cabin. Behind is a fully equipped galley and sleeping area.

'Just some unfinished business, Marcel.' Kohler smiles, satisfied with the outcome of this morning's meeting.

'That doesn't answer my question, KK. Last time you met Novchenko must have been the middle of 2001. I met him in October, he was fucking apoplectic about you. Screamed at me, said that you had reneged on a deal. I almost got thrown out of his villa!'

'For that, I apologise, Marcel. It was just a misunderstanding.'

'Oh really? Then I don't hear from you for ages and then out of the blue, a phone call, 'Please Marcel, see if you can find Novchenko, I need to talk to him.' Huh!'

'Don't take it so personally, Marcel.'

'I do take it personally! That meeting in Paris, I was dismissed like some servant. Then today, 'wait in the waiting room, Marcel, whilst the big boys talk,' ha!'

'Alright, Marcel, I didn't mean to offend you. I just don't want you involved in this deal with Novchenko. It's better that you don't know anything about it.'

'I thought we were friends, KK?'

'We are friends, I can assure you, just don't push me on this one.'

'Ok, have it your way. A word of warning though, I hope you know who you're dealing with.'

'Yes, Marcel, I do.'

'Novchenko traded the Army for the Mafia, just be bloody careful, I've seen them at work.'

'What do you mean?'

'I've had other dealings with Novchenko.'

'For what?'

'Maybe it's better that you don't know about it, KK.'

'Ok, I asked for that. Sometimes I worry about your neck, Marcel.'

'I'm more worried about yours at the moment.'

'Don't worry, I know what I'm doing. Now, more champagne.' Kohler snaps his fingers. The stewardess appears at his side, tops up their glasses. 'I think we'll have the smoked salmon, caviar and blinis. See what Franz wants, will you?'

'Of course, Herr Kohler.' The tall blonde, wearing a short blue skirt and tight white blouse, makes her way forward.

'Have you screwed her, KK?' Dubois leans forward to catch a glimpse of her shapely legs, gives Kohler a nudge.

'That's more like you, Marcel, crude and to the point. And no, I haven't. Never do it on your own doorstep is my motto and please put your tongue back.'

'Just asking.'

'Why, are you interested?'

'Ha! With a body like that, who wouldn't be.'

'I'll see what I can arrange, Marcel. That's what friends are for, after all.' Kohler laughs.

CHAPTER TWENTY

After a lobster salad, Novchenko lies on the bed, in the darkness of his bedroom. He often has a siesta after lunch, has discovered that some of his more innovative ideas come to him as he dozes. He is thinking about this afternoon's guest. He looks at his watch, time for a shower first.

Half an hour later, Novchenko sits under the same umbrella, beside the pool. It's mid afternoon, the hottest time of the day. Even the cicadas seem to be hiding from the heat. The only sound is from the distant waves, pounding the beach.

He's grateful for the balmy breeze from the sea. He lights a cigarette, tapping the table slowly with his gold lighter. He sees Dmitri approaching, his visitor in tow. This is the visitor's first time here. Novchenko's visitor is of medium height, olive-skinned, receding black hair. He is wearing a white cotton open-necked shirt, cream linen trousers and light tan loafers. At least he's not wearing a stupid fucking suit, Novchenko thinks, as he rises to greet him.

'Mr Habtoor, so glad that you could come at such short notice.'

They shake hands across the table.

'No problem, especially when you provide such an efficient mode of transport.' Habtoor gives a slight bow. Habtoor had flown by Egyptair from Cairo to Nicosia, where he'd been met by Novchenko's private jet for the flight to Faro.

'Something to drink, perhaps?'

'No, I'm fine, thank you.'

Novchenko dismisses Dmitri with a wave. Both Novchenko and Habtoor sit down.

'I trust there were no problems at the airport?'

'No, everything went very smoothly.' For this trip, Habtoor had used his Moroccan passport.

'Good, the Portugese are not too fussy, don't want to scare away the tourists.' Novchenko chuckles to himself.

Habtoor sits watching his host, wondering about his accent, probably Russian. He's also wondering how this Novchenko had got his name. Someone called Feodor had found him, had made the proposition. Which was why he was here.

'Mr Habtoor, your return flight is in three hours, so, as they say, I will not beat about the bush. My associate informs me that you have a client who would be interested in a product that I have to sell.' Novchenko lights another cigarette.

'That is correct.'

'Your client being…?'

'I am not at liberty to reveal his name.' Habtoor gives an apologetic shrug.

'No matter, as long as he can pay.'

'And how much would he have to pay?'

'Thirty million dollars.' Novchenko flicks some cigarette ash onto the pool deck

Habtoor does not react to this amount, he's been in this game too long to show any emotion. 'And this figure…?'

'Thirty million dollars. For that you get a 500 kiloton warhead.'

Habtoor gives a sharp intake of breath.

'I also have two conditions. Firstly, the device is not to be used in Europe or Russia. Secondly, payment, in full, is to be made one month before delivery.' Novchenko sits back, studying Habtoor's reaction.

Habtoor has often had to think fast on his feet, but the enormity of what is being offered is only slowly sinking in. He's only here because Bin Laden has specifically retained him to purchase nuclear weapons. He has already been contacted by the German again, Bin Laden could get two for the price of one. Thirty million dollars was not a problem to Bin Laden, and Habtoor's fee was ten per cent – three million dollars. Enough to put his retirement plans into action. A 500 kiloton bomb would be devastating, would blow up a major city and more. I'm going to have to be careful where I retire to. Despite the heat, he feels he's skating on thin ice, very thin ice.

'The money should not be a problem, nor your first condition. But payment in full before delivery is rather unusual.' Habtoor finally replies.

'Mr Habtoor, we are dealing with an unusual purchase. The terms and conditions are not negotiable.'

Silence falls between them. Novchenko lights another cigarette and gazes across the pool, the water gently rippling in the breeze. He looks back at Habtoor, deep in thought, 'So?'

'I think we have a deal.' Habtoor nods.

Novchenko smiles to himself. That part was easy, this may be slightly more difficult.

'I understand that you have been dealing with a certain Herr Kohler.'

'What! How do you know that?' Habtoor's eyes widen.

'In my business, it is necessary to know such things. I believe that you like Vienna, Mr Habtoor.' Novchenko smiles across the table.

'Yes, it's a very nice city.' Habtoor starts to sweat and it's not from the heat.

'Indeed, so convenient for meetings, don't you think?' Novchenko is enjoying himself, watching Habtoor wriggle in front of him.

'May I ask where this is leading to?'

'Of course! You're a sharp man, Mr Habtoor, I can see that. I assume that you have worked out that I am also supplying the first bomb via Kohler.'

'That had crossed my mind, yes.'

'You see, you are sharp! But, regrettably, Kohler is no longer in the picture.'

'That I don't understand.'

'From now on, you will deal only with me. I'm offering you the two bombs for fifty million dollars!'

'What! But Kohler offered one for free.'

'Maybe you didn't hear me, Habtoor, Herr Kohler is out of the picture. What's the problem? I'm offering you two bombs at a discount, you'll save ten million dollars!'

'But fifty million dollars!'

'Well, you'll just have to soak a few more Saudi princes, won't you?'

Habtoor says nothing for a few moments, he's thinking fast. The price is high, but Bin Laden wouldn't pass up this chance, regardless of the cost. And my fee has just gone up by two million dollars.

'I shall have to talk to my client but in principle, I agree.'

'Excellent! Payment will be made thirty days before delivery. You will be given the bank account details. Upon receipt of payment, the devices will be delivered to a port of your choice, within reason, of course. After that, it's up to you. You will deal in future with my associate, Feodor. Now, unless there's anything else, I think our business is concluded.' Novchenko stands up, Habtoor follows.

'Of course. But what about Kohler?'

'You will act as if nothing has happened. He will contact you with the shipping details. When he does so, reconfirm with Feodor.'

They shake hands, Novchenko can feel the sweat on Habtoor's palm, also knows it doesn't come from the heat of the day. He snaps his fingers and Dmitri appears from nowhere.

'He will show you to the car. Have a safe trip back, Mr Habtoor. Remember, Feodor will be in touch,' Novchenko smiles broadly.

Habtoor gives a brief bow and follows Dmitri into the house.

Novchenko watches him disappear, his smile has quickly disappeared. He sits down slowly. So, a profitable day's work. Two clients, eighty million dollars. But only one will receive the bombs. He thinks for a few minutes, the answer is quite simple. This Kohler is an amateur, a fool and German. Habtoor is a different matter. From Feodor's investigations, through his old Stasi connections, he knows that Habtoor is a front man for Osama Bin Laden. Now, Novchenko is a powerful man, but doesn't necessarily want to get entangled with that madman nor double-cross him. He knows the stated aims of Bin Laden – the destruction of Israel and America. Novchenko couldn't care less about Israel, in his words the Middle East was a fucking mess. Now, America, that would be interesting. A Soviet bomb going off in New York, huh! A certain irony in that, the old Politburo would have been pleased! His thoughts turn to Habtoor, again. He knows from Feodor that Habtoor supplied the Mujahideen in Afghanistan. 'How many deaths of my comrades was he responsible for?' he says out loud.

The decision has been made. Time for a swim. The pool deck is deserted, Svetlana and her sister are shopping in Faro. Novchenko didn't want any distractions this afternoon. He steps out into the still hot sun, slowly sinking in the west. He thinks after dinner a game of chess would be nice. Wants to try out a variation of his opening pawn gambit with Dmitri. As he dives into the pool, all thoughts of Kohler and Habtoor are banished from his mind. Their fate has already been decided.

PART THREE

Apocalypse Now
Francis Ford Coppola

CHAPTER TWENTY ONE

Gare du Nord, Paris. I step down from the Eurostar from London. I check my watch, midday, dead on time, how do the French do it? I've always thought it a shame that the Eurostar arrives at this station, not one of the most elegant in Paris. And not one of the safest; first time visitors should be beware of the ticket touts and pickpockets. I am in Paris to meet Henri Lefevre, hoping that he can help me. I step out into the morning sunshine, the heat of a cloudless July day building. I see Henri's driver, Pierre, just beyond the taxi stand, leaning against a black Peugot 307. He flicks his cigarette away, gives me a wave. I get in beside him, we drive off with a squeal of tyres. The interior of the car is hot, I undo my tie.

'Ah, pardon, Monsieur Stevens.' Pierre leans forward and switches on the air conditioning. Cool air wafts over me.

'Merci, Pierre.' I make sure my seat belt is secure. Pierre drives very fast and we are in Paris, after all. Pierre is from the Basque country, near the Spanish border. I find his particular patois difficult to understand, but I usually get the drift of what he's saying. Today it is the usual litany of complaints, Paris traffic and French politics, in particular the President. Pierre also has the unfortunate habit of taking both hands off the wheel to gesticulate about something and looking at me at the same time. I stare straight ahead, praying that we don't hit anything. After several near misses, honking of horns, waving of fists, we squeal to a stop in front of the Brasserie Lafayette, Henri's lunchtime haunt.

I step onto the pavement, legs slightly shaky, the 307 screams off into the distance. I enter the cool interior, past the old zinc bar, see Henri sitting at the rear at his favourite table. The place is already busy, waiters toing and froing between tables, carrying full plates or empty plates, orders being shouted through to the kitchen adding to the cacaphony of noise. I squeeze past and approach Henri.

'Richard! How are you? You look a bit pale. Still not used to Pierre's driving?' Henri grins at me, rises up to shake my hand.

'How does he manage not to have an accident?' I sit down on an old wooden chair, opposite Henri.

'Ha! I pay him not to have accidents, Richard.' Henri's grin turns to laughter. 'Anyway, I'm glad you could come today. We're celebrating the end of Project Phoenix!'

'Yes, congratulations.' I watch Henri pour some red wine, from a half-full carafe, into my glass. 'I got your email, so it was Andrew Johnston.'

'Yes, thanks to you, and Yvette, of course.'

'Ah, the famous Yvette.'

'I told you her mouth could work wonders, you know she...'

'I don't think we need the details, Henri.' I sip my wine, it's pale and fruity and very good.

'Ok, ok. You were right about the golf, that's where he met the Americans.'

'And the money?'

'You know, for a guy who was so intelligent, he was also very stupid. He kept it in his locker in the golf club. Can you believe it? A hundred thousand dollars in old plastic shopping bags! Dumb!' Henri laughs to himself, refills his glass. 'Do you like the wine?'

'Very good, Henri.'

'It's the vin de la maison, how do you say?'

'House wine.'

'Yes, house wine. It's a Bourgogne, I prefer it at lunchtime, not so heavy as a Bordeaux.' He lifts his glass up, studies it through the light. 'And it's cheap, Richard.' Henri laughs again. 'And it's a double celebration! I'm going to be promoted!'

'That's great news, Henri, you deserve it.' We clink our glasses.

'And what about you?'

'Probably demoted.'

'Ha, that's what I like about the English, their sense of humour.'

'Except it's not funny, Henri.'

'Ah, still problems with Mr Forsyth, then?'

'You could say that. That's the other reason that I'm here.'

'I received the two names from you, Habtoor and Kohler.'

'And?'

'Let's eat first, Richard, I don't want to spoil my lunch. I've ordered steak and frites, the best in Paris.' With that, he snaps his fingers in the direction of the bar. Within moments, two plates appear on our table, a silver pot of Dijon mustard, and another carafe of red. I think Henri has settled in for the afternoon.

The steak is medium rare, cooked to perfection, the frites as only the way the French can do them. As I eat, I let Henri babble on about his wife, two kids, the state of French education. He's now talking about redecorating his apartment. I can remember being invited to his place in Versailles. It's bloody huge, with high ceilings and full of antique furniture. I was quite depressed when I returned to my pokey little flat. Maybe it's time I moved into something bigger.

'Very good.' Henri pushes away his now-empty plate, wipes his mouth with a white linen napkin. 'You see, French beef is just as good as English beef, yes?'

'Yes, Henri, on this I must agree with you.' I finish the last of my frites.

'So, these names that you're asking about?' Henri leans back in his chair, fishes out a crumpled packet of Disque Bleu from his jacket pocket. He takes out an even more crumpled cigarette and lights it with a cheap plastic lighter.

I take another sip of wine and tell him about Kruger. Henri asks the occasional question, puffs on his cigarette, toys with his glass.

'And so, the whole thing is turning into a bit of a nightmare. Both Baxter and Kruger are dead, I have no proof of any of this and all I do have are these two names.'

'Mmm, so the BND are off-limits?'

'As decreed by Forsyth.'

'What about the Americans and the Israelis?'

'Forsyth is handling them himself.'

'I hope that's correct, Richard, for if any of this is true and they're kept in the dark, the shit will hit the fan.'

'I am aware of that, Henri.'

'Just don't get hung out to be dried, my friend.'

'Don't worry, I'm watching my back.'

'Good. Now, first of all Habtoor. I'm not sure how much more we have on him than you do. As far as I'm aware, he's never stepped on French soil, so he's not on our priority list.'

'But you know what he has supplied and to whom?'

'Of course, but he is not considered a direct threat to the state of France.' Henri shrugs his shoulders, stubs out his cigarette.

'Ok, so what about Kohler?'

'Ah there, I might be able to help.' Henri smiles across the table.

'I need all the help I can get, Henri.'

'I won't bore you with who and what Kohler is. His recent high profile, however, is causing a certain unease in the Elysees Palace.'

'Why?'

'It is no secret that if elections were held tomorrow in Germany, Kohler would become chancellor.'

'And?'

'There is also the rumour that he's about to form a new political party of the right of centre.'

'So maybe Kruger was correct, maybe Kohler is a fascist.'

'Yes, which explains the unease in Paris. We don't want 1939 again.'

'You're not being serious?'

'I hope not, but there are a lot of problems in Germany at the moment. Unemployment has risen again, the former East Germany is still causing Bonn a big headache. Kohler will be attractive to a lot of people, particularly the young.'

'I see,' I pause, drink some more wine. 'You said that you may be able to help.'

'Ah yes.' Henri lights another cigarette. 'KK Industries have done work in France, usually as a joint venture with Dubois Construction. Now, Marcel Dubois owns the company and is a very good friend of Kohler's.'

'So?'

'If there is anything going on, maybe Dubois knows about it. I should tell you that Dubois is a bit of a slippery customer, has some rather dubious friends. His father was the same. Now, as far as I am aware, Marcel has never broken the law. But he sails pretty close to the wind sometimes. His company is particularly active now, in Spain and Portugal. We know that some of his clients are connected to the Russian Mafia. I suggest that I will keep a close eye on Dubois over the coming weeks, see if he's up to anything, you never know.'

'I'd appreciate anything, Henri.'

'So, what's happening on your side?'

'Not a lot, I'm afraid. We're no closer to finding Baxter's or Kruger's murderer.'

'Maybe it was Haller.'

'Well, the hotel video is pretty inconclusive, we never did get a frontal shot. He is the same height and build as Haller but…'

'Haller would be capable, you know.'

'You think so?'

'When Haller was sixteen, after his father died, he got in with a bad lot. They were running contraband across the border into France. One time they were caught, there was a fight, Haller put a gendarme in hospital. He was jailed for five years and then we kicked him back across the border. Kohler took him under his wing and now he's Kohler's personal assistant. Fiercely loyal, will do anything for his master.'

'Including murder?'

'Well, if anything of what you've told me is true, what's the death of two old men in the scheme of things?'

'You could be right. But otherwise, I have to tread carefully with Kohler, he's evidently a personal friend of our Prime Minister.'

'Kohler seems to be the personal friend of most politicians in Europe. I understand your problem.'

'And Habtoor? I only have an out of date photograph. All our embassies are on alert for any information about him, but, so far nothing.'

'You understand that you may have to contact the BND, eventually?'

'Yes, but as a last resort.' I finish my wine.

'We'll have coffee and two cognacs, eh?' Henri waves his hand to the bar.

'Are you trying to get me drunk, Henri?'

'Come on, Richard, we are not going to solve the problems of the world today. Relax. Sometimes you are too, how do you say, straitlaced?'

'I'm fine, honestly,' I watch as two coffees and two large cognacs appear.

'Listen, Richard, Yvette is in the office this afternoon, maybe I could ask her to join us. I could introduce you.'

'Henri, I actually have a new lady friend.' I put some sugar in the coffee.

'Mon dieu! Wonders will never cease! What's she like, eh?'

'She's very pretty.'

'Then, I must meet her.'

'Only when your wife is present!'

'But, Richard! I am a happily married man. My wife says that I can look but I cannot touch, ha!' Henri lifts his cognac, 'Salut!'

'Salut!' I smile and shake my head.

'You know, Richard, what you need is a holiday.'

'I don't have time for holidays.'

'Rubbish! You should take this pretty lady away somewhere, forget all this crap. Why not Biarritz or Saint Jean de Luz? It's beautiful down there, clear your head, make love all day.'

'Thank you, Henri, I get the picture.' I try the cognac. 'Actually, I was going to ask you something else, you've just reminded me.'

'What?' Henri has finished his cognac, orders another.

'When this is all over, I think that I'll get out, before Forsyth throws me out. I don't want to give him that pleasure. And so, where to go? I was thinking about the Dordogne, Henri.'

'The Dordogne? No, it's now full of English! Don't laugh, it's true. No, better to be further south. I'd choose somewhere near the Pyrenees, probably Pau.'

'Why there?'

'It's hot in the summer, you can play golf, go fishing, whatever, and in winter, there's the skiing. Listen, if you go to Biarritz, Pau is only an hour away, go and have a look.'

'Good idea, Henri, maybe I'll do just that.'

CHAPTER TWENTY TWO

10th August, Berlin.

Haller sits opposite Kohler, waiting for the phone call. Kohler sits at his desk, leafing through his morning's correspondence. Suddenly, Haller's mobile rings.

'Yes?'

'The package is ready, Herr Haller.' Feodor's halting German sounds distant.

'Good, we've been waiting.'

'As agreed, the payment is thirty million dollars. The bank account has changed, I will send you the details by email.'

'Ok.'

'Upon receipt of the payment, I shall contact you about the shipment details, understood?'

'Understood.' Haller places his now silent phone on the desk.

'So?' Kohler looks up from his papers.

'Everything is ready, but the account has changed, he'll email me the details.'

'Good.' Kohler resumes his reading.

'Kurt, you are taking a big risk, what happens if you pay the money and he doesn't deliver?'

'The whole venture is a big risk, Franz. However, Dubois assures me that the one good thing about Novchenko is that he keeps his promises.'

'Well, I hope your French friend is right.' Haller looks at Kohler, sitting there, apparently without a care in the world. 'You know that once you pay, that's it, there's no stopping what is going to happen.'

'Of course I do, that is the whole point of this, Franz.'

'But the size of this device! It's twenty times bigger than what was dropped on Hiroshima!'

'So? It doesn't matter whether it's five, ten, forty times bigger. It's the act itself that matters!'

'But you're talking about the deaths of hundreds of thousands of people, for Christ's sake!'

'Don't get cold feet now, Franz, we've been through all this before. My mind is made up, there will be no further discussion. Now, once you get the details, send the money. Do I make myself clear?'

'Perfectly, Kurt, perfectly.'

Kohler looks across at his favourite view of Berlin. When I'm elected, I shall return Berlin to its rightful place as the seat of government. Shut down that liberal, pinko nest in Bonn. Kohler reluctantly returns to his papers, carries on reading the contract in front of him. De Vries is finally going to get his hotel in Rotterdam, but as Kohler signs the contract, he's more concerned about Haller. He's beginning to crack, look at him, fidgetting in his chair. I'm going to have to keep a close eye on him, I need him to do one more thing. Kohler puts down the signed contract, places his pen on the desk.

'You realise, Franz, that after this is over, Schroener will have to be taken care of.'

'What do you mean?'

'He knows too much, he could be dangerous,' Kohler pauses, stares out the window. 'Yes, he'll have to be taken care of, I'll tell you when.'

Haller begins to sweat, but it's the cold sweat of fear. So, it's come to this. First Pieck, then Kruger and now it's Schroener's turn. Kohler is getting rid of the evidence, I wonder if I'm next?

26th August, Langley, Virginia.

'Harding? Where the hell have you been?' Kelly lights another cigarette.

'Around and about.'

'You were supposed to phone me back about our friend Mr H.'

211

'I've been busy,' comes the abrupt reply.

'Where are you anyway?' Kelly rolls his eyes to the ceiling.

'That's on a need to know basis.'

'We are supposed to be on the same side, you know.'

'So they say,' Harding is silent for a few moments. 'What's happening at your end anyway?'

'Zilch. My superiors think I'm wasting my time. They're more concerned about events in Tehran.'

'Maybe they should be.'

'Yeah and if anything does happen, who's first in the firing line?'

'That's what you're paid for, I guess.' Harding gives a faint chuckle.

Kelly inwardly fumes. Harding can be a right prick when he wants to.

'So, you have nothing to tell me?' Kelly stubs out his cigarette.

'Not exactly.'

'Meaning?'

'You know Kelly, when there's a storm approaching, all the birds in the trees go quiet?'

'What are you driving at?'

'Well, it's the same over here, it's all gone quiet, too quiet.'

'So, you think something's going to happen?'

'That last time I remember it like this was just before 9/11.'

'Shit! You haven't got any information?'

'Nope. All my contacts are either unavailable or have disappeared.'

'And nothing on Mr H?'

'Just a rumour.'

'What?' Kelly looks around his desk for the cigarette packet.

'We keep some Afghans in pocket money. One of them came over the Pakistan border, two weeks ago, selling some dope. Claims he saw Mr H in the foothills.

This guy is generally reliable, so if he says he saw Mr H, then it's probably true.'

'Didn't you send people in to have a look?'

'Kelly, I'm not in the area, not in my jurisdiction.'

'Jesus, the fucking bureaucracy sometimes!'

'You said it, not me.'

'What's your best guess, if he was in Afghanistan?'

'Well, he wasn't up there admiring the view. He was meeting someone, you can guess who. Listen, I have to go, people to see, places to be. Just keep your ass covered, Kelly. Maybe a good time to take a vacation. I am.'

Kelly replaces the phone. He finds the cigarette packet in his Out tray, fishes out a cigarette and lights it, inhales deeply. Bastard Harding! Two weeks he's known about this sighting of Habtoor. Why didn't he call? I've known Harding for a long time now. He sounded worried, but in his line of business, that shouldn't surprise me.

Four months have passed since Kelly first learnt about Habtoor. And since then, he's been hitting himself against a brick wall. Nobody knows nothing! And he's getting lukewarm support from above. All this money that we spend on intelligence and I'm praying for a break, even a tiny break. Mind you, the Brits aren't doing any better. This Stevens has had to enlist the help of the French, he must be desperate!

Take a vacation? Harding must be fucking joking!

CHAPTER TWENTY THREE

7th September, George Cinq, Paris.

'So, what's the celebration, KK?' Dubois settles back on the sofa in Kohler's suite.

'Life is good, Marcel, and it's just about to get better.' Kohler smiles as he pours champagne into two crystal flutes. He hands one to Dubois.

'Sante.' They toast each other.

'I hear that your new political party will have its inauguration next month.' Dubois savours the dry sparkling wine.

'You hear right, Marcel, there are exciting times ahead.' Kohler sits down beside Dubois.

'Congratulations, KK. Chancellor Kohler has a certain je ne sais quoi.'

'Quite, Marcel. And German politics is not going to know what hit it!'

'Someone told me that you're right of Attila the Hun, KK.'

'Oh, come on, Marcel. So I have some right wing views, what's wrong with that? How much money do you give the French National Front, Marcel?'

'Enough. But I don't want to become its leader.'

'Ah, Marcel, some of us are born leaders. Have some more champagne.' Kohler refills their glasses. 'Anyway, Marcel, the press always exaggerate. I just want Germany to play a more important role on the world stage. There's no harm in that, is there?' Kohler laughs, walks across to the window, looks out. 'You know, there could be an invitation to the White House before the year is out.'

Just then, Kohler's mobile phone rings. He crosses the room, picks it up from the table.

'Yes... ah, Andrei. Yes, of course... Excellent, so the shipment is on the 10th September... Where? That's near Stettin... at the Polish border, yes? And it will be in

Hamburg by evening, very good… Sorry? Ha! By Red Star container, I like the irony in that… I'll tell Haller, he'll brief our other friend… Yes, same to you.' Kohler does a little jig in front of Dubois. 'Today just got even better, Marcel!'

'What was that all about?'

'My business is now concluded with Novchenko. You can relax now, Marcel.'

There is a knock at the door, Haller enters.

'Franz, you've just arrived in time!' Kohler goes to greet him, whispers something in his ear, then laughs.

Marcel watches, notices that Haller apparently doesn't get the joke, then hears the name Habtoor mentioned. Haller says nothing, just nods, walks past Dubois into the bedroom, without acknowledging him. He hears Haller's muffled voice talking to somebody on the phone.

'Right, Marcel. All this exciting news has made me rather hungry. Time for lunch!'

7th September, Ryanair Flight 372

The captain has just told us that we will be arriving shortly in Biarritz. I look out the window, the blue calm sea comes up to meet us. Helen grips my hand tightly. I've discovered that she hates flying. I look across, she gives me a nervous smile. The plane is full, mostly English voices, old and young couples, no children, they're back at school.

I've taken Henri's advice, a few days in south west France, just me and Helen. Several days ago, I received a copy of the latest Joint Intelligence Committee report which has downgraded the terrorist threat level to Britain. And being typically British, everyone has gone on holiday. Forsyth is fly-fishing in the Scottish borders somewhere, so I thought, bugger it, I'm having a few days off as well. My investigations into Kruger's allegations have stalled. I'm beginning to think that Forsyth considers the whole thing as a wild goose chase.

But I have nagging doubts about this affair, things are quiet, too quiet.

With a couple of bumps, we're down. We step out into a cloudless blue sky, it's five o'clock and still very warm. We pick up our bags, pass through passport control and head for the Hertz rental office. Within half an hour, Helen and I are driving away in a little red Peugot 207, heading for the mountains. Henri has recommended a small village called Sare, in the foothills of the Pyrenees. It only takes 30 minutes, up a winding road, to reach Sare. The Hotel Ithurra is situated in the middle of this pretty little Basque village. The hotel is family run, we're welcomed by a young lady who I assume to be the daughter of the owners.

The bedroom is a good size, with old antique furniture. Our window overlooks the pelotte court, the traditional Basque ball game. I place our bags on the luggage rack. Helen eyes up the bed.

'Why don't we try it out before dinner?' She smiles at me.

Next morning, fortified with orange juice, thick black coffee and croissants to die for, we set off for Pau. We travel along the Autoroute 64, mercifully devoid of traffic. Within 90 minutes, we're standing in the centre of Pau. Henri was right, it is a beautiful town, gentile, the French might say. In the distance, you can see the snow-capped mountains. We spend all day doing the tourist trail, just happy in each other's company. We leave, reluctantly, in the early evening and head back to Sare.

We have dinner again in the hotel restaurant, Henri was right again about the cooking. Afterwards, I order coffee and two cognacs. I settle back in my chair, tired, but pleasantly tired. Good food, beautiful countryside and accompanied by a beautiful woman. Helen is dressed tonight in a simple white linen dress. I think she must have a different outfit for each evening, judging by the size of her suitcase. At this moment, she's looking for her cigarettes.

'That's what I like about the French, so civilised,' she lights up. 'After a very good meal, you can sit and relax, coffee and brandy, and a cigarette.' She smiles.

'I remember one night with my friend, Henri, in a Metro station in Paris. On the other platform, a well-dressed man appeared and sat down on a bench opposite us. He proceeded to light a cigarette, despite a 'no smoking' sign above his head.'

'You see, if that was in London, he'd be arrested or lynched!'

'Probably. The French are generally a law abiding nation, except if they don't like a law, they just ignore it. I think it's something to do with being a Republic.' I take a sip of cognac.

'I think this is the first time that I've seen you so relaxed, Richard.'

'Being away from London helps.'

'You were upset about the death of that German, weren't you?'

'Murder is always upsetting, Helen.'

'And no one was caught?'

'No, just another statistic for unsolved murders in London.' I shake my head. 'Anyway, enough about that, I'm on holiday.' I try to smile and toast Helen with my glass. She smiles back, drinks some cognac.

'So, what are we doing tomorrow?' she stubs out her cigarette.

'Well, I thought in the morning we'd go to Biarritz and then in the afternoon, Saint Jean de Luz.'

'Perfect. The Spanish border is very close, isn't it?'

'Very, and you can nip over and buy cheap cigarettes.'

'That's a must, I'm running pretty low.' Helen examines an almost empty packet.

'You know, Helen, this isn't just a holiday, it's also a scouting trip.' I look at Helen, not sure how she'll react to my proposition.

'A scouting trip?'

'Yes, you see, I've had an idea for some time of getting out, that is out of London.'

'But that's where you work.' Helen looks puzzled.

'Ah yes, but if I didn't work, then the world is my oyster, so to speak.'

'You mean that you would quit your job?'

'It's not a question of quitting, Helen, it'a question of retiring before I'm forced out.'

'Oh, I see.' Helen takes out another cigarette.

'I've not said anything about this before, Helen, well, we haven't known each other that long. But I'll get a good pension, the flat in Docklands will bring a decent price. And so, I've thought about selling up and moving down here.' There, I've said it. Now I wonder what the reaction will be. Helen just sits there, gazing out the window, into the darkness.

'I know this is a bit sudden for you, Helen, but I thought it only fair to let you know what I'm thinking. I thought maybe that you would...'

'Don't ask, please, Richard,' Helen looks at me, a slightly pained expression on her face. I think I've made a mistake. Fool!

'As you've said, Richard, we've known each other for such a short time, I don't know if I'm ready to...'

'Of course, it was presumptious of me to think.....'

'I think we should call it a night, don't you think? Helen stubs out her cigarette, picks up her bag and stands up.

I look around me, the restaurant is empty, we seem to make a habit of being the last to leave. We climb the stairs in silence, which continues in the bedroom. We both undress, I lie on my back, staring at the ceiling. I feel Helen's hand on my chest and then her whisper.

'But I need you tonight, Richard.'

CHAPTER TWENTY FOUR

I'm in a field, the sun is shining, I see Helen running towards me. We have a son and daughter, they trail behind her, laughing. Then the phone rings. I slowly become conscious, my eyes become accustomed to the darkness. I realise that the ringing is coming from my mobile, on the bedside table. I reach across and pick it up.

'Yes?' I rub my sleep-filled eyes.

'Richard, it's Henri.'

'Who? Bloody hell! What time is it.' I look at my watch, six o' clock.

'I'm sorry to disturb you so early,' Henri's voice sounds faint, maybe it's because of the reception up in the hills.

'Well, you have disturbed me, what's so important that you....'

'We picked up Dubois last night.'

'And?' I hear Helen stirring beside me.

'You have to come to Paris.'

'What? When?'

'I've arranged for the Gendarmerie in Biarritz to pick you up. They should be at the hotel within the next half hour.'

'Half an hour!' I sit up in bed, my dream long forgotten about.

'They'll drive you to Bordeaux, there's an Air France flight to Paris at 10.20, everything has been arranged.'

'But I'm here with my girlfriend.'

'I know, she will have to make her own way back to London.'

'This had better be bloody important, Henri.'

'It is, see you in Paris.' Henri cuts the connection.

I get out of bed, stumble towards the bathroom.

'What's happening, Richard?' I hear Helen's sleepy voice behind me.

'I have to go to Paris.' I call out.

'What?'

'Paris. Sorry, it's a bit of an emergency.' I step into the shower, hoping that the stinging, hot water will clear my brain. I quickly dry myself, wrap a towel around me. Helen is now sitting up in bed, I open the curtains, the dawn sun lights up the bedroom.

'Am I coming?'

'No, sorry, this is business.' I put on the clothes that I wore last night, stuff the rest of my belongings into my bag. 'Look, I'm sorry Helen, but the police are picking me up in,' I look at my watch, '15 minutes.'

'But what am I to…?'

'Contact the airline, see if you can get an earlier flight back to London. You'll have to drop the car off as well.' I stand there, suddenly seeing Helen vulnerable for the first time. I sit down on the bed beside her, stroke her tousled hair. 'I really am sorry, Helen, this was supposed to be us having some time together, alone. My wife, ex wife, used to complain that I was always dashing off some place. I said to myself that it must not happen with you but…'

'I think I understand, Richard,' she squeezes my hand.

'I must go,' I look at my watch again. ' I'll phone you as soon as I can. I know this is probably not the right time but I… I think I love you, Helen.' I look at her, sitting up in bed, the sunlight glinting in her blonde hair. That's the way I'll always remember her.

The Air France flight arrives five minutes early. Pierre is waiting for me in the Arrivals Hall at Charles de Gaulle airport. As usual, Pierre is in a hurry. This time, he has a blue flashing light on the roof of the Peugot. We join the Periphique, cars scatter in front of us.

'Ou est Henri?' I ask through clenched teeth, as we miss a van by a whisker.

'Place de Republique,' Pierre looks at me as we overtake a lorry, horn blaring, fist being waved. 'C'est une cachette sure.' Pierre looks ahead for his next victim.

Une cachette sure? Henri has mentioned that before, what is it? Ah yes, a safehouse. I wonder why Dubois is being held at a safehouse and not Henri's headquarters. We take the Porte De Lilas exit, cutting up another poor hapless driver. Pierre drops his speed fractionally as we encounter heavier traffic. We go around the Place de Republique then take a right. Pierre mercifully slows down, he's looking for somewhere to park. It's a typical tree-lined Parisian street, turn of the century apartments on either side. Pierre finds a space which looks too narrow for me, but somehow he shoe horns the car into it. We both get out, I take my bag from the back. Pierre leads me through large double entrance doors, inside it's quite dark, the entrance hall has a slight musty smell to it. We climb well worn stone steps to the first floor. Pierre knocks on the first door on the left, it's opened by someone that I don't recognise. He nods to Pierre, I follow him in.

'Ah, at last!' Henri gets up from an old armchair to greet me.

We shake hands, he gestures to another armchair for me to sit down. The room is large, probably quite grand at one time. The curtains are closed, the room is in darkness except for a small table light. This room also has a slight musty smell, overpowered however, by stale cigarette smoke. I'm aware of two men sitting behind Henri.

'Richard, let me introduce Jean Paul and Raymond, they're helping me with our investigations.' Henri waves behind him. The two men look up, give me a brief nod, continue their whispered conversation.

'So Henri, what's so important to drag me out of bed from the arms of my beloved?'

221

'Ha, you're lucky to have been in bed. We picked up Dubois last night and I haven't seen my bed since.' Henri stifles a yawn.

'Where is he?'

'Next door, been shouting for his notaire amongst other things. Fortunately, this place is soundproof.' Henri leans across, takes a cigarette from the packet on the table. I notice the overflowing ashtray on the floor at Henri's feet.

'Why is he here and more to the point, why am I here?'

'Ok, Richard, here's what we have.' Henri lights his cigarette, flicks some ash onto the floor. 'After our meeting in July, I made some enquiries about Dubois. I discovered that our Douane, our customs people, were increasingly concerned about drugs coming over the Spanish border near Irun, just south of Saint Jean de Luz.'

'I've just come from there.'

'Yes, ironic, isn't it? Anyway, our friend Dubois has been a naughty boy.'

Henri flicks more ash onto the floor.

'Go on.'

'As you know, Dubois is a contractor. He's been very busy in Spain and Portugal. Now, being a good Frenchman, he promotes French products. So for all these projects, he's been shipping in sanitaryware, ironmongery, etc. But of course, he's then left with empty lorries for the return journeys. So, he decided to go into the pottery business.'

'Pottery?'

'Bear with me, Richard, all will become clear. He bought up local pottery, in Portugal especially, direct from the factories. They were blanks, shipped them back to France, imprinted the Dubois name, made a profit of fifty per cent.'

'Nothing wrong with that, is there?'

'Ah well, you see our Douane received a tip-off, they stopped one of Dubois's lorries yesterday morning. Five hundred empty pots, except six were full of cocaine, street value around two million euros. Our friend is in deep shit, as you would say.' Henri smiles for the first time.

'But where do I fit into all this?'

'Look Richard, I have Dubois by the balls! Maybe we squeeze them a little, find out what he knows about Kohler.

'Maybe he doesn't know anything.'

'It's at least worth trying, don't you think?'

'I suppose so.' But I'm not convinced.

'Ok, time for you to meet him. His English is pretty good. If there's any problem, I'll translate for you.' Henri stands up, drops his cigarette into the ashtray. I follow him, as he opens the door into the next room. This room is smaller but just as dark, the curtains are also drawn. Dubois is sitting at a table in the middle of the room. A lamp on the table is again the only light. Dubois looks up, maybe he's been sleeping. He's unshaven, his grey suit crumpled. A half-finished cup of coffee sits in front of him.

'Where's Villebois and who the fuck is he?' Dubois points at me with a stubby little finger. I notice his eyes for the first time, they're coal black.

'Your notaire will be here, eventually. And this gentleman is Richard Stevens, he works for British Intelligence.' Henri and I sit down opposite Dubois.

'British? What's he doing here? This trumped-up charge is a French affair, non?' Dubois leans back, folds his arms in front of him.

'Quite, but the drugs business is now an international concern.' Henri pulls out another cigarette.

'Pah! If you say so. And must you smoke these filthy things in here?'

'Listen Dubois, you're on my territory now, I do what I like.' Henri blows some smoke across the table, Dubois tries to wave it away.

'Now, where were we?'

'You arrest me in the middle of the night, bring me to this dump, try and implicate me in some drugs shipment, that's where we are!'

'Come on Dubois, your construction manager and the driver of the lorry are down at the Prefecture, singing like canaries. Your manager will testify that he was carrying out your personal instructions.'

'Ha, he'll say anything as long as you pay him enough!'

'Paying him enough? Maybe it was you not paying enough. They're just trying to save their skins, maybe you should do the same.'

'What do you mean?'

'You'll be found guilty, Dubois, make no mistake. You'll get twenty years, you'll be an old man when you get out. Think about it.'

Dubois says nothing, but I can see him do the mental arithmetic in his head.

'Ok, I'm thinking about it.'

'If you were to assist us, then maybe you'd get five years, out in three if you behaved yourself.'

'And what would I have to do?'

'Just tell us how the whole operation worked.' Henri drops another cigarette on the floor, uses a shoe to put it out.

Dubois sits there saying nothing, minutes pass.

'We haven't got all day, Dubois. If you don't want to help us, then we can leave now. But once we leave, there is no deal on offer, this is your last chance.'

Dubois still says nothing, but I can see him weighing up his options.

'Well, it would appear that I have little choice in this matter,' Dubois leans forward, a decision has been made. 'It was very simple really. My lorries picked up the pots from various locations, some of the pots were prepacked with… er drugs.'

'Where did the drugs come from?'

'Listen, if I tell you that, then I'm going to need protection.' Dubois's voice almost becomes a whisper. For the first time, I see fear in these coal, black eyes.

'Why?'

'The drugs were supplied by the Mafia, the Russian Mafia.'

'Who in particular?'

'I'm telling you, these people are fucking dangerous!'

'Who, Dubois?'

'It was…' Dubois takes out a handkerchief, mops his brow.

Henri looks across at me, he's thinking this man is really scared, '…a client of mine. A man called Andrei Novchenko.'

'Who's he?'

'He's a retired Russian General, owns a big haulage company, Red Star or something.'

'And he provided the drugs?'

'No, not personally. He has an associate called Feodor, it was his son, Dimitri, who dealt with the shipments.'

'What about the shipments?'

'They came in by speedboat, dropped off near Faro. This Dmitri transferred them to the pottery factories. I'm giving you this information, but you can't use my name, they'll kill me!' Dubois's voice sounds hoarse, pleading, the early defiance gone.

'I believe that you are a close friend of Kurt Kohler?' It's the first time that I have spoken.

'Who?' Dubois looks confused by this change in direction of the conversation.

'Kurt Kohler,' I speak slowly, 'I believe that you are a close friend of his.'

'Yes, but he's got nothing to do with this.'

'I didn't say he did, I'm just asking about your relationship with him.'

'Well yes, we are friends, both social and business. We've done many projects together…'

I let Dubois ramble on, but I'm thinking about this Novchenko. A retired Russian General, owns a haulage company, into drugs, I wonder?

'Did Kohler know Novchenko?' My question cuts across Dubois like a knife.

'What? Who told you that?' The fear returns to Dubois's eyes.

Bingo!

'Nobody, but you just have.' I look at Henri, who smiles. 'So, what did Kohler have to do with Novchenko?'

'It was business.'

'What kind of business?'

'I don't know!' Dubois looks at Henri for help. But Henri lights up and stares at the ceiling.

'But, you are his friend, he must have told you.'

'Well, he didn't.'

'When did they first meet?'

'All these questions…' Dubois rolls his eyes.

'Just answer them!' Henri shouts at Dubois.

'Alright, alright, no need to shout. Let me think, it must have been the middle of 2001, in Paris.'

'What did they discuss?' I resume the questioning, not sure where this is leading to.

'I told you, I don't know. I was excluded from the meeting.'

'And then what happened?'

'Whatever they had agreed, well, it fell through. I saw Novchenko in October, he was furious with Kohler, I don't know why. You should be asking Kohler these questions, not me!'

'Don't worry, we will. Now, did they meet again?'

'Not for a few years, then suddenly, Kohler asked me to set up another meeting.'

'When was that?'

'This spring, in Faro. I'd built a villa for Novchenko, that's where the meeting was held.'

'And were you present at the meeting?'

'No, again I was excluded'

'I thought you were a close friend?'

'That's what I said to KK, he was treating me like a servant. But he said that it was better that I didn't know anything.'

'And has he met him since?'

'Not that I'm aware of. But KK spoke to him two days ago.'

'Where?'

'Here, in Paris.'

'Kohler is in Paris?' I must sound surprised.

'Yes, at the George Cinq, didn't you know?' Dubois looks at Henri, he gives me a blank stare.

'So what was the phone call about?'

'I'm not sure, it was about some shipment or other.'

'Dubois, think very carefully, this is important.'

'OK, OK,' Dubois pauses, collecting his thoughts. 'KK was in a very good mood, we were drinking lots of champagne. And then his phone rang, it was Novchenko. It was about a shipment coming over the German – Polish border, near Stettin, I think. It was being delivered to Hamburg on the night of the 10th. He joked that it was coming by a Red Star container. That was it.'

'Nothing else?'

'Then Haller came into the room, I heard KK mention someone called Habtoor to him.'

'What was that name again?'

'I'm sure it was Habtoor, then Haller went into the other room and spoke to someone on the phone. Do you know this Habtoor?' Dubois looks at us both.

I turn to Henri, 'We need to talk.' We get up to leave, I can hear Dubois behind us.

'What about our deal?'

'Fuck your deal,' I hear Henri mutter under his breath.

Henri leaves the door open, turns to Jean Paul, 'Stay with him, he's not going anywhere.'

We slump down in the armchairs, say nothing for a few moments, the enormity of what Dubois has just said, slowly sinking in.

'Mon dieu,' Henri lights a cigarette, 'I think your friend Kruger may have been right.'

'I think so too,' I nod slowly.

'You've got your connection between Kohler and Habtoor.'

'Yes, but where does this Novchenko fit in?'

'Maybe he's supplying the weapon. Being a general, he could have access to such material. It wouldn't come cheap, but Kohler has the money, of that there is no doubt. I'll ask my people to check on Novchenko, see if we have anything on him. So, what do we do now?'

'Why don't you pick up Kohler?'

'What, on the say so of Dubois, a suspected drug smuggler? I'd be laughed out of court! In any event, this has serious political repercussions. I'd have to go to the top to approve such a thing.' Henri draws heavily on his cigarette, the tip burns fiercely. 'You'll have to go to the German border, try and intercept the container. Tomorrow is the 10th, remember.'

'Needles in haystacks, comes to mind.'

'Whatever, if the shipment is to reach Hamburg by night, it will have to cross by early morning.'

'Maybe,' I say thoughtfully.

'And, you're going to have to involve the Germans.'

'That had crossed my mind, Henri. Anybody in mind?'

'I could have. I've been thinking since our last meeting. Remember Wolfgang Riesner? He was at that inter-allied intelligence meeting in Brussels last year. He was briefly involved in Operation Phoenix, looking after Daimler Benz interests.'

228

'Yes, vaguely. Tall, crewcut hair, no sense of humour?'

'That's him.'

'Would you trust him?'

'He seemed pretty straight to me, what other options do you have?'

'None at the moment.'

'Ok, I'll call him, but before that you have to get to Berlin. I think that would be the nearest airport. Raymond, your laptop, please.' Raymond appears, lays his laptop on the table. Henri opens it up, logs onto the internet. 'Let's see, Stettin. Yes, Berlin is closest. Now flights. There's an Air France flight out of Charles de Gaulle at 18.55, arrives Berlin at 20.40.'

'Nothing earlier?'

'Richard, in case you haven't noticed, there's a French air traffic go slow, half the flights have been cancelled.'

'Ok, but speak to Riesner first.'

'What do I tell him?'

'Keep it simple. Something about a joint French and British operation, concerning illegal shipments etc.'

'Nothing about a nuclear possibility?'

'Christ no! We're not even sure what is in this container, if we find it. And I don't want to scare off Kohler and Novchenko.'

'Ok, we'll play it your way.'

'Anyway, thanks Henri, this may be the break I've been looking for, but in some ways, I hope to god it isn't.'

'I know what you mean, Richard. It's funny how things work out in our business, little bits of meaningless information come together and, hey presto, it all opens up.

'I just hope it's not a Pandora's box we've opened up.'

'If it is, you'd better keep it shut, mon ami.'

CHAPTER TWENTY FIVE

My flight arrives at Berlin-Tegel Airport, half an hour late, thanks to French Air Traffic Control. Wolfgang Riesner is waiting for me in the Arrivals Hall. He is taller than I remember, dressed in a black leather overcoat.

'Herr Stevens, welcome to Berlin.' A brief smile, followed by a firm handshake.

'Thank you, what has Henri told you?'

'All a bit mysterious, if you don't mind me saying so.' Riesner's English is good, if heavily accented.

'You will appreciate that this is a very sensitive operation, Herr Riesner.'

'We are always willing to help our French and British colleagues, but I think that you will have to be more specific.'

'Maybe we can discuss this somewhere more private.' I look around at the milling crowds.

'Of course, please, follow me, I have a car outside.'

We leave the airport terminal, a black Mercedes is waiting, just beyond the taxi stand. At this time of night, the air is quite chilly. I can understand why Riesner is wearing an overcoat. I only have my jacket, I've left my bag with Henri. We both get in the back of the car, I'm not introduced to the driver.

'Henri said that this shipment was coming from Stettin. The nearest border crossing would be Pomellen and Kolbaskowo, that's about an hour from here.' Riesner unbuttons his coat, settles back. 'I have some of my people there already.'

'Thank you for your help.' I watch the airport disappear from view.

'So what is this all about, Herr Stevens?'

I'd decided on the flight here that I would give Riesner a sanitised version of events. I tell him that we are investigating an illegal shipment of nuclear waste.

'I see. And why haven't we been told about this before now?'

'We only received details about the shipment today.' At least I'm not lying about that.

'Mmm, I wish your French friend had been more explicit. I shall have to get one of our Radiation units to the border, we don't want any accidents, do we?' There's a slight edge to Riesner's voice, I don't think he is amused by this turn of events. He takes out a mobile phone, presses a number.

My German is rudimentary, so I don't understand his rapid fire conversation. He ends the call, he appears satisfied.

'A unit will be there by morning,' He leans back, closes his eyes. 'I've booked us into a hotel near the border for the night.'

'Shouldn't we wait at the border?'

'I've told you, my people are already there. They have been instructed to stop any Red Star container lorry. If you wish to spend the night in the back seat of this car, please feel free.' Riesner opens his eyes, looks at me then closes his eyes again. End of conversation.

I look in front of me. The powerful headlights pick out an empty autobahn ahead. I begin to see signs for the Polish border, then we exit the autobahn. We're on a minor road, again very little traffic. I see a sign for Prenzlau-Ropersdorf, where the hell are we? Minutes later, we arrive in front of a hotel, the Hotel Am Uckersee. Riesner wakes up. The driver parks near the entrance, the three of us get out. It's now after midnight, a sleepy clerk gives us our room keys.

'We'll meet at 5am, the border is only fifteen minutes from here. If anything should happen in the meantime, I'll wake you up.' Riesner gives me a slight bow and heads off down the bedroom corridor. I think he's seriously pissed off. Mind you, so would I be if the roles had been reversed. I look at my room key, number thirteen, typical! The bedroom seems to have had a

Scandinavian designer, everything is in pine, the bed, the wardrobe, table, even the doors. I lie down on the bed, take out my mobile, try Helen again. No answer, that's the fourth time I've phoned her and no reply, where the hell is she? I think of phoning Henri but he told me before that he would keep Dubois under wraps until we know what's in the shipment. I look at my phone again, the battery is low. Damn! And I've left the charger with Helen, I hope she brings it back with her. I can't be bothered getting undressed and fall into an uneasy sleep.

A hammering on the door wakes me from a deep sleep.

'Herr Stevens! We'll be leaving in ten minutes.' I hear Riesner on the other side of the door.

'OK, I'll be with you.' I open one eye, look at my watch, 4.50 am, bloody hell! I stumble towards the bathroom, undress, stand under the hot shower for a good five minutes. I towel myself dry, put my clothes back on, wishing that I'd brought my bag with me, for a change of shirt at least. I look at the misted-up mirror, not a pretty sight, and I need a shave. I make my way to Reception, Riesner is waiting for me, he has an exaggerated look at his watch. He also looks immaculate, which doesn't improve my humour.

'Come, my car is ready, the hotel bill has been settled.'

We step outside, I shiver in the cool morning air. The sky to the east is pink, dawn is approaching. I'm aware of a lake nearby, a church spire in the distance. We get into the Mercedes and set off for the border. There's a small town to my right which I assume to be the almost unpronounceable Prenzlau-Ropersdorf.

'There have been no Red Star containers crossing the border so far, mind you this crossing tends to be quiet during the night.' Riesner looks out at the passing countryside, coming into view as the sun slowly rises. Suddenly his phone rings, he listens for a few moments, answers the caller, turns and looks at me.

'We may be in business, Herr Stevens, we've just stopped a Red Star container, destination Hamburg!'

'Brilliant!' I feel the adrenalin race through my blood.

'We've isolated the truck, it's being checked for any signs of radiation.'

Five minutes later, we approach the border. I can see German and Polish flags fluttering in the early morning breeze. Riesner gives the driver instructions, we approach a lorry park, empty except for one lorry containing a Red Star container. The lorry is surrounded by several German policemen, a man wearing a white vest and blue jeans is arguing with one of them. We come to a stop and get out of the car. A police officer approaches Riesner, they have a quick conversation.

'So, Herr Stevens, the container is clean externally, no sign of radiation.'

'Thank god for that at least. Who's the guy in the white vest?'

'He's the driver, he's Polish and he's not very happy. Says he's been driving for thirty years and never been stopped once.'

We approach the lorry, I look at the container. It looks like any other container you see on the roads, except this one is painted red, with Red Star painted in large white letters on the side with Russian Cyrillic letters below. Looks innocent enough, but what's inside? The driver continues his argument with the nearest policeman, Riesner joins me, he's holding some papers.

'This is the cargo list, let's see… originated in Warsaw from the Pidulski Plastics factory, being sent to the Hapalg agents in Hamburg. Contents are three hundred and fifty mannequins.' Riesner gives me a puzzled look.

'What?' I look at him in disbelief.

'Mannequins, you know dummies.'

'Open up the bloody thing!' I don't believe this. I walk to the back of the container, Riesner follows me. He shouts to two policemem to open it up.

Twelve women stare at me. They are all bald, blues eyes, red lips. I can't see their bodies properly, they're covered in clear plastic sheets. I hear someone sniggering behind me. 'Unload them!' I say, my anger mounting. Five minutes later, I'm surrounded by three hundred and fifty dummies, and I feel like one of them at this precise moment.

'So, Herr Stevens, no nuclear waste then?' Riesner gives me a stoney stare.

'Obviously.' I storm off towards the car. I lean against the bonnet, take a few deep breaths to calm down. What the hell is going on? I've been sent on a wild goose chase. I've been made a fool of, that bastard Dubois! My phone rings.

'Stevens, where the hell are you?' The dulcet tones of Forsyth assail me.

'At the German – Polish border.' I look skywards, count to ten.

'So I've heard. I've just had my German opposite on the phone asking what the hell is going on, something about illegal nuclear waste shipments. What are you playing at? I am supposed to be on holiday, you know.'

'I had a tip-off yesterday,' I see Riesner approaching. I walk away from the car. 'The nuclear device was supposed to be in this shipment.'

'And?'

'Nothing.' I decide not to mention the mannequins.

'So, if it's not there, where the hell is it?' I can hear Forsyth's voice rising.

'I don't know, I have to get back to Paris.' I watch as the dummies are loaded back into the container, the Polish driver is still arguing.

'No you're not.'

'Sorry?'

'I've also had the Americans on the phone, they've got wind of your escapades. Some German has tipped them off. I told you not to involve the Germans!'

'I had no choice.'

'Well, the Americans are furious and it's all your fault! They want explanations, you'll have to go to Washington.'

'Washington?'

'Yes, everything is arranged. You'll go to Frankfurt, you're booked on the 13.10 Lufthansa flight.'

'But I…'

'Don't argue with me, Stevens, just be on that plane.'

'What do I say to the Americans?'

'Just bring them up to date with your investigations. This is all your fault, you've put me in a very difficult position.' Forsyth hangs up.

Bastard! I hear footsteps on the gravel behind me. I turn around, Riesner stands there.

'Problems?'

'You could say that, my superior is not very happy.'

'Ah, Herr Forsyth, yes?'

'Have you met him?'

'Only once, in Brussels. A rather self-opinionated man.'

'You could say that.' I give a rueful smile. 'Anyway, he said that your boss had been on the phone to him.'

'Yes, your disclosure about a nuclear connection got quite a few people out of bed last night.'

'I'm sorry if I've inconvenienced your…'

'What is going on, Herr Stevens? What are you actually looking for?'

So here I am, standing in the middle of a lorry park at the German – Polish border. I don't think I have ever felt so alone. I watch the driver climb into his cab, start up the engine, drive off in a cloud of black exhaust fumes. He sticks one finger out of the window, I think it's directed at me.

'I'm waiting, Herr Stevens.'

'Did you know a man called Otto Pieck?' I glance at Riesner, looking for his reaction. I may regret this, but I'm going to have to trust this man.

235

'Pieck? Yes, he died at the beginning of the year, very sad. What has he to do with this?'

'It was suicide, yes?'

'Officially.'

'And unofficially?'

'Well,' Riesner pauses, looks at the ground, 'some of us thought that the circumstances were suspicious.'

'Was he murdered?'

Riesner looks up, walks towards me, takes my arm, 'Let's take a walk, shall we?'

We head towards the high fence, surrounding the lorry park. I look through the chainlink, see a pretty farming landscape in front of me. I tell Riesner about Pieck's investigation, the death of Kruger in London. Riesner says nothing, just stares ahead.

'You should have contacted us earlier,' Riesner finally says.

'I wasn't allowed to.'

'Forsyth?'

'Yes.'

'And German nationals are involved in the purchase of this weapon?'

'That is correct.'

'And they are?'

'I'm not allowed to give out that information.'

'Forsyth again?'

'Yes.'

'Your Herr Forsyth is leaving you in a rather exposed position, yes?'

'Don't I know it, Herr Riesner.' I laugh, but there is a hollow ring to it.

'There were rumours that Pieck was onto something,' Riesner pauses, 'and yes, there is a faction within our organisation with its own agenda. But, what is your English expression? One bad apple…'

'Quite.'

'So, what do you do next?'

236

'I'm instructed to go to Frankfurt, then onto Washington. We seem to have offended our American friends.'

'Easily done, I can assure you. Well, you can take my car and driver, Frankfurt is a couple of hours from here. When's your flight?'

'Eh, 13.10.'

'No problem.'

'And you?'

'My instructions are to stay here, all Red Star containers are to be stopped and searched. For your information, this applies to all border crossings with Poland. If it's coming by road, we'll find it.' Riesner tries to give me a reassuring smile. But for some reason, deep down, I think we are all too late.

'Well. I must be going.'

'Yes, come.' Riesner leads me back to the car.

'Thank you for your help, Herr Riesner.' We shake hands.

'I just hope we're not too late.' Maybe he can read my mind. 'Good luck, Herr Stevens, I think that you're going to need it.' He gives me a half-salute, shouts instructions to his driver.

We're soon on the autobahn again. I'm sitting in the front, alongside Riesner's driver, who I quickly discover doesn't speak any English. I take out my mobile, try Henri but my phone is dead. I gesture with my mobile to the driver but he just shrugs his shoulders. Dammit! I'll have to phone Henri from the airport. I think about Riesner, he was right, we should have contacted the Germans earlier. Forsyth is going to come under extreme pressure to release Kohler's name. Serves him right! We should have brought Kohler in at the beginning, saved ourselves a lot of wasted time and effort. Ah, hindsight is a wonderful thing. I'm now also worried about how much the Americans actually know. We approach Berlin, the traffic here is much heavier. I look at my watch,

11.00 am, should be fine. Then we hit a traffic jam, I see an overhead gantry, flashing lights indicate an accident ahead. We crawl forward for the next half an hour, I'm starting to get anxious. We finally pass a jackknifed lorry, the road is clear ahead. We arrive outside Frankfurt airport at 12.15. I thank the driver with my elementary German, hurry into the departure hall. I approach the Lufthansa information desk. I'm told that my ticket is waiting for me at check-in desk 21. I discover that the check-in desk is for first class, at least Forsyth has got something right.

'Ah, Herr Stevens, we've been waiting for you.' A pretty brunette looks at my ticket. 'Seat 1a has been reserved for you, boarding will start shortly.'

'I need to make a phone call.' I look around for a payphone.

'You can use the phones in the first class lounge, but I don't think you'll have time. There are phones over there, but please hurry.'

I thank her, grab my boarding pass, make for the bank of phones. I pick the nearest one, insert my Visa card, trying desperately to remember Henri's phone number.

'Henri?' I get through after the second ring.

'Yes, Richard, where are you?'

'Frankfurt, I'm just about to board a flight to Washington. I meant to phone you earlier but my phone has packed up.'

'No matter, Riesner phoned me, told me what was happening. You've divulged a lot to him, yes?'

'I'd no choice, Henri. Listen, what about Dubois?'

'I'd like to break his neck! I'm going back to take him down to headquarters, I'll squeeze him dry, the little bastard!'

'Maybe he doesn't know anything else.'

'I think he does, he's already let slip that Kohler has bought an apartment in Paris, nobody else knows that.'

'Do you think Kohler is there now?'

'I'll check it out after I've deposited Dubois at Headquarters. I'll email you the address, it's on the Left Bank somewhere.'

'Ok, I must go Henri, my flight is being called. I'll phone you once I've reached Washington.'

'Bonne chance, mon ami.' He cuts the connection.

I hurry to the departure gate, I'm the last to board. The First Class section is half full, I settle back into the large comfortable seat. The plane takes off at exactly 13.10, typical German efficiency; the stewardesses aren't bad looking either. Damn! I didn't try Helen again. We soon reach our cruising altitude, chilled champagne is served. I devour a plateful of nuts, discover that I'm starving since I haven't eaten much during the last two days. I look out at the brilliant blue sky, think about Henri and wonder how he's getting on with poor Dubois. Little did I know then that events in Paris and around the world were about to change everything.

CHAPTER TWENTY SIX

Mohammed Habtoor stretches and yawns as he looks across the lounge, through the open French windows. Beyond the manicured lawn, he can see the brown sluggish waters of the Nile. In the distance, an Arab dhow, sails limp in the morning heat, drifts southwards.

Habtoor has come to a decision the previous night. He's decided to retire; he's made more than enough money in the arms business. He has bought and sold all kinds of arms, but never a nuclear bomb. Bin Laden has paid him well, he always did. But whenever or wherever these bombs explode, the shit as they say, will hit the fan.

Egypt has been a safe haven for him for many years. He's sold arms to all the various groups, Hamas, Hezbollah, the Taliban. But his best customer is al-Qaeda. Several Egyptian officials have been bribed to turn a blind eye to his nefarious activities and offer protection. And so he's felt safe, even from Mossad. He knows, however, that this recent acquisition by Bin Laden is destined for America or Israel. Then even Egypt wouldn't be safe for him. No, time to pack his bags. Several years ago, he'd bought, under a different name and passport, a large chalet near Grindelwald, in the Swiss Alps. Although a Saudi by birth, Habtoor loves the Western way of life, loves Switzerland, although Austria is a close second. The warm summers, the cold, snowy winters, the clear crystal air. Yes, Switzerland is perfect for his retirement. The Swiss aren't inquisitive people, don't pry into your affairs, particularly if you are rich. And over the years, Habtoor has deposited a lot of money into various Swiss bank accounts.

But Habtoor has one last rendezvous. Although in his late fifties, he still enjoys sex. He'll miss Fatima, her houseboat on the Nile, her young nubile body. Yes, one last lunch, a lazy afternoon in her bed and then goodbye.

Habtoor hurries to his bedroom, lays out a pair of slacks, cotton shirt and white leather loafers. He showers quickly and gets dressed. He looks around the lounge, Abdul will lock up. He goes to the steel reinforced front door, undoes the three bolts, unlocks the heavy Yale security lock. Habtoor is a careful man, one has to be in his profession. He steps outside into the heat of the mid morning sun. He squints his eyes skywards; the sun looks hazy, even the pollution from Cairo reaches here. Where the hell is Abdul? Lazy bastard! At least he's brought the car out of the garage. Habtoor is driving today, Abdul doesn't know about Fatima. But he should have opened the gates, damn him! Habtoor looks up the driveway, the gates are still shut. It is then that he sees the dirty old beggar, standing on the other side, rattling a metal cup across the railings. How many times have I told Abdul to keep these people away from here, Habtoor shakes his head, gives the neighbourhood a bad name. Habtoor crosses the cobbled driveway and opens the front door of his BMW 7 Series saloon. Thankfully, the interior is still cool from being in the garage. He loves the smell of the leather, the solid build quality of the car, typically German. For a split second he thinks of that German he'd met in Vienna. He puts the key in the ignition, the engine purrs into life immediately. He glances over his shoulder, a least the beggar has gone. He picks up the auto gate control from the dashboard. He is thinking about Fatima as he presses open.

There is a blinding flash, followed by a roar and then a loud explosion. Half the garage is demolished, all the windows in the front of the house are blown in. The front door hangs askew off its hinges. There is very little left of the BMW, just part of the chassis and engine block. The shredded tyres are alight, already sending black, acrid smoke into the air. Mohammed Habtoor has disappeared, been vaporised, as has his servant, Abdul, who has been in the boot with a bullet in the back of his head.

If anyone had noticed the old beggar before, as he shambled up the street, trailing his left leg behind him, they would have been surprised to see him suddenly running, after the explosion, towards a waiting car. Even more surprised that he got into the car. But the beggar is in a hurry. He has a plane to catch. The afternoon flight to Moscow.

Paris 1710 hours local time.

Pierre drives Henri Lefevre back to the apartment off the Place de la Republique. Lefevre is in a foul mood, his meeting has not gone well. The Elysses Palace is stalling about arresting Kohler, he's even had to call off his surveillance of the George Cinq. His only hope is Dubois, I'll break that little shit yet!

They squeal to a halt outside the apartment, Henri leaps out.

'Hey boss,' Pierre calls out, 'I missed lunch, can I...?'

'OK, Pierre, there's a place at the end of the street, no more than half an hour, OK?'

Henri runs up the stairs, Raymond opens the door.

'Has he said anything?' Henri searches his pockets for his cigarettes.

'No, same old story,' Raymond shrugs, 'and he's screaming for Villebois.'

'I'll give him Villebois, right up his backside!' Henri crosses the room, enters the study. 'So, Dubois, let's stop with the lies and let's have the truth, eh?'

'What do you mean? I've told you everything I know!' Dubois screeches at Lefevre, stands up; he is beginning to panic.

'My English friend went to meet this container and found nothing.' Henri lights a cigarette, paces around the room.

'But that's impossible! I told you exactly what Kohler said... unless?'

Dubois slowly sits down.

'Unless what?' Henri stops in mid stride, looks at Dubois.

'I've been thinking, I haven't had much chance to do anything else in this dump. You know, Novchenko never liked Kohler, I was surprised that he agreed to deal with him,' Dubois pauses, a smile slowly crosses his face. 'The crafty Russian bastard! What if he never meant to deliver, eh?'

Henri walks slowly towards Dubois. Christ! What if he's right? This bloody bomb could be anywhere, and if Kohler doesn't have it, who does?

'You,' Henri points at Dubois, 'are coming with me.'

'What about Villebois?'

'You can ask my superiors that at headquarters. Raymond, get this piece of shit out of here!'

Henri watches Raymond frogmarch the protesting Dubois out of the apartment. Henri looks at his watch, what time does Richard arrive in Washington? I need to speak to him and soon. His mobile rings, he looks at the number and sighs.

'Yes, dear, no, I'm not forgetting. Yes, your parents are never late and yes, I'll remember to pick up the fish. I'll try and be there by eight, promise.' Henri shakes his head, puts his phone back in his jacket pocket. He crosses the room to his laptop on the table, sends Kohler's address to Fleming. He picks up the laptop, leaves the flat, locks the door, and descends the stairs.

Outside, Raymond keeps a firm grip of Dubois's arm. Henri looks around the deserted street. Where's Pierre? Dammit! Just then, he sees Pierre running up the street towards them.

'Sorry boss.' Pierre pulls out the car keys.

'Your stomach is going to be the death of you one of these days, ha! Come on, let's go.'

The tall blond figure stands at the end of the street. He'd followed the driver to the cafe, watched him order a sandwich and a beer, plenty of time therefore for him to do his work. The figure watches the four men get into the car, turns and starts walking. He hears the engine turn and then ducks as he feels the blast on his back, hears the sound of the explosion echo off the surrounding buildings, hears the screams, the panic. Car alarms go off, bits of metal rain down on the street. He turns the corner, people run past him, he turns his face. Dmitri does not want to be remembered. He smiles to himself, fifty pounds of Semtex under the car, with a motion detector detonator had done their work. That's taken care of Dubois and those other interfering Frenchman. Dmitri waits outside the Place de la Republique Metro station, watches police cars, sirens wailing, career around the Place. A plume of smoke rises above the skyline from the street that he has just left. One by one, his three colleagues join him. They've been the surveillance team, ordered by Novchenko, to keep an eye on Dubois. They'd watched as Dubois had been picked up, either by the police or the security services, held in that apartment. Novchenko had sanctioned the hit. The only mystery was the identity of the man who had arrived yesterday. They'd lost him, maybe he'd been heading for the airport, no matter.

'So, you know what to do?' The three men nod. 'Ok, take up your positions at the George Cinq.'

Now for the next two, I hope they're as easy.

CHAPTER TWENTY SEVEN

Autoroute 26, one hour north of Paris, 1800 hours local time.

The Aire de Cercles is one hour's drive from Calais on the A26. Jean Marie and his brother Claude exit from the autoroute, drive slowly around the rest area, looking for the container lorry.

'Over there.' Jean Marie points to a white cab and container, parked under some trees. Claude stops the old Citroen alongside the cab. Jean Marie looks around him, the lorry park is empty except for this one. He walks over to the cab, feels under the front wheel arch, finds the key. He unlocks the driver's door, climbs up into the cabin. His hand searches under the seat, finds the envelope, gets down from the cabin. He quickly opens the envelope, counts the money, ten thousand euros. He whistles to himself, this must be an important cargo. He walks back to the car, Claude winds down his window.

'Here.' Jean Marie hands over the envelope. 'Whatever is in that container,' Jean Marie looks over his shoulder, 'well, just make sure that I don't get caught.'

'We've been alright so far.' Claude looks up at his older brother, always worrying, he smiles to himself.

'There's always a first time,' Jean Marie glances around him.

'Don't worry, I'll take care of everything. You'd better get going.'

'Yes,' Jean Marie looks at his watch. 'Remember, it's the 21.15 P&O ferry, I think it's the Pride of Kent, OK?'

'I know, I know, don't worry, see you there.' Claude gives his brother a smile and a wave and drives off.

Jean Marie stands there for a few moments, hears the hum of traffic from the autoroute, watches his brother disappear. He and his brother have been doing this for two years now, picking up illegal shipments from various

Aires around Calais and transporting them to England. Jean Marie is the driver, Claude is a French Customs officer in the Port of Calais. It's Claude's responsibility to make sure of Custom clearance and so far so good. Jean Marie, however, is worried about this particular shipment, they've never been paid this much before. It had all started two years ago, in a dingy little bar near the port. A stranger had approached Jean Marie and his brother, they started chatting. One drink led to another, the stranger then made his pitch. Would they be interested in ferrying certain shipments across the Channel into England? For a fee, of course. The fee was discussed, Jean Marie did some quick mental calculations. In three years, he and his brother could buy that bar that they always wanted, be their own boss.

Jean Marie's only condition was that it wasn't to involve human trafficking; that was now too dangerous. He knew of one driver who had been picked up by the British and he was still in jail. The stranger agreed; the first shipment was to be the following month.

Another lorry comes into the rest area, the driver gives Jean Marie a brief wave, Jean Marie thinks that he recognises him, better get going. He climbs into the cabin, starts up the Daimler Benz engine, releases the air brakes and sets off. He's used to all types of lorries but you need a few minutes to get the feel of each one and this one feels heavy, he'll need to be careful.

Jean Marie guides the lorry through the outskirts of the Port of Calais. He hands over his passport and ticket at the P&O booth. He proceeds to Customs, sees Claude chatting to some other officers. One officer turns as Jean Marie approaches, Claude pulls him by the arm, says something to him, they laugh. Jean Marie continues to Gate Fifteen, breathes a sigh of relief. That bit was easy, I don't know how Claude does it, now for the English side.

The crossing takes one hour twenty-five minutes. Jean Marie sits in the bar, drinks two coffees. After docking, the cars leave first, then the lorries follow. As usual, it's very busy. There is a queue of lorries in front of him, going through Customs. The last hurdle, must stay calm, he says to himself. He sees a large van being pulled over, the driver gets out, speaks to several Customs officers. Jean Marie crawls forward, he shows his shipping documents to a harassed-looking officer. The officer, after a quick glance, waves Jean Marie through. I've done it, he smiles to himself, easy money really!

He leaves Dover by the A20 and then stops at a lorry lay-by. He rereads the instructions that came with the ticket. He's to stay here overnight, arrive in London no later by midday tomorrow. He locks the cabin doors, climbs in the back, there's a small bunk bed. As he settles down for the night, he thinks about the shipping document. Mannequins? What will they think of next?

1800 hours local time, Haifa.

The SS Bosphorous Seas steams slowly into the port of Haifa. The pilot is on board and he is not happy. This ship is late and he is therefore late. It is his son's Bar Mitzvah party tonight. Myra will kill him if he's not there by eight o'clock. He paces impatiently around the bridge.

'You should have been here four hours ago.' The pilot glares at the ship's captain.

'I'm sorry, we'd a problem with the engines.' He shrugs his shoulders.

The pilot is a Russian Jew, originally from Kiev. He's seen many ships in his time but this is the worst. Tramp does not even begin to describe it, more rust than anything else. Problems with the engines? Huh, I'm surprised it made it out of Istanbul harbour. He looks again at the captain, tall, hooked nose, black beard, dark brown almost black eyes. Some of these Arabs can be right arrogant sonofabitches and he's one of them. The pilot shakes his head and closes his laptop.

'You'll dock at pier 12,' The pilot glances at the manifest again, five thousand tonnes of cement. No doubt for more settlers' homes. 'You won't be able to start unloading until tomorrow, you know.' You've made me wait, you arrogant prick, so I'll make you wait.

'That is not a problem. Tomorrow will be fine.' The captain smiles at the pilot, much to his annoyance. The tall Arab turns and walks slowly across the bridge and looks westward. The sun is setting on the far horizon, like a large orange ball of fire. He slips his hand into the pocket of his white trousers and grasps the remote control, his thumb caressing the activate button.

'Yes, tomorrow. Tomorrow will be just fine.'

The 11th September.

'Inshallah.'

CHAPTER TWENTY EIGHT

1600 hours Eastern time. Dulles International Airport. Washington D.C.

The Lufthansa jet rolls to a stop, the pilot cuts the engines, I hear the generator kick in. I undo my seatbelt and stand up. The flight was uneventful, food was pretty good, I must have slept for five hours. At least I've had a shave, a splash of Armani makes me feel more human. The chief stewardess approaches.

'Herr Stevens, I hope that you have enjoyed your flight with us. There is an American government official waiting for you, you'll disembark first. Please, follow me.'

I walk past the other passengers as they get ready to disembark. The cabin door swings open. Various uniformed, Lufthansa officials are waiting, a young man in a grey suit steps forward.

'Mr Stevens? I'm Jeff Connors, CIA. I've been sent to meet you.' He smiles nervously, somehow he reminds me of Bradbury. We shake hands briefly, I follow him up the gangway. I'm ushered through passport control, I'm obviously expected. We step outside, the air is warm and humid. The concourse is busy, passengers with baggage trolleys, looking for taxis or friends. A black Ford Explorer, with black tinted windows, draws up in front of us. Connors gets in the front, I sit in the back. Connors says something to the driver, we drive off.

'Where are we going?' I ask Connors, who so far has said very little.

'Langley, you're expected.' Connors turns around, gives me a half-smile.

We leave the airport and join Interstate 66, heading east, past Fairfax on our right. Near Falls Church, we join Interstate 495 and travel north. We turn off soon afterwards, I see signs for McLean. Several minutes later we arrive at the entrance to the CIA headquarters, our car is waved through, past security. The buildings are situated within a parkland, not quite what I was expecting. We approach the main building, a 1960s-style slab block. We stop outside the main entrance, Connors and I get out. Inside, we cross the famous floor emblem of the CIA. At the security desk, Connors arranges my visitor's pass. We go to a bank of elevators, we come out on the fourth floor, Connors leads me to a small meeting room.

'Mr Kelly will be with you shortly. Help yourself to coffee.' Connors points to a small sideboard and leaves.

I wander over to the sideboard and pour some coffee from a half-full coffee pot, add some sugar. In the middle of the room is a table with six chairs. The room is predominately grey, walls, carpet and furniture. I sit down, look out the window over the parkland in front. I sip my coffee, it tastes quite bitter. Well, not the warmest welcome I've received, let's see what happens next. The door opens behind me, a stocky-looking man in a dark blue suit enters.

'Hi, I'm Dick Kelly.' He gives me a brusque handshake, sits down opposite me.

Kelly must be about my age, close cropped silver hair, craggy looking face.

'So, you're the famous Richard Stevens,' Kelly says with a faint hint of a smile.

'Really? I didn't know my fame has spread this far.'

'You roughed up a friend of mine, O'Connor?'

'Ah yes, Toulouse.' I smile at the thought.

'I hear that you play hardball, Stevens.' Kelly looks at me, folds his arms in front of him.

'Only when necessary. We don't like you playing in our backyard, especially when you don't have our permission.'

'OK, but that's in the past,' Kelly pauses. 'I believe that we have a more immediate problem.'

'How much do you know?'

'Only that you're chasing around Europe looking for a nuclear bomb and that a certain Mohammed Habtoor is involved.'

'That's a fair summation,' I drink some more coffee. 'What about Kohler?'

'Who the hell is Kohler?' Kelly looks puzzled.

Oh dear, this is what I was afraid of. Forsyth has been less than communicative with our American friends. And I now know why I'm here and not Forsyth. So, I decide that I have no choice but to tell the Americans everything that I know. I settle back in my chair and recount my meeting with Kruger, the death of Pieck, then Kruger himself. Kelly sits there patiently, although I can see his irritation mounting.

'Two days ago, Dubois in Paris gave us our first real proof of the connection between Kohler and Habtoor. And then of course, this Novchenko has entered the frame.' I look across at Kelly, deep in thought. He finally stands up, walks towards the sideboard, pours himself some coffee.

'We knew about Habtoor but nothing about Kohler, why was that?' Kelly turns around, stares at me.

'You'd have to ask Forsyth that question.'

'Oh, we will, don't worry.' Kelly smiles to himself. 'And what about this Novchenko?'

'As I said, he's only come to our attention through Dubois. I need to talk to Henri Lefevre.'

'Feel free.' Kelly points to the phone on the sideboard. 'I have to speak to some people, I'll be back shortly.' He leaves me in the room alone.

I pick up the phone, dial the international code for France, then Henri's number. No sound, nothing, how strange. I sit down again, wondering if I should call his office. My more immediate concern, however, is Forsyth. What the hell is he playing at? Either he's going for personal glory, as usual, or he never believed in any of this in the first place. And if the Americans have been kept in the dark, I bet the Israelis haven't been told either. Forsyth is playing a dangerous game and I'm in the middle of it. I'm rather surprised by Kelly's reaction, I'd expected histrionics on his part. But so far, he's been quite calm. The door opens, Kelly and another man enter.

'This is a colleague of mine, Harding.' Kelly points to the tall figure beside him. We shake hands, they sit down opposite me.

'We've also been looking for Habtoor.' Harding says. He is taller than Kelly, face weather-beaten, cold blue eyes. He's dressed casually, blue denim jacket, faded grey slacks. Definitely not a desk man, unlike Kelly.

'An hour ago,' Harding continues, 'I received a communication from our Cairo office. They'd been told by a source in the Egyptian government that Habtoor had been killed by a car bomb in his house, just south of Cairo.'

'The Israelis?' I ask Kelly.

'So far they're denying it, but knowing Mossad, who knows…'

'I doubt it,' Harding interrupts. 'It would be unusual for them to operate in Egypt.'

'Unless they had permission?' Kelly looks at Harding.

'Yeah, but I've been in close touch with Tel Aviv over the past few months. I don't think they really knew where Habtoor was, certainly not Cairo.'

Silence descends between the three of us, each wirh our own thoughts. The door opens, Connors enters, passes a piece of paper to Kelly. He sits there, frowns as he reads it.

'You'd better read this.' Kelly slides the piece of paper across the table.

I look at the typewritten message.

REUTERS FLASH   Paris, 10th September 1805 hours.

'Car bomb explodes near Place de la Republique, four dead, several injured – End.'

My heart sinks as I read on.

252

REUTERS FLASH Paris, 10th September 1904 hours.

'Car bomb - Police have confirmed that Henri Lefevre, senior French intelligence agent, amongst dead. Two other intelligence officers thought to be also dead. The identity of the fourth fatality is not yet known. Police treating bombing as a terrorist act. No group has so far claimed responsibility – End.'

I sit there stunned. Henri, my god, Henri dead. I feel sick.

'I'm sorry, Stevens… this must come as a great shock to you.' Kelly says quietly.

I sit there for a few moments, trying to collect my thoughts. I can't get the image of the jovial Henri, my friend, out of my mind. He was always so careful, how could this have happened?

'So, two car bombs, hardly coincidental, wouldn't you think?' Harding looks across the table at me. His face is expressionless, he reminds me that there's no room for sentimentality in our business.

'I think I know who the fourth person is.' I finally say, trying to focus on the job in hand. At least I owe Henri that.

'Who?'

'Dubois.'

'Mmm, looks like someone is getting rid of any witnesses.' Kelly adds thoughtfully.

'But who?'

'Could be Bin Laden.' Harding looks at Kelly.

'What about Novchenko?' I look at the two Americans, Connors has left the room. 'If he's the one supplying the bomb, he'll want to cover his tracks.'

'The Germans haven't found anything trying to cross their borders yet.' Kelly stands up, paces around the room.

'Maybe we're too late.' I say quietly.

'Meaning?' Kelly turns around sharply.

'I'm not sure. I just have a hunch that Novchenko and Habtoor have been working to a different timetable.'

'So, the bomb has already been delivered?'

'That would explain why Habtoor is dead, his usefulness has come to an end.'

Kelly and Harding look at each other, Harding stands up.

'Well, Mr Stevens, you'll appreciate that we have a lot of work to do.'

Kelly makes for the door, Harding follows.

'You'll have to pick up Kohler, you know that.'

'That matter is with the State Department, there is evidently a sensitive political angle to consider.' Kelly turns and pauses, 'But we will do what is necessary.'

'And Novchenko?'

'The Director is speaking to Moscow, at this minute. We'll find that sonofabitch, don't you worry.'

'I would like to help, you know.'

'Look Stevens,' Kelly sighs, 'we've got our hands full. I'm instructed to deliver you to the British Embassy, evidently your political masters are waiting. I'll send Connors in, there's a car waiting for you downstairs.'

'Very well,' I get up from my chair, ' I don't seem to have much option.'

'If anything happens, you'll be the first to know about it, OK? If something does happen, of course, there's going to be hell to pay.' Kelly looks at me, purses his lips, shakes his head and is gone.

CHAPTER TWENTY NINE

2305 hours local time. Le Cinq restaurant, George Cinq hotel, Paris.

'That was excellent as usual,' Kohler carefully folds his napkin. 'The lobster was superb.' Kohler looks at his watch. 'Now I must be going, Franz, Dubois is picking me up.'

'Why so late?' Haller looks up from his unfinished plate.

'Oh, you know Dubois, always wanting me to meet somebody.' Kohler stands up, admires the grey and gold decor of the restaurant.

'You know that I don't like you going out late at night on your own.'

'Don't worry, Franz, I'm with Dubois. I'll see you tomorrow.'

Kohler strides out of the restaurant, makes for the hotel entrance then appears to change his mind. He fumbles in his jacket pocket as though he has forgotten something. He turns, walks past the receptionist and takes the lift to the fifth floor. Kohler walks down the wide corridor, past the door to his suite and enters the service stairs. At the ground floor, he is confronted by the exit door which has an alarm fitted, just in case a guest decides to do a midnight flit. And so Kohler turns left, opens an unmarked door. Inside, left luggage is stacked to the ceiling on timber shelving. At the end of the room is another door to the outside. Kohler passes an array of Louis Vuitton and Cartier leather cases, sees the old Vietnamese polishing shoes at an old desk. The old man looks up as Kohler approaches him, a faint smile of recognition shows on his face. Kohler places a one hundred euro note on the table, between two black patent shoes. He lifts his finger to his lips in a silent gesture. The old man just nods and pockets the note before Kohler has had time to open the door.

Outside, in the warm evening air, Kohler smiles to himself. All this deception is necessary of course, ever since he discovered that Schreiber has been following him, especially for his nocturnal visits. Buying the apartment had been Kohler's idea, Dubois had done the rest. Satisfied that he is alone, Kohler hails a passing taxi, gives the driver an address on the Left Bank. As he settles back in his seat, Kohler thinks about tonight, thinks about the young Estonian and Latvian being delivered in an hour's time. He feels himself being aroused at the thought of these two in his bed.

Haller watches Kohler leave the restaurant, sees the waiters bowing and scraping, as usual. He calls the head waiter over, signs the bill, leaves a hundred euro tip. He thinks of following Kohler but decides against it. For tomorrow, Haller is leaving for good, his flight to Barcelona booked. Ever since the transaction with Novchenko, Haller has been making his own plans. Time to get out, he's made enough money. There's a large German expatriate community in the Costa Brava, the weather is better too. Stay a couple of months, see which way the wind is blowing, then he'll decide what to do. If this bomb does go off, then Kohler will be hot property and Haller doesn't want Mossad chasing him for the rest of his life.

Haller enters his room, adjacent to Kohler's suite. He looks at the half-packed suitcase on the bed, crosses to the mini bar, pours himself a whisky. He switches on the television, sits down in a leather armchair, watches adverts but his mind is elsewhere. He looks at his watch, midnight, a late night news programme comes on. The lead story is about the car bomb, which had been the talk of the hotel that evening. He's thinking about Spain when he hears the name Dubois mentioned by a reporter at the scene of the bombing. He spills his whisky as he leans forward to turn up the sound. The reporter mentions that three French security officers were killed along with Marcel Dubois, a leading contractor in France. Haller listens for a few more moments, then switches off the television. He sits there thinking furiously. Dubois dead, my God! What the hell was he doing with French security people? And what had he been telling them? Suddenly, Haller feels afraid. I need to get out of here and now. What about Kurt, what was all that nonsense about meeting Dubois when he's been dead for six hours? Unless of course, Kurt doesn't know that Dubois is already dead. I have to phone him. He hears a double knock at the door, maybe that's Kurt now, bet he's forgotten his key again.

'Kurt, I…' Haller opens the door but stops in mid sentence. 'But you're… Dmitri, yes?'

'Yes, Haller, and I have a present from Andrei,' Dmitri stands there in a house boy's uniform, his left hand holds a silver tray covered with a white napkin. His right hand slips under the napkin and pulls out a revolver, fitted with a silencer.

'No, no…!' Haller steps back.

Dmitri fires twice, the first bullet hits Haller in the chest, the second straight through his heart. The force of the bullets throws Haller backwards onto the bed, his head collides with the suitcase. Dmitri steps into the room, checks for a pulse, none. Haller's mouth is open, his unseeing eyes stare at the fresco ceiling.

As Dmitri leaves the room, he takes the Do Not Disturb sign and slips it over the outside door handle, makes sure the door is firmly shut. The corridor is empty, no one has heard a thing. Dmitri knocks again at Kohler's door, no answer, where the hell is he? He stands there for a few moments then makes for the service stairs. Time to meet Novchenko.

Dmitri comes out the hotel, the black Mercedes is waiting, the back door opens. He gets in and closes the door.

'Taken care of?' Feodor asks

'Yes, no problem.' Dmitri replies. 'But Kohler has gone missing.'

'What!' Novchenko growls from the back.

'He left the restaurant, went up to his suite, but he wasn't there.'

'Shit!' Novchenko takes out a cigarette and lights it, fingers thrum on the leather armrest as he thinks what to do next. 'Right, leave your boys outside the hotel, Dmitri, Kohler has to come back here. Take him out, I don't care if it's in broad fucking daylight!'

'But...' Dmitri starts to protest.

'Just give the instructions! This is your fault, you lost Kohler! Now phone Igor, they're being paid enough money anyway.'

Dmitri says nothing, takes out his mobile, speaks to Igor.

'Good.' Novchenko leans forward and taps Feodor on the shoulder, 'Orly.'

Novchenko settles back in his seat as the car speeds off. Kohler was a fool, he thinks, as he watches the darkened streets pass by. Did he really think that he would know the actual details of the shipment? Think that it would really end up at Hamburg docks, ha! Novchenko had switched containers, the real containers had ended up at Calais and Marseille, on schedule. Habtoor had done the rest. Before his usefulness had come to an end. Only one loose end, Kohler. Well, Igor will take care of that.

'So, my friends, I believe Brazil is very nice at this time of year!' Novchenko smiles to himself. He is leaving Europe, maybe for good. The private jet is waiting to fly him to Rio de Janeiro. Feodor had been there six months previously, his brief simple. To buy a ranch, about two hours drive from Rio or more accurately, 15 minutes by

258

helicopter. A suitable property has been purchased, including five thousand acres. The ranch house already has new security fencing, Dmitri's associates are on 24-hour guard duty. To the rear is a large outbuilding, big enough for the three containers which, at this moment, are halfway across the Atlantic. Novchenko has decided to sell the three devices, when the time is right, to the next highest bidder. Maybe Bin Laden will be back. Eighty million dollars was now in The First Cayman Bank, along with the rest, close to three hundred million dollars. More than enough for my retirement!

The car slows as it approaches the entrance to Orly airport. Novchenko looks at his watch, the 11th September. Tomorrow, his first appointment is with Brazil's finest plastic surgeon. Andrei Novchenko is about to disappear.

CHAPTER THIRTY

10th September 2331 hours Eastern Time, British Embassy, Washington D.C.

The British Embassy sits at the north end of Embassy Row. The Ambassador's residence was built in 1929, designed by the famous architect Sir Edwin Lutyens. But I can't see much of it, as we arrive in darkness. I'm met by James Meldrew, the Ambassador's personal secretary. The Ambassador is evidently attending a reception at the Chilean Embassy, no sign of great concern here then. I'm ushered in to the study, photographs abound of the Ambassador with prominent world leaders. I sit down in a leather armchair.

'I can rustle up some sandwiches and coffee, if you'd like?' James stands attentively beside me.

'Yes, that would be fine, thank you.'

'Mr Watson will be along shortly, he's in the Chancery, seems to be a bit of a panic on.' Meldrew rolls his eyes to the ceiling and flounces out of the room. So, Watson is here, another of Forsyth's cronies; I wonder what he wants. I know that he doesn't like me and the feeling is mutual. James enters carrying a tray, puts it down on a small table beside me.

'Will there be anything more, Mr Stevens?'

'No, thank you.' I survey the plate of sandwiches, choose the smoked salmon.

'I'll show Mr Watson in, when he arrives.'

I'm left alone thinking about what's happened over the last few days. I'm still coming to terms with Henri's death. I just hope that he didn't die in vain. I'm halfway through the sandwiches when the door opens.

'Ah, there you are, about time too.' Stuart Watson enters, that arrogant swagger that I so dislike. He picks up a sandwich without asking, rude bastard!

'Help yourself, please do,' I say, but my sarcasm is lost on him; he wouldn't understand the word.

'You were supposed to contact us when you arrived, you know.'

'The CIA met me off the plane, I didn't have much choice in the matter.'

'We'd a driver waiting for you, he came back, said that you weren't on the plane. It's not good enough, you know.'

'Then Forsyth should have been more explicit in his instructions. I picked up my ticket in Frankfurt, there was no message.'

'Mmm, that ham is damn good.' Watson sits down opposite me, examines a half-eaten sandwich. 'So, what's all this about anyway, eh?' Watson doesn't sit, he lounges in his chair. 'Messages flying all over the place between London and Washington. Had to work bloody late, missed a date with a cracking blonde from the State Department, huh!' Watson appears severely piqued. What a shame.

'Anything from Forsyth?' I pour myself coffee, don't offer any to Watson.

'He's bloody pissed off with you, says this is all your fault!' Watson eyes the last sandwich, I pick it up and eat it.

'Well, if he'd told the Americans in the first place, we wouldn't be in this mess.' I fire my opening shot.

'This was supposed to be a British affair, Stevens, get one over on the Yanks.'

'Is that what this is all about?' I shake my head in disbelief, 'Getting one over on the Yanks, when we probably have a nuclear bomb which has now gone AWOL.'

'That's if you believe all this stuff, where's the proof?'

I eye up this baffoon in front of me, why waste my breath on him. Just then the door opens, the Ambassador breezes in.

261

'Ah, Stuart there you are,' Sir George Bingham is a large man, a florid face. He's wearing a dark grey, pinstriped suit. 'And you must be Stevens.' He looks at me, undoes his tie. 'Ah, that's better.' He crosses to a drinks cabinet, takes out a decanter. 'Anyone for a nightcap?'

I decline but Stuart of course doesn't. Bingham sits behind his desk, they toast each other, it's as though I'm invisible. Bingham starts some story about the Chilean Ambassador's wife.

'Excuse me, Ambassador, but we do have a possible crisis on our hands,' I interrupt him in mid joke.

'What?' Bingham looks annoyed.

'It's about the message from Mr Forsyth, George,' Stuart has a smirk on his face.

'Oh, that, I see,' Bingham drinks more whisky, looks at me. 'But that's intelligence stuff, got bugger all to do with me!' He now takes out a cigar, looks for a lighter.

'May have to calm some ruffled feathers, George.' He leans across and lights the cigar. Smarmy bastard!

'Yes, Forsyth said that this was all your fault, Stevens.' Bingham puffs on his cigar, stares up at the ceiling.

I refrain, with great difficulty, from getting up and ramming that cigar down his throat. If anyone else says that this is my fault, I'm going to punch them. I suddenly feel tired, maybe it's jet lag. There's no point discussing this any further with these two idiots, Forsyth has them in his pocket. I am the bogey man. 'Well, if you don't mind, I'd like to call it a day.' I stand up. 'I'm meeting the Americans early tomorrow, at least they're treating this seriously.' I glare at Watson, who seems more interested in getting a refill.

'Well, you'd better phone Forsyth in the morning, brief our side first, eh?' Bingham tops up both glasses. 'You'll be staying in the Chancery tonight, James will show you across.' Bingham waves his hand then continues his story about the Chilean Ambassador's wife.

I leave the study, I'm livid. What do they say about lunatics running the aslylum?

James leads me across to the adjacent Chancery. After passing through security, I'm shown to a small bedroom on the second floor. I collapse onto the single bed, I'm exhausted, I can't be bothered undressing. I'm dreaming of Helen, we're on a beach somewhere, all alone. Then I see a figure running towards me, he's shouting my name.

'Stevens, Stevens, wake up!' Someone is shaking me, I open my eyes, there's a young man standing beside the bed. 'You'll have to come quick, something terrible has happened in Israel!'

I roll out of bed, try and get my bearings, remember where I am. The young man is Miller, the Night Duty Officer, I follow him down the stairs. He's talking so quickly I only catch half of what he's saying. We enter his office, there's a television set, showing CNN news

'I got a call from London saying switch on CNN,' Miller just points at the television.

I look at the Breaking News headline – '…Major explosion in Haifa, many casualties… maybe a nuclear explosion, unconfirmed reports from Tel Aviv… El Al jet reports seeing large mushroom cloud over city…'

I turn up the sound, the CNN anchorman cuts to their correspondant in Tel Aviv.

'What are you hearing, Ed?'

'Well, John, at the moment it is all very confusing. We do know that around 7am this morning there was a huge explosion in the Port of Haifa. Now there are unconfirmed reports, I repeat, unconfirmed, that it was a nuclear explosion. We are not aware of any nuclear facilities near Haifa, so…'

My legs feel weak, I sit down in a chair. I stare, unbelieving, at the television, not taking in what is being said. It's actually happened, those mad bastards have actually done it. The desk phone rings, Miller answers it.

'Yes? Stevens? Yes, he's here.' Miller, white faced, hands the phone to me.

'Stevens.' My mouth is dry.

'You heard?' It's Kelly.

'Yes, I'm watching, right now.'

'There will be a car at the Embassy in fifteen minutes, we need to talk.' He hangs up.

It's 2.30 am in Washington, 9.30 am in Tel Aviv. I'm sitting in Kelly's office.

The world is waking up to the terrible events in Haifa. Another 9/11, but on a scale that most people will not comprehend. I watch the television in the corner of the room. The pictures are from a direct feed from the Pentagon, will be heavily edited before being shown in public, if they are ever shown. The camera from a Blackhawk pilotless drone shows what's left of Haifa. A pillar of ugly, dark brown smoke rises above the city. Below the smoke, it's difficult to determine if there ever was a city, very few visible signs remain. I can see the port area, identifiable only by its adjacency to the coastline. Even the sea looks angry. The camera pans southwards, it's just possible to make out where buildings once stood, burnt squares or rectangles bordering pale strips of what were streets. The camera zooms in, stumps of buildings appear, a wall here, a pile of blackened rubble behind. Further from the epicentre, the camera starts to pick out what looks like burnt matchsticks. I realise these are bodies. I turn away, I feel sick.

Kelly watches with me, occasionally shakes his head, every so often I hear a muttered oath under his breath. He looks back to his desk, sifts through papers in front of him. Every so often, a flustered-looking Connors comes into the room, deposits more papers onto Kelly's desk.

Kelly looks up, leans back, rubs his eyes. 'Our seismologists picked it up first, thought there had been an earthquake. From their readings, we calculate the blast was in the five hundred kiloton range.'

'Jesus Christ!'

'Haifa had, and I repeat had, a population of two hundred and fifty thousand people. I don't think there will be many left alive, pity the poor bastards who are. We're looking at a dead city.' Kelly picks up a cigarette packet, lights a cigarette, stares into space. 'Kohler wasn't playing with smarties, was he?' Kelly looks like he's aged since yesterday, probably I do too. But I haven't looked in a mirror recently, maybe I don't want to.

'I just can't believe this has happened.' I shake my head again.

'We believe the epicentre was the Haifa port area.' Kelly still stares into space.

'I bet it was in a bloody container!'

'Possibly. We're going to have to contact all the shipping agents in the region, see if we can trace the ship, if it did come by ship.'

'My bet is that it did. That's why they picked Haifa. Much more difficult to bring it in across the Israeli borders.'

'You could be right. And it's going to take a lot of hard work and cooperation from some governments, who are not particularly our best friends at the moment, to find it.'

'What about Kohler?'

'We're talking to Bonn. They don't believe us.' Kelly stubs out his cigarette

'They must, they've got to find him!'

'That's out of my hands at the moment.' Kelly shrugs.

'So, what happens now?'

'Try and find Novchenko. Our people in Lisbon are now on their way to the Algarve, at least we found out where his villa is.' Kelly lights up another cigarette.

'He'll be long gone.'

'Yes, but where?' Kelly pauses, picks up a piece of paper in front of him. 'We've talked to Moscow, they don't believe us either. The blame game is about to start, Stevens. The Israeli government is in emergency session, their Prime Minister has already been on the phone to the President. You should realise, Stevens, that our Director has already briefed him. Naturally, the Director is covering his ass and blaming the Brits. Your name has been mentioned.'

'Tell him to speak to Forsyth.' I glare at Kelly.

'Oh, he will,' Kelly puffs on his cigarette, 'after the President has spoken to your Prime Minister. I'd like to be a fly on the wall during that conversation.' Kelly smiles faintly.

'I should get back to the Embassy, speak to Forsyth.' I start to get up.

'Hold, hold on,' Kelly waves me back down. 'You can phone him from here, anyway I prefer you to be here.'

'But, in theory, Watson is the one, he is my superior here in Washington.'

'Who? That prick! No thanks, I want you here.'

'I'm not being kept prisoner, am I?'

'Not yet,' again a faint smile. 'You know Stevens, I kinda feel for you. You've been investigating this with one hand tied behind your back, a bit like me really. And you're all I've got, so you stay.'

Connors comes in, hands a piece of paper to Kelly who quickly scans it.

'Well, well, well, another piece of the jigsaw,' Kelly purses his lips. 'A Franz Haller was found shot dead in the George Cinq hotel this morning by a housemaid. Haller was the personal assistant to Kurt Kohler, the well known German magnate. Mr Kohler was also staying at the hotel but has evidently gone missing. The French police are treating his disappearance as suspicious.' Kelly looks up at me.

'I bet they never find him.'

'You could be right. Novchenko's work?'

'I think so, everyone involved in this are now dead. He's taken them out, one by one.'

'Then just as well you're safe here with me, isn't it?' Kelly smiles faintly. His phone rings, he frowns as he listens to the caller. 'I'll need to leave you for a while, don't go walkabout, OK?' Kelly gets up from his desk.

I wait for Kelly to leave then quickly cross to the computer on his desk. I type in my email address and password. There are three messages from my daughter asking where the hell am I, she'll have to wait. And there's Henri's message, a message from the dead. I click on it and write down the address, somewhere on the Left Bank, Henri had said. I check the address again then delete the message and sign out.

I sit back in my chair. Maybe Kohler is not dead, maybe he's still in Paris. And I owe it to Henri to find Kohler if he is still alive. The problem is, how do I get to Paris?

CHAPTER THIRTY ONE

11th September 8.04 am, A20 outside Dover.

Jean Marie climbs down from his cab, stretches, shivers slightly. The morning air is still cool, despite the sunshine. He wanders over to the snack bar, an old white caravan. Several other drivers stand around chatting, he doesn't recognise any of them. He orders a coffee, winces as he tastes the bitter liquid. He lights his first cigarette of the day, maybe I should have had the tea, he thinks as he listens to the other drivers. Most are Poles or Czechs, how things have changed. Used to be only French and German drivers, Jean Marie shakes his head, now the majority are from Eastern Europe, taking our jobs. They're paid less, so they drive longer, not taking the official breaks. These cowboys are an accident waiting to happen. Another shake of the head as he hands back his half-finished coffee. He heads back to his lorry, walks around it once, checking everything is in order, don't want to be stopped by the police. Satisfied, he climbs into the cab, puts the key into the ignition. Before he starts the engine, he looks again at his instructions. The delivery is to be made to an address in Canary Wharf. He's never been there before, usually it's to some warehouse in the east side of London. He has a quick look at the map, his finger traces the route. So, join the M20 then onto the A2, I might have to ask for directions when I get closer. He looks at his watch, yes, plenty of time.

11.32 am. Southern Approach, Blackwall Tunnel, London.

Abdul Rashid leaves his uncle's shop, hurries along Old Mauritius Street. He's received a strange call from his brother in Birmingham. He's to go to the Southern

Approach road and look out for a white container lorry. When he sees it, he's to phone the number that he has been given. Rashid stands on the pavement, surveys the oncoming traffic. At least the rush hour is over, easier to see what's coming. He glances at his watch, it should be here by now. Then, in the distance he sees the white cab, container behind. The lorry passes him, he reads the signage – ODESSA Freight Lines, stencilled on the white container, that's the one. He takes out his mobile, taps in the numbers he's been given and presses send.

'Oh, it's you Helen, I was hoping it was Dad,' Anna watches Helen come into the flat.

'Well, I was hoping that Richard would be back by now,' Helen drops her shopping bag in the kitchen, walks into the lounge.

'Where is he anyway? Thought you were both in Biarritz?' Anna is sitting at the coffee table.

'We were, then he had to rush off to Paris. I haven't heard anything since.' Which is not exactly true, Helen admits to herself. I know he's been calling me. But I don't want to tell him on the phone, I need to tell him in person.

'Bet he's forgotten to charge his phone, he's always doing that.' Anna bends down, takes a cigarette packet from her bag, lights it.

'I'll make some coffee, want some?'

'No thanks,' Anna eyes the other packet on the table, hears Helen busy in the kitchen. A couple of minutes later, Helen reappears holding a mug.

'Helen, this probably isn't any of my business but I found this in the bathroom.' Anna point to the blue and white packet in front of her.

'Ah... ah yes,' Helen blushes slightly, 'that's mine.'

'And?'

'I took a test yesterday, I'm pregnant.'

'What?' Anna forgets about her cigarette, stares at Helen.

'Yes, I found out yesterday.' Helen clasps both hands around her mug.

' Does Dad know, I mean it is Dad's?'

'He doesn't know yet and yes it is his.'

'This is a bit sudden isn't it?' Anna stares at Helen. 'I mean, you've only known Dad for a few months.'

'Well, yes, I suppose so,' Helen turns, looks out the patio windows. 'I'm going to hand in my notice at the school,' she looks out across the harbour. 'I'll put the flat in London up for sale, move in with my parents in Bath. They're delighted at being grandparents at last.'

'What about Dad?'

'He can visit at weekends.'

'What do you mean at weekends? Aren't you going to get married or at least live together?'

'I don't think so,' Helen turns, faces Anna. 'Bit of an age difference, don't you think?'

'Oh, I get it,' Anna says slowly. 'You've just used him, haven't you?'

'Used is a rather unfortunate word. You see, my husband was killed just before we were going to start a family. I've wanted a baby ever since. I went out with a few men, it was ghastly, these strange men pawing at you. Then I met Richard, he was so different, kind and gentle.'

'You've planned this all along, haven't you? You scheming bitch!' Anna spits it out.

'Really, Anna, such language doesn't suit that pretty mouth,' Helen turns, opens the patio doors, steps outside. It is a beautiful day, things couldn't be better. She looks skywards, sees a plane making its final approach to the nearby City airport. The roar of jet engines blot out her happy thoughts.

Abdul Rashid listens to his phone, no reply from the number he has just dialled. He calls his brother, 'I've called that number but there's...'

'What number did you call.'

Rashid repeats the number.

'It ends in seven you idiot, not eight! Dial it again! Now!' Rashid's brother hangs up.

Rashid redials the number. What's wrong with my brother today? Shouting like that. And why is he in Birmingham? He hates Birmingham. Rashid looks along the expressway. As he presses Send, the white container lorry has disappeared into the Blackwall Tunnel.

Jean Marie is lost. He knows that he's taken a wrong turning somewhere, shouldn't be amongst all these office buildings. Merde! Ahead he sees the security guards, wearing bright yellow jackets, wave him to stop. Jean Marie winds down his window.

'Where are you going, mate?' The elderly guard asks him.

'I look for Argus Trading Company,' Jean Marie replies, in his halting English.

'Argus Trading Company? Never heard of them. Sure you're in the right place?' The guard turns to his colleague, smiles as he raises his eyebrows. Bloody French!

'It says Canada Place, Canary Wharf,' Jean Marie glances at his shipping documents.

'What you got in there anyway?' The guard points to the white container.

'It's mannequins.' Jean Marie stares ahead of him, this is not going to plan. If they ask me to open the container, I'm off.

'Mannequins?' The guard studies the driver, sees the sweat on his forehead. Something's not right here, he thinks to himself. Since this morning's news about Haifa, security around Canary Wharf and London has been heightened.

'Maybe we should have a look inside, eh?' The guard smiles up at the driver.

Jean Marie makes his decision. He shoves the cab door open, catching the guard on the head, who falls to the ground. He jumps down and starts running, not knowing where. He hears the other guard shouting after him.

'Oi, you! Stop!'

But Jean Marie doesn't stop, looks around desperately for an escape route, doesn't see the woman coming out of the ground floor office. He runs straight into her, sending the young woman onto the pavement. She screams, her briefcase bursts open, papers flutter across the road. Jean Marie doesn't look back, keeps running. Then he sees a sign for the Jubilee Line. Yes, the Underground, must get there, then I'll be safe.

Sergeant Tom Phillips receives the call at 11.58 – security guard assaulted at the western entrance to Canary Wharf. Phillips takes in the scene as his car comes to a stop. The container lorry, the driver's door open, a security guard sitting on the kerbside, trying to staunch blood streaming from a head wound, another guard standing, talking into a walkie-talkie.

'What happened then?'

'Bloody driver slammed the door in my face! Ran off.' The guard moans, points down the street.

Phillips examines a nasty cut on the guard's forehead, 'Better phone for an ambulance,' Phillips looks at the other guard who nods, speaks again into his walkie-talkie. Satisfied, Phillips walks down the length of the container lorry. So, what's in this container that made the driver run off? Phillips removes his cap, scratches his head. A large brass lock confronts him at the rear of the container. He jogs back to the cab, takes the ring of keys out of the ignition. He tries several before the lock springs open. Phillips uses one of the metal lugs to pull one of the doors open.

'Christ! This is heavy!' Phillips peers into the gloomy interior, stands back and gasps, 'Bloody hell!'

Abdul Rashid stares at his silent phone, cursing his brother. What the hell is going on? I've tried this number three times now and still no reply. Rashid looks around him, cars and lorries pass him by. Well, I'm not standing here any longer, I've got better things to do. Uncle doesn't like me being away from the shop too long, he'll already be annoyed. Rashid starts walking back, still wondering about his brother. Wait until he gets back from Birmingham, I'll give him hell!

CHAPTER THIRTY TWO

6.57 am local time, CIA Headquarters, Langley.

Conference Room B is bigger than the room I was in yesterday. It has a bigger table, can seat twelve, but the grey interior is the same. I am waiting for Dick Kelly and the Director of the CIA, this will not be an easy meeting. I feel that I am being held incommunicado; there has been no contact from Forsyth or the embassy. I don't know whether that is good or bad, probably bad. I sit at the table watching the bank of muted television sets recessed into the end wall. Each set shows a different news channel, ABC, NBC, CNN and BBC World. Above the televisions, rows of digital clocks show the local time of various capital cities around the world, London, Paris, Moscow, Beijing and Tokyo. It's now four hours since the nuclear explosion in Haifa; the first grainy footage of the devastation in and around that city is being aired. As I suspected, so far it is heavily edited. Soundless anchormen and women talk over Breaking News headlines, the death toll is now estimated at three hundred thousand. Various experts are paraded in front of the screens, subtitles indicate their professions, mostly military. The Israeli Foreign Minister appears on CNN; I see tears trickle down his cheeks.

I look at London, the clock shows 12.30 am. Another Breaking News appears on BBC, something about a suspicious lorry in Canary Wharf. I get up from my chair, wander over to the far wall. I examine the television, notice that there are controls below, turn up the sound. A woman newscaster is saying that a container lorry has been stopped in Canary Wharf. My pulse quickens, not another bomb, surely? Another reporter appears saying that an office worker, on a cigarette break outside, saw everything. The cab door hitting the security officer, the driver running away, knocking over a woman, a police car then arriving. The area is now cordoned off, the police are declining to comment so far. Someone out of camera, hands the reporter a piece of paper. He quickly reads it, frowns, then says that the rumour is that the container contains a bomb, no other details as yet.

I pull a chair across and sit down in front of the televisions. I can see CNN and ABC now reporting the same story. I watch mesmerised, knowing for sure what is inside that second container. I haven't been chasing one nuclear device, there were two all the time. Why didn't I know about it? I try to think back to the beginning. Kruger only mentioned one device, Dubois said that Kohler talked about one container. If this is a second nuclear bomb, where has it come from?

Fifty minutes later. I'm back in Kelly's office, he's smoking another one of his interminable cigarettes.

'So, it's been confirmed then,' Kelly frowns at me. 'Our embassy in Grosvenor Square has just heard through a source from the British government that it was a nuclear device. Same size as the Haifa bomb.'

'Bloody hell!' I shiver at the thought if it had gone off in the middle of London.

'Your Bomb Disposal people have defused it. It should have been triggered by a phone call, probably by a mobile.' Kelly stubs out his cigarette into an overflowing ashtray.

'Why didn't it go off then?'

'That's what they're trying to figure out. Maybe, just maybe, they were very lucky. Anyway, it doesn't bear thinking about what would have happened if it had gone off, does it?'

'No, quite.' Images of Haifa come back to me.

'You understand that this raises more questions than answers?'

'Meaning?'

'You only mentioned one bomb, not two.'

275

'I realise that and I've been thinking.' I watch Kelly light another cigarette, the room is now filled with a blue haze. 'Our friend Novchenko must have sold two devices to Habtoor and Kohler didn't know about the second one.'

'Possible,' Kelly nods thoughtfully.

'Bin Laden uses one on Israel, the obvious target, and the second one on London, which by the grace of god, didn't explode.'

'Why not New York or here?'

'That, I can't figure out, unless...' I stare out of the office window.

'Unless what?' Kelly leans forward.

'Just think, Israel is in turmoil, the Middle East is like a powder keg. If the bomb had gone off in London, there would have been chaos. Not thousands dead but millions! And Britain would have been decapitated, so to speak.' I stare at Kelly, feel a chill go through me.

'And America would have lost its two staunchest allies, interesting theory, Richard.'

'Maybe there is a method to his madness after all?' I say quietly. 'Isolate America.'

'There is another thing,' Kelly pauses. 'What if Novchenko has more of these containers?'

'That's why we have to find him.'

'My Director is at the White House now, that's why you didn't meet him. Moscow is going to come under extreme pressure to find Novchenko. After Haifa and now London, they can't deny his involvement...' Kelly's phone rings, he picks it up.

'Ah, Sir Clive... yes, a close shave. What? Oh, I see... yes he's here... when? OK, you want to speak? No? I'll see to it... yes, same to you.' Kelly replaces the receiver. 'That was Sir Clive Cadogan, you know him?'

'Yes, we've crossed swords a couple of times.' Particularly over the dodgy dossier, I think bitterly. Cadogan is a Permanent Secretary to the Foreign Office, a right cold fish, no sense of humour.

'You're wanted back in London.'

'Thought that would have been Forsyth.'

'Ah, it seems that Mr Forsyth is in a spot of bother, evidently heads are going to roll.' A slight smile crosses Kelly's face.

'Mine included, probably.'

'That I wouldn't know. Anyway, I'm to book you on the BA flight tonight.'

'I want to go to Paris.' I say bluntly.

'Why?' Kelly's smile is now replaced with a frown.

'I want to see Henri's wife, that's the least I can do.'

'The world is going up in flames and you want to pass on your condolences?'

'Something like that,' I return Kelly's quizzical stare. 'Anyway, I want to meet up with Henri's people, well, the ones that are still alive,' I say bitterly. 'Kohler may still be alive and in Paris and if he is, I'm not going to find him in London, will I?'

'You know something that I don't know?' Kelly draws heavily on his cigarette.

'Of course not,' I bluster. 'Look, you'll cover for me, yes?'

Kelly slowly stubs out his cigarette, 'OK, I'll give you 48 hours, then I have to tell London. I think there's a United flight out of Dulles for Paris in the afternoon, I'll get you on it.'

'I'll need a gun.'

'What? Going to shoot Henri's wife or something?' Kelly's eyes are now hard, staring at me.

'I don't know what's going to happen in Paris. Do you?' I stare back at him.

Kelly nods slowly, 'I'll have someone meet you in Paris, OK?'

'Thanks, you'll call me about Novchenko, yes?' I stand up.

'Sure.' Kelly lights another cigarette, I'll be glad to get out of this fug.

'A couple of questions before I go.'

'Shoot.'

'When we first met, how did you know about Habtoor's involvement?'

'That's my little secret.'

'Couldn't involve Cadogan, could it?'

'What's your second question?' Kelly taps his lighter on the desk.

'And Bin Laden?'

'Harding, remember him? On his way right now to Afghanistan. If anyone can find Bin Laden, it's Harding. Let's just hope he does.'

'Yes, I suppose hope is the best word, under these circumstances.' I look back at Kelly, puffing on his cigarette, wondering if we'll ever meet again.

Kelly watches Stevens leave the room. That bastard knows something but what? Kelly thinks for a few minutes then picks up the phone and dials a number. 'Harding, you still in D.C.? Good, slight change of plan. Tyson's Corner, one hour.'

CHAPTER THIRTY THREE

Kurt Kohler wakens slowly on the morning of September 11th. He's still tired from the exertions of the night before. These two girls were good, he thinks to himself, feeling himself harden again below the silk bed sheet. He glances at his watch on the bedside table. Christ! I'm late. He slides out of bed, enters the marble bathroom. He showers first cold, then hot. He dries himself quickly, pulls on a white bathrobe. He hurries through the bedroom into the lounge, picks up his mobile from the glass coffee table. No messages, that's strange. Haller will be going nuts because I haven't phoned him. He presses Haller's number, looks around him, sees the upturned champagne bottle in a silver cooler, feels his mouth still dry. The girls have already gone, that's the arrangement.

'Hello?' A strange voice answers.

'Franz?' A puzzled Kohler replies.

'Who is this?' The voice hardens.

Kohler immediately breaks the connection. Shit! Someone has got hold of Haller's phone, that means something has happened to Haller. Kohler paces around the lounge, barefoot, cold against the marble floor. Dubois's contractors had done the renovation work and it still had cost Kohler a small fortune. But Kohler is not thinking about that, he's thinking about Haller. The coldness of his feet spreads through his whole body. He sits down slowly on the leather settee and switches on the television. The CNN channel is showing the first footage of Haifa. Kohler stares at the screen in disbelief. Jesus H Christ! The ragheads have actually done it! Haller is forgotten about as he listens to the reporter from Tel Aviv describing what has taken place in Haifa. A smile slowly spreads across Kohler's face. Well, I've done it, kept my side of the bargain. I hope Schreiber is watching television this morning, this will make him choke on his cornflakes! Kohler laughs to himself, heads for the bedroom, dresses quickly. He returns to the lounge, flicks through the news channels, Haifa is on every channel. Then he notices on BBC, the first reports about a possible bomb in London, maybe nuclear. Kohler sinks slowly onto the settee. What the…? That wasn't part of the deal, what have these fucking idiots done! Kohler sits there, mind racing, half hearing the television. This is Novchenko's doing, the bastard! Habtoor must have received two bombs, what a fool I've been! Novchenko has been working to a different agenda, I'll fix that Russian bastard! Then he's suddenly reminded about Haller. He flicks over to a French news channel, something about a car bomb near the Place de la Republique. Pictures of the dead flash across the screen; it's then that he sees Dubois's face. Kohler leans back, heart pumping, this can't be happening, this can't be fucking happening! He cries to himself. He drags his eyes back to the screen, he sees another reporter standing outside the George Cinq, something about a tourist, believed to be German, found murdered this morning, in his room. 'Franz! Oh no!' Kohler shouts at the television. He buries his head in his hands, Kohler's world is beginning to unravel.

Kohler is not sure how long he sits there, images of Haifa pass again in front of his unseeing eyes. He then finds himself in front of the drinks trolley, he picks up a crystal decanter, pours himself a large measure of brandy. He swallows it in one, feels the fiery liquid course down his throat, notices his hand holding the glass, shaking. He walks back to the settee, legs slightly unsteady. He sits down again, puts the empty glass on the table. This has to be Novchenko's work, typical gangster, rubbing out the witnesses and I'll be next if I'm not careful. So, I have to get out of Paris and for that I'll need help. He picks up his mobile and presses a number.

'Yes?' Schreiber's gruff voice replies.

'You've seen the news?' Kohler grips the phone tightly.

'Oh yes, very good Herr Kohler, pity it wasn't Tel Aviv though.'

'I gave them the bomb, I didn't choose the destination.' Kohler replies curtly.

'Maybe you should have…'

'Look, Israel will never recover from this, her neighbours may take this chance to pounce.'

'And there again they may not. This has not been thought through, has it, Herr Kohler?' Schreiber's tone sharpens.

'Don't tell me…' Kohler starts to protest.

'What about London?' Schreiber's voice cuts across him.

'That had nothing to do with me, it must be that idiot Novchenko, he…'

'You are in control of the situation, Herr Kohler?' Schreiber's voice turns to ice.

'Of course! But I…' Kohler pauses.

'Yes?'

'There have been complications,' Kohler pauses again.

'Go on.'

Kohler quickly tells him about the death of Dubois and the probable death of Haller. Schreiber is silent for a minute or two.

'Well?' Kohler breaks the silence.

'The death of Dubois does not concern us and we regret Haller's death. But the involvement of the French Security services does concern us. What did Dubois tell them?'

'I don't fucking know, he's dead!' Kohler shouts down the phone.

'No need to shout, Herr Kohler, a cool head is required at this moment.'

'OK, OK,' Kohler tries to calm down. 'You need to get me out of Paris and fast!'

'That may not be so simple, Herr Kohler, we have to protect our own interests.'

'What do you mean by that?' Kohler appears stunned.

'The situation has changed,' Schreiber pauses, 'with the involvement of the French and now possibly the German Security Service. I have to protect my own people.'

'You're hanging me out to dry, you bastard!' Kohler shouts.

'Really, Herr Kohler, if you are going to be offensive, I shall terminate this conversation now,' Schreiber's voice has an air of finality to it.

'Alright, alright! I'm sorry, I just need to get out of Paris,' Kohler pleads for the first time in his life.

'Are you in a safe place?'

'I think so,' Kohler is thinking about Dubois, did he tell them about the apartment?

'Well, stay put, I will phone you as soon as possible, I have to consult with others.' Schreiber terminates the call.

Kohler stares at the silent phone then leans back, stares at the ceiling. What have I done? Why did I get myself involved with this? Franz was right, he usually was, I should have listened to him. Suddenly Kohler sees his face staring back at him from the television screen. He turns the sound up. Paris police are looking for him in connection to a murder enquiry of one Franz Haller, his private secretary. It now dawns on Kohler that Schreiber is his only hope, but will he deliver?

CHAPTER THIRTY FOUR

Charles de Gaulle airport is not my favourite airport in the world and at 7.30 in the morning, my opinion does not change. The cool September air pervades the already cold, concrete interior. The National Guardsmen in Dulles airport are replaced in Paris by France's elite paratroopers, red berets at a jaunty angle, impassive faces below, eyeballing each passenger as they pass by. A Garuda flight from Jakarta has also landed, a long line of Muslims wait as each one is methodically questioned at passport control, I think that they will have a long wait. It would appear though that a white caucasian with a British passport has no such problems. I'm waved through with just a cursory glance, a sign of the times that we now live in, the world that has changed forever.

In the Arrivals hall, I'm not expecting someone holding up a card with Richard Stevens MI6 on it, so I make for the taxi stand outside. Just before the exit, a young man walks up to me. He's dressed in a dark blue suit, matching tie and white shirt.

'Mr Stevens?' he enquires with a slight smile, 'I'm Bob Hopkins, American Embassy, Mr Kelly asked me to meet you.' We shake hands briefly, his handshake firm, confident.

'That's very kind of him, I…'

'Please, follow me, I have a car waiting.'

Outside, there's a black Ford Explorer with black tinted windows, parked in a no waiting area, engine running. This car seems to be vehicle of choice for the CIA, as a terrorist I'd know what to look for. Two gendarmes are talking to the driver, one of them laughs, the other keeps an eye on anyone coming out of the Arrivals hall. The rear doors open automatically, we get in. The gendarmes stand back, give a mock salute, as we drive off. I notice Hopkins nodding to someone on the other side of the road. So there are minders around, just to make sure the no one slips something untoward under the car.

We join the Periphique, as usual the morning traffic is heavy. I see the Stade de France outlined against a cloudless blue sky. A few words pass between Hopkins and the driver who is also American, the car accelerates. Hopkins picks up a manila folder from the seat, opens it and starts reading. I notice that the driver has an ear piece and mike, he mumbles occasionally to somebody. I guess that there is a second car behind us, just making sure that we are not being tailed.

'You guys are not taking any chances, are you?' I look across at Hopkins.

'What?' Hopkins's head jerks up.

'The minders at the airport, the second car behind us.'

'Yeah, you could say that,' Hopkins smiles briefly.

'Am I in danger?'

'We're all in danger, Mr Stevens,' The smile vanishes, he returns to his folder. The journey is not as hectic as it was with Henri's driver but just as fast, the driver using the car's bulk to muscle its way past other cars. Speed limits are ignored, the advantage of having diplomatic plates no doubt. We exit at the Porte de Lilas and head for the Place de la Republique, the scene of Henri's murder, the reason that I am here.

'You're booked in at the Crillon, by the way,' Hopkins closes his file.

'No expense spared, eh?' I reply. The CIA's expense account is obviously greater than ours. Hopkins says nothing, just nods.

The car slows as we head down Rue de Faubourg, the traffic is backing up from the Place de la Republique. I see why as we eventually enter the square. Gendarmes are stopping every car, checking papers, looking in the car boots. As we approach, the gendarmes must see the diplomatic plates and wave us through. We exit on

Boulevard Saint Denis, on the other side I see a street cordoned off with red and white striped tape, more gendarmes, that must have been where the bomb went off.

'Heard about your friend, sorry.' Hopkins says quietly.

I say nothing, just stare out of the window, thinking about Henri and the good times that we had together, determined to find the man who caused his death, Kurt Kolher. Within minutes, we are outside the Hotel Crillon on the Place de La Concorde. As the car rolls to a stop, Hopkins leans forward, picks up a large brown envelope from the front seat and hands it to me.

'For your security,' he says simply.

I glance inside, there is a Walther PKK and silencer.

'Don't worry, it's untraceable,' he pauses, hands me a card, 'that's my number, 24/7 if you need anything.'

I thank him, get out of the already open door. The car speeds off as I enter the hotel. I pick up my room keys from a harassed-looking receptionist, more people are checking out than checking in, maybe they have decided that after Haifa and London, business is not so important, returning to loved ones and friends is. My room overlooks the Place; in other times I would stand and admire the view, but not today. Two Scorpion armoured cars straddle the central statue, gun turrets pointed towards either the Champs-Elysèes or the Louvre. More paratroopers patrol around the Place, you can feel the tension in the air. I shower and change. I bought two shirts and some underwear in Dulles airport's shopping mall. At least I feel human again. I check my mobile, still no word from Helen. Room service has delivered coffee. I drink two cups black, feel the caffeine kick in. Now to find Kohler's apartment.

I take the lift down to the hotel foyer, stand there for a few moments, just taking in my surroundings, looking for the watchers. Kelly hasn't provided all this out of the kindness of his heart. He's guessed that I know something, just wants me to lead him to whatever it is. The foyer is too crowded to pick out any of his people, mostly they are all business suits, the ocassional smartly dressed woman. I pass the Crillon Bar, it hasn't opened yet. Henri and I spent a few late nights there, drinking Irish coffees, supposed to be the best in France even in Europe. After the second one I didn't disagree. The other attractions were the beautiful women that frequented the bar at night. Henri would gaze admiringly as they passed him by. He used to say, 'I can look but I cannot touch,' and give that throaty laugh. I miss that laugh. Anyway, time to move on.

I walk outside, pass the luxury cars parked alongside the entrance. I stop to admire a Ferrari, quickly turn around, don't see anyone behind me. I would guess that there are about six watchers, two inside, two outside, the other two as back up, probably in a car. I turn eastwards, cross the Place de la Concorde and walk down the Rue de Rivoli towards the Louvre. As I pass the expensive art and antique shops on my left, I try Henri's home number but there's no reply, maybe his wife has gone to her parents in Normandy. I stop and pretend to admire an overpriced piece of modern art, look back up the street, seeing if I recognise anyone from the hotel lobby. A group of Japanese tourists pass me, little Rising Sun flags held high, I fall in behind them. I've decided that if some of the Americans are using a car, I'll even up the odds. As the Japanese cross over to the Louvre, I quickly enter the Metro station. Inside, I buy a carnet of tickets and take the first train. The first stop is Les Halles, I get out, watch who gets out with me, still I don't recognise anybody. Either they're bloody good or I'm getting too old for this. I take the next train, ten minutes later I'm crossing the Place de la Republique. It's beginning to get warm, I feel the perspiration on the back of my shirt under my jacket. My briefcase feels heavy, but I don't mind, inside is my gun. I approach the street where

Henri's driver took me, was that only two days ago? Stony-faced gendarmes stand in front of steel barriers. Beyond, I can see a large white tent in the middle of the street, that must have been where the bomb went off. The trees around have been shredded, like some First World War scene. Several of the buildings look badly damaged, very few windows are intact, that must have been some explosion. There are several bouquets of flowers propped up against the barriers. I see a young girl selling red roses, buy one and lay it gently amongst the rest. I bow my head, remember Henri, feel my eyes moisten. I find a cafe nearby, take off my jacket, order a Badoit, sit under an umbrella. I feel better after drinking the ice cold fizzy water. I glance to my left, there's a newsagent next door, see the headline of the Figaro 'Qui est le prochain?' above a photograph of what is left of Haifa. Who is next? A very good question. I take out my street map of Paris, courtesy of the hotel, and look for Kohler's address. Henri said it was on the Left Bank but the printing is so small, maybe I need glasses. And then I see it, just off the Rue du Bac, between the 6th and 7th Arrondissements.

Rue de Tabac is about halfway down Rue du Bac. I've taken the Metro here, changed trains twice, but still can't pick out any followers. As I cross the street, I forget that I'm in France and look right instead of left. A cyclist in a bright pink T-Mobile vest almost knocks me down. I hear a shouted 'Merde!' as he continues on, fist shaken in the air. I enter Rue de Tabac; on the left is an elegant row of four-storey townhouses, sandstone facades recently cleaned. As I walk down, I see shiny black painted entrance doors, brilliant white window frames, everything looks very new. On the other side of the street is a rather strange-looking building. It looks like a warehouse and it too seems to have been recently renovated. A large white canopy projects from the entrance. I can see gold lettering on one of the windows, Hotel de Tabac.

Halfway down, I stop at number six, opposite the hotel entrance. I look at the brass nameplates, all are French except for the top right apartment which is blank, that must be Kohler's. I also see the security camera, above the entrance door, eyeing me up and down. I turn quickly, cross the street and enter the hotel. The foyer is double-storied, large wooden beams criss-cross the ceiling. I find out later that this used to be one of the drying halls, you can still smell the tobacco in the air. An elegant-looking man, in a black suit, stands behind the reception desk, studies me as I approach.

'Monsieur?' He enquires as he takes in my crumpled jacket, sweat-covered shirt.

'I would like a room, one night only,' I reply in my best French.

'I see,' he pauses, studies a computer screen, 'I have one room at the front and one at the rear, the rear one has a very nice view of the garden, it's...'

'I'll take the one at the front,' I interrupt quickly.

'As you wish,' he types something into the computer, 'and your luggage?'

'Held up at the airport,' I shrug my shoulders.

'Quite, that will be four hundred euros for the one night,' he smiles faintly, no doubt thinking that I will now turn on my heels.

But I call his bluff, take out four one hundred euro notes and place them on the desk. I fill out the reservation form, giving the name of Kelly. I place another one hundred euro note in front of him, saying that I'm expecting a friend and do not wish to be disturbed. The money is swept up into a jacket pocket, private assignations are bread money for Paris hoteliers.

My room is almost directly over the entrance canopy, on the same level as Kohler's apartment. I'd learnt from the television in my room at the Crillon about the death of Franz Haller and that the police were looking for Kurt Kohler. I'm hoping, praying, that Kohler is in his apartment. Without Haller, he'll need help to get out of

Paris, maybe his Nazi friends are going to help. I pull up a chair, settle down in front of the window, stare across at the drawn curtains. If he's not there, then I've wasted a lot of time and effort, and I'm not sure what to do next. Then I see the curtains move. Bingo! He's there!

Kohler looks out from a gap between the curtains across at the hotel entrance. He'd watched the man approach his front door, staring at the nameplates then entering the hotel. Maybe just a stupid lost tourist, but you can't be too careful. He closes the curtains, paces the lounge floor. He's been stuck in his apartment for 48 hours now and he's not happy. There have been several acrimonious phone calls with Schreiber, who's supposed to phone back confirming that Kohler will be picked up tonight. He wanders into the kitchen, looks in the fridge. He's tired of a diet of smoked salmon and caviar, six eggs stare back at him. How do you make an omelette? His culinary thoughts are disturbed by the phone ringing.

'Yes?'

'There will be a black Mercedes 600, Hamburg plates, waiting at the end of your street at 11.30 tonight, be there.' Schreiber hangs up.

Cheeky bastard! Kohler fumes. Anyway, at last I'm getting out of here, I'll deal with Schreiber when I get back to Germany. He looks back at the fridge, to hell with food, it's time for champagne!

Darkness falls. I see lights come on in Kohler's apartment, the rest of the building is in darkness. Now is the time to act, I can't wait any longer. I open my briefcase, take out the Walther PKK and fit the silencer, slip on my jacket, close the case. In the foyer, two loud Americans are checking in, a pretty receptionist doesn't see me leave. Across the street, I stand in front of number six and press the bell for Kohler's apartment.

'Ja?' A guttural German voice answers.

'Herr Kohler, I'm Richard Stevens, British Intelligence, we need to talk.'

'I'm sorry,' the reply is in stilted English, 'you must have the wrong apartment.'

'Herr Kohler, I know you are in there, Dubois gave me your address.'

There's a long pause then, 'I'm sorry, we have nothing to discuss.'

'Look Kohler, I know about Novchenko, about the containers.'

'I don't know what you're talking about, now if you don't mind....'

'I do mind and I'm tired standing here. If you don't open up, I'll have the gendarmes around here in five minutes and they'll break the door down!'

Again a pause, 'Very well, you may come up.'

Inside the apartment, Kohler looks at Steven's face on the security monitor. He was the man here looking at the entrance this afternoon! British Intelligence? What the hell do they want? And Dubois! That little French prick! I knew he'd talk! Kohler's mind is racing, I need a weapon. Haller said that I should always carry a gun but I never needed one, I had Haller. He hurries into the kitchen, looks around, sees the pristine set of kitchen knives. He picks one, feels the weight in his hand, perfect! He retraces his steps, places the knife between two decanters on the drinks trolley. He looks at his watch, two hours before the car arrives. I have to stall this Englishman or kill him.

The black painted door opens automatically. I enter a large foyer, a marble staircase spirals upwards. At the fourth floor, I approach the door to Kohler's apartment, again it opens automatically. Beyond the lobby, I see Kohler standing in the middle of a large lounge. He's taller than I expected and quite muscular, a man who works out obviously. He's wearing an open-necked white shirt, black trousers, black patent shoes and stands there, hands on hips, legs apart, confident, arrogant.

'And so, what do we have to discuss, Herr…?' Kohler makes a show of inspecting perfectly manicured fingernails.

'Stevens, British Intelligence,' I reply as I approach him.

'Ah yes, British Intelligence, now what do they have to do with me?' He looks at me with feigned indifference.

'Haifa,' I say simply, looking for some kind of reaction but there's nothing, his face like a blank canvas.

'Haifa? Terrible, watched it on the television, couldn't believe it,' Kohler pauses, 'but that has nothing to do with me, Herr… Stevens.' The blank canvas is replaced with a smirk.

'Not according to your friend Dubois.'

'Ha! Dubois was a builder, he was…' The smirk becomes a smile.

'Your friend and before he was killed, he told us everything about Novchenko, the Red Star container.'

'Yes, I'll admit he was my friend but these other names mean nothing to me.' Kohler sits down on a black leather settee. 'His death came as a great shock to me.' He shakes his head, at least the smile has disappeared.

'Why would someone blow up a builder, Herr Kohler?' I sit down opposite him in a matching armchair, rest my briefcase on my knees.

'That is for the police to find out,' Kohler says sharply.

'And Haller?' I keep probing.

'Another tragedy, a robbery gone wrong, who knows?' Kohler shrugs his shoulders, his face now impassive again.

I say nothing for a few moments, taking in my surroundings. The colour scheme of the room is like Kohler, all white and black. White walls and ceiling. Black furniture rests on a white marble floor. The only colour comes from several paintings of vivid red slashes. I look back at Kohler, staring at me.

'Don't you find it extraordinary that your closest associate and closest friend are murdered on the same day?' I finally say.

'If you are looking for coincidence, Herr Stevens, I don't believe in it, I only believe in fate,' Kolher pauses, starts to get up from the settee.

'Several months ago, I met Ernst Kruger.'

'Kruger?' Kohler sits down again, maybe a look of uncertainty in his eyes for the first time.

'Yes, Kruger, used to be an officer in the Stasi. He'd come to England to meet Baxter, an old friend of mine. Kruger told me his reasons for coming to England, to expose a plot by neo-Nazis to buy a nuclear bomb.'

'Preposterous nonsense! Ha, and where did this Kruger get this rubbish from?' Kohler rolls his eyes to the ceiling.

'From a friend in German Intelligence, Otto Pieck,' I look at Kohler, he's staring at me, that look of uncertainty again. 'And Pieck was murdered, and regrettably so was Kruger, before he could tell me the destination of the bomb, Israel. My friend Baxter was also murdered. It would seem that anyone who comes close to you, Herr Kohler, winds up dead and we haven't discussed Haifa yet.' I lean back, hands resting on my briefcase, ready, just in case. Kohler says nothing, stares straight ahead. He's a cold fish, completely devoid of emotion, all these people dead, no guilt, not one iota. 'How much did you pay Novchenko for the bomb?'

'What? More nonsense!' Kohler shakes his head. 'Look I met Novchenko on several occasions. He had a villa built in Portugal, he was very rich, we discussed some new building projects, that was it.' Suddenly Kohler stands up, glances at his watch, walks across to the window, parts the curtains, looks outside. 'Anyway, Herr Stevens, I have a busy schedule,' he continues to stare outside. 'You've wasted enough of my time with this ridiculous story.' He turns to face me. 'Just supposing any of this was true, where's the proof, eh? It would appear that your er... witnesses are all dead, Pieck, Kruger, Dubois and where's Novchenko? Really Stevens you'll have to do better than this,' Kohler smiles across the room at me.

It's then that I open my briefcase, take out my gun and point it at him.

'Ah, of course! You're armed, how careless of me. I should have frisked you, isn't that the term?' Kohler doesn't seem surprised nor, more worryingly, concerned about having a gun pointed at him. That look out the window, someone is coming for him, and then I realise the obvious, that ever since I stepped foot inside this apartment, one of us is not going to leave here alive.

Kohler strides across the lounge, stops in front of one of the red slash paintings.

'I paid a lot of money for this, but he's a good painter, I'll double my money in a few years,' he stands there staring. 'How much do you want, Stevens?'

'What?' I keep my gun trained on Kohler's back.

'How much money?' Kohler spins around, 'One million, two million? I have deep pockets, you know.' The smirk has returned.

'It's not about money,' I say quietly.

'It's always about money, you fool! The world goes around because of money...'

'It's about justice!' I shout back at Kohler.

'Justice? Ha! A fool and an idealist! A deadly combination,' Kohler laughs to himself, walks slowly towards a drinks trolley. 'A car will be picking me up shortly, I'll be in Germany in four hours.' He stops, his back towards me.

'What about Haller? The police?'

'Taken care of,' he pours himself a drink. 'You see, I left the hotel before midnight on the 10th, had to return urgently to Berlin on business.' There's a mirror above the trolley, I can see Kohler's face staring back at me. 'I have the witnesses to prove it and you have none,' he says with a snarl.

It's the speed of Kohler that surprises me, he whirls around, throws something. In a split second I see a flash of steel, something punches into my left shoulder. Christ it hurts! Kohler dives to his left, I see a leg, fire once, think I've missed him, and then I hear a scream. I can see Kohler's left shoe, twitching, then it disappears behind the settee. I look at my shoulder, a kitchen knife slowly eases out of my jacket and clatters onto the floor. I feel inside my jacket, my shirt is wet, I'm cut but not deeply, the knife hit my shoulder bone, it could have been worse. I hear Kohler, dragging his body across the floor, cursing and moaning. I stand up rather shakily, see Kohler crawling towards the kitchen, dragging his left leg, a smear of red on the floor behind him. I place myself between the kitchen door and Kohler.

'Run out of knives, have we?' I sit down on my haunches, point the gun in Kohler's face.

'You shot me, you fucking shot me!' Kohler screams at me, spittle runs down his chin. 'I need a doctor, get me a doctor, I'll pay anything, anything.'

'The car bomb which killed Dubois also killed a very good friend of mine,' I keep the gun pointed at Kohler's left eye.

'I had nothing to do with that!' Kohler starts pleading. How different from that arrogant sonofabitch a few minutes ago.

'Not personally, I suppose. We think Novchenko planted the bomb, but you employed Novchenko.'

'Not to blow up your friend! Please I…'

'No, but to blow up Haifa, you bastard! Do you know how many have died? Three hundred thousand innocent civilians and counting,' I feel my hand starting to shake, shock is setting in.

'So what, they were Jews, fucking Jews, I wish they'd killed the whole fucking lot!' Kohler snarls, eyes defiant.

294

And that's when I blow his brains out. I ease myself up slowly, look down at what's left of Kohler's head, see the white floor turning red. I walk into the kitchen, put the gun inside my jacket pocket, wash the blood from my hands, rinse my face. My shoulder is now beginning to really hurt, must find something for it. I enter the bedroom, the bathroom is about the size of my flat. There is an array of bottles, uppers, downers, even Viagra. I find some paracetamol, swallow three with a glass of water, carefully clean my prints from the glass. Looking in the mirror, my face is pale but fortunately I don't seem to be losing much blood. I was lucky, very lucky. I retrace my steps, find myself in Kohler's bedroom. The bed is unmade, clothes are strewn on the floor, a half-filled suitcase lies beside the door. I see the fitted wardrobe along one whole wall. It's filled with suits, more than I've owned in a whole lifetime. I walk down the line of beautifully cut material in blues and greys, at the end there's one in black. I pull the hangers back and there is a complete Nazi uniform, jacket, trousers, jackboots and cap, the Death's Head face staring at me, eyeless. Below, there is an expensive Canon Reflex camera and tripod, alongside what looks like a shoe box. I bend down, use a handkerchief to lift off the lid. Kohler's face leers at me from a photograph, he's having sex with a young girl. I feel sick, there are dozens of photographs of Kohler in different sexual poses, all with young girls, some very young. What perverted mind could have done this? I pick up the box and empty the photographs over the bed, that should give the police something to think about. At the last moment, I pick out two of the more offensive photos and slip them into my jacket pocket.

I re-enter the lounge, don't even bother looking at that piece of shit lying on the floor, pick up my briefcase and head for the door. I'm just about to leave when something about the photographs makes me stop. Just to the left of the door is a small wall panel, I open it. Inside

295

is a television monitor, I can see the street from here and as I suspected, there's a video recorder. I press the eject button and pocket the tape. Now to get the hell out of here.

I arrive at street level, it appears deserted, even the lights of the hotel are dimmed. I hurry towards Rue du Bac. Suddenly a figure appears from a darkened doorway, I reach for my gun.

'Well?' The disembodied voice enquires.

'Harding! What the hell are you doing here?' I say with more relief than shock as I see him step towards me.

'Kelly thought that you might need some help,' he looks up at the building behind me, 'and Kohler?'

'He's dead, I killed him,' I suddenly feel very tired.

'You OK?'

'The bastard threw a knife at me,' my hand goes to my shoulder.

'Come on, I've a car waiting, we'll get you fixed up.'

I follow Harding to another black Ford Explorer waiting at the corner of Rue de Tabac. I'm about to step in when I notice the black Mercedes parked further down the street, I can make out the glow of a cigarette behind the steering wheel.

'Friends of yours?' I turn to Harding.

'Nope, they turned up about fifteen minutes ago,' Harding shrugs.

'I bet they've come to pick up Kohler.'

'Well, they'll have a long fucking wait then, won't they? Come on let's go.'

As we speed through Paris, Harding takes out a first aid box and dresses my wound, 'You were lucky, another two inches and you would have been a stuck pig.'

I say nothing, slip on my shirt and jacket. 'What would have happened if Kohler had come out instead of me?' I turn to look at Harding.

'He wouldn't have got very far,' Harding stares out of the window.

'I could have been killed, you know.'

'Kelly had great faith in you, said you had balls and he was right.' Harding turns, smiles slightly.

'He knew I was coming after Kohler, didn't he?'

'Well, he didn't believe the grieving widow business, decided to let you run with it. Said you deserved to be in at the kill, so to speak.' Harding stares out of the window again, 'We were just along for the ride.'

'I didn't pick out your people, they were good.'

'Well, if it's any comfort, they thought you were pretty good, especially on the Metro, you made them earn their money,' Harding chuckles to himself.

'But the Rue du Bac?'

'The guy on the bike, remember?'

'He almost killed me!'

'Christ, you almost killed him!'

'The two Americans in the hotel, yes?'

'Yeah, bit loud, weren't they? Wait till Kelly finds out about his name in the register, ha!' Harding's smile slowly fades, 'And now?'

'I have to go back to London, face my masters, who are not going to be well pleased,' It's my turn to stare out of the window.

'Well, I'll drop you off at the Crillon, get some rest. I'll phone first thing, get you on the first flight out of here.'

'What about Kohler?'

'We'll let him rot for a few hours, then there will be an anonymous phone call to the police. Don't worry, you'll be long gone.'

'Thanks, Harding, you know, for everything that you've done.'

'Don't mention it, pal, we're on the same side aren't we?'

'Yes, we're on the same side,' I return Harding's smile. But I don't tell him about the photographs. Well, we don't need to tell each other everything, do we?

CHAPTER THIRTY FIVE

The first thing that I notice about Heathrow is the amount of soldiers on duty, in twos or threes, sometimes accompanying armed policemen wearing black bulletproof vests. They all look serious, intent. There's tension in the air, as if something is about to happen. Harding kept his word, his car picked me up from the Crillon at dawn, I managed to get the first British Airways flight out. I phoned Bradbury, told him to have me picked up from Heathrow, he gabbles on about me being in trouble, so what else is new? I shut Bradbury up, tell him that I must meet Cadogan this morning. My shoulder is stiff but at least the pain has lessened. I'm met by a government chauffeur, maybe Cadogan's, he doesn't introduce himself.

We leave the airport in a dark green Jaguar, squeeze through a checkpoint of two Saladin armoured cars, more grim-looking soldiers. We head into London, but the going is painfully slow. I then see why. Another checkpoint, more armoured cars and soldiers. A show of force, but against whom?

We eventually reach Whitehall, draw up in front of a pale grey edifice, recently cleaned. The driver points to a discreet, old oak door.

'Second floor, you're expected.' The first and last words spoken by my driver.

I ease myself out of the Jaguar, feel the first drops of rain from a leaden sky. As I approach the door slowly swings open, I'm being watched. I enter a dimly-lit hallway, climb stone-flagged stairs, the lighting is not much better. I open another oak door on the second-floor landing, enter a brightly lit corridor, a man in a dark grey pinstripe suit is waiting for me.

'I'm Symonds, Sir Clive Cadogan is waiting.' His words are clipped, definitely public school.

We proceed down the corridor, the carpet, deep red, is thick and deadens any noise. It is quite eerie, as there is no sound, maybe just the gentle hum of machinery somewhere. Halfway down, we stop, another oak door. Symonds knocks gently, opens the door. I step inside a large room; whoever designed the interior likes oak, floor, walls and ceiling. Various portraits of stern-looking men stare down at me. Maybe they're Cadogan's ancestors. If power has a smell, then its scent emanates from this room. The man himself sits behind a large desk, he gives me a casual wave, points to a high-backed chair opposite him. I sit down, watch Cadogan as he continues writing. He looks older since we last met but still perfectly groomed. Swept back silver hair, pale complexion, gold-rimmed spectacles perched on the end of an aquiline nose. Impeccably cut dark grey suit, some regimental tie contrasting against a white silk shirt. I look at the portrait hanging above him, yes, definitely his father. Cadogan finally stops writing, signs off with a flourish, lays down his gold pen. He looks up, leans back in his red leather armchair, focuses pale blue eyes on me.

'You're late, where the hell have you been?' No welcome back, no nice to see you again. Typical Cadogan, economical with words.

'Paris,' I say simply.

'Paris! You were told to report back here, really Stevens, you…'

'Kohler is dead,' I cut him off in mid sentence.

'What?' Cadogan's eyes narrow.

'He's dead, I shot him.'

'You what? Are you mad?' Cadogan splutters.

'No, just doing the world a favour.' I'm savouring this, watching Cadogan's reaction, putting him off balance.

'You are mad,' Cadogan says slowly, eyeing his desk phone nervously, maybe he thinks he needs some help. 'You just can't go around shooting people, you need authority…'

'I am licensed to kill.' I smile at Cadogan.

'You're not bloody James Bond, Stevens, and you can wipe that smile off your face,' Cadogan sits back in his chair, adjusts his glasses, tries to regain control of the situation. 'I'll give you five minutes to tell me what happened. It had better be good, otherwise I shall personally see that you end up in jail and they'll throw away the key!'

And so I tell him the whole sorry tale. About Dubois, Novchenko and Kohler, the death of my friend Henri. 'So, you see, Kohler was key to the whole thing, it was his idea, his baby,' I pause for a moment. 'Kohler was right about one thing though, all the witnesses wound up dead.'

'And so you decided to be judge and jury,' Cadogan leans forward, eyes now icy blue.

'Look, there was a car waiting in Paris to take Kohler back to Germany. Once he was back there, we couldn't have touched him. A man in his position could hire the best lawyers, we'd have been laughed out of court.'

'But to kill him?'

'If I hadn't done it, the Americans would have.' I meet Cadogan's stare.

'The Americans?' Cadogan's eyes narrow to slits.

'Let's just say that they helped me, provided backup. They'll tip-off the police, Kohler's body should be found today.'

'You don't work for the Americans, Stevens, you work for us, but for how much longer is a matter of debate,' Cadogan straightens his cuffs. It may be my imagination, but the temperature in the room seems to have suddenly dropped.

'I have no regrets about what I did.' I take the two photographs from my jacket and carefully place them on the desk in front of Cadogan. He looks down, picks them up.

'What the hell! Oh my God.' Cadogan's eyes widen, he drops the photgraphs as if they're radioactive.

300

'You see, the once future chancellor of Germany was also nothing more than a dirty little paedophile. As I said, I think I did the world a favour.'

Cadogan says nothing, stares disbelieving at Kohler's sexual antics. He pushes the photographs towards me, as though their proximity will contaminate him.

'This whole affair is a bloody mess,' Cadogan finally says.

'At least the bomb in London didn't go off.'

'I bet the people of Haifa would have wished the same.' Cadogan's words are slow and precise.

'I don't think we could have stopped it.' I stare back at Cadogan, who averts his eyes, studies something behind me.

'Meaning?' He looks back at me.

'I wasn't allowed to talk to the Israelis, the Germans or the Americans. If I had, events may have turned out differently.' I sit back, fold my arms. One thing that I am not doing is to take the blame for this fine mess, as Cadogan calls it. I'm also not having Haifa on my conscience.

'You weren't allowed to?'

'Mr Forsyth's instructions. He said that he himself would deal with the Israelis and the Americans. The Germans were off-limits because of what Kruger had told me.'

'Forsyth gives a different story, Stevens.'

'He would, wouldn't he?'

'Perhaps, but we'll come to Forsyth's role in all this later.' Cadogan picks up the gold pen, toys with it between his long fingers. 'If any of this is made public, there will be hell to pay. The Israelis will be apoplectic about being kept in the dark.' Cadogan studies his pen. 'And what about our American friends?'

'Pacified. I think I've got Kelly onside. He did sanction the hit on Kohler.'

'Ah yes, Kelly, good man,' A faint smile appears.

'You know him, don't you?' A stab in the dark.

'We have met, on occasion.'

'Did you tell him about Habtoor?'

'What?' Cadogan looks up sharply, his pen drops to the desk. 'Just remember, Stevens, I'm the one asking the questions.' Cadogan makes a show of straightening his jacket cuffs.

At least I've found out Kelly's source. But why didn't Cadogan tell him about Kohler?

'And Kohler?' Time to twist the knife.

'What about Kohler?'

'Why weren't the Americans told about Kohler? It's a simple question.'

'See, that's your problem, Stevens. You are never aware of the politics of the situation.' Cadogan sighs as though this is all frightfully boring.

'The politics?' I feel my anger rising.

'Kohler could have been the next German chancellor. And what did we have to go on? The musings of some old German? What would have happened if it had all been untrue? Anglo-German relations would have hit rock-bottom, huh!' Cadogan glances again at the photographs. 'Of course we didn't know about his sexual preferences then.'

'So because of politics, as you put it, three hundred thousand are lying dead in Haifa!' I answer angrily.

'No need to raise your voice, Stevens,' Cadogan replies, eyebrows raised. 'That's why none of this is to be made public, understand?' His voice now more like a hiss.

I say nothing, just stare back at him, despising him for what he is. But I smile inwardly for I've decided not to tell him about the other photographs, the ones now lying on Kohler's bed. When the police finally find them, there's going to be a right royal scandal, some important people are going to be very embarrassed, maybe even our Prime Minister. Cadogan is going to have his hands full, serves the bastard right!

'I want your report of this affair on my desk tomorrow, for my eyes only.' Cadogan settles back in his chair, thinking he's back in control.

'Forsyth should be sacked, you know.'

'Mr Forsyth is not your concern,' Cadogan pauses. 'It's not feasible to sack him now, the press would have a field day, even those idiots can put two and two together. Maybe in six months or so, given a peerage, kicked upstairs.' Cadogan stares at the ceiling.

'And his replacement?'

'Not you, Stevens, oh no, not you.' That faint smile reappears. 'Digsby, perhaps.'

'Digsby!' I'm incredulous. 'He's a pen pusher!'

'I rather liken him to a safe pair of hands,' Cadogan nods to himself, satisfied with his assessment.

'And me?'

'We'll need to read your report first.'

'You can have my resignation now.'

'I don't think so, not yet anyway. You see there is some unfinished business.'

'Which is?'

'The Bomb Disposal team's intial report indicates that the detonator should have been triggered by a mobile phone call.'

'But the call wasn't made, was it? Otherwise you and this building wouldn't be here.' My turn to smile.

'How droll, Stevens,' Cadogan doesn't return my smile. 'But the call may have been sent. You see, we've picked up the lorry on CCTV. It came in by the Blackwall Tunnel and as you may know, there are dead spots in the tunnel for receiving calls. The tunnel may have saved us.'

'Which means we have a suicide bomber on the loose?'

'Precisely, or a sleeper unit. And if they are prepared to use a nuclear bomb, what else are they prepared to do, eh?'

'But this is internal security, MI5's area.'

'Quite, but with your knowledge, you may be useful to them, call it a secondment.'

'I'll have to consider it.' I sit there thinking. If what Cadogan has said is true, then we are still in serious danger.

'Please do, it would be nice to have closure…'

'What about Novchenko?'

'Ah, the Russian. We and the Americans are talking to Moscow, Putin is under a lot of pressure. We'll assist in any way we can, but it's basically their show.'

'I'd like to help.'

'Noted, but first your report, on my desk tomorrow, first thing.' Cadogan picks up a file from his desk, starts to flick through it. 'By the way, just keep to the facts, won't you? Don't want any of your personal opinions, like for instance on the Iraq dossier.' Cadogan's fixed smile is glacial.

'Of course, Sir Clive, mustn't land you in the shit, must we?' Before he can reply, I'm out of my chair and out of the room. I hear a strangled epithet behind me. Symonds is waiting for me.

'This way, please,' he points down the corridor.

'No thanks, I'll use the stairs. I had to come in by the tradesman entrance and I'll leave by it.' I leave Symonds open-mouthed. For some reason I feel a lot better.

CHAPTER THIRTY SIX

Two months after 11th September.

Andrei Novchenko paces around his study. He looks at his watch again, they should be back by now. He passes the large mirror on the wall and examines his face again. Not bad, most of the scars have healed. He touches his cheek, the skin is still a bit tight. The surgeon has said that it will soften in the next month or two. Novchenko is pleased with the results, thinks he looks younger, he's even lost some weight. He hears a soft knock on the study door and returns to his seat behind the desk.

'Come,' he says and picks up a cigar in front of him.

Feodor and Dmitri enter. Their T-shirts and jeans are muddy, sweat glistens on their faces and arms.

'Mission accomplished, I trust?' Novchenko lights the tip of his cigar.

'Yes, Andrei, no problems.' Feodor leans across the desk and hands him a piece of paper, there are several numbers written on it.

'Good, why don't you shower and change. Let's say, meet on the verandah in an hour. Champagne tonight, you've both done well!'

After Feodor and Dmitri have left, Novchenko sits there, puffing on his cigar, thinking about the last two months. He couldn't believe it when he'd woken up in his hospital bed, the terrible events in Haifa and the attempt on London. He'd raged at Feodor about that double-crossing motherfucker Bin Laden, the device was not to be used in Europe. But over the next couple of weeks, his mood had changed. He had come to the conclusion that, in fact, Bin Laden had been quite brilliant. Instead of attacking America, he had attacked and disabled a close ally.

And so, Andrei Novchenko, now Alonso Xavier was putting his affairs in order. He knew that, eventually, the remaining Intelligence services around the world may find out about the containers, someone always talked. He'd also heard from Moscow, that the Berkut, Russia's elite police force, were becoming very aggressive. They were no longer going after the small fry, they wanted the leaders of the Mafia. Putin didn't want one of these devices in his backyard.

Novchenko had decided to dispose of the other three containers. He'd seen the destruction that one had caused, nobody was going to get their hands on the other three. Another one in Europe, now that would be bad for business.

But how?

It had been quite simple, really. Bury them. Feodor had arranged the hire of the excavator and crane, the transporter was already on site. Feodor, his cousin and Dmitri had taken the vehicles and the containers, one by one, about thirty kilometres north, just to where the jungle starts. They'd cleared the area, excavated a large pit and buried the containers. It had taken them three days, but within six months, the jungle would reclaim the land, just as if no one had been there. Nobody would know.

Novchenko lifts the piece of paper from the desk. He looks at the printed numbers, the GPS location of the containers. He takes his lighter and sets the piece of paper alight. He drops the ashes into the ashtray. There, even I don't know. He looks at his watch, time for drinks, his favourite time of day. Sitting on the verandah, watching the setting sun, sipping vintage champagne. Life couldn't be better!

Dmitri comes out of the shower. He quickly dries himself and slips on a new pair of jeans and cotton shirt. He crosses the cool, tiled floor and picks up his muddied jeans. He takes a piece of paper out from the back pocket. He looks at the numbers, the same ones given to Novchenko. He smiles to himself as he folds the piece of paper, puts it back into his pocket. He looks at himself in the mirror, not bad, maybe put on a bit too much weight recently. But, what is there to do here? The ranch is situated in a small clearing, surrounded by miles, hundreds of miles of fucking jungle! At least there is a pool where he can exercise but it's just so boring already. He misses Russia, the cut and thrust of the drugs business. He tries not to think about that bomb and what happened in Israel. He has no particular feelings about the Jews, but what was Novchenko thinking about? He must have known something like this would happen. And what about London? That really doesn't bear thinking about. Christ, I've got friends living in London!

The thought of his friends depresses him further. Dmitri slowly buttons up his shirt. Is this my life from now on, stuck in the middle of nowhere? I have to get out of here, I have to persuade Andrei to let me leave. And what about Andrei himself? It's so difficult to get used to, that face, the different hair, even his body now looks different. It's like talking to someone that I don't even know.

Dmitri zips up his jeans. Ha, the only entertainment is at the weekends when high-class hookers are flown in from Rio. But Dmitri prefers blondes, thinks about Svetlana in Portugal, remembers her lithe tanned body. His erotic thought are interrupted by his mobile ringing.

'Yes?'

'Dmitri, how are you?'

'Who is this?'

'Voronov.' The voice is indistinct, there's an echo on the line.

'Voronov? Major Voronov?' Dmitri suddenly feels cold, despite the warmth of the room.

'It's Colonel Voronov now. I've been assigned to the Berkut.'

'How did you get my number?' Dmitri sits down slowly on the bed. The Berkut, shit!

'Ah well, you see I've got Viktor Krasny in front of me. He's a stubborn man, you know. But after we broke his left leg, then his right leg, he gave me your number. They always do.' Voronov laughs.

'What do you want?' Dmitri shivers slightly.

'Your boss has been a naughty boy, Dmitri. The Kremlin are not amused, in fact they're seriously pissed off.' The laughter gone, replaced by chill words.

'I had nothing to do with it, it was all Novchenko's idea,' Dmitri tries to protest, 'I…'

'Well then, you have nothing to fear, have you, dear boy? You see it's Novchenko we want.'

'What do you mean?'

'Don't be stupid! We want Novchenko, dead or alive, preferably dead!'

'How do you know where he is?' Dmitri feels himself start to sweat.

'Simple, after I broke Krasny's left arm, he told me about the ranch in Brazil.'

'You know about that?'

'Oh yes, and the shipping details, even the address of the ranch. How careless, Dmitri, you've gone soft, forgotten your training.'

Dmitri holds his head in his hands. Novchenko had told him to use a different shipping agent from Rio to the ranch, but Krasny said that he would arrange everything. Christ! This is all my fault.

'So, I'm phoning you because of our former friendship, Dmitri. You were a good soldier, could have been very good. But you chose another life. I am, however, prepared to give you a chance.'

'What do you mean?'

'We have Spesnatz Commandos arriving in Rio tomorrow, at midday. Their destination is, of course, the ranch. They have been instructed not to take any prisoners, do you understand?'

'Yes.'

'Good, so here is my offer. You take care of Novchenko by tomorrow midday and the rest of you will be spared.'

'You want me to kill Novchenko?'

'That is the general idea.'

'I can't, he's like an uncle to me,'

'Then think of your father! Do you want to see him shot down like a dog!'

'No, no, of course not.'

'Then do as I say! You and your father will be allowed to return to Russia. I can't promise you anything, but at least you'll live.'

Dmitri looks at his now-silent phone. He lays it on the bed beside him, notices that his hand is shaking. He leans forward, buries his head in his hands, thinking furiously. What am I to do? He recaps the phone call in his head. Voronov didn't mention the other containers. But maybe he wouldn't, because even Krasny didn't know what was in them. I may have an insurance policy, a life insurance policy. He takes out the piece of paper again, looks at the numbers, but he now knows them all by heart. He quickly gets up, crosses to the bathroom. He stands in front of the toilet, tears the paper in shreds, drops them into the bowl, flushes the toilet.

He picks up his watch, looks at the second hand ticking around. Time for drinks. Time to kill my uncle.

He hears Novchenko's laughter before he sees him. He climbs the stone steps to the terrace, sees his father sitting beside Novchenko. Both are drinking champagne, Novchenko laughs again. Better to die happy, Dmitri thinks briefly. As he approaches, his father turns, gives him a quzzical look, doesn't see the Makharov pistol until too late.

'Dmitri! What the…?' Feodor's shout is like a screech

Dmitri aims at the base of Novchenko's head, fires once, there's a soft phut from the silencer. Novchenko

309

pitches forward out of his seat, knocks over the tray of drinks, there's a dull thud as his body hits the tiled terrace floor. His body twitches once, twice, then is still. Dark red blood from the gunshot wound pools on the terracotta. Feodor is half out of his chair, he slowly sinks back in disbelief, his crystal glass drops and shatters.

'What… what have you just done, Dmitri?' Feodor finally says, his tanned face now ashen.

'I'm sorry, Father,' Dmitri looks at Novchenko then his pistol, shakes his head. ' Voronov, remember him? He called me an hour ago, the Berkut know where we are, know where he is.' Dmitri points the pistol at Novchenko. 'They know about the bombs, they wanted him dead. A Spesnatz team is arriving here by tomorrow evening. Either I killed him before that or they would kill us all. It was an offer that I couldn't refuse.'

'But you should have told me, we could…' Feodor just sits there, still in shock.

'What? Make a run for it? Do you want to spend the rest of your life on the run?' Dmitri turns, faces his father.

'I just think…'

'Don't think, it was him or us. I decided to save the life of my father, not my uncle. The choice was quite simple.'

Silence falls between the two of them. Flies start to buzz around Novchenko's head. The sun starts to drop in the west, the only sound is from the night life in the nearby jungle, slowly awakening.

'I knew something terrible like this would happen,' Feodor finally says, wiping a tear from his eye. He looks away from the body in front of him, stares at the setting sun. 'He saved my life, you know, in Afghanistan. Pulled me out of a jeep that had hit a mine. He was quite fearless then, cared for his men. But that changed after the war was over and then that drugs business. He had these three soldiers shot like dogs after the delivery to Krasny. I knew one of them, just a young conscript, happy to be going home, a survivor, ha!' Feodor looks up at his son. 'I wish he'd never met that fucking German! That's where he got this idea of power, this nuclear bomb business. I never thought that they would explode one of them.' Feodor sighs. 'All these people dying for what? More money than I could dream of, huh! Andrei always said that I was good at running the truck business, but never saw the bigger picture. I was always his sergeant, Dmitri, with the oldest excuse in the book. I just followed orders.'

'We're all guilty of that,' Dmitri says slowly, looks at his father, suddenly sees a man much older than his age.

'What will they do with us, Dmitri?'

'Who, Voronov? He's promised our lives.'

'Do you believe him?'

'No, but I have something to trade.' Dmitri smiles for the first time.

'To trade?'

'Yes, numbers.'

'Numbers?'

'The co-ordinates of the containers.'

'Ah, of course! Clever boy, you see that proves my point, you're the officer and I'm still just a sergeant.'

'No, you're not a sergeant, you're my father.' Dmitri gently rests his hand on Feodor's shoulder. 'Now, I'll clean up this mess, you go and get packed. You're leaving for the Motherland tomorrow!'

CHAPTER THIRTY SIX

Friday afternoon, end of another bloody awful week. It's two months since I've written my report about the past events. I've told it as I see it, warts and all. It won't please Sir Cadogan, but I really don't care. My personal life is in a mess too. I've spoken several times to Helen, she's reluctantly agreed to meet me on Sunday in Bath. I may be the father but I'm not going to be her husband. I know that I've been used but I can't get her out of my mind.

I'm sitting alone in my office, still in Newton House. I'm being isolated, in quarantine so to speak. I've not seen Forsyth either, we're being kept apart. They probably know what I would do if I did meet him. The Welsh dragon has also departed, maybe a sign of Forsyth's weakened position. Bradbury has been recalled to Vauxhall Cross, maybe they don't want him corrupted by me.

I did manage to go to Paris to attend Henri's funeral. It was a very sad affair. I'll miss Henri, who was a good intelligence officer, but he was also my friend. I spent some time with Henri's wife, Nicole. She held up pretty well, considering the circumstances. I also met Yvette, she of the famous mouth. I gave her the still photographs from the security video from Kohler's apartment but didn't tell her where they're from. There were several different men on camera, usually accompanied by one or two young girls. I told Yvette that we were trying to break-up a paedophile ring and these men are the French connection. I hope she finds these bastards. The other photographs of Kohler's sexual activities did cause a scandal, as I thought. There's been severe embarrassment to several top European politicians, another reason why I'm in trouble with Cadogan.

My daily task is to read through MI5's briefings, on the hunt for the sleeper cell. There is very little to go on, no CCTV images, no witnesses. At least the French picked up the lorry driver. Evidently he and his brother have been involved in illegal shipments across the Channel for months. But this is also a dead end as they only received a phone call where and when to pick up the lorries, never knew who the contact was, always paid in cash. The only certainty is that the nuclear device was Russian. The manhunt is on for Novchenko, but so far nothing.

I look at my watch, time to go home. But first I decide to phone Kelly, it's a month since we've last spoken. The news wasn't good, Harding was missing in Afghanistan, Kelly was depressed. I dial his number.

'Dick? Hi, it's Richard.'

'Hey, Richard, I was just about to phone you, good news.'

'Harding?'

'No,' Kelly pauses, 'afraid not. We've had a Rangers team working the Afghan-Pakistan border, but they haven't found anything yet.' Kelly takes a drag on his cigarette. ' But Harding has gone missing before, so we live in hope.'

'So what's the good news?'

'What? Oh yeah, well, we've just been briefed by the Russian ambassador. Novchenko's dead!'

'How?'

'Well, being Russian it's a bit convoluted. They found out that he was holed up in some ranch north of Rio de Janeiro.'

'Brazil? How did he end up there?'

'That the Russians won't say, you know what they can be like sometimes. Anyway, Novchenko had two sidekicks, Feodor and Dmitri, heard of them?'

'Yes, I think Dubois mentioned them.'

'Well, Moscow cut a deal with this Dmitri, to kill Novchenko. They sent in a Spesnatz team to recover the body. But when they arrived, the Spesnatz officer couldn't identify Novchenko. This Dmitri said that he had undergone plastic surgery. I'm not sure exactly what happened next, but there was an argument, nobody knows who fired the first shot. In the ensuing firefight, Feodor and Dmitri were killed, the Spesnatz lost five men. Huh, typical Russian fuck-up!' Kelly laughs. 'So they bring Novchenko's body back to Russia. He's been identified by his army dental records. By the way, the Russians didn't find any more containers, so there were only two.'

'Well, thank god for that.' I feel that I can relax for the first time in a long time.

'Yeah, looks like we've got closure.' I can hear Kelly light another cigarette. 'So, how are things with you, Richard?'

'Deciding whether I jump before I'm pushed.'

'That bad, huh?'

'You could say.'

'Listen, I said it before, you did the best with the hand that was dealt to you.'

'Maybe, I just can't forget that video of Haifa, all these people dead.'

'Nobody who saw that will ever forget, Richard. It's funny though, how out of tragedy comes hope. So many countries in the Middle East have come together to help Israel. A lot of people have looked into the abyss and didn't like what they saw. We have to hope, Richard.'

'Yes, well…'

'Listen, I've also just heard that a Helmut Schroener has been made head of the German BND.'

'Who? Never heard of him.'

'Precisely, has caused quite a stir in German intelligence circles.' Kelly pauses, 'A little birdy also tells me that Schroener knew Franz Haller.'

'You think…?'

'Let's just say that we're going to keep a close eye on Herr Schroener.'

314

'OK, I'll pass this info onto our people, if I'm still in a job.'

'Listen if things go pear-shaped over there, I could always use a good freelance agent.'

'I'll bear that in mind, Dick.'

'You do that.'

'Best of luck with Harding, he really helped me in Paris.'

'Thanks, stay in touch.'

I put down the phone. Working for the Americans? No, I don't think so.

It's now six o'clock, I need a drink.

I haven't been in the Star since the last time I met Helen. I nod to a few of the locals, still the same old faces. I settle myself at the bar, order a large malt. This time the barmaid is Swedish, another student and quite a looker. Tall, blonde hair, the palest blue eyes. She smiles as she hands me my glass, perfect white teeth greet me. The first malt doesn't touch the sides, I order another. The rear view of the barmaid is almost as good as the front view. Someone sits down beside me. I turn, Saunders!

'Hi, Richard, long time no see.' Saunders doesn't look at me, he's also admiring the view. 'Make that two, Helga.'

'You know her?'

Saunders says nothing, just gives me a wink. Two glasses appear in front of us, Saunders smiles, the Swede blushes.

'You know the last time we met, you got me into trouble.' I concentrate on my malt, trying not to look at the Swede as she leans across the bar to pick up some empty glasses, bare flesh exposed between her blouse and tight fitting jeans.

'But I didn't reveal my source, did I?' Saunders talks to me but he's not looking at me.

'But Forsyth guessed.'

'Ah yes, and how is Mr Forsyth these days?' Saunders finally looks at me.

'Why don't you ask him?'

'If only I could, very difficult to get hold of these days, Mr Forsyth. Strange, thought he would be basking in the glory of thwarting a nuclear attack on Britain. But, de nada. Odd, don't you think?'

I say nothing, toy with my half-empty glass.

'You know, Richard,' Saunders leans over, I catch a whiff of aftershave, 'there are rumours that it was all a bit of a balls-up. That your lot knew about it, but did nothing.'

I finish my malt, turn and face Saunders.

'You know I couldn't possibly comment.'

But I did...

EPILOGUE

REUTERS FLASH – Rio de Janeiro 16th April 2020

Brazil's Chernobyl?

Brazilian Health Authorities and the World Health Organisation are increasingly concerned and mystified by radioactive pollution found in the Oroko river. At least eight natives in the region have died, wildlife has also been affected.

A WHO source has said, quote – 'We do not understand the high levels of radioactivity being found in the Oroko river. The Oroko river and its tributaries cover thousands of square miles, to find the source of the radioactivity could take months. Our immediate concern is that the latest pollution has been found fifteen miles north of the capital. If it continues its southward movement to Rio, we could be facing an environmental and humanitarian disaster.' – end of quote.